P9-BZQ-549

**Also available from
Victoria Alexander**

The Lady Travelers Society

VICTORIA ALEXANDER

THE LADY TRAVELERS
GUIDE TO

Happily
Ever After

HQN™

HQN™

Recycling programs
for this product may
not exist in your area.

ISBN-13: 978-0-373-80407-8

The Lady Travelers Guide to Happily Ever After

Copyright © 2019 by Cheryl Griffin

www.HQNBooks.com

Printed in U.S.A.

This book is for all of you who have traveled with me

down the roads of my imagination

For my friends, who pushed and pulled

and cheered me along the way

For Nancy, who helps me navigate the unexpected turns

For Tory and Alex—the best parts of my journey

And for Chuck, who has held my hand every step of the way

Happily Ever After

really is

just the beginning

PROLOGUE

London, 1882

RICHARD BRANHAM, THE EARL OF ELLSWORTH, stood at the window in his library gazing at the back gardens, his hands clasped behind his back. One could tell by the set of his shoulders this was to be one of those discussions. Said discussions usually centered around his nephew's—his heir's—poor behavior, lack of responsibility and questionable future. Although James Branham thought his future had been rather firmly settled yesterday.

"Uncle Richard?" James braced himself. "You asked to see me?"

Uncle Richard turned from the window, the late-morning light emphasizing the lines of aging in his face. But then the man had passed his seventy-fifth year. "I thought we should talk."

"It seems to me we've done nothing but talk the last few days."

His uncle studied him for a long moment. "I'm proud of you."

"I beg your pardon?" Not exactly what James had expected.

"You did the right thing." Uncle Richard crossed the room and took his usual seat behind his ancient mahogany desk. "It wasn't easy."

James shrugged and sat in the equally old wingback

chair in front of the desk. They'd faced each other countless times across this desk since James had come to live
with his uncle at the age of nine when his parents had
died. Fifteen years later, James's behavior was still a matter that warranted discussion.

"There wasn't much of a choice." It seemed to James
it came down to his future, or hers. He would survive a
scandal. Men with money and titles always did. Violet
would have been ruined. And it was entirely his fault.

"You saved that girl from scandal and probably a life
alone. A young woman's fate rests on her reputation."

"I am well aware of that." It didn't seem at all fair that
Violet should have to suffer for his mistake. What had
he been thinking? Or had he been thinking at all? Apparently, there was a great deal of guilt that went along
with selfish errors of judgment, even when one ultimately
did the right thing.

"Public indiscretions, even those we might deem
minor, are rarely forgiven by society. Being kissed by
a man whose engagement to another woman is about to
be announced is not something that is easily forgotten."

"She did slap me," James pointed out. "Hard."

"Yes, I saw that as did everyone else." Uncle Richard's
lips twitched as if he were holding back a smile. He met
his nephew's gaze directly. "It *was* a mistake, wasn't it?"

"Yes, of course." James nodded, perhaps a bit too ve-
hemently. There was no need to change his story now.
He had kissed Violet Hagen on a dark terrace at the ball
where his engagement to Marie Fredericks was to be
announced. Admittedly, in the light of day, one would
never confuse Violet with Marie, but then it hadn't been
the light of day. And he had possibly drunk more than
was wise. And...

And marrying Marie had looked more and more like a fate worse than death. He should have come up with a better way to escape marriage to her but he'd tried to convince himself he was simply experiencing the kind of apprehension most men felt when coming face-to-face with an eternity tied to the same woman. Regardless, that night, with his engagement moments from being publicly announced, he could feel a noose tightening around his neck. A wiser man, a *better* man, would have simply called it off. Only a true idiot would have seen the silly challenge of his friends to kiss his almost-fiancée as a chance for escape. Only a stupid ass—or a coward— would have allowed the world to think he had mistakenly kissed the wrong woman, knowing full well that very public *mistake* would lead to calling off any engagement. It had seemed a brilliant idea.

He never for a moment thought it would also lead to a fast marriage with the mistake in question.

"Do you like her?" Uncle Richard said without warning.

James frowned in confusion. "Who?"

"Your wife?" A hard tone sounded in Richard's voice. "The one you married yesterday?"

"Ah, Violet." He nodded. "Well, yes, certainly. She's quite pleasant. Quiet, rather shy I would say. But witty under that terribly reserved exterior, as well. And not unattractive." Indeed, as he had been courting Marie he'd grown to know Violet. The idea of kissing her had not been an entirely new one. But then that particular idea occurred to him with most of the women he knew.

"What do you intend to do now?"

"Now? Honestly, Uncle Richard." James shook his head. "I have no idea. I don't think I am ready for marriage."

VIOLET'S BREATH CAUGHT. She'd been about to enter the library to greet her new husband and his uncle. Obviously James had no idea she'd be up and about but then it was already late morning. She suspected James rarely rose before noon.

"And yet you are married," Lord Ellsworth said.

What was one supposed to do when hearing one's husband of less than a day proclaim he was not ready for marriage? Violet Hagen—now Branham—was not given to eavesdropping under ordinary circumstances. These were scarcely ordinary.

"Well, yes but…"

Uncle Richard's voice hardened. "But?"

"None of this is Violet's fault. She shouldn't have to pay for it." James paused. "I've legitimately made her my wife, given her my name. I was thinking Violet and I would have one of those modern marriages. You know, the sort where we go our separate ways for the most part."

Violet bit back a gasp. Her heart twisted in her chest. *No!* Twenty-one years of quiet, reserved, proper behavior, of not standing up for herself, of doing what was expected up to and including marrying a man who had no desire to marry her, shattered with his words.

"She and I could—"

"She and I could what?" Violet swept into the room. Both men jumped to their feet.

"Good morning, Violet," Lord Ellsworth said pleasantly. "I trust you slept well?"

"Quite, thank you, my lord." She moved closer. "I couldn't help overhearing. As you and James are discussing my marriage and my future, don't you think I should be present?"

"Of course." James offered her a chair.

"I'd prefer to stand." She braced herself. "Correct me

if I'm wrong, but you're suggesting that you and I continue our lives as if we were not married? You go your way and I go mine?"

"Well, yes, something like that."

"I see." Good Lord! The man really didn't want her. A lump lodged in her throat. She ignored it. Now was not the time to feel sorry for herself. She'd thought, she'd *hoped*, that he liked her well enough to make a success of this marriage. She more than liked him, she'd been secretly smitten with the man very nearly since the moment she'd met him. What an idiot she was. "Then last night was…" She steeled herself, not sure if she wanted the answer. Still, only a coward wouldn't ask the question and the time for cowardliness was past. "An obligation? The responsibility of a dutiful husband?"

"No, not entirely." He paused to choose his words. "But last night does erase any question of the legality of our union. It protects you should something happen to me. Death or something of the like."

"That's certainly the best idea I've heard today," she snapped.

Lord Ellsworth cleared his throat.

"I say, Violet, that's uncalled-for." James frowned.

"Really? And I think that's the very least that is called for!"

"Didn't you say she was shy and reserved?" Lord Ellsworth said in an aside to James.

"She was."

"Shy and reserved will not serve me well at the moment, my lord." She clenched her fists by her side, as much to still the trembling of her hands as from anger.

The oddest look of what might have been admiration shone in the older man's eyes. Any other time she would have reveled in it. Now, she was fighting for her future. Her husband—her *new* husband—was about to turn her into that most pathetic creature: a wife in name only. *Absolutely not!* She squared her shoulders. "I will not return to my family's house."

"We shall find you a house," James said quickly.

"She shall stay here." Lord Ellsworth shot him a hard glance. "This is her home now."

"Yes, of course." Unease shaded James's words. He was no doubt thinking exactly what she was—being under the same roof would be exceptionally awkward if indeed they were living separate lives.

"I'm not sure I wish to." Violet crossed her arms over her chest. "In this marriage you're proposing, you are free to continue your reckless and scandalous ways?"

"Yes, I suppose, although calling them reckless and scandalous does seem a bit harsh."

She ignored him. "And I may do as I wish, as well?"

"I hadn't really considered…" James's brow furrowed in confusion. Obviously the man didn't like the sound of that. Good. "I would think so."

She smiled slowly. He didn't seem to like that, either. "Now that we have agreed to the rules—" she turned to Lord Ellsworth "—I hate to be indelicate but I would like to discuss finances."

His lordship nodded. "James will provide you with an allowance suitable for your position. Yours to spend as you please."

James nodded.

She looked at her new husband for a long moment. Silly of her to think that simply because she had feelings for him, because they shared a certain friendship, that this sham of a marriage would succeed. She shifted her gaze back to his uncle. "Given our arrangement, London is going to be uncomfortable for both of us. I have always wanted to travel. Can that be arranged?"

"Yes, of course." Lord Ellsworth glanced at his nephew. "Unless, you have any objection?"

"Whatever she wants," James said quietly. It really was the least he could do and the man knew it. He'd ruined her life. Destroyed any real chance of a good match and put her at the center of scandal. Now he could make amends by financing her freedom.

"Very well then." She met her husband's gaze directly. "I do agree with you, James. I don't think you're ready for marriage. For that matter, I doubt you're ready for any significant responsibility whatsoever."

"Come now, Violet." The man actually had the nerve to sound indignant. "I should be given some credit. I did marry you and in doing so saved you from ruin. One might say I rescued you."

"After it was you who put me in an untenable situation in the first place." She ignored the fact that she had kissed him back with all the enthusiasm of unrequited love. "And destroyed my life in the process."

"Not deliberately," James said as if that made a difference. "That was never my intention."

"I'll arrange an appointment with my solicitor." Lord Ellsworth smiled at his new niece. "I know it's difficult at the moment, but regardless of where your travels take you, I do hope you will consider Ellsworth House your home."

She forced a smile. "Thank you, my lord." She turned her attention back to James. Resolve hardened her voice. "As for you, I never want to see you again."

"There will be occasions—"

"Never!" She fairly spat the word, ignoring the pain squeezing her heart. Apparently, this was what true heartbreak felt like. No doubt made worse by the hope that last night… She thrust the thought aside. "I'm quite serious, James. Never."

He stared, a stunned look on his handsome face. As if only now did he realize the consequences of what he'd done, of how he'd crushed her hopes and her heart. "Very well, never."

"Now, if you will excuse me." Violet nodded and headed toward the door. It was all she should do to keep her pace calm and sedate when what she truly wanted was to flee and then weep. Possibly forever.

"That appears resolved," his lordship said behind her. "I must say, I'm rather disappointed."

Tears blurred her eyes and she started toward her rooms. This was not the future she'd envisioned yesterday when she'd said vows that apparently only she really meant.

"It's for the best, uncle." James's voice trailed after her.

Maybe in that at least, James was right.

Part One

London

CHAPTER ONE

Nearly six years later...

"HAVE I TOLD you how fortunate I am to be dancing with the loveliest woman here?" Lord Westmont said in his most charming manner. A manner designed to persuade whatever lady he was speaking to that he had never said those words—or words at all like them—to any other woman.

"Why no, my lord, I don't believe you have." Violet Branham followed his lead flawlessly. Westmont was an excellent dancer but then so was she. She flashed him a knowing smile. "At least not tonight. Although you might have mentioned it last year when we danced together at this very ball. And I believe the year before that, as well."

His eyes widened in surprise. Poor Evan never would have expected a woman—a mere woman no doubt—to be so horribly honest. It was not how the game was played. But then Violet was tired of playing games by other people's rules.

A stunned moment later, he laughed. "Lady Ellsworth, you are as outspoken as ever. I don't know why I didn't notice how truly delightful you are years ago."

"Years ago, I wasn't particularly delightful. But you don't recall meeting me years ago, do you?"

The most charming look of panic crossed his face.

"Goodness, Evan, we met some nine years ago during

my first season and again during my second and third
seasons, as well. You simply weren't, oh, *aware* of me,
I would say."

He frowned. "That's a dreadful accusation."

"My apologies." She widened her eyes in an innocent
manner. "Was I supposed to be kind?"

"I'm beginning to suspect I don't deserve kindness,"
he said slowly.

"Not in that respect. It was indeed a dreadful thing
to do, you know. At least it seemed so at the time." She
shrugged. "Although you were not alone in your complete
lack of acknowledgment of my very existence."

He winced. "My apologies, Violet. All I can say in
my defense is that I was much younger, rather full of
myself and somewhat stupid. Well, extremely stupid."
He paused. "You may object, should you feel the need."

"Oh, no, please continue."

It was rather fun, making Evan pay, as it were, for
the rudeness of his youth. There was a time when she
never would have thrown his vile behavior back in his
face. But she was not the same girl he had ignored all
those years ago. It wasn't so much that she had blossomed
as she had simply come into her own, aged like a fine
wine. When she had first come out in society, she had
been one of those vast numbers of girls who were not so
pretty as to catch the eye of every available gentleman,
but not so dull as to be considered a true wallflower. Admittedly, that changed with every passing season as her
prospects for marriage grew dimmer. There was hope for
Violet, her mother had often said, if only Violet would
pay more attention to her appearance and at least pretend
to enjoy flirtatious chatter and social occasions even if
she thought such things inane. No, much to Mother's annoyance, Violet preferred her own company and the soli-

tude to write bad poetry or read Lord Byron's works or ride alone. No wonder men like Lord Westmont tended to overlook her.

Those days were past. Years of travel abroad, meeting fascinating people and having assorted adventures had polished her. Provided her with the kind of confidence one could only acquire from living life. And she knew it. She was not the girl she used to be. Nearly six years of a separated marriage was enough to change anyone. As well as force them to grow up and discard silly thoughts of love and romance and other such nonsense.

"And I was rather shallow as well it appears." Genuine regret shone in his eyes. Perhaps she wasn't the only one who had changed. "Once again, my apologies for my thoughtless behavior. But tonight, I do think you are the loveliest, as well as most interesting, woman in the room."

"And tonight, my lord," she said, and smiled up at him, "I will believe you."

"Am I forgiven then?"

"Perhaps."

He laughed then sobered. "Why don't you come back to England more often? Allow me to make up for the past."

"I am considering it."

He gazed into her eyes and smiled. "Good."

She returned his smile but was not so foolish as to believe his words. Evan was an outrageous flirt and Violet had no intention of becoming any man's conquest.

In spite of any number of admittedly silly concerns, it was good to be back in London. It was always good to come home. Although the house in Mayfair she resided in when she was in the city was scarcely home. But as it was her husband's house, it was hers, as well. She refused to stay with her parents. Returning to the house of her girlhood would be an admission that her marriage was a dreadful failure. It was true, of course, and everyone in London knew it, but she had no desire to listen to her mother tell her exactly what she had done wrong.

Violet knew all too well that she had allowed a bit of foolish girlhood longing and a remarkable kiss to sweep aside all reason, overcoming good sense and any sort of primal instinct of self-preservation.

The music faded. She stepped out of Evan's arms, and he escorted her off the dance floor.

"In spite of your painful candor—" Evan raised her hand to his lips "—I would very much like to call on you. I would be honored if you would allow me the opportunity to make amends for my past stupidity." He grinned. "I do so like a challenge."

"You do realize I'm a married woman."

He gasped in an overly dramatic manner. She doubted if anyone in London was not aware of her sham of a marriage. How she and James had married and then gone their separate ways. It was a long time ago but society had a very long memory. "Violet, you misunderstand. I only wish to further our friendship."

"You are no more than a breath away from becoming a true cad, aren't you, Evan?"

He grinned, then caught sight of something over her shoulder and froze like a frightened bunny. And she knew.

"Lord Westmont," the voice that shouldn't be at all familiar and yet was recognized somewhere in the vicinity of her soul, sounded behind her. Her heart clenched.

"Ellsworth," Evan said with far more composure than she would have thought he had a moment ago.

Violet summoned the most awful sense of determination. She had anticipated this moment, planned for it ever since she had finally accepted he had absolutely no interest in her whatsoever. She turned and smiled politely, ignoring the hitch in her throat. He had always been the handsomest man in the room with his dark hair and deep blue eyes. No doubt if she'd stayed with him, he would have broken her heart. Again. The man didn't have a faithful bone in his body. "Lord Ellsworth."

His gaze bore into hers. She refused to flinch.

"Lady Ellsworth." He took her hand and raised it to his lips, his gaze never faltering from hers. If she were a fanciful sort, she would have thought a hush fell over the entire ballroom, all eyes on the estranged Lord and Lady Ellsworth. Once, the very thought would have terrified her. Now, she didn't care. "Never is a very long time."

"Apparently, not long enough."

The look in his eyes was an interesting mix of caution, curiosity and challenge. But then they hadn't seen each other face-to-face in close to six years. God knew what her eyes were saying to him. "I believe this is our dance."

"Is it?" She tilted her head. He appeared exactly as she remembered. His shoulders were as broad, his gaze as endless, his hair as thick and dark and just the tiniest bit disarrayed—as if it was the last stronghold of the rebellious nature of his youth.

Oh, certainly, over the years she'd seen him on occasion from the window of her room as he was leaving the London house, scampering off to the country or wherever he went so as to avoid her during her visits home, thus keeping a promise he'd made long ago. But this was the closest they'd been to each other since the day after their wedding. On further consideration, he wasn't entirely unchanged. There were a few creases around the corners of his eyes but beyond that, something had shifted, matured perhaps. The look in his eye had once been carefree and flirtatious and brimming with ill-concealed amusement.

Now it was direct, firm, compelling. His lighthearted manner six years ago was that of a young man with no particular cares or responsibilities. The air of assurance and confidence about him now was that of a man who had no doubt of his place in the world. This was no longer the happy-go-lucky young man she been forced to wed when she had just turned twenty-one and he was twenty-four. But then she was not the quiet, pale creature she'd been then, either. "Are you sure you're not mistaken?"

"Violet," Evan interrupted. "Do you need my assistance?"

What a surprisingly gallant thing to say. Perhaps she had misjudged him.

"No, Evan, but I do appreciate your offer." She smiled in polite dismissal then paused. "Although might I request a favor?"

"Anything," he said with a smile.

"Do you see the young ladies over there?" She nodded toward a group of young women sitting together, desperately trying to appear as if they were having a wonderful time and not counting the minutes until they could flee for the safety of home. "They are no doubt reserved and quiet but are probably quite interesting and very nice. Would you ask at least one of them to dance?"

"I shall do better than that," Evan said gallantly. "I shall ask my brother and a few of my friends to dance with them, as well."

She cast him a brilliant smile. "In which case you are most certainly forgiven."

Evan grinned and took his leave.

Violet turned her attention back to James, who, as of two months ago when dear Uncle Richard had passed on, was now the Earl of Ellsworth. The man who had ruined her life. Her husband.

"There are any number of things I may be mistaken about. Nonetheless, this *is* our dance." James leaned in and spoke softly. "People are staring."

She laughed as if he had just said something amusing. "Of course they are, James. We've never been seen together in public before. No doubt everyone is expecting we'll do something they can talk about for days. Now the question is—will we?"

"Shall we disappoint them instead?" He held out his arm. "Dance with me, Violet."

"There's nothing I'd rather do." In truth, there were any number of things she'd rather do including walking on hot coals and being thrown into a lion's den. There was little difference and little choice. She placed her hand on his arm and allowed him to escort her onto the floor.

Regardless of how often she'd practiced exactly what she'd say when this moment came she couldn't quite summon the right words. Perhaps because it was deeply unsettling to be in his arms again where she never should have been in the first place.

Six years ago, on the night his engagement was to be announced to her friend Marie Fredericks, he had kissed quiet Violet Hagen on the shadowed terrace—later claiming he'd mistaken her for Marie as they were both red-haired and wearing blue gowns. Although really one was a sky blue and the other a sea foam, and Marie's hair was more blond than red. Aside from that, Violet was decidedly taller and not as curved as Marie. His friends also admitted they had challenged him to give his fiancée a real kiss—the kind of kiss a man gives the woman he intends to marry—and had directed him to the terrace where they later swore they truly thought Marie was. There was as well far more partaking of spirits than was perhaps wise. Unfortunately, in their zeal to witness this real kiss, they tangled in the draperies covering the windows overlooking the terrace, ripping them down in the process and directing the attention of everyone in the room to the *real kiss* currently in progress right outside.

It wasn't bad enough that he had kissed her but that she had kissed him back with a shocking amount of enthusiasm for a girl who had scarcely been kissed at all up to that point. And really did the hesitant brush of lips she'd experienced previously with two cautious young men even count as legitimate kisses? Admittedly, Violet had thought them rather thrilling until James had kissed her. She'd been shocked when he'd swept her into his arms. Then, with no more than a moment of hesitation, she had wrapped her arms around him, thinking surely he had realized Marie was the wrong match for him and Violet was so very right. When their lips met and his body pressed against hers, she'd discovered a passion she'd never imagined. It was a *real* kiss, or at least she had thought it was. She didn't question the why of it. Stupid, as it turned out. She had no idea he had mistaken her for Marie until he raised his head and realized what he'd done. And that was the first crack of her heart.

The second was the shock on his face and he'd uttered, "Bloody hell, it's you."

What could she do but slap him hard across his face?

Still, the damage was done. Which apparently, in the more scandal-prone minds of society, was in the intensity of the embrace—just to add yet another layer of humiliation—rather than the slap. All in all it was the Holy Grail of gossip. A man whose engagement was about to be announced found in a compromising position with the friend of the intended fiancée. Her parents had then insisted on marriage as the scandal was such her mother warned she would never make a decent match now. James's uncle Richard, the Earl of Ellsworth, had left James's decision up to him but left unsaid the questions of honor and responsibility involved. In spite of James's devil-may-care reputation, no one had ever questioned his word. Violet had protested—obviously James had no desire to marry her. It was pointed out James no longer had a choice, nor did she. James did what was expected and two days later they were married.

Through the years Violet did wonder what might have happened if she had refused to marry him. If she had stood up for herself.

She certainly did the morning after their wedding night when she learned he intended for their marriage to be little more than a pretense. When her heart had shattered. Violet had truly thought, up until that moment, there was the possibility they might make the best of this. They had been friends of a sort. If she had, in the back of her mind, wanted more, well, that was a silly thought. But she absolutely would not stay with a man who didn't want her.

A week later, Violet engaged a companion—Mrs. Cleo Ryland, a delightful widow only a few years older than Violet—packed her bags and headed to Paris. James had provided her with the resources she needed to see everything she had ever read about, everything she'd ever dreamed of seeing. If he did not intend to be her husband, she intended to take full advantage of his generosity.

She had earned it.

"IT'S BEEN A long time since we danced together," James said mildly.

He had danced with Violet any number of times before their marriage as he couldn't dance exclusively with Marie. There were rules about that sort of thing. Violet and other friends and acquaintances were always with

James and Marie and the couple was quite properly never
alone. Marie wanted a dashing, handsome husband with
a respectable title and a tidy fortune to provide her an
unsullied position in society. She was not about to let so
much as a hint of impropriety jeopardize that. In Marie's
eyes, James was a perfect fit.

"It's been a long time since we've spoken." Violet
summoned a nondescript smile.

"Pride is a cruel mistress, Violet."

"One of many mistresses, no doubt," she said lightly.
Regardless of how rarely she was in London, gossip about
his numerous liaisons inevitably reached her, thanks to
her mother and a handful of well-meaning friends. She'd
ignored them for the most part. He had his life and she
had hers.

"Regardless of what you might think of me, I meant
that with all due sincerity." He paused. "I am trying to
admit to my past mistakes."

"And then what?"

"Then atone for them." He met her gaze directly.

She drew her brows together. "I'm not quite sure what
you're trying to say, James, but I am certain the dance
floor in the middle of Lady Brockwell's annual ball is
not the best place to do it."

"On the contrary, my dear." He grinned and for a moment she saw the man she'd married. "We would make
Lady Brockwell's ball the talk of London."

"Oh, I'd rather not. I've never particularly liked her."

"Are you staying at Ellsworth House?" he asked.

"I always do." She paused. "You had warning, I sent
a telegram from Lisbon." Whenever she headed toward
London she sent a telegram to Andrews, James's butler,
to give the household notice as to her impending arrival.
And give James the time he needed to escape.

"Thoughtful of you as always." He cast her his most charming smile. "Now, may I escort you home?"

"I'm not sure I am ready to leave."

"Forgive me if it sounded like a question. It wasn't."

She raised a brow. "Is that an order, then?"

He hesitated then grimaced. "Of course not. Sorry, I've never dealt with a wife before."

"Not one of your own, you mean."

His eyes narrowed slightly, as if she had pushed him too far. Good.

"And I've never dealt with a husband. But one dance and then we're off?" She shook her head. "Won't that set them all to talking? *Why are Lord and Lady Ellsworth leaving so early? What do you think they're up to?* That sort of thing."

"Probably, but only until the next interesting tidbit comes along. Should be no more than a day or two."

It really was pointless to argue with him. And they did have things to talk about that were best discussed in private. She wasn't sure she was prepared to do so tonight, however.

The music ended and he tucked her hand in the crook of his arm and steered her in a relaxed manner toward the door, stopping here and there to exchange a word with acquaintances. As if there was nothing at all out of the ordinary for Lord and Lady Ellsworth to be in the same room together let alone departing as a couple.

Once they had settled in the carriage, Violet let out a resigned sigh. "You do realize my mother will hear of this and will probably be calling on us by morning."

"My apologies."

She chose her words carefully. "I'm not sure I would have attended the ball if I had known you were going to be there."

"Whereas I knew you were going to be there and thought it better to greet you in public."

"Oh?"

"I wasn't sure you'd come," he said abruptly. "To London, I mean."

"I am here because of Uncle Richard, of course," she said coolly, ignoring the catch in her throat. "I was so saddened to hear of his passing. I wish I had come to see him again."

Uncle Richard had never thought it necessary to vacate the premises upon her visits home. He and Violet had spent long hours together during her stays, playing cards or chess, attending plays or lectures, and discussing whatever happened to pass through their minds. He'd been ill for some time but on her last visit a year ago, she'd thought he had improved. He was the only person who had ever accepted her for who she was rather than who she used to be or who she should be. Sorrow stabbed her at the thought of never seeing him again.

"You didn't come when he died two months ago."

"It seemed pointless."

"I assume you received notice from his solicitor about tomorrow's meeting?"

She nodded. The letter had insisted she return to London as soon as possible, as per Uncle Richard's instructions. It was followed by a telegram confirming her attendance at tomorrow's meeting. "Do you know what it's regarding?"

"Uncle Richard's final wishes." He shrugged. "Beyond that, I have no idea."

"Then we shall both be surprised," she said under her breath.

While it did strike her as an ordinary conversation, tension fairly bounced off the walls of the carriage. Idle chatter seemed absurd. There was so much of importance to say, issues that needed to be resolved. And yet here and now, she couldn't bring herself to say anything. What did one say to a husband one hadn't spoken to in nearly six years? Silence was far wiser at the moment. But it was past time. One of them had to be honest enough to do what needed to be done. It was more than likely to be her. Goodness, hadn't she been working up her courage for years? Still, it might be better to hear what the solicitor had to say. Another day or two would make no real difference.

James helped her from the carriage and escorted her into the grand house near Grosvenor Square. Andrews greeted them, handed her wrap to a footman and promptly vanished, no doubt within calling distance should he be needed. The butler was the very soul of discretion. Regardless, Violet suspected he and any number of other servants were observing them from some unseen location.

"I usually have a glass of brandy in the library before bed," James said in an offhand manner. "Would you care to join me?"

"I'm afraid I've had a very long day. I would prefer to retire for the night." She smiled politely and turned toward the stairs. *Coward*, a voice whispered in the back of her head. A civilized brandy in the comfort of Uncle Richard's library would be the perfect opportunity for calm, rational discussion. Regardless, she simply wasn't ready. She'd assumed she wouldn't see him until they met in the solicitor's office. She never imagined she'd see him, dance with him, tonight.

"I had hoped we could talk."

She turned back to him. "Now?" She narrowed her eyes. "Why?"

"It just seems like an opportune time. That's all." He paused. "We've never really talked."

"No, we haven't." *And whose fault is that?* She bit back the words and heaved a weary sigh. "It's been almost six years, James. Surely whatever you have to say can wait another day."

He gazed at her for a long moment then nodded. "Of course." He paused. "That was very nice of you. Encouraging Westmont to dance with those girls."

"I am very nice." Her gaze met his. "And I know how they feel."

"Yes, I suppose you do." He looked as if he wanted to say something else, then thought better of it. "Good night, Violet."

"Good night, James." She nodded and started up the grand staircase, refusing to look back at him. She knew he watched her, felt his gaze on her as if his eyes were burning into her back.

Her room was at the farthest end of the hall from his. Aside from a single night, she and James had never before slept under the same roof. That thought alone was enough to keep her from getting so much as a wink of sleep. Add to that, Uncle Richard's mysterious final wishes and her own desire to at last resolve things between them and move on with their lives and anything approximating true rest was impossible.

Beyond all else, she couldn't get James's comment out of her head. Was he truly ready to face his past mistakes? Did those mistakes include her?

And how on earth did he intend to atone for that?

CHAPTER TWO

"AND SHE'S BACK," Ophelia Higginbotham said under her breath and resisted the urge to slide under the covers and pull them up over her head.

"How are you feeling, Effie?" Persephone Fitzhew-Wellmore sailed into the room like a ray of unrelenting sunshine. She glanced at Lady Guinevere Blodgett, sitting nearby in Effie's bedroom and currently perusing the obituary section of the *Times* as she had done every day in recent years. "How is she?"

Gwen didn't look up from the page. After all, it wasn't as if she hadn't been asked the question every time Poppy entered the room. "Much better I think."

"I am." Effie nodded in her healthiest manner. "Oh, I am indeed. I feel much, *much* better. Why, I daresay I'll be out of bed in no time."

"I doubt that." Poppy's brow furrowed and she eyed the other woman closely. "I think you look extremely pale. Doesn't she, Gwen?"

"Oh my, yes," Gwen murmured.

"There, you see? Gwen agrees with me," Poppy said firmly. "They'll be no more discussion about it. Although you may read today's post if you feel up to it." She set a small stack of correspondence on the tray on Effie's lap.

"And I do." Effie voice rang with eagerness. Even invoices would be a respite from the endless boredom of being waited on hand and foot. Still, it couldn't be helped.

"We'll see how you feel tomorrow." Poppy shook her head in a chastising manner. "This is your third relapse of whatever illness has been plaguing you." She paused. "Perhaps we should have Dr. Wrenfield—"

"No," Gwen and Effie said at the same time.

"You know how Effie hates to be a bother," Gwen said quickly. "Besides, the doctor has been here once already and was unable to identify the true nature of her illness."

"Yes, but I wasn't here when he called," Poppy said. "Perhaps if I were to give him my observations, it might help him in determining what the problem is."

"I really can't afford another visit," Effie added.

It was the one thing Poppy couldn't argue with.

Finances were more and more distressing for the three widows. Their husbands had all died within the past few years—Gwen's Sir Charles and Poppy's Malcomb three years ago, followed the next year by Effie's dear William. The men, who had all lived lives of adventure and exploration and excitement, had been felled by the most ordinary of circumstances—Sir Charles had succumbed to a recurrent bout of malaria, Malcomb passed on in his chair in front of the fire so peacefully it took Poppy several hours to realize he had indeed left this life and Effie's dear William, having had a long and illustrious career in Her Majesty's army without scarcely a scrape, fell from a ladder he shouldn't have been on in the first place. It was scant comfort to Effie that she'd told him not to climb the blasted ladder.

While they were excellent husbands—even if they were scarcely ever present, which, depending upon one's point of view, might have contributed to their long and happy marriages—they'd not given enough thought to providing for their wives' financial futures in the event of their demise. Gwen suspected, as they had survived any number of perilous adventures, they never imagined their days would be cut short in the relative safety of home. The end result of their lack of foresight was that their widows were slowly and inevitably running out of funds. The three friends had each saved some money through the years, and Effie did have a small military pension, but they estimated it would not be long before they would all be penniless. Being penniless as well as in one's seventies was not a pleasant prospect.

"Of course." Poppy sighed. "We really have to do something about that." She straightened her shoulders. "For now I shall see if your cook has the broth ready."

"Oh, goody." Effie forced a cheery smile. "Broth."

"You're fortunate your cook is so skilled at broth." Poppy cast Effie an encouraging smile and took her leave.

"Mm-mm, more broth," Gwen said softly, the corners of her mouth twitching in an effort to hold back a laugh.

"I hate broth." Effie let out a resigned breath. "This won't be nearly as funny next week when you're the one in bed."

Gwen lowered the paper. "Oh, no. We agreed there should be at least two to three weeks between illnesses so as not to arouse her suspicions."

"I'm not sure I can do this again." Effie shuffled through the envelopes on the tray. "There's nothing worse than being forced to stay in bed when there's nothing whatsoever wrong with you."

"And who knows better than I?"

It had been Gwen's bout with a persistent cold that had given them the idea of feigning illness in the first place. It had seemed a brilliant idea at the time. Neither of them had imagined how terribly draining acting ill could be. But it was all they could think of and they had agreed something must be done about Poppy's melancholy state.

The three had been friends—no, sisters—for more than forty years now, drawn together by the absence of husbands wandering the world in search of adventure. Aside from Gwen's niece and great-nephew, none of them had any real family nor had any of them been blessed with children. But through thick and thin, for most of their lives, they could count on each other. Now, Poppy needed them even if she would never admit it.

She was the youngest of the three by two years and had always been the cheeriest of the group. Nothing in Poppy's estimation was so dire it would not ultimately work out for the best. Gwen was the most practical of the trio and Effie had long accepted she was the one more prone to sarcasm, snide comments and an often too-colorful vocabulary. She had once decided the three of them were very much like ancient Greek goddesses. Poppy was the goddess of peace and love and all things bright and happy. Gwen was the goddess of wisdom and practicality. Effie was the goddess of war. She rather liked that.

But the bright light that was Poppy had dimmed since Malcomb's death. Oh, Effie and Gwen had mourned the loss of their husbands every bit as deeply. One would have thought, as they had lived much of their lives without their spouses, their passing would have been easier. But it was one thing to fear the man you loved might never come home and something else entirely to know that he wouldn't. Perhaps because Effie and Gwen did not see the world through the rose-colored haze that Poppy did, it was somewhat easier to face whatever life now had in store.

Gwen had thought, and Effie agreed, that it wasn't just Malcomb's death that had depressed Poppy's spirits. Her husband's passing had been followed that same year by Sir Charles and then William the following year. Gwen had likened it to a plague only without the locusts. She and Effie had agreed, unlike so many widows of their acquaintance, they at least knew how to take care of themselves. Of course, they hadn't realized the perilous state of their respective finances and they never expected Poppy's melancholy to linger.

It was quite by accident that they discovered when she was busy, she almost seemed her old self. They had then cunningly guided her into volunteering to reorganize the library and collections of the Explorers Club. That in itself took nearly a year and far more of their own time than they had planned on. Who ever would have suspected Poppy had the talent of a general for barking orders and delegating tasks. Effie had always considered her a bit scattered. When one of the ladies on the board of the club's Ladies Committee resigned to move to York to be with her daughter's family, they had encouraged Poppy to stand for that seat. She was universally liked and no one ran against her but the position did not take up nearly as much of Poppy's time as Effie and Gwen had hoped. Then Gwen had come down with a nasty cold and Poppy had charged in to help with her care, and her friends realized this would indeed give her a project of sorts to fill her time. At least until they could come up with something better.

"We're going to have to think of something else soon, you know. Something to occupy her days and her mind." Effie sorted her mail into two stacks—the accounts due she could fortunately still pay, and correspondence of an interesting nature. That stack was sadly comprised of only one crisp, cream-colored envelope.

"I am trying to think of something. I have no desire to take to my bed again." Gwen returned to her study of the obituaries. "Oh look, that nice Mrs. Hackett died. What a shame."

"I thought you detested Mrs. Hackett." Effie picked up the envelope and examined it. The stationery was of excellent quality, the handwriting unfamiliar and a bit unsteady. She turned it over. Some sort of embossed seal was on the flap. How very interesting indeed.

"I did, but now she's dead." Gwen thought for a moment. "In the scheme of things, one could say I won."

"Whoever is left standing wins?" Effie slit the envelope with a letter opener, a replica of a sword her husband had owned.

"Something like that." Gwen settled back in her chair. "I don't know why I insist on reading these death notices. It seems there is at least one acquaintance listed nearly every day. Why, everyone we know is dropping dead."

"These things tend to happen when one reaches a certain age." Effie pulled several pages from the envelope and started to read.

My dear Ophelia,
Forgive me for taking the liberty of calling you dear. In my heart, you have always been my dear Ophelia. But I knew the moment I introduced you to my good friend, William, on that summer night all those many years ago that I would never have the opportunity to call you my dear aloud.

Effie's breath caught. *Richard.*

"Still, one does hate to be uninformed," Gwen continued. "Imagine if I were to have a party. It would be dreadfully awkward if I were to invite someone who is already dead." She paused. "Of course, they wouldn't come so it might not be so awkward at that."

*I hope you received my letter of condolence
upon William's passing. He was a good, true friend
and I have missed him. It is one of the many regrets
of my life that we drifted apart.*

*What a pity it is to recognize your regrets when
it's too late to do anything about them. My greatest by far was not fighting for your affections. But
the way you and William looked at one another on
that very first meeting was as if there was no one
else in the world. I knew any hope I had was futile.
So I chose to step back. And while I still believe it
was the right thing to do, I have discovered if one
is haunted by any single word in life it is* perhaps.

Shock rippled through her. Surely she wasn't reading
this correctly.

"Although a séance would be interesting," Gwen
mused. "I wonder if one sends invitations to the dead."

*I have been ill for some time and I know my re-
maining days are few. I fear if you are reading this,
I have breathed my last. This letter is in the form
of my final request, which I am leaving in your capable hands.*

"That would be a great deal of fun," Gwen said
thoughtfully. "Although I daresay we couldn't afford a
real spiritualist. But I think Mrs. Addison has a cousin
who dabbles in contacting the spirits from beyond. She's
quite good at it from what I hear and I doubt she would
charge a fee."

*I can do nothing about the past but, even from
the grave, I may be able to influence the future. In*

*my life I have witnessed three great loves. The first
was between you and William. The second was my
love for you. It seems I can confess in death what
I never managed to say in life. Please do not allow
my revelation to distress you. I refused to interfere
with your happiness and knowing you were happy
was enough.*

"Still," Gwen continued, "the last thing Poppy needs
is to see Malcomb again. I can't imagine that would be
the least bit helpful."

*I am convinced I have seen one more great love
even if those involved refuse to acknowledge it.*

"Gwen," Effie said sharply. "In all those obituaries
you read, have you seen a notice about the death of the
Earl of Ellsworth?"

"Ellsworth? I'm not sure. It does sound vaguely familiar." Gwen thought for a moment. "Yes, I think I did
see that name. A few weeks ago perhaps? Or longer I
suppose. Certainly within the last few months. Did you
know him?"

Effie nodded. "I had once thought he might be the
man I would marry but then I met William."

Gwen's eyes widened. "Oh?"

Effie scanned the rest of the letter. Good Lord. Surely
the man wasn't serious? She held it out to Gwen. "Read
this."

Gwen started to read then looked at Effie. "Are you
sure you want me to read this? It seems rather personal."

"I'd tell you everything it says anyway."

"There is that." Gwen returned her attention to the
letter.

She was certainly taking her time. Still, Effie had been so shocked she had done little more than skim the rest of the letter. She drummed her fingers on the tray impatiently.

At last Gwen looked up. "This man spent his entire life in love with you."

Effie winced. "I had no idea."

"He never gave you a hint as to his feelings?"

"Of course not. Besides, William was like a brother to him, at least when they were young. They went their separate ways as the years went on. The army sent William all over the world and when he left the military, he followed on the heels of your husband. You know as well as I he was hardly ever here. I rarely saw Richard after William and I married."

Although Effie supposed it was possible that it was difficult for Richard to see William given his feelings for her. "On those occasions when I ran into him he was cordial and pleasant, as any old friend would be, but nothing more than that."

Gwen nodded. "How very noble of him not to let you know how he felt."

"Yes, I suppose it was." And if she had known of Richard's feelings? "It would have been terribly uncomfortable if he had declared himself."

"And would you have done anything differently had you known of his feelings?"

Effie shook her head. "No."

"Did you ever once lead him to believe there could be anything between you once you met William?"

"Of course not."

"Then you have nothing to feel guilty about."

"I don't feel guilty," Effie said. "I had nothing to do

with this. But I do feel badly for him. It's quite sad, don't you think?"

"Unrequited love usually is."

"He was a wonderful man, very charming and quite nice. He was very nearly perfect I suppose. William wasn't the least bit perfect." Effie smiled.

"Are you going to take up this challenge he has set for you?"

"It does seem like a lot of effort."

"It was a man's dying wish. You really can't say no to a dying man's wish." Gwen paused. "Besides, he says you'll be paid for any expenses you incur as well as re-ceive a stipend as he anticipates this will take a great deal of your time." She grimaced. "Do you think he knew of your financial difficulties?"

"I hadn't thought of that." Effie shook her head. "I couldn't possibly accept his money under those circum-stances. I should have to return it."

"You can't return it—he's dead."

"Then I shall give it to charity," Effie said staunchly.

"We'll be charity in no more than a year ourselves," Gwen pointed out.

For a few minutes, Effie had forgotten about their fi-nancial difficulties. "That does put it in a different light."

"It also seems to me—" Gwen chose her words with care "—this man's last thoughts were not for himself but for those he loved, which apparently included you."

"If I agree to do this, I am to meet with his solicitor and the parties involved tomorrow."

"And?"

"And I suppose when a man who is no longer with us wants to do something rather lovely, it would be bad form for the living to refuse."

Gwen adopted a casual tone. "You are doing it then?"

"Yes, I suppose I am. But I'm not doing it alone."

"I wouldn't expect you to."

Effie drew her brows together. "Still, it's a matter of love. It doesn't seem like the sort of thing one should do for money."

"You're not doing it for the money. You're doing it because a man who cared deeply for you has asked for your help. It's the only thing he ever asked of you. The money is simply a delightful bonus. He doesn't need it anymore but with any luck, it will sustain you until we can come up with a way to avoid destitution."

"Sustain *us*," Effie said firmly.

Gwen grinned. "Even better."

Poppy stepped into the room, carrying a tray with the dreaded broth steaming in a large bowl. "What's even better?"

Effie and Gwen traded glances.

"I believe, my dear old friend…" Effie smiled in a manner she had been told was more than a little wicked. "We have a new project."

CHAPTER THREE

"ARE YOU *MAD*?" The question blurted from James's mouth before he could stop it. Still, if anything seemed to warrant the questioning of sanity it was the words the solicitor had just dropped like a sudden whiff of something unexpected and extremely unpleasant.

"This is not my idea, James," Marcus Davies said in a patient manner. He had no doubt been practicing for this particular meeting. He and James had attended school together but hadn't become friends until after James's marriage, brought together initially by their shared affinity for raucous living and having a great deal of fun. A few years ago, both men put their respective pasts behind them as Marcus joined his father's firm—the firm that had long handled Uncle Richard's affairs—and James had become involved in Uncle Richard's business interests and estate management. In short, they had grown up. While they had once been cohorts in disreputable antics, they had eventually discovered the advantage of respectable comportment. More's the pity. "This is entirely your uncle's doing."

"He'd never do something so preposterous."

"Don't be absurd." Violet shot him a look of chastisement or annoyance or exasperation or some twisted female combination of all that and more. Women had thrown him all kinds of looks in his life but they were usually far more pleasant and inviting. "It's exactly the kind of thing he'd do. I never paid a single visit here wherein he didn't bring up how it was time to reconcile our differences. Indeed, it was his favorite topic." She glanced at the older lady sitting in a chair strategically placed off to one side of Marcus's desk. "Mrs. Higginbotham? What do you think?"

"I certainly don't think Richard was mad, if that's what you're implying, my lord." Mrs. Higginbotham cast him a look shockingly similar to Violet's. "According to the letter he sent me, he wanted to, well, correct a mistake or right a wrong or prevent a great loss, something of that nature." The widow was once apparently a good friend of Uncle Richard's, although James couldn't recall ever hearing her name. Regardless, his uncle had thought highly enough of this Ophelia Higginbotham to place James's fate in the lady's hands. She nodded at Marcus. "I suggest you continue as there will no doubt be further outbursts—" both ladies cast James that unnerving glance again "—and I daresay we don't want this to go on longer than necessary."

"Very well." Marcus shot James a pointed look, a warning to keep his mouth shut. While his firm handled Uncle Richard's affairs, Marcus personally managed all of James's legal needs. He was at once James's friend, legal advisor and, on occasion, protector. The solicitor cleared his throat. "As I was saying, while you do inherit your uncle's title, his properties—including the country estate and the house in London, as well as his fortune—were his to do with as he pleased."

James waved off the explanation. "We know all that. Go on."

"I simply want to make certain you and Lady Ellsworth are clear on all the various aspects of your uncle's will so there are no misunderstandings." The others might not realize it but it was apparent to James that his old friend was somewhat amused by Uncle Richard's will. They would have to discuss later how this was not the least bit amusing. "As his only heir, the argument can be made that you are certainly entitled to his property and his fortune but his lordship was very specific about the conditions under which you would receive it all.

"First, as I'm sure you remember my saying a minute ago—"

"Burned into my brain," James muttered.

"—you and Lady Ellsworth are to reside together for a period of two years, eleven months, one week and three days. That length of time is based on the date of today's meeting as per your uncle's instructions. He wished this meeting to be held as soon after his death as possible. But as Lady Ellsworth was abroad, it did take some time to contact her."

"Uncle Richard always knew exactly where I was," Violet pointed out. "We corresponded regularly."

"The blame for any delay falls entirely on us." Marcus cast Violet an apologetic smile. "As I was saying, for two years, eleven—"

"Three years," James said. "You might as well call it three years."

"For the sake of expediency, very well, three years it is." Marcus continued. "With no more than a total of fourteen days spent apart during the course of any given year."

"This residing together begins—" Violet held her breath "—when?"

"Today," Marcus said. "From this moment on."

"I see," she said faintly.

"Secondly, you must appear as a couple—a cordial couple—several times a week—"

"Three," Mrs. Higginbotham said.

Marcus nodded and continued. "Said appearances are to be in a public setting or in the presence of witnesses."

James frowned. "What do you mean *the presence of witnesses*?"

"That is left to the discretion of Mrs. Higginbotham." Marcus smirked.

"And we have to appear to be happy?" Violet asked.

"You certainly shouldn't appear to be unhappy. Blatant unhappiness with each other in public would no doubt cause tongues to wag. You will want to avoid that as the third stipulation requires there be no scandal whatsoever. No hint of impropriety, no faint whiff of unpleasant gossip. No rumors, no innuendoes, no insinuations." His gaze flicked to Violet. "Regarding either of you." And back to James. "Do you understand?"

"Completely." James shrugged. "That won't be the least bit difficult." Three pairs of skeptical eyes fixed on him. "My name has not been so much as whispered with regards to anything the least bit untoward in quite some time." Quite some time being defined rather loosely, at least in his definition.

"One more thing." Marcus glanced down at the papers in front of him to hide his smile. "You are forbidden to mourn or to wear black."

"He hated black," Violet and James said in unison.

He glanced at her, but she ignored him.

Violet nodded at the elderly lady. "Is Mrs. Higginbotham the authority on what constitutes scandal, as well?"

Mrs. Higginbotham smiled.

"Mrs. Higginbotham is the sole judge and arbitrator in any dispute or query. In this matter, her power is absolute and she has a great deal of discretion. She may do exactly as she thinks best, even allow for an exemption to any of the stipulations should she deem it necessary. In the case of unforeseen emergencies and the like." Marcus glanced at James, a note of apology in his voice. "His lordship was quite clear on this matter. He had no doubt Mrs. Higginbotham would wield the authority he has given her in a wise and competent manner as befitting the widow of a colonel and a woman he had long admired."

"Let me make certain I do indeed understand," Violet said thoughtfully. "In order for James to receive his inheritance we have to live together, appear as a congenial couple and avoid anything the least bit scandalous for two years, eleven months, one week and three days?"

"Three years," James said under his breath.

Marcus nodded.

"And if we succeed?" Violet asked.

"James will inherit everything except for a few gifts for charitable institutions and his late lordship's servants," Marcus said. "And you, Lady Ellsworth, will receive double your current allowance as well as an annual stipend for expenses for the rest of your life. Your financial independence will be assured. The two of you will also be free to resume your lives as they have been up to this point."

"I see." Violet considered Marcus's words for a moment. "And if we don't manage this?"

"Then nearly everything goes to charity." Marcus shrugged apologetically.

Violet slanted James a quick glance. "What if either of us refuses to abide by Uncle's Richard's conditions?"

"Again, charity will benefit."

"So we have no choice," James said flatly. This was not the least bit fair. Hadn't he done everything he could to prove to Uncle Richard he was worthy to be his successor? He'd learned how to manage the estate, strategies for investment and all the sundry details of business and management. Why, hadn't Richard's fortune grown at James's hand?

Still, James should have expected something like this. Uncle Richard had never made any secret of the fact that he considered James a bit of an idiot when it came to Violet. And of course he was right. But Uncle Richard was a good man who had never done anything disgraceful in his life. He could never comprehend how the burden of guilt could trap a man and keep him immobile.

"I've had a copy of his lordship's conditions made for each of you. There are some minor details we have not discussed but I assure you they are insignificant. Over the course of the next three years, your joint financial support will be substantially reduced as you will be supporting only one household. Other than that, your income and expenses will remain as they are now. Are there any questions?" Marcus glanced at the gathering.

Violet shook her head slowly. James could almost see the gears and flywheels of her brain sorting through the details of Uncle Richard's terms. But then she had always been clever. It was one of the things James had liked about her. A familiar sliver of guilt stabbed him, as it tended to do whenever he thought about Violet.

"I daresay, there will be questions, Mr. Davies." Mrs. Higginbotham glanced at Violet, then James. "At the moment, it's clear Lord and Lady Ellsworth are still a bit stunned." She stood, the gentlemen immediately springing to their feet, and pinned James with a firm look. "Might I suggest we join you for dinner tomorrow night at your residence? We shall discuss all of this and I will be able to answer any questions that may have come to mind between now and then. I shall bring my friends,

who will be assisting me in this endeavor." She turned to
Marcus. "Perhaps you should join us as well, Mr. Davies."

It wasn't a question. Marcus smiled weakly. "I can't
think of anything I'd rather do."

"Excellent." She nodded at James. "When you return
to Ellsworth House you'll find your staff has prepared
the master suite—with separate bedrooms of course—for
the two of you, as per your uncle's instructions."

If his uncle's ultimate purpose was in doubt, it certainly wasn't now. "Did he think of everything, Mrs.
Higginbotham?"

"I would hope so, my lord, but we shall see." She
smiled pleasantly. "Until tomorrow evening, then. Good
day." She nodded and took her leave.

James waited until the door closed behind her. "Where
on earth did Uncle Richard find her?"

"Apparently he knew her many years ago," Marcus
said thoughtfully. "Before she was married."

James sank back down into his chair. "We don't need
a governess, Marcus."

"You don't have a choice."

"I don't like putting my fate in the hands of a woman
I don't know."

"Again, no choice."

"Why didn't you warn me about this?"

"Sorry, old man." Marcus shrugged. "There are rules
regarding confidentiality that even I hesitate to break.
And your uncle specifically asked me not to say anything
to you. I was fond of him, you know."

"Everyone liked Uncle Richard." James blew a frustrated breath. "Is there any way out of this? Contest the
will or something of that nature?"

"I'm afraid not. We drafted it to your uncle's specifi-
cations and made certain every detail was in order. My

father and one of his brothers worked with your uncle for months to ensure it was exactly as he wanted as well as make certain it could not be challenged. They are very good. Even so, I am going over every detail."

"What if we—"

"I beg your pardon." Violet glared. "Perhaps you have forgotten but I am sitting right here. As this scheme cannot succeed without me, I suggest either include me in the conversation or shut up altogether."

Both men stared. This was not the quiet, rather meek woman he'd married. His mind flashed back to the last time he'd seen her—the morning after their wedding. She hadn't been the least bit meek when she'd informed him in no uncertain terms she never wanted to see him again. James hadn't heard her raise her voice before. He didn't know she could. His thoughts on occasion returned to that morning. Violet had been a tall, fire-haired tower of indignation and anger. There'd been a distinct touch of magnificence about her. Uncle Richard had noticed. Pity James hadn't.

Her demeanor then was attributable to justifiable anger. Last night, it was obvious she was not the same girl he once knew. The difference in her manner was apparent in the set of her chin and the look in her eye. The way she carried herself said without words this was a woman confident of her own worth. This was a woman who would hold her ground. She had changed in other ways, as well. He didn't remember her red hair being so glorious or her green eyes so captivating or her figure so enticing. There was somehow *more* to her now. As if she had once been a pencil drawing and was now a painting in oil. She was vibrant. Alive. Remarkable. And far lovelier than he remembered.

"Apparently you are not the only one without a choice,"

she said sharply, her eyes flashing with annoyance. "If I do not accept my role in this little farce, I will have virtually nothing to live on. Isn't that right, Mr. Davies?"

"Yes. Furthermore, there will be no more money for traveling—"

"Yes, yes, I understand that." She rose to her feet. "Mrs. Higginbotham was right. There will be questions." She pinned Marcus with a hard look. "Come prepared to answer them." She nodded curtly and strode out of the office.

James stared after her.

"I thought you said she was timid?" The vaguest hint of awe sounded in Marcus voice.

"She's changed."

Marcus chuckled. "Apparently." He paused. "You're going to have to stay on her good side, you know, if you want to pull this off."

"Yes, I know. She's not overly fond of me."

"From what you've told me, she has good reason for that." Marcus sat down. "This will certainly require a great deal of effort on your part. It won't be easy for you."

"Your confidence in me is heartening." James retook his seat.

Marcus pulled open a desk drawer and pulled out a bottle of fine Scottish whiskey and two glasses. He filled one and passed it to James.

"I shouldn't. She's probably waiting for me in the carriage."

"Or she's taken the carriage and left you to fend for yourself." Marcus chuckled. "I wouldn't put it past her."

"Nor would I." James sipped the whiskey. Nothing like good whiskey to put a thing in perspective. Although perhaps not today. "What am I going to do?"

"There's nothing you can do but abide by the terms of the will. I assure you, I have studied it thoroughly. As I said, my father and his brothers are very good." Marcus considered his friend for a moment. "She's quite lovely and you've always had an inexplicable charm for women. And she is your wife after all. Is there any possibility that you and she—"

"No. Maybe." James shook his head. "I don't know. It's been a long time." Even so, the memory of their wedding night—memories of Violet—had always dwelled in the back of his mind. No doubt the reason why he hadn't been with another woman in a very long time. "Uncle Richard thought Violet and I were destined for one another. That in my avoiding marriage to the wrong woman I had somehow ended up with the right woman. This is his way of forcing us together."

"He was nothing if not determined." Marcus paused. "May I ask you something?"

"Why not?" James settled back in his chair.

"If I recall correctly, quite some time ago, in an inebriated state of maudlin self-pity, you told me Lady Ellsworth was the biggest regret of your life."

"And?"

"And you said that on more than one occasion."

"You must admit, it's a rather significant regret." He shrugged. "I ruined her life."

"Yes, you've said that, as well." Marcus eyed him thoughtfully. "You've also said you were young, stupid and about to be engaged to the wrong woman."

"Hence the regret."

"Understandable." Marcus nodded. "But among all those things you've said about your ill-fated marriage, there's one thing you've never said."

"And what is that?"

Marcus met his gaze. "You've never once said it was a mistake."

JAMES INSTRUCTED HIS driver, then climbed into the carriage. "I didn't think you'd wait for me."

"That would have been rude." Violet smiled pleasantly. "I am never rude."

"I wouldn't think you were," he said slowly.

"We have a decision to make."

"I don't see that we have a choice."

"Of course we do," she said. "There are always choices, some better than others. From what Uncle Richard has said about you in the last few years, you seem to have a talent for business. Should either of us decide not to abide by the terms of the will, you would have to seek employment."

He had no doubt he could find employment of a sort. But if he'd learned nothing else about the world of business he had learned *who* you were was every bit as important as your skills or intelligence. A disinherited earl would not be especially sought after.

"I would indeed." He shifted in his seat. It wasn't just the fortune—although its loss would be painful—but losing the properties that had been in his family for generations twisted his soul. The country estate where his father had taught him to ride and to swim, as had his father before him. The London house Uncle Richard had made James's haven. The places James had always called home. "My life would certainly change. As would yours."

She hesitated. "Yes, of course."

He had the oddest feeling there was something she didn't wish to say.

"Although, as your husband, it would be my responsibility to provide your support."

"You would have to find good employment." She eyed him thoughtfully. "You've been very generous through the years."

He shrugged off her comment. Generosity apparently went hand in hand with guilt.

"Was that at Uncle Richard's urging?"

Did she think so little of him? He couldn't blame her if she did but it was annoying nonetheless. "Would it matter if it was?"

"Perhaps not." She paused. "But it is something I have always wondered."

"You could have asked my uncle."

"I'm not sure he would have told me," she said with a sigh. "He was very fond of you and rather proud of the man you've become."

Good to know. "No, your financial support had nothing to do with Uncle Richard."

"I see." For a long moment she was silent. "You're asking for three more years of my life. It's a very long time."

"Perhaps it is better to think of it as two years, eleven months, one week and three days after all."

"Not really." She pinned him with a hard look. "You do realize the significance of two years, eleven months, one week and three days, don't you?"

He scoffed. "Of course I do." What the hell was she talking about?

"Oh?" She studied him closely. "Can you tell me why Uncle Richard stipulated two years, eleven months, one week and three days?"

"Of course I can." At once the answer struck him and he wondered if Uncle Richard was looking after him from above. He leaned forward and met her gaze firmly. "Five years, ten months, two weeks and six days is—as of today—how long we've been married. Two years, eleven months, one week and three days is exactly half that. The stipulation was that the length of time be based on the date of today's meeting." He shrugged. "If you had returned to London sooner, the requirement would have been shorter."

"Very good, James." She nodded coolly. "Given your reaction in Mr. Davies's office, one might have thought you didn't realize that."

"One would have been wrong," he said in a superior manner and sent a silent prayer of gratitude to his uncle. "Still, it does seem excessive."

"Uncle Richard probably considered it fitting. An appropriate penance of sorts."

"Or a sentence?"

"Also appropriate, I suppose." She shook her head. "Uncle Richard never failed to lecture me about the absurdity of our circumstances. Every time I saw him, he said this had gone on long enough and I should return to England to stay." She met his gaze, and challenge shone in her eyes. "I told him I hadn't been asked."

"Would you have come back if I had?" It scarcely mattered now but it did seem important.

"It's rather a pointless question. You didn't ask."

"But if I had?" he pressed.

She stared at him for a long moment. "I don't know," she said at last and shrugged. "It's water under the bridge now. Nothing can be done about the past."

"Better to move on from here, then," he said. Still, there was a great deal of the past that remained to be resolved. "We should have expected something of this nature." And really, hadn't Uncle Richard warned him? Hadn't he said on more than one occasion that if James wouldn't do something about his marriage, someone should?

She smiled wryly. "He's proving a point you know, even in death."

James chuckled. "I am aware of that."

"It seems that we have no choice." She sighed. "Regardless, I shall have to consider this. If I agree to abide by the terms of the will, well, my life will be remarkably different."

"Apparently my fate is now in your hands."

"Yes, I suppose it is." She settled back in her seat. "Rather ironic when you think about it," she said under her breath and turned toward the window.

Violet continued to gaze silently at the passing streets, apparently lost in thought. He had no idea what she was thinking. Every now and then he caught a glimpse of her expression, at once serene and determined. He suspected it did not bode well. Beyond that, there was something she wasn't telling him. Violet was entirely too unconcerned about the potential loss of James's inheritance. After all, if he lost everything, so did she.

The moment they entered the house they were met by a blonde woman Violet introduced as Mrs. Ryland, her companion and secretary. A few years older than Violet, she was quite lovely, or she would have been had she not glared at James as if he were the devil incarnate. Violet announced they had errands to run and would be back late in the afternoon.

"Will you be joining me for dinner tonight?" he asked.

Violet glanced at the other woman. "I think we'll take dinner in our rooms tonight."

He raised a brow. "Don't we have a great deal to talk about?"

"And I have a great deal to think about." She smiled politely, nodded at Mrs. Ryland, and the ladies took their leave.

He stared after them. This was not the Violet he remembered. Not the girl he had known. He had liked the old Violet. This new Violet was an unknown. And most intriguing.

Violet Branham was a woman any man would be proud to have by his side. She was strong and confident, independent and elegant—a woman of the world. And a challenge. Six years ago he hadn't especially liked challenges but he was not the man he used to be, either. At the moment she didn't seem to like him. It was entirely possible she wouldn't agree to the terms of the will. But if she did… A lot could happen in the next two years, eleven months, one week and three days.

Violet Branham, the Countess of Ellsworth, *his wife* might indeed be the right woman for him. Six years ago he'd been too young or too stupid or too scared to realize it or possibly accept it. Now, however…

For a fleeting moment, he could have sworn he heard Uncle Richard chuckling in the distance.

CHAPTER FOUR

"APPARENTLY, JAMES HAS a legitimate office." Violet stirred a dollop of cream into the Turkish coffee she preferred that Richard's—or rather James's or now her cook, she supposed—always had on hand for her visits. Thanks to a restless night, Violet had slept later than usual and it was nearly noon before she came downstairs to join Cleo in the cozy breakfast room where the widow was sorting through Violet's correspondence. "And keeps business hours."

"Who would have thought." Cleo bit back a smile. Apparently, her companion found the fact that Uncle Richard's comments in recent years about how much James had changed, the responsibilities he'd taken on, his head for management and business and his accompanying maturity did have a basis in fact and were not simply the ramblings of a loving uncle, to be most amusing.

Cleo Ryland had been Violet's companion, secretary and dear friend almost from the very day Violet had hired her. A scant three years older than Violet, the pretty young widow had been the first person to answer Violet's advertisement when she had decided to use James's financial support to travel. Violet liked her immediately and the feeling was mutual. Cleo was well-educated, intelligent with a clever wit and a desire to do something with her life other than marry the first man who came along simply for financial salvation. She was also tired of her family's—particularly her mother's—constant harping on how she needed to find a new husband before she was too old to do so. She and Violet had a great deal in common when it came to mothers. Within days, Violet had Cleo's references checked and the two women were off to see the world.

"It's most convenient, really. I'd prefer not to be around him every minute." Especially as Violet had no desire to continue yesterday's discussion quite yet. Still, it had remained on her mind throughout the long night. As much as she hated to admit it, James was right. There was little choice but to abide by the terms of Uncle Richard's will. "Unless he was at one of his many clubs, my father was always in the house. Usually in his library."

Violet glanced around the morning room. It could use a bit of freshening. In fact, the entire house could stand refurbishment. It had been a bachelor abode for entirely too long. That might be something she could take on during the next three years. She'd never been the mistress of a house and it sounded rather like fun. She had, after all, been trained for the position. It was the only thing she'd been expected to do with her life.

"In spite of the circumstances, I am glad to be back in London." Violet sipped her coffee, savoring the hearty aroma and the deep flavor mellowed by the rich cream. "This time it feels different, as if I have indeed returned for good."

"I suppose even the lure of the adventure to be found in travel pales in time."

"Perhaps." It had indeed been the grandest of adventures. "One does like to pause now and again. To catch one's breath."

"Three years is more than enough time to catch one's

breath." Cleo studied her curiously. "You're going to do it, aren't you?"

Violet met her friend's gaze. "I am."

Cleo glanced at the door as if to make certain they were alone then lowered her voice. "What are you going to do about you-know-who?"

"Quite frankly," Violet winced, "I haven't given him a second thought."

Cleo's eyes widened. "That's rather telling, isn't it? I thought you and he were—"

"We're not," Violet said firmly. "Admittedly, we have discussed the possibility of something more, as well as the possibility of divorce, but there's never really been anything more between us. I've been very clear about how I feel. He's been a good friend and he's a very nice man. And if I were free, well…" She shook her head. "I can't ask him to wait three years in hopes that my feelings will become more significant than they are."

"I see." Cleo considered her. "But you *are* going to spend three years with a man you haven't spoken to in nearly six?"

Violet knew Cleo wouldn't understand. Cleo believed James had ruined Violet's life and therefore was the root of all evil in the world. "I know you don't like James—"

Cleo snorted.

"—but I owe him a great deal."

"Nonsense." Cleo sniffed. "You don't owe him anything."

"On the contrary, Cleo." Violet blew a long breath. "He could have made my life miserable. You and I both know women whose husbands have tired of them or never especially wanted them in the first place. Their lives look fine on the surface but everyone knows how dreadfully unhappy they are. They are the subject of quiet ridicule and blatant pity. James saved me from that." She shook her head. "He married me because of a silly mistake that nonetheless would have ruined my life. He deserves some credit for doing the right thing."

"He married you and then went his own way. According to everything we've heard, he's behaved exactly as he did before he was married." Cleo pinned her with a firm look. "I think you should tell him to shove off."

Violet laughed. "You are a good friend but in this, you're wrong." She thought for a moment. "In providing generous financial support, as well as freedom and independence, James gave me the world.

"I wouldn't have become who I am and I certainly would never have met you, Cleo, had he insisted on my being an expected sort of wife. Think of the things we've seen, the things we've done, the people we've met and those we've helped in some small way. James made it all possible and for that I'm grateful." She shrugged. "I didn't say it would be easy and I'm not especially happy about it. And yes, three years is a long time, but James saved me once. Now it's my turn to save him."

"Are you going to tell him how you feel?"

"Don't be absurd. I'll tell him I've decided to abide by the terms of the will, but I certainly won't say I'm grateful to him." She adopted a wicked smile. "It would go straight to his head and that wouldn't be any fun at all. Nor do I intend to make this easy for him."

"That sounds something like revenge."

"I prefer to think of it more as retribution. If he wants his inheritance, I intend to make him work for it. I'm not sure how at the moment, but I'm certain opportunities will arise." She paused. "Besides, I like the idea of his being in my debt."

"I hadn't thought of that." Cleo nodded. "Very clever."

Violet sipped her coffee. "Aside from everything else, this was Uncle Richard's last wish. I owe him, as well."

Still, as grateful as she was for the life James had given her, there were some things she could not ignore. He never made any attempt at a real marriage with her. He never saw her, never spoke to her. Admittedly, she had said she never wanted to see him again, but that sort of thing did tend to mellow with the years. There were any number of times—especially in the first few years— when she would have been receptive to overtures, even reconciliation. When she might well have returned to truly be his wife. But he'd made no effort whatsoever. And he'd certainly never asked her to come home. Oh, she could have taken the first step toward him. Whether it was a matter of pride or simple stubbornness or apprehension, Violet refused to do so. James had made the decision as to the type of marriage they'd have, he had determined the path of their lives and it was up to James to change that path.

She might be willing to give him three years but forgiveness was another question entirely. It scarcely mattered how much these years apart had changed either of them. The moment she saw him again, she knew somewhere deep inside she would have to keep her distance and guard against the resurfacing of any of those feelings she'd once thought she had for him. The man was not to be trusted, at least not with her heart. Regardless of his intent, and whether he realized it or not, he had broken her heart all those years ago. She would not allow him to do so again.

"It might even be fun." Violet grinned. "Being Lady Ellsworth, that is."

"One can only hope." Cleo smiled. "You are already

in high demand. There are a number of invitations here
to consider."

"So soon?"

"According to his lordship's secretary, the earl is routinely invited to nearly everything of note, although his
attendance is rare. Even though you weren't here, invitations were always addressed to Mr. and Mrs. Branham
and now, of course, to Lord and Lady Ellsworth." She
paused. "Everyone in society is going to be talking about
your reconciliation, you know. The attention on the two
of you will be unrelenting."

"Thank you for the reminder." Violet had very nearly
put the stipulation about appearing as a happy couple
out of her head.

She knew full well there was no possible way for the
two of them to appear in public without causing a tidal
wave of gossip. Violet Branham may be clever, confident
and sophisticated when it came to the rest of the world
but here in London, she had always feared she might slip
back into the docile creature she used to be. That when
presented with the unforgiving, unrelenting judgmental
nature of London society—of her mother and people exactly like her—time would reverse itself and she would
again be the unassuming wallflower she had once been.
Precisely why she never stayed long in England. That
would be yet another challenge of the next three years.
"Let's wait to decide what to accept until we speak to
Mrs. Higginbotham and her friends tonight. I'm sure they
will have some suggestions."

"Lady Ellsworth." Andrews appeared at the door.
"Lady Cranton is here."

Cleo winced.

"Tell her I'm not at home," Violet said.

A distinct look of distress washed over the butler's face.

Violet grimaced. "She knows I'm here, doesn't she?"

"I'm afraid so, my lady."

"It can't be helped I suppose." Violet sighed. "Please show her into the parlor. Oh, and then ask the kitchen for tea and a tray of biscuits." Violet glanced at Cleo. "You know how she'll be if I don't offer her something."

Cleo shuddered.

"Anything else, my lady?" Andrews asked.

"A pot of coffee as well, I think." Violet nodded. "That will do. Thank you, Andrews."

The butler nodded and hurried off.

"You do realize, living in England for the next three years, seeing her will be unavoidable."

"I hadn't thought of that. Although that in itself is enough to make me change my mind," Violet added and rose to her feet.

"Are you sure you want to talk to her alone?"

"Not really, but this is my house and I'm not going to put up with her nonsense in my own home." She started toward the parlor. "But do say a little prayer for me, Cleo."

"I daresay a single prayer will not be nearly enough." Cleo's words trailed after her.

Violet paused before the parlor doors, summoned every ounce of confidence she possessed, adopted a pleasant smile and pushed open the doors. "Good morning, Mother."

Margaret, Viscountess Cranton, was as tall as her daughter with hair a few shades darker. That, Violet had always thought, was where the similarities ended. While Mother was still a fine figure of a woman, she was stern and unrelenting in her pursuit of what she deemed to be required or proper. Mother's unyielding nature was evident in her manner and her speech and showed on her face. Mother, Violet had long suspected, had never been especially happy. She would have felt sorry for Father but he didn't seem to care.

"Please God, Violet, have you at last come to your senses?"

"Delightful to see you again, Mother." Violet smiled coolly. "I thought I'd see you before now. Lady Brockwell's ball was the day before yesterday, after all."

"I've been in the country. We returned last night." Mother glared. "I demand to know what's going on."

"Do be seated, Mother." Violet waved at the sofa, then settled in a nearby chair.

Mother glanced around the parlor, no doubt assessing the quality and cost of every item in the room. She probably hadn't stepped foot in Ellsworth House since James's ill-fated engagement party all those years ago.

"Well, go on."

"I'm not sure what you want to know."

"Don't be evasive." Mother's brows drew together. "You know exactly what I'm asking."

A discreet knock sounded at the parlor doors before they opened and Andrews rolled in a tea cart. Mother set her jaw impatiently. It would never do to be caught discussing private matters with servants present.

"Would you like me to pour, my lady?" Andrews asked.

"I'll do it. Thank you, Andrews." Violet smiled and nodded in dismissal.

Andrews took his leave, no doubt grateful to escape.

"Would you care for tea?" Violet said, even as she poured a cup.

"At least you haven't forgotten everything you were taught." Mother accepted the cup and added sugar.

"I assure you, Mother, I've forgotten absolutely nothing." Violet poured herself a cup of coffee.

"Is that coffee?" Disapproval furrowed Mother's brow.

"It is." Violet widened her eyes innocently. "Oh, I do apologize. Did you prefer coffee?"

"Don't be absurd." Mother considered coffee a drink of the lower classes and therefore beneath her. "No doubt you picked up a taste for it in some godforsaken foreign coffeehouse."

"No doubt."

Mother cautiously selected two biscuits, as if she wanted to assure herself of their quality before indulging. Violet's jaw tightened.

"Why are you here, Mother?"

"Instead of waiting for you to call on me?" Mother's brow soared upward. "Who knows when that might happen."

"Come now, Mother. I join you and Father and Caroline for dinner whenever I'm in London." As much as neither Violet nor her mother enjoyed it, Violet always paid an obligatory call on her family, which usually included dinner. An ordeal no one especially enjoyed. Conversation inevitably centered around what a perfect daughter twenty-year-old Caroline was with her brilliant prospects for a match and the disastrous state of Violet's own marriage. A failure that was obviously her fault. Truth was never especially important to Mother.

The fact of the matter was Mother had never forgiven Violet for being the subject of scandal, compounded by her not becoming the perfect Mrs. Branham, now Lady Ellsworth, she was expected to be. She should have been a force in society, a renowned hostess and mother of a respectable number of offspring. A daughter an ambitious mother could be proud of. And Violet had never forgiven her mother for leaping at the chance to marry her off. Not merely because of a relatively minor scandal but because she thought this was Violet's only chance for an acceptable marriage. Which might well have been true but was beside the point nonetheless.

No one ever said aloud what the real problem was between mother and daughter. The true crux of the difficulty between them was simply that the day after her wedding, for the first time in twenty-one years, Violet Branham had at last found her courage, her voice and—thanks to James—her independence. There was nothing Mother hated more than a daughter she could not control.

"How is Father? And Caroline?"

"Your father never changes." Mother shrugged. Father was a good enough sort, Violet supposed, although she barely knew the man. He might have had more of an interest in his children had they been born sons but as they were female he had abdicated all decisions regarding Violet and her sister to Mother.

"Caroline is about to be engaged to the son of a duke." Mother paused. "Not his heir, mind you, but a younger son with three brothers ahead of him. Still, he has a significant income and one never knows what might happen in the future. Your sister could be a duchess one day."

"We can only hope," Violet murmured. One did wonder if Caroline's prospective fiancé's family should be warned as Mother would cheerfully do away with an entire line of succession to achieve her ambitions. If she couldn't be a duchess herself, a daughter for a duchess would do.

"The engagement will be officially announced at a ball next month, as befitting such an august match. I expect you to attend." Mother pinned her with a firm look. "Will you still be here?"

"My plans are uncertain at the moment." She was not about to tell her mother she would be staying in England before she told James.

"Your plans are always uncertain." Disapproval rang in Mother's voice. "You wander aimlessly around the world and rarely return to England—where you should be."

"On the contrary, Mother. It's not the least bit aimless."

"It's not the way a proper wife should behave." Mother's lips thinned. "There have been rumors you know."

"Yes, I know, Mother. You never fail to write me about every rumor or bit of gossip about my husband, for which I am most grateful."

"The rumors are not just about him." A warning sounded in Mother's voice.

"Oh, good. I would hate for him to have all the fun."

For a long moment Mother glared and Violet glared right back. There was a time when Violet would have backed down. Said something placating and apologized. It was easier and peace would be restored. She'd stopped that years ago when she'd realized capitulating to her mother would make no difference in their relationship but would make a great deal of difference in how Violet felt about herself.

"I assure you, Mother, any rumors about me are greatly exaggerated with no more than a morsel of truth in them at best."

"I should hope so!" Mother studied her intently. "You and Lord Ellsworth were seen dancing together."

"He's an excellent dancer and he *is* my husband."

"That has never seemed to matter to you before."

Violet shrugged. "You wanted me to have a husband and I have one. You never particularly cared how he and I felt about one another."

Mother ignored her. "And you left the ball together."

"We *are* married and we do reside in the same house."

"No one has ever seen you together before." Mother's eyes narrowed as if she were trying to see into her daughter's very soul. "Have you and your husband reconciled?"

"It's really none of your concern," Violet said blithely.

"Of course it's my concern. I am your mother. I have only your best interests at heart."

Best interests? It was all Violet could do to keep her temper in check. "Really, Mother? When did you begin having my best interests at heart?"

"I have always put you and your sister above all else," Mother said in a lofty manner, which might have been most effective had Violet been able to recall even once when that was true.

"Did you put my interest above all else when you forced me to marry a man who didn't want to marry me?" And there it was. The charge she had avoided making for almost six years.

"You were ruined!" Mother's eyes widened in indignation. "My insistence on marriage saved you from a life of being alone."

"And what do you think my life has been thus far?" The words were out of Violet's mouth before she could stop them. She wasn't sure why she'd said that. She hadn't been alone these past years. Far from it. She'd had Cleo and any number of friends abroad. Why, she was the least alone person she knew. And if she didn't have a husband who cared for her, well, that was the price to be paid for independence.

"Your life would have been perfect if you hadn't been so headstrong."

"You know nothing about my life, Mother."

"I daresay I know far more than you suspect." Mother

stood. "Has your husband finally put his foot down and demanded you return home and pick up your responsibilities as his wife?"

Violet rose to her feet. "My husband does not put his foot down nor would I allow him to do so."

"That might be one of the problems." Mother sniffed.

"You simply will not accept that you forfeited the right to ask me anything when you forced me into marriage."

"Nonetheless, I *am* asking if you and your husband—"

"Why do you care? What possible difference does it make to you?"

"People talk, Violet, and they've been talking about you for nearly six years. It's a source of constant humiliation for the entire family. Why, we're lucky your scandalous life hasn't affected Caroline's impending engagement!"

"Well, he is only a younger son, Mother."

"If you and your husband would just come to your senses and—" Mother gasped. "Dear Lord, you're here to ask for a divorce, aren't you?"

"That is no concern of yours."

Mother sucked in a sharp breath. "There has never been a divorce in this family. The scandal will ruin us all. I insist—"

"For God's sakes, Mother," Violet snapped, "that's quite enough. I am not asking for a divorce and yes, I am back to stay." She drew a deep breath. Mother was an expert at the art of gossip and might well be useful at dissipating any untoward rumors about Violet and James's apparent reconciliation. "After all these years apart, James and I have at last acknowledged we share the kind of mad, passionate love every woman dreams of! There now, are you happy?"

"Not at all because that's utter nonsense and I don't

believe you for a moment." Mother huffed. "One doesn't stay away for years then wake up one morning to discover true love was there all along."

"Actually, Mother…" Violet raised her chin. "One does."

"My dear, darling wife." As if on cue, James strode into the room, pulled her into his arms and gazed deeply into her eyes. "It's been but a few hours and yet it seems like an eternity since I left your side."

"Does it?" What on earth was he doing? Violet gazed up into his blue eyes, dark and endless and…amused?

"When we're apart, I count the minutes until we're together again." He lowered his head to hers as if he intended to kiss her.

Violet's breath caught.

Mother cleared her throat.

"Oh, I am sorry. I had no idea anyone else was here." He released Violet, but slid one arm around her waist in a blatant display of affection. Blatant displays of affection were every bit as bad in Mother's view as wives not being *proper*.

"James, you remember my mother."

"Yes of course." His arm tightened around her in a manner that could only be called possessive. It was oddly satisfying.

"Lord Ellsworth." Mother eyed him suspiciously. "I should take my leave."

"Delightful to see you again." He nodded toward the door. "Andrews will see you out."

"Violet, I expect your attendance at your sister's ball."

"Good day, Mother."

"Good day, Lady Cranton," James said and nuzzled the side of Violet's neck as if Mother wasn't there. A shiver ran down her spine. She really should protest but how would that look?

"Dear Lord," Mother muttered and marched toward the door.

Violet steeled herself against the melting sensation of James's lips against that surprisingly sensitive spot where her neck met her shoulder and waited until the parlor door closed behind her mother. Even then it was far harder to get the words out than one would expect. She drew a deep breath. "What do you think you're doing?"

CHAPTER FIVE

"I'M CONVINCING YOUR mother as to our reconciliation."
James kissed that delicious juncture of neck and shoulder. Her scent—an arousing mix of jasmine and spice—wrapped around him and it was all he could do not to pull her tighter against him. "As she is one of the most notorious gossips in London, it seemed an excellent idea."

"Well, she's gone now." Violet pushed out of his arms. "You can stop that."

He grinned. "I rather enjoyed it."

"You would."

Given the charming flush on her cheeks and the look in her eyes, so did she, although she'd never admit it. Still, it was interesting. His grin widened.

"Nonetheless, it was entirely inappropriate. This is a farce, James. Nothing more. You do need to remember that." Her voice was firm even if there was the tiniest breathless quality to it. That too was interesting.

"Did you say that just to annoy your mother?"

"Probably." Her brows drew together in confusion. "Say what?"

"That you and I had reconciled. That after all these years we share a mad, passionate love."

"Surely I didn't say anything of the sort." A blush washed up her face. Oh, he liked that. "Did I?"

"Your words exactly."

"One says all sort of things when one fails to give due

consideration to one's words." She blew a long breath. "Yes, I suppose I did say some of it to annoy her. But really, what one says in the heat of—"

"Passion?"

"*Annoyance* cannot be taken as irrefutable." She cast him a questioning look. "So you remember my mother?"

"She continues to haunt my dreams." He shivered. James would never forget how adamant Lady Cranton had been that they marry. How angry she'd been at him—justifiably—but how angry she'd been at Violet, as well. It wasn't at all fair. As if any of this had been Violet's fault.

"There is nothing my mother finds more scandalous or improper than mad, passionate love."

"Actually, I was wondering about the rest of it." He adopted a casual tone. "About staying in London. With your husband." He held his breath. "Did you say that part to annoy her, as well?"

"No. I had already come to that decision." She squared her shoulders. "I like my life, James. Three years seems a small enough price to pay for my independence and my freedom."

"So you'll do it for the money?" he said slowly. Relief mixed with a tinge of disappointment. Surely he couldn't expect her to do it for any other reason. Still…it had been a long night and he'd done a great deal of thinking. All about her. Or rather, about them. Although he'd never not thought about her in one way or another through the years.

In the beginning, he'd gone on with his life as if he'd never married at all. In truth, his drinking, carousing and meaningless encounters with women had increased after Violet left. James blamed it on guilt. It was easy to forget what a cad be was, how he had ruined her life, if he was inebriated or had an anonymous woman in his bed. After he passed the second anniversary of his marriage, the appeal of raucous behavior, random women and drunken stupors began to fade. It was around that time too that Uncle Richard had been struck by a violent but blessedly brief illness and James had begun learning what was required to follow in his uncle's footsteps. Upon later reflection, he acknowledged that was the true beginning of adulthood.

Violet raised a shoulder in a casual shrug as if money was as good a reason as any.

His brow rose. "You needn't act as if you were doing me a great favor."

"Oh, but I *am* doing you a great favor."

"You have as much to lose as I do."

She met his gaze directly. "No, I don't."

"Oh?"

She hesitated then shrugged. "It's not important at the moment." She turned and headed toward the stairs.

"It sounded important." He strode after her.

"I'm not going to discuss this now." She reached the grand stairway and started up. "But I'm not agreeing to this because I have no other choice."

"Yes, I've heard about your choices," he called after her.

Violet Branham, Lady Ellsworth, *his wife*, might not be aware of it but there had been nearly as much gossip about her over the past six years as there had been about him. He knew the truth about his behavior, but he had no idea if the stories he'd heard about her were accurate. Of course, some came from Duncan, Viscount Welles, who had mentioned running into Violet somewhere in Europe in recent years. Welles was an old friend, one of the very men who had issued the ill-fated challenge to kiss his fiancée on that night six years ago. Even so, the information was not firsthand. Regardless, what James heard about Violet's behavior had grown increasingly bothersome as his own conduct had become more respectable.

"My choices?" She swiveled on the stairs and glared down at him. "What do you mean by that?"

"Never mind." He waved off her question. Discussing this now was a mistake. After all, they had three years ahead of them. "It doesn't matter."

"I suspect it does matter," she snapped.

Apparently, she was not going to let the subject drop. Very well. Let the games begin. "You have not been entirely inconspicuous these past six years. There have been rumors, gossip."

Her eyes narrowed. "What, exactly, have you heard?"

"You said yourself nothing can be done about the past." It was his turn to adopt an offhand manner, as if none of this was of any significance. "What's done is done."

"Nonetheless, I would like to know what you have heard."

"I doubt that." He turned and strode toward the library. This was not the sort of talk a man had with his wife without the benefit of spirits.

"You cannot make vague, unsubstantiated charges and then just walk away," she called after him.

"Actually, I can." He stepped into the library, snapped the door closed behind him and crossed the room to the cabinet where Uncle Richard kept convenient bottles of brandy, whiskey and assorted spirits.

A moment later the door crashed open and he tried not to grin. He'd suspected this new Violet wouldn't be able to resist continuing the conversation.

"If you want to start something like this at least have the courage to finish it!"

James took a bottle of whiskey and poured a glass. "Would you like a glass?"

"Goodness, James, it's barely past noon."

"If we're going to start the first day of the next three years reliving our sordid pasts, I for one am going to need fortification."

"No doubt." She moved to him, plucked the glass from his hand and took a sip. "My past is not the least bit sordid, thank you very much."

He eyed the glass. "I believe that's mine."

"Not anymore." She smirked and took another sip. "And I prefer to think of it as clearing the air. If we're going to spend the next three years together as a *happy couple* in public, I daresay it's best to get everything out in the open. To alleviate the possibility of untoward surprises."

"We wouldn't want that." He poured a glass for himself.

"I'd rather not appear shocked when some well-meaning acquaintance decides it's time I was informed of all of my husband's indiscretions."

He sipped his drink and studied her. As curious as he was about the rumors regarding her behavior, he wasn't at all sure confessing his own transgressions was wise. Fuel on the fire and that sort of thing. "It seems to me, we have a great deal to discuss regarding the past six years. Are you certain you wish to start with this particular topic?"

"Why not?" A distinct challenge shone in her eyes. "I must say I'm surprised you've had the time to pay any attention to rumors about me when there's been so much gossip about you."

His tone sharpened. "One does tend to note gossip about one's wife."

"As one tends to note rumors about one's husband."

Her voice hardened. "Something like, oh, say, his dalliance with an opera singer."

"Or her liaison with a French count."

Her teeth clenched. "His affair with an American actress."

"Hers with an Italian sculptor," he said sharply. That tidbit came straight from Welles.

"His with any number of merry widows!"

"Hers with some talentless Greek poet!"

Her eyes widened. Apparently he'd hit the mark with that charge. Not that it gave him any satisfaction. Until now, he wasn't sure he really believed any of the rumors. This was Violet, after all.

She choked back a laugh.

Although she had certainly changed. "You find this amusing?"

"Yes, actually I do." She grinned. "Don't you?"

"No!" he snapped. "I don't find any of this amusing."

"You used to find much of life amusing."

"I am not the same man I used to be."

She snorted in disbelief.

"I shall make a deal with you, Violet," he said evenly. "I won't throw your affairs in your face if you don't throw my affairs in mine. We'll leave the past in the past."

"I don't know. Throwing your indiscretions in your face sounds rather enjoyable to me." She sipped her whiskey and considered him. Apparently, she was not going to make this easy.

"What I'm proposing is a truce."

"I was unaware we were engaged in battle."

His gaze met hers directly. "We have been engaged in a game of warfare since the night I kissed you on a darkened terrace."

"Nonsense." She scoffed. "We haven't even seen each other."

"Am I wrong?"

"I suppose it has been something of a battle albeit a silent one."

He sipped his drink. "Perhaps we could be, well, friends again."

"Unwilling partners perhaps but friends?" She tossed back the rest of her whiskey in a manner any man would be proud of. "I don't think I can be your friend."

"Nonetheless, you are my wife."

"Six years ago, you didn't want a wife."

Six years ago I was an idiot. "And yet I have one who now apparently has to act like a wife." He drew a deep breath. "As I intend to act like a husband."

Her brow arched upward. "Do you?"

"It's what Uncle Richard wanted." He paused. "We were friends once, Violet, you and I."

"Once was a very long time ago, James." She set her glass down on a nearby table and headed for the door. "Lady Higginbotham and her friends will be here for dinner at half-past seven. Don't be late. And do dress appropriately."

"That sounded very much like a wife to me," he called after her.

She glanced over her shoulder. "Oh, my dear James, that's just the beginning."

"Excellent dinner, Lord Ellsworth," Lady Blodgett said with a pleasant smile. "Do give my compliments to your cook."

"Mrs. Clarke will be pleased to hear you enjoyed it." James smiled.

Lady Blodgett and Mrs. Fitzhew-Wellmore were the

friends of Mrs. Higginbotham's she'd said were going to help her oversee the conditions of the will. All three ladies were of advanced years although one could see they must have been quite lovely in their younger days. Marcus and Mrs. Ryland completed their company. Marcus had noted privately earlier in the evening how he and James were horribly outnumbered and they should be on their toes. If this was indeed a game there were three distinct factions as evidenced by the seating at the table. James sat at the head at the table, Violet opposite at the far end. Mrs. Ryland sat next to Violet and beside Marcus who was on James's right. The three older ladies sat on the other side.

Mrs. Higginbotham proclaimed before they were seated that there would be no discussion of Uncle Richard's will until after dinner. Both James and Marcus spent the better part of the meal doing their best to charm the females at the table. Which did seem to work well with the exception of Violet—who even while she directed the conversation around the table was cool and aloof at least toward James—and Mrs. Ryland, whose distaste for James was only barely concealed. Although she did not appear entirely immune to Marcus's charms even if it did seem the widow was trying to resist the engaging solicitor. Apparently, she was reluctant to throw her lot in with the enemy.

All in all the meal was pleasant enough if one ignored the superficial nature of the conversation and the currents eddying just below the surface.

"So." Mrs. Higginbotham looked around the table. "Shall we begin?"

"Perhaps we should retire to the parlor," Violet said in her best lady of the house manner. Her mother would be proud. James stifled a laugh.

"Oh, I think here at the table where we are all on equal footing is preferable," Mrs. Higginbotham said and looked at James. "Unless you object?"

"Not at all, Mrs. Higginbotham." He smiled at the older lady. No doubt the next three years would be fraught with problems regarding her interpretation of Uncle Richard's stipulations. It was not too soon to try to get her in his corner.

Her eyes narrowed slightly as if she knew exactly what he was thinking. "Excellent."

Violet signaled Andrews, who nodded and left the room, returning almost at once with decanters of brandy, port and sherry. Andrews obviously anticipated the company staying at the table and James wondered if Violet and Uncle Richard had done so during her visits.

Once the table was cleared and they all had glasses of brandy or port, the older ladies insisting they preferred the more traditional lady's offering of sherry, Mrs. Higginbotham began. "I gather the two of you have agreed to abide by the terms of the will."

James met Violet's gaze and they nodded.

"Excellent." Mrs. Higginbotham looked at Marcus. "Shall we take Richard's stipulations one at a time?"

Marcus nodded. "Whatever you prefer."

"Very well." Mrs. Higginbotham thought for a moment. "First, is the requirement that you live together for the next two years, eleven months, one week and three days or rather two days now with no more than fourteen days spent apart in any given year." Mrs. Higginbotham's gaze circled the table.

"That seems fairly straightforward to me. Are there any questions?"

"Is there any requirement as to where we reside? Are we confined to England?" Violet asked.

"As long as the two of you are living together, under the same roof, not at all." Mrs. Higginbotham paused. "Although it would be most difficult for Lady Blodgett, Mrs. Fitzhew-Wellmore and myself to oversee the terms of the will if you chose to live abroad. In Rome for example."

"In which case, Effie, Poppy and I would feel it necessary to reside with you." Lady Blodgett smiled in an agreeable manner that in no way negated her threat.

"I for one have always wanted to live abroad." Excitement rang in Mrs. Fitzhew-Wellmore's voice.

"I don't intend to live anywhere but England." James's tone was more than a little pompous. Where on earth had that come from? He'd never been even remotely pompous before. "And I don't consider it confinement."

Violet's jaw tightened but her tone was cordial. "I wasn't suggesting we *live* somewhere else. I was simply wondering if it was possible to travel."

"Of course it is, dear." Mrs. Fitzhew-Wellmore, who did seem the nicest of the older ladies, smiled at Violet. "You'd simply have to take him with you."

"I have no desire to travel," James said in an offhand manner. His reticence to travel had more to do with the violent reaction of his stomach to being on a ship than anything else. Even the rocking motion of lengthy train trips, especially those through mountainous areas, brought on a nasty queasiness. When he had discovered that tendency he had blamed it on an overindulgence in spirits. He really didn't care to find out if he was right or not.

"Travel is the grandest of adventures, James," Violet said. "There's an entire world beyond England's shores, you know."

"I traveled the continent after I left school and found that more than sufficient."

"Ah yes, the grand tour young men of privilege take to indulge in scandalous pursuits under the guise of culture." Violet smiled pleasantly, belying the look in her eye that clearly indicated what she thought of young men on grand tours.

He ignored her. "Besides, I have entirely too many responsibilities here to take the time needed for traveling."

At once five pairs of skeptical eyes fixed on him. Marcus nodded encouragement. James smiled and sipped his brandy.

Violet opened her mouth to say something, then apparently thought better of it and pressed her lips together.

"The second condition," Lady Blodgett began, "requires you to be seen as a couple three times a week."

"That seems rather a lot," Violet said.

James leaned forward and met her gaze. "Don't you want to be seen with me?"

"Not particularly."

He smiled slowly. "You don't really have a choice."

She ignored him and turned her gaze to Mrs. Higginbotham. "What constitutes an appearance as a couple?"

The ladies exchanged glances.

"We've been discussing that very thing," Lady Blodgett began. "We don't believe it's necessary to attend a ball or soiree or anything of that nature three times a week."

"That would be most exhausting," Mrs. Fitzhew-Wellmore added.

"Appearing as a couple is not at all complicated," Mrs. Higginbotham said. "Why, tonight's dinner is certainly the two of you as a couple with others."

"Perhaps you should have dinner with us every night," James said wryly.

"Sarcasm, my lord?" Lady Blodgett pinned him with a hard look, and James resisted the urge to squirm in his seat.

"Sorry," he murmured.

"We couldn't possibly be here every night," Mrs. Fitzhew-Wellmore said then sighed. "Although the food was excellent."

"We feel something as simple as guests for dinner would be acceptable to meet that obligation," Mrs. Higginbotham said. "Especially in the beginning. We propose the three of us join you for dinner once a week although you may certainly invite other people. That takes care of one weekly appearance and will allow you to keep us informed as to the other two appearances, as well."

"We have taken the liberty of asking your secretary, my lord," Lady Blodgett said, "as well as Mrs. Ryland—"

Violet shot a surprised look at her friend who winced.

"—to gather the invitations you've received of late. We shall compile a list of those which would be suitable for your initial public appearances."

James drew his brows together. "I think we are more than capable of handling our own social engagements."

"No, she's right." Violet cast the older woman an admiring look. "While I have kept up on the comings and goings of London society there are no doubt nuances I have missed. And it might be best to ease our way into this new life rather than leap in headfirst."

"I've always liked leaping in head first." James smirked. Marcus bit back a grin.

"And that has proved to be so successful for you in the past," Violet said in an overly sweet tone.

"We also suggest rides in Hyde Park, either on horseback or in a carriage, visits to galleries, attendance at lec-

tures, the theater, exhibitions, concerts, that sort of thing."
Lady Blodgett smiled. "It might be quite enjoyable."

"That would be four hundred and twenty-four appearances as a couple. I figured it out." Mrs. Fitzhew-
Wellmore paused. "Well, four hundred and twenty-three
given this evening counts as one."

"I'm not sure it was necessary to calculate the number of appearances, Poppy." Mrs. Higginbotham's gaze
shifted from Violet to James and back. "I believe you've
frightened them."

"It does sound rather overwhelming," Lady Blodgett
noted.

"Nonsense." Mrs. Fitzhew-Wellmore waved off the
comment. "I can't imagine much of anything scares either Lord or Lady Ellsworth."

"I'm certainly not afraid of spending time with my
wife." James met Violet's gaze. "I cannot speak for Lady
Ellsworth however."

"Goodness, James," Violet said coolly. "The last thing
I'm afraid of is you."

"Excellent." Mrs. Fitzhew-Wellmore beamed. "Then
the final stipulation is the one prohibiting scandal or gossip." She paused. "Although gossip about how Lord and
Lady Ellsworth have reconciled their differences and
are apparently quite happy would certainly be acceptable. Agreeable gossip as opposed to scandalous rumors.
You understand."

Mrs. Higginbotham's gaze circled the table. "While
neither Lady Blodgett, Mrs. Fitzhew-Wellmore or myself
are prone to gossip—"

Mrs. Fitzhew-Wellmore choked. Lady Blodgett smiled
serenely.

"—we are not without connections. We are well aware

of the past gossip involving each of you. That is at an end."

"I have no difficulty with that." Violet smiled.

James nodded. "Nor do I."

"To everyone outside of our little circle here, the two of you will appear to be happily reconciled. I believe it would be wise as well to keep the stipulations of the will private—to avoid undue gossip." Mrs. Higginbotham turned to Violet. "You do understand that you will be taking up management of the household as per your position as Lady Ellsworth."

Violet nodded. "I assumed as much." She glanced at James. "Will I have a free hand? To manage the staff as I see fit? And with regards to all matters pertaining to the residences?"

"Of course," James said. He really hadn't considered that there was now a lady of the house. It was rather a nice idea. "Regardless of how little time you've spent here in the past, this is your home as is Ellsworth Manor. You are Lady Ellsworth, after all."

"The first Lady Ellsworth in quite some time, given Richard never married," Mrs. Higginbotham pointed out.

Violet smiled with satisfaction, a bit too much satisfaction really.

"However, even the most loyal of servants do gossip you know," Lady Blodgett said. "Which means even here you will have to behave in a cordial manner toward each other."

Violet shook her head. "This feels like a poorly written French farce."

"Then perhaps you need to rewrite it, dear." Mrs. Fitzhew-Wellmore smiled pleasantly.

"I have no desire to lose the property that has been in my family for generations but aside from all else…"

James chose his words with care. "This is what Uncle Richard wanted. I am not thrilled with the manner in which he is forcing us to abide by his wishes but if Violet is willing to do so, I am, as well."

"I told his lordship earlier today, I would abide by the terms of the will. For Uncle Richard," Violet added and smiled at Mrs. Higginbotham. "He really was a wonderful man."

"Then allow me to propose a toast." Marcus rose to his feet. "To his lordship, Richard Branham, the late Earl of Ellsworth."

The toast echoed around the table and James swallowed against a lump in his throat. As much as he would have preferred Uncle Richard had found some other way to encourage a reconciliation with Violet, James knew the determined old man had only done what he thought was best. His methods were questionable but his heart was not.

"And here's to Lord and Lady Ellsworth and the next three years," Marcus added. The gathering responded with varying degrees of enthusiasm. James was fairly certain only he heard the rest of Marcus's words. "God help you both."

WASN'T IT NICE of his lordship to send us home in his carriage?" Poppy snuggled back against the tufted leather seats.

"I'd say it's the least he could do," Effie said. "We are, after all, the only thing that might save his future."

"Not, of course, the main purpose of his uncle's will," Gwen pointed out.

"Richard's letter was very clear on that point," Effie said. "There was no doubt in his mind that these two people potentially share a great love and belong together.

I don't see it myself but we shall take Richard's conviction on faith. He has charged us with making certain that happens and has given us three years to accomplish it."

"Three years might not be enough. This is going to be harder than I thought." Gwen frowned. "I don't remember the last time I've attended a more awkward meal."

"But the food was excellent," Poppy murmured.

"Surely you didn't think Richard could simply throw them together and all would be well?" Effie scoffed.

"I had rather hoped that would be the case," Poppy said. "As his late lordship did think they were fated to be together it seems to me, fate really should lend a helping hand."

"One cannot count on fate," Gwen said. "Fate however, can count on us."

"No one said this would be easy." Effie drew her brows together. "I agree that the evening was awkward and there was a palpable sense of tension in the air."

Gwen nodded. "A great deal was left unsaid at that table."

"At least they're not at each other's throats," Poppy pointed out.

"That's something, I suppose." Gwen sighed.

"Actually, I don't think it is." Effie considered the evening. There was something missing… "There was no particular, oh, I don't know, *spark* between them. There were moments of course but all in all, he was pleasant and she was polite. At least if they were arguing, if their blood was at a boil, that would indicate some sort of, well, passion."

"Passion?" Poppy's voice rose. "What on earth are you thinking?"

"She's thinking's there's a fine line between the passion of anger and passion of another sort." Gwen grinned. "I must say that's brilliant."

"There is nothing more satisfying than scratching a persistent itch." Effie smirked.

"I don't understand." Poppy shook her head. "We're going to make them itch?"

"In a manner of speaking," Gwen said. "From tonight's observation, I suspect James is more amenable to reconciliation than Violet. While they both seem quite stubborn, it would appear Violet is extremely wary, as well. Perhaps our next step should be to determine how they really feel about each other."

Effie nodded. "The more information we have, the quicker we can move this along. We would hate for them to fall into the habit of merely existing together. No, we need to strike while the iron is hot."

"One does prefer to avoid being mercenary," Poppy said slowly, "but the longer this takes, the more Effie will be paid."

"That is a consideration," Gwen added. "We do need the money."

"Richard's money is nothing more than a momentary respite." Effie forced a note of confidence even she didn't believe. "It simply gives us a bit of room to come up with a way to salvage our sagging finances. Nonetheless, financial considerations will not influence our efforts. And I will not have a dead man's final wish hanging over my head for the next three years. Richard believed James and Violet belong together. And together they shall be." Effie set her chin stubbornly. "Whether they like it or not."

CHAPTER SIX

VIOLET JOTTED DOWN another idea regarding refurbishment of the house in the notebook beside her plate, ignoring James's entry into the breakfast room. She'd retired to her room the moment their guests had left last night, once again politely declining James's invitation to join him in the library.

"Good morning," he said in a pleasant enough manner, bypassing the table for the breakfast offerings on the sideboard.

"Good morning," she murmured, her gaze still on the page before her.

"I trust you slept well."

"Quite well, thank you." In truth she'd barely slept a wink. Dinner with Mrs. Higginbotham and her friends had driven home just how difficult and challenging the next three years would be. Beyond that, she couldn't get James's suggestion that they be friends again out of her head. Their friendship had once been the first step toward heartbreak. She would not make that mistake again. Polite cordiality while maintaining an aloof distance was the right path to take if Violet was to survive the next three years with her heart intact.

She really hadn't considered the game they'd be playing. They would be together continually, pretending to be a happy couple. More than once through the long hours of the night she had revisited her decision to adhere to

the conditions of Uncle Richard's will. And more than
once she had aimed disgruntled comments toward Uncle
Richard in the hereafter.

Most annoying of all was that his uncle had put James's
future squarely in Violet's hands. Which did seem only
right, all things considered, but was still a nasty burden
to bear. Unless Violet was mistaken, James had no idea
she had financial resources of her own.

Before their wedding, Uncle Richard had set up a private trust for Violet that, according to the terms of their
marriage agreement and the myriad papers she and James
had both signed, was to be hers and hers alone. A few
years ago, Violet had asked Richard if he had provided
her with her own financial security because he didn't
trust his nephew. Richard had simply said James was a
good man who would one day also be reliable, depend-
able and responsible. Until then, Violet's private finances
were a reserve against disaster. A reserve Richard was
confident she would never need. Indeed Violet had never
touched any of the money and the trust had grown to a
tidy fortune thanks to clever investing and sage advice.

Which made Richard's will all the more mysterious.
He knew she could do without his money. That threaten-
ing not to give it to James wouldn't really affect her. Apparently Richard was counting on her to go along with
the stipulations to save his nephew. Whether the earl
thought she would do so because she still had feelings for
her husband or because James had given her opportunities she would not otherwise have had or simply because
she was a decent enough person she would never know.

James filled his plate and sat down at the table.

"Did you sleep well?"

"I had an excellent night's sleep," he said in a hearty
manner she didn't believe for a moment. She knew better.

The master suite dressing rooms separating his bedroom from hers were not deep enough to muffle sound. And James's bed creaked. Loudly and horribly like the moaning of the hounds from hell.

Violet had slept on any number of hotel mattresses and she couldn't recall even one that was worse. Judging by the incessant creaking of his bed, the man had tossed and turned all night and he'd had no more sleep than she. If there was one thing that drove her mad, it was not being able to sleep.

"Where is Mrs. Ryland this morning?"

"She had a family matter to attend to." After Violet's mother's visit yesterday, Cleo decided she should call on her own before her family learned she was back in London. While Cleo's family was not in the same circles of society as Lady Cranton, one of her sisters had married the brother of a viscount and was usually well informed of the latest gossip.

"Are you going to your office today?"

He chuckled. "I go to my office every day."

"Every day?" She turned a page in her notebook. "That's impressive."

"Is it?"

"It implies you are serious about the responsibilities you have taken on."

"Did you think my office was simply some sort of ploy? Something to fool the world into believing I have accepted my obligations? That I am now the man my uncle hoped I would be?"

She looked up and met his gaze. "I'm not sure what to think. In the past few years, Richard wasted no opportunity to talk about how you have matured. Accepted your position. Given up your wild ways, that sort of thing."

"Well, not all of them." He grinned in an altogether too

wicked manner, and her heart fluttered, as unexpected as it was annoying. She ignored it. His tone sobered. "Apparently, I now have to prove it to you."

The sincerity in his eyes was unmistakable. Still, reconciling this new James with the man she had married was difficult and might well be impossible. "There's no need to prove anything to me."

"Oh, but there is." He selected a piece of toast from the rack on the table and slathered it with jam. "If we are to survive these next three years, you need to understand that I am not the man I used to be."

"We shall see," she murmured and returned her gaze to the clean notebook page in front of her. She scribbled the first thing that came to mind, ignoring the fact that she had written the very same line on the previous page.

For several minutes he didn't say a word, but she could feel his gaze on her. "I like having an office," he said at last, "and I admit it is a symbol of sorts. More of independence than anything else really.

"Uncle Richard used to take care of all his business here, in the library, as most men do. When I started learning to manage his affairs, I worked at a table near his desk. But as I gradually handled more and more and hired a secretary, my needs outgrew the table. At the same time, his supervision of his business endeavors and property management and everything else grew less and less. Some days I would look over to see he was doing nothing more than reading the *Times*."

She glanced up at him.

"The desk in the library has been in the family for generations. It was his father's and his grandfather's before him for at least the last century. My uncle once told me one of his strongest memories was of his grandfather sitting behind that carved mahogany beast. It's really quite intimidating, you know."

Violet smiled wryly. "Yes, I know."

"Be grateful you never had to sit in front of it to be taken to task for your sins." He shuddered.

"I can well imagine how daunting that might be." Although she had sat in front of the desk during her visits when she and Uncle James would discuss her accounts and investments, he had never chastised her for anything. But then, in spite of gossip about her, there had never been anything to chastise her for.

"Daunting?" He scoffed. "Try terrifying."

For a moment, she could see James as a boy sitting in one of the chairs positioned in front of the desk, waiting for whatever judgment Uncle Richard might deem suitable for any transgression James had committed.

"The desk has always been a symbol, the sacred altar of authority. It's always been used by the head of the family." He paused. "Even though Uncle Richard offered the use of the desk, my doing so was like saying his time was at an end. That he was no longer useful or necessary or wanted." He shook his head. "I couldn't do that."

"So you acquired an office," she said softly. She'd never doubted James's affection for Richard but that was based on Richard's comments alone. Here and now it was obvious how much her husband had cared for the old man.

"I did." He nodded. "Aside from this house and Ellsworth Manor in the country, my uncle owns—" his brow furrowed "—I suppose I own them now at least for the time being—several professional buildings here in London. I took a suite in one of those buildings. Now that my uncle is gone I could give it up, I suppose, but I rather like leaving the house every day. Being out in the world.

Being part of the world." He smiled in a self-conscious manner.

"Do you?"

He nodded. "I know it sounds rather odd for someone of my background, but the world—Uncle Richard's world and the world of all those earls that came before him—is changing rapidly. Family fortunes used to be dependent on land but that will soon no longer be the case. We have to change with the times or in time we will be left behind. We are approaching the dawn of a new century, you know." James speared a piece of sausage and popped it in his mouth.

Violet had no idea what to say.

James continued to eat his breakfast as if he hadn't just said something rather clever and profound and insightful. And damned impressive.

"One other thing." He took a sip of coffee. "In spite of the family heritage, I've always hated that desk."

"Really?"

"Good God, Violet, have you looked at it?"

"It is rather imposing."

"The legs are carved with writhing mythological beasts devouring unrepentant sinners."

"I never noticed."

"Perhaps because you've never been a ten-year-old boy sitting in front of it at eye level with a dragon or a snake consuming a screaming villager, awaiting your own fate."

"Yes, well, I can see where that might be disheartening."

"At the very least." He shook his head. "I have no desire to put my children through that."

"You want children?" she said without thinking.

He raised a brow. "Don't you?"

"Well, yes, but…"

"But that is a discussion for another time." He took another sip of his coffee and set his serviette beside his plate. "What are your plans for today?"

"Oh, this and that. Nothing of any particular importance." She squared her shoulders. "Lady Ellsworth might as well begin making public appearances. Mrs. Higginbotham and her friends invited me to join them for tea."

"They're a dangerous group," he warned with a smile. "I would watch myself if I were you."

"I shall be alert at all times."

"See that you are." He grinned and stood. "I should be off. Good day, Violet."

"Good day, James."

With that he took his leave.

Violet tapped her finger absently on her notebook. That was certainly unexpected. Oh, they had conversed any number of times before their marriage when he was courting Marie but that had always been lighthearted and vaguely flirtatious and of no consequence whatsoever. They had never spoken of anything even remotely serious.

It struck her that she really didn't know anything about the man she had married and now suspected she never had. She had fallen head over heels for him based on nothing more than flirtatious banter and a wicked smile. How dreadfully shallow of her. And how stupid.

There was obviously more to James than she had thought, then or now. Which didn't mean there could ever be anything between them.

Of course, a tiny voice whispered in the back of her head, it didn't rule it out either.

"...AND WE DO think the spring ball at the Explorers Club the week after next would be perfect for your first no-

table public appearance." Effie tapped the first line of a
long list of social engagements she had placed in front
of Violet. Mrs. Higginbotham and the other ladies preferred Violet call them by their given names as they were
inevitably going to spend a fair amount of time together
in the next three years and would surely become great
friends. "It's going to be quite special in recognition of
the Queen's anniversary year. She won't attend, of course,
but the ball is in her honor."

"I'm not sure we are invited to that," Violet murmured,
staring at the list. It was longer than she had expected
and filled with names of people she hadn't seen in years.
People she wasn't at all sure she wished to see.

"Of course you are, dear." Gwen smiled. "And if you
hadn't been we would have made certain you were."

The ladies had asked to meet here at the ladies' reading room at Fenwick and Sons, Booksellers for refresh-
ments and a chat.

Violet scanned the lists. "Why the Explorers Club
Ball? I had no idea James was a member."

"Indeed he is, as was his uncle before him." Poppy
lowered her voice in a confidential manner. "The vast
majority of the Explorers Club membership comprises
men who will never do anything more adventurous than
maintaining their membership. But they do like belong-
ing and they provide financial support and a certain elite
status, as well. You understand."

Violet nodded.

"We thought this particular event would be suitable
for, oh, dipping your toes in the societal water so to
speak," Gwen said. "While the very fact that Lord and
Lady Ellsworth are at last residing together will be the
subject of a great deal of discussion nearly everywhere
you go, the Explorers Club is not quite as socially con-

scious as something like Lady Scarsdale's annual ball or the charity fete for military widows and orphans, or the Queen's garden party or any number of other events you've been invited to."

"Although you will have to face some of those sooner or later," Effie warned.

"Beyond that," Poppy continued, "we will be at the ball should you have need of us."

"That's very kind of you." For good or ill, these women were going to be a part of her life for the next three years. Best to get everything out in the open. "Do you know how James and I came to be married?"

The ladies exchanged glances.

"As you are well aware," Gwen began, "London society is a world all its own and there are subtle divisions. Our husbands were men of adventure. Effie's husband William was a military man for much of his life. My dear Charles and Poppy's Malcomb—"

"God rest their souls," Poppy said under her breath.

"—were engaged in exploration. None of us married wealth or titles. My husband was knighted long after we were married. Our friends and acquaintances were not quite the same as his late lordship's although the earl, William and Effie were great friends in their youth."

"Just tell the girl." Effie huffed and met Violet's gaze. "While we are not in the same social circles, we do have a great number of connections between us. And the story of a passionate kiss between a man about to be engaged—"

"Don't forget the slap." Poppy grinned. "I thought the slap was the best part."

"—is a juicy bit of gossip that does tend to spread widely." Sympathy shone in Effie's eyes. "So yes, we knew all about the circumstances of your marriage when it occurred, long before I received Richard's instructions regarding his will."

"I daresay there probably isn't anyone in London who doesn't know." Poppy winced. "Although it was a long time ago," she added helpfully.

"I assumed as much." Violet smiled weakly. "At least it saves me from having to tell the tale now."

Poppy leaned forward. "Do you hate him?"

Violet widened her eyes in surprise. "Hate who?"

"James, of course." Effie's brow furrowed. "Although I suppose you might hate Richard now as well for putting you in this situation."

"I'm not especially happy about it, but no." Violet shook her head. "I loved Uncle Richard. I could never hate him."

"And James?" Effie's gaze locked with hers.

"James made a stupid mistake six years ago." Violet chose her words with care. "But even though he had no desire to wed, he did the honorable thing and married me." She thought for a moment. "I thought he had ruined my life but recently I've come to the realization that he in fact saved my life. He gave me the freedom and the resources that made me the woman I have become. And I like her. I like me." She shook her head. "I could never hate him."

"Excellent." Poppy beamed.

"However," Violet added, and Poppy's expression deflated. "He didn't want a wife at all and he certainly didn't want me." She drew a deep breath. "Rather upsetting to discover the man you've just married doesn't want you."

The ladies nodded as one.

"I have never forgotten that nor have I forgiven him. While it does appear that James is decidedly different from the man he once was—as I am not the same woman I was six years ago—I don't know that I can trust him."

"Understandable." Effie raised her chin. "Trust has to be earned."

The other ladies nodded in agreement.

"But you don't *dis*like him?" Poppy asked.

"I only just today realized I barely know him." Violet shook her head. "I don't dislike him but I can't say I like him, either."

"Trust." Poppy nodded. "It's all about trust."

"For the next three years I intend to keep him at arm's length." Violet squared her shoulders. "I shall be cordial and polite."

"Cordial and polite is certainly a beginning," Gwen said. "But we did think you were a bit, oh, docile last night."

"Docile?" Violet frowned. "Me?"

"Men will walk all over you if you let them," Effie warned.

It had been six years since Violet had been anything approaching docile. "I thought I was appropriately aloof."

"Well, that's a discussion for another time." Effie waved off the comment. "We were wondering what your thoughts were regarding your position as Lady Ellsworth."

"Well, I'm assessing the house as to needed refurbishment. Other than that, I really haven't given it much thought." Right now all Violet could think about was *docile*. Dear Lord, if she was docile after three days what would happen after three years? She absolutely would not become the woman she once was.

"Oh, you should, you really should. You have a unique place in society now and society will expect a great deal from you," Gwen said. "Your every action will be noted and commented upon."

Violet shrugged. "That's nothing new. I daresay I've been scrutinized every time I've returned to London."

"Then you are most assuredly up to the task." Poppy smiled. "We've heard nothing but wonderful things about you."

"That is good to know." Violet sipped her tea, still trying to get *docile* out of her head.

"We've no doubt you will be a brilliant Lady Ellsworth, at least publicly." Effie paused. "Privately is another matter."

Violet's brow rose. "Oh?"

"James is used to an all-male household." Gwen shook her head. "He no doubt thinks life will not change for him. Men get set in their ways. For most of James's life, he and Richard lived a carefree bachelor existence with no significant female presence."

"You are about to change that," Poppy added firmly. "It's important to start this relationship on the right foot."

"I did think—"

"Men like to believe they're in charge but we know better." Effie nodded. "You must carve out your position right from the beginning. Grab the bull by the horns as they say. Take the reins, my dear."

"Men do need to be, oh, what's the word?" Poppy glanced at her friends.

"Managed," Gwen said. "As you would manage a household." She frowned. "Do you know how to manage a household?"

"I never have but I'm confident I can." For that at least her mother could be credited.

"Although it is best if men don't *know* they're being managed." Effie refilled her cup from the pot of tea on the table. "Male pride and all that."

"I'd never really considered—"

"Most men expect women to be biddable, subservient creatures dedicated to making the lives of men comfortable."

"I daresay—"

"You're a clever, independent woman who has spent years traveling the world," Gwen said.

"Assert yourself my dear." Effie nodded. "Be the woman you've become."

Violet drew her brows together. "I intend to be."

"It's never too soon to begin." Poppy selected a biscuit from the tiered plate on the table.

"For good or ill, the man changed the course of your life," Effie said. "Now, he's depending on you to save the rest of his."

"And he did give you a free hand." Poppy smiled sweetly but there was a determined look in her eye. "We suggest you take it."

"After all." Effie met Violet's gaze. "You are Lady Ellsworth. The first Lady Ellsworth in quite some time."

"We know you're up to the task." Confidence rang in Gwen's voice.

"Indeed I am." Violet raised her chin. Docile indeed!

"Excellent." Poppy beamed. "Now then, you must tell us all about your travels."

"Our husbands were always traveling but none of us have been anywhere at all." Effie nodded toward Poppy. "Oh, Poppy visited Paris as a girl."

"And we did once spend a few weeks in the Lake District," Gwen said.

Poppy nodded. "We can't imagine a greater adventure than seeing all those places one merely reads about. And we do so want to hear all about your adventures."

"*All* about my adventures? Are you sure?" Violet asked with a smile. "I have been traveling for some time now."

"Oh, my, yes." Gwen nodded. "It will be as if we were there with you."

"Well…" Violet thought for a moment. "Where would you like to begin?"

"I have always wanted to travel to Italy." Poppy's eyes shone with excitement. "And Switzerland."

"India," Effie announced. "Definitely India. And perhaps…"

It seemed there wasn't anywhere in the world the threesome didn't want to see for themselves.

"Very well, then. I shall start at the beginning." She thought for a moment. "After my marriage, the first place I traveled to was Paris." She glanced at Poppy. "But as you've been there perhaps I should start with someplace else?"

"Oh, no." Poppy shook her head. "It's been so long since I was there I scarcely remember it at all."

"Photographs of Paris, even paintings, do not do it justice," Violet began. "Paris is as much a state of mind as anything else. The first thing one notices…"

For the next hour or so Violet regaled her new friends with stories of the City of Light, of the fascinating sights she had seen and equally fascinating people she had met.

The ladies were right. If she didn't stand up for herself, no one else would. She was willing to act as James's wife for the next three years but she was not about to become the woman he had married.

And docile was the last thing she intended to be.

CHAPTER SEVEN

"OH, YES, JAMES, yes, yes, yes."

Violet's red hair spread across the pillows, strands of twisted solid flames. Her fingers dug into his shoulders and she writhed beneath him. He thrust into her over and over, faster and harder. Moans of pleasure sounded deep in her throat, matching his own, spurring him on. He lost himself in the feel of her delectable body beneath his, the heat of her flesh, the press of her tightened nipples against his chest, the delicious scent of her wrapping itself around his soul. The headboard banged against the wall, knocking louder and louder with every thrust of his cock deep into her. At last she was his and he was hers. So very good. So very right. Meant—fated—to be. Pleasure and need spiraled within him and her body rose up to meet his. The pounding increased, echoing through his blood, his body, his soul. Louder and faster and—

James jerked upright in bed, the dream of Violet moaning his name abruptly shattered. "Bloody hell!"

He scrambled off the bed, threw on his dressing gown, strode to the door and flung it open. "What in the name of all that's holy is going on?"

Violet stood before him, dressed in a riding habit the exact emerald shade of her eyes, hand raised to knock yet again.

"Did I wake you?" she asked in an innocent manner. Her gaze flicked over him, pausing at the obvious evi-

dence of his arousal beneath his robe. "Or perhaps I interrupted?"

Now was probably not the best time to confess she
had awoken him from a dream about her—about them—
nor was it the first erotic dream he'd had about her. "I
was asleep!"

"My apologies." Her gaze returned to his eyes, the
most delectable blush washing up her face. "Shouldn't
you do something—" she fluttered her fingers in the general vicinity of his erection "—about that?"

Under other circumstances, he would have stepped
behind the door in an attempt at modesty. But *she* had
pounded on *his* door and he wasn't the least bit happy
about it. Even now the urge to pull her into his arms and
finish what he'd started in his dreams was damn near
irresistible. He crossed his arms over his chest. "What
would you suggest I do?"

"I don't know. Something."

"Are you offering your assistance?"

"Don't be crude, James," she said in a weak voice, then
cleared her throat. "I thought we could take a ride in the
park. It will fulfill one of our obligatory appearances."

"Now?"

"Unless things have changed dramatically in the years
I've been away, no one who is anyone rides in the park
until ten at the earliest. Therefore, we shall have the place
to ourselves."

He shook his head in an effort to clear it. "It's still
dark."

"The sun will be up in a few minutes. Which gives
you just enough time to dress."

"So you have awakened me before dawn to ride in
the park?"

"Oh, I've always enjoyed a nice, invigorating ride in

the park, especially early in the morning. I find it most stimulating," she said, then apparently realized what else her words might mean. Her blush deepened.

"I would hate to deprive you of stimulation," he said wryly.

"Excellent." She adopted a pleasant smile but the blush did not recede. Interesting in a woman of her rumored experience. "I shall see you downstairs, then." She turned and swished off down the hall, her nicely bustled ass swaying behind her.

He refused to hurry to dress, taking a bit more time than was necessary although he did need to alleviate his current state of arousal. He certainly couldn't ride a blasted horse like this. Besides, it was too damn early in the morning to be up and about.

This wasn't the first time he had dreamed about her. Dreams that had increased in frequency in the last few years. For that he blamed Uncle Richard's incessant campaign to bring them together—as well as his own sense of guilt and possibly the fact that he couldn't remember the last time he'd been with a woman. Surely celibacy also played a role in his nocturnal amorous adventures. But the dreams he'd had since she'd taken up residence in the room next to his were far more intense and intimate and passionate than any he'd had before. This most recent dream had been the worst. Or possibly the best. Perhaps it had been triggered by their comments about wanting children. There was only one way to have children.

He wanted her back, although really he'd never had her in the first place. Now, thanks to Uncle Richard, he would have to do something about that. Even he knew it was past time. She was willing to be his wife in little more than name only at the moment. It wasn't enough. He wanted more. He wasn't sure when he had realized that, but he had. He wanted her in his life for more than three years. He wanted her in his bed. And he wanted her heart. She had claimed his with that first kiss on the terrace even if he'd wasted years refusing to accept it. What an idiot he'd been. He'd never set out to make a woman fall in love with him before, but this was different. This was his wife. This was Violet.

James made his way downstairs to the front entry to find it empty. Jonas, the lone footman, who did not look particularly awake, opened the door a split second before James reached it. Violet was outside, already mounted, the reins of a second horse held by a sleepy stable boy.

"I am so pleased you were *finally* able to join me, my lord." Violet flicked her gaze over him. "And people claim women take a long time to dress." She turned her horse in the direction of the park.

He mounted his horse and guided the beast into place beside her. "Oh, I wouldn't have missed this. One can never start the day with too much stimulation."

She shot him a sharp glance. He ignored it.

They maneuvered their horses around the few early-morning vehicles they encountered and in no time had entered Hyde Park and made their way to Rotten Row.

"You're right." He drew a refreshing breath. "This is an excellent time of day for a brisk ride. I should do it more often."

"It does require getting out of bed at an early hour, you know." The tiniest hint of what might have been amusement quirked the corners of her lips. "You don't seem inclined to do that."

"I would rather stay in bed, but as there was nothing to keep me there—" he bit back a grin "—and you were most insistent, here I am. I see you're as good a horsewoman as you always were."

"How on earth can you say that?" She slanted a glance at him. "I don't recall us ever riding together."

"Someone must have mentioned it to me."

"Marie, no doubt. Although I daresay it wasn't a compliment," she said coolly. "She was never particularly impressed by anything that wasn't involved with clothes or parties or social position."

He was hard-pressed to deny it. Indeed, even at the time he had realized Marie's shallow, self-involved nature was not something he wished to be trapped with for the rest of his life. "That friendship always struck me as odd. You and she had nothing in common."

"Our mothers were friends and insisted we be friends, as well." She shrugged. "Marie liked having me around. I was no threat to her."

He chuckled. "That's not how I remember it."

"Then your memory is faulty."

"A possibility perhaps." He paused. "I remember you as being very quiet and reserved. It did strike me then that you preferred being in the background."

"Yes, I suppose I did." She fell silent for a moment. "It was easier to keep my mouth shut, keep my opinions to myself, rather than run the risk of being chastised or worse—ostracized."

"You were quite well-read and knowledgeable."

Her expression tightened. "Not something encouraged in a girl."

"And you were very easy to talk to."

"About nothing of substance if I recall."

"I rarely talked about anything of substance in those days." He chuckled. "But I remember you and I talking a great deal about any number of subjects."

"No, James. You talked, you charmed, you flirted outrageously and I listened attentively and nodded in agreement, whether I agreed or not." She shook her head. "We might have thought we knew each other then, but we were mistaken."

"And yet I thought we did." Even so, it was not an attractive picture, at least from her perspective. "We danced quite a lot, as well. You were an excellent dancer."

"Thank you. I had excellent teachers. My mother made sure of it." She fell silent for a moment. "Do you ever regret not marrying her?"

"Marie? I regret the manner in which it ended," he said simply. "But not marrying Marie was the second smartest thing I've ever done."

"Only the second?" Her brow rose. "And what was the first?"

"Marrying you."

She reined her horse to a stop and glared at him. "Good Lord, James. Do you honestly expect me to believe that?"

"I'm being honest with you."

"Is this part of you making amends for your mistakes?"

"Not entirely. It has more to do with accepting my responsibilities. Facing the future." He met her gaze directly. "And understanding what I want in life."

"And do you know what you want?" Challenge sounded in her voice and shone in her eyes.

He stared at her for a long moment. "It's taken me six years but yes, I do."

"Utter nonsense." She scoffed and urged her horse to a brisk trot.

He directed his mount to keep pace with hers for a time when she spurred her horse to a canter. But when she took off at a gallop, he slowed, mesmerized by her, the very vision of freedom and independence. He couldn't imagine having to sit sideways on a horse but had to admit the grace and beauty of woman and horse moving as one was striking. This was a woman to admire. Hadn't Uncle Richard been telling him that for years? His stomach tightened. And she was his. Legally, anyway.

They scarcely spoke on their return to the house. He slid off his horse the moment they reached the front walk and turned to help her before she could protest.

"Mine is not the memory that's faulty." He kept his hands on her waist and gazed into her eyes. "You did far more than simply listen and nod. You told me you loved the writings of Jane Austen because the heroines in her stories were strong and defiant. You think Lord Byron's words are the most romantic ever written. You like Charles Dickens and while you agree with him regarding social reforms, you do not like being preached to in the guise of entertainment."

Her eyes widened in surprise and he continued before she could say a word.

"You enjoy the works of Gilbert and Sullivan but aren't fond of serious opera. You believe women should and will someday be allowed to vote and you think chocolate is a gift of the gods." He nodded sharply. "You didn't just listen and nod, Violet. And I didn't just talk and flirt, although I admit I did a great deal of that. But I listened, too." His gaze bored into hers. "Whether we like it or not, Uncle Richard gave the two of us a second chance. I, for one, intend to take it."

"Don't you think it's a bit late for that?"

"No, I don't. I have made some terrible decisions and dreadful mistakes."

"And now you intend to atone for them?"

"Indeed I do." He released her and started up the front

steps. "I'm going to change, then I'll be down for breakfast."

"When do you plan to start on this path to atonement?" she called after him.

"I already have." A distinct sense of satisfaction washed through him. He would win her affections if it was the last thing he ever did. Admittedly, he had no idea how at the moment.

He hadn't courted a woman since Marie and to call that a courtship at all was being generous. Marie had practically fallen into his arms with no more effort on his part beyond his usual flirtatious nature and the fact he had wealth and was heir to a respectable title. It took very little to win Marie's heart and in hindsight he realized he never had. Marie wanted *what* he was, not *who* he was.

Violet would be far more difficult. And entirely worth it.

The man he was six years ago was not up to the task. The man he was today refused to fail. Not at this.

He had laid down a gauntlet of sorts. Whether or not she picked it up remained to be seen.

And in many ways, the game had just begun.

THE DOOR TO the library swung open with far more force than was necessary. The tiniest sense of triumph trickled through him.

Violet stood in the doorway. "We need to talk."

James leaned back in the chair behind Uncle Richard's desk and considered her. "You didn't particularly wish to talk at breakfast this morning after our ride. And while you and Mrs. Ryland talked a great deal at dinner, you did not think it necessary to include me in your conversation."

"That might have been rude of me."

His brow rose. "Might have been?"

"I am not usually rude. My apologies."

"Accepted." He stood and circled the desk. "Brandy?"

"Dear Lord, yes."

He chuckled, poured her a glass then crossed the room and handed it to her. His fingers brushed against hers and she sucked in a quick breath.

"Thank you." She moved away from him and took a bracing sip.

"Would you like to sit down?" He nodded at the chair in front of the fireplace.

"No. Yes. I don't know." She huffed and glared at him. "Why did you say that today?"

"I said any number of things today." He returned to the desk and picked up his brandy.

Her eyes narrowed. "Let's start with your terrible decisions and dreadful mistakes."

He grinned. "It's going to be a long night."

"This is not amusing," she said sharply.

"Come now, you have to admit, it is a little amusing. Two people who married to avoid scandal then lived separate lives now forced to live together for three years and appear to the world as a happy couple? All while avoiding yet another scandal?" He sipped his drink. "It has all the markings of a Shakespearean comedy."

"Don't be ridiculous," she said, but the tiniest glint of amusement shone in her eyes.

"You're the one who said it was a poorly written French farce."

"You may have a point, but it's of no importance. Now, we're discussing your terrible decisions and dreadful mistakes. Which would you like to talk about first?"

"Where should I start?"

"Oh, why don't you choose?"

"You have no intention of making anything easy for me, do you?"

"No." She smirked. "I do not."

"Very well then." He sifted through his long list of errors in judgment. "It was a mistake to go our separate ways, not to attempt a real marriage with you."

"I can agree with that."

"However." He paused. "We would have both been miserable. I was young and stupid and arrogant. I would have made a horrible husband."

She snorted. "Go on."

"I would have broken your heart." He shrugged. "The only thing I did right was to admit I wasn't ready for marriage."

Violet studied him for a long moment. "Possibly."

"My next mistake was agreeing never to see you again."

"That was my edict."

"And I abided by it." He shook his head. "I shouldn't have. At least not as long as I did."

"At any point in the last six years, you could have asked me to come home."

"Yet another mistake. You may add it to the list."

"I will." She was softening, not overtly, but he could see it in her eyes. "Is there more?"

"Undoubtedly." He grimaced. "But nothing else comes to mind at the moment." James raised his glass to her. "I shall let you know when something else occurs to me."

Suspicion shone in her eyes. "You also said you intend to take the second chance Uncle Richard has given you."

"Given *us*."

"Given us." Reluctance sounded in her voice. "What did you mean?"

"I mean, my dear Lady Ellsworth, I have three years

to prove to you that I am not the man I used to be." He stepped toward her. She stepped back. "Three years to change your mind about me."

"Change my mind?"

"It's obvious you don't like me." Again he took a step toward her. Again she took a step back, the look in her eye wary. How very interesting.

"I don't *dis*like you."

"You liked me once." He stepped closer. She moved back, her eyes widening when her delightful derriere hit the desk.

"As nothing more than a friend."

He swirled his brandy in his glass and gazed into her eyes. "You said you don't want to be my friend."

She sidestepped him and made her escape. "No, I said I didn't think I could be your friend."

"Why not?"

"We haven't seen each other in six years. I daresay we really have nothing in common—"

"Except for marriage."

"Yes, well, there is that. But this whole idea of a second chance…" She threw back the rest of her drink and shook her head. "I don't know. Perhaps we could be friends at that."

He thought for a moment. "I'm afraid friendship is no longer possible."

"What?"

"I want more."

Her brow furrowed. "I don't understand."

"I want my wife," he said simply.

"You mean me?"

"You're the only wife I have." He moved to the brandy decanter, then returned. She held out her empty glass.

"And the only one I want." He filled her glass, set down the decanter and moved toward her again.

"Wait." She held out her hand to stop him. "You want me as your wife and everything that entails?"

He nodded. "I do."

"Including the more…intimate aspects of marriage?"

He grinned. "I certainly wouldn't rule that out."

"I see. That is interesting." She eyed him thoughtfully, the most intriguing look on her face.

He wasn't sure if that look was good or bad but it did seem the air—the balance—in the room shifted slightly.

"You're right, James, friendship will probably not do for either of us." She smiled. "But this wife idea does have merit."

"It does?" Caution edged his voice. What was she up to?

"I will certainly give it due consideration." She thought for a moment. "In spite of your innate instincts, this is not something we can leap into all at once."

"Probably not," he said slowly.

"So I will abide by the terms of the will with a great deal of enthusiasm. And perhaps at the end of three years, I might indeed embrace the intimate parts of marriage. When it becomes my choice, without the threat of losing your inheritance hanging over us." She leaned toward him and smiled sweetly. "When I decide."

She turned and started toward the door. "And until then, I shall be the best Lady Ellsworth the world has ever seen. You wanted a wife and a wife you shall have." She glanced back at him. "You did mean it about a free hand, didn't you?"

"You are Lady Ellsworth."

"Excellent. Good night, James." She paused. "Sleep well." The door shut behind her.

What on earth had just happened? He'd had the upper hand, but somehow she'd wrested control. But she'd also admitted she didn't *dis*like him, which left the door open for something more in the future.

He grinned.

And for now, that would do.

CHAPTER EIGHT

"SHE'S DRIVING ME INSANE. Stark raving mad." James signaled to the server for another whiskey. He and Marcus sat in their favorite chairs in their favorite section of Prichard's, their favorite gentlemen's club. A club not so conservative in nature as Uncle Richard's preferred club, with membership generally younger. Still, it was respectable, venerable and had been in existence since before Victoria was crowned. It was a male sanctuary and today, exactly what James needed.

"You don't look insane," Marcus said.

"Look closer," James muttered.

"Now that you mention it, you do look a bit mad." Marcus aimed a pointed figure at his friend. "Right there. Around the eyes. There's a definite hint of madness." He considered his friend curiously. "Not going well with the lovely Lady Ellsworth?"

"It's not going badly, I suppose," James admitted grudgingly. "But I wouldn't say it was going well, either." He paused. "Or perhaps it's going too well."

"Apparently, I was wrong." Marcus grinned. "You are mad."

James leaned forward in his chair. "She said she intends to be the best Lady Ellsworth imaginable. I'm not entirely sure what that means but I think her intention is to drive me—"

"Yes, yes, I know." Marcus waved the comment away. "Why on earth would she do that?"

"Revenge," James said darkly.

"Might I point out she did agree to your uncle's stipulations. She didn't have to."

"She does have as much to lose as I do."

"I'm not sure about that," Marcus said thoughtfully. "I ran across a notation in your uncle's file the other day that I intend to look into."

"A notation about what?"

"I don't know yet so I don't want to say anything more at the moment."

James frowned. "You do love being at once vague and suggestive."

"Indeed I do. It's a gift." Marcus grinned. "So how exactly is she driving you mad?"

"The woman has completely taken over my life. And my home. She says the house has been the purview of bachelors for far too long and needs refurbishing. It's now been invaded by an army of tradesmen armed with paint and wallpaper and fabric. The library is the only place still safe. Still *mine*."

"Well, she is Lady Ellsworth." Marcus paused. "And she might have a point."

"There's nothing wrong with the house," James said firmly. "Beyond that, she is unwaveringly polite, chipper, cheery and a smile never fades from her face. But not one of those sweet and pleasant the-world-is-a-wonderful-place sort of smiles, but rather an I'm-biding-my-time smile or a just-you-wait smile." He aimed his glass at his friend. "That smile does not bode well."

Marcus chuckled. "Scared, are we?"

"Not for a minute. Oh, I am treading with caution

but—" James smiled reluctantly "—I have to admit, I'm rather enjoying this game we're playing."

"Well, that's something, isn't it?" Marcus paused. "I thought you were going to employ the more charming aspects of your nature to work your way into her affections."

"I am being charming. I am being as bloody charming as any man can possibly be." He accepted a new glass of whiskey from the waiter and took a much needed sip. "She barely says more than what's necessary. Unless we are appearing together publicly, I rarely see her." His jaw tightened. "Even when she joins me for breakfast or dinner that watchdog of hers is almost always present."

"Ah, the delightful Mrs. Ryland."

James scoffed.

"You don't find her delightful? With all that blond hair and those enchanting blue eyes?"

"I tend not to appreciate women who despise me," James said dryly.

"I see your point." Marcus chuckled. "She doesn't despise me."

"Then you should marry her and get her out of my way." James straightened in his chair. "That's an excellent idea."

"For you perhaps." Marcus snorted. "I'm not going to marry a woman just to make your life easier."

"You did say she was delightful."

"Even so—"

James sank back in his chair. "I'd do it for you."

Marcus laughed. "No, you wouldn't."

"I expect better from you," James said in a lofty manner.

"My apologies for disappointing you." Marcus grinned. "It can't be that bad."

"I think Violet intends to torture me for the next three years."

"In the event she doesn't drive you mad?"

"It's a two-pronged attack."

"You haven't seen each other for nearly six years. A period of adjustment is to be expected. It's only been a little over two weeks, after all."

"Two long, endless weeks." Two weeks in which, aside from anything else, he'd had very little sleep.

How could he sleep when he was so very aware of her presence in the room next to his? Awareness that led to all sorts of thoughts. To wicked, longing desires. And his dreams. Good God. If he wrote them down, they'd be banned. And rightfully so. Every night he'd had to take himself in hand just to relieve the aching need.

"I haven't heard from Mrs. Higginbotham so I'm assuming you're abiding by the terms of the will regarding the necessity of public appearances."

James jerked his attention back to his friend and nodded. "Mrs. Higginbotham has given us a great deal of leeway in that regard. Apparently an early-morning ride in the park—entirely too early by the way—counts as a public appearance even though we have yet to run into anyone we know. So every morning—we ride."

Marcus's brow rose. "How early?"

"Dawn." He shuddered. "The first time Violet pounded on my door, the sun was barely on the horizon. I thought the house was on fire."

Marcus choked back a laugh. "You've never been fond of early mornings unless they were a continuation of the night before."

"Those days are over."

Admittedly, their morning rides were surprisingly enjoyable and an invigorating way to start the day. It had

been his experience that riding with ladies in the park
was a dignified, tranquil, relatively boring experience
and good for little more than engaging in conversation.
With Violet it was another matter entirely. As there were
few people in the park during their early-morning out-
ings, she felt free to alternate between brisk canters and
spirited gallops. Yesterday, she had even challenged him
to a race. Worse, she had beaten him, which he claimed
was only due to his innate sense of chivalry. Her eyes
had flashed with delight and she'd said he was rather endearing in his self-delusion.

"So Lord and Lady Ellsworth have yet to appear at a
social engagement?"

"Mrs. Higginbotham suggested it might be wise to
ease our way into society. Violet seems in no particular hurry."

"Maybe she's afraid." Marcus shrugged.

"Violet?" James raised a skeptical brow. "I can't imagine she's afraid of anything. Once, perhaps, but not now."

"Come now, James." Marcus rolled his gaze toward
the ceiling. "Think about it. She left England right after
a titillating bit of scandal and has rarely spent more than
a few weeks here since then. I can't imagine anyone who
wouldn't be apprehensive about reentering that particular world."

"I doubt it. Uncle Richard always took great delight in
telling me Violet routinely attended any number of social
events during her visits."

"A temporary stay is a far cry from permanent resi-
dency."

"It's possible, I suppose. The ladies suggested our first
significant social outing—the Explorers Club ball tomorrow night." James eyed his friend hopefully. "Would you
like to join us?"

"The Explorers Club ball?" Marcus grimaced. "I can't think of anything less exciting."

"Perhaps if Mrs. Ryland was to come along…"

"What are friends for?" Marcus grinned. "I'd be delighted to join you."

"Good." He sipped his drink. "At least if I'm dancing with Violet, she can't escape. I thought I had known her all those years ago although I see now I barely knew her at all."

"Oh?"

"She was something of a wallflower. More interested in books and poetry than anything else. But she had a quick wit, even if it rarely surfaced. Odd, we both remember those conversations differently now." He grinned. "But I distinctly recall every now and then, I'd catch her staring at me as if I were something quite remarkable."

"And then you broke her heart."

"Rubbish. She wasn't the only woman who looked at me that way. I was considered quite a catch. I may have ruined Violet's life but I didn't break her heart."

"Are you sure?"

"Yes, of course." Was he? The idea had never occurred to him before now. Did Violet have feelings for him beyond friendship six years ago? Surely he would have noticed. But in truth, hadn't he been just as self-centered as Marie? "Good God, what if you're right?"

"It would certainly explain why she's so standoffish now."

"That paints an entirely different picture, doesn't it?" At once, the morning after their wedding flashed through his mind. He'd thought she'd been offended—understandably so—but perhaps it had been something deeper he'd seen in her eyes. And when she'd insisted

she never wanted to see him again… "How could I have
been so blind?"

Marcus wisely said nothing.

"Bloody hell. What an arrogant ass I am. Was," he
added quickly. "I *was* an arrogant ass. I would hope I'm
a better man now."

"We all hope that." Marcus grinned then sobered.
"Perhaps some of her reticence to be alone with you is
because she doesn't trust you. If she did indeed have feelings for you once, if she was hurt by your, well, rejec-
tion of your marriage, it's entirely possible she fears the
return of those feelings."

"I never imagined…" He shook his head. "I'm going
to have to earn her trust, aren't I?"

"At the very least." Marcus thought for a moment.
"How do you feel about her?"

"I was fond of her all those years ago."

"And now?"

"Now, I find her…intriguing. Fascinating. Exciting."
He thought for a moment. "She's determined. And clever.
In a terrifying sort of way. She doesn't hesitate to speak
her mind. She's, well, a challenge."

"You've never really faced a significant challenge,
have you?"

"Not for a moment." James shrugged. "Things come
easily for me. I'll not apologize for that."

"You realize arrogance will not serve you well."

"Yet another challenge."

Marcus raised his glass. "I have confidence in you."

"That's one of us." He braced himself and met his
friend's gaze. "I want more than three years. I want the
rest of my life with her."

"You what?"

"You heard me."

"Even so, it's hard to believe."

"I assure you, you're no more surprised than I." James grimaced. "Now that she's here, I can see what I've missed and what I want."

Marcus stared. "Are you in love with her?"

"I don't know. I'm not sure I'm ready to call it that quite yet but…perhaps I always have been." He paused to gather his thoughts. "Maybe I was just too young and stupid and arrogant to realize it." Or maybe he had known it the moment his lips had touched hers. "Maybe I've been a bloody fool for the last six years." He drew a deep breath. "I think Uncle Richard was right."

"Yet another unexpected development."

"Isn't it, though?" James wasn't quite sure he believed it himself. "Who would have thought the only woman I want to seduce would be my wife."

JAMES ABSENTLY HANDED his hat and gloves to Jonas and started toward the library. His talk with Marcus had given him a great deal to think about. The idea that Violet might have felt something beyond friendship for him had never so much as crossed his mind. It certainly did explain her unyielding determination to keep her distance.

He glanced into the parlor and groaned. Rolls of fabric and wallpaper littered every available space. Everywhere he looked, workmen measured the floors, the windows and the walls. Others covered furniture with sheeting and rolled up the carpets. He stepped back to avoid two men carrying a large piece of covered furniture out of the room. Mrs. Ryland stood in the middle of it all directing the activity.

"Where is she?" He glared at the woman.

Mrs. Ryland glanced at him. "Good day, my lord."

"Good day," he said in a disgruntled manner. "Where is my wife?"

"I believe she's in the library."

"*My* library?"

She smiled politely but a wicked gleam sparked in her eyes.

"Bloody hell." He started toward the library then paused. "You don't like me very much do you?"

"I didn't know I was expected to," she said in an overly pleasant manner then turned to finish her discussion with a short, balding man holding a large notebook.

"I suppose not," he muttered, and headed toward the one room in the house he considered his sanctuary. The scene of organized confusion in the parlor was echoed in the dining room, the breakfast room and every other room he passed.

He reached the library and threw open the library door. "What are you doing in my library?"

Violet glanced up from behind the desk—*his* desk—and smiled that deceptively pleasant smile of hers. "*Our* library, James." She scribbled something in her ever-present notebook. He was starting to hate notebooks. "I didn't expect you to return from your office so early."

"My hours are my own." He snapped the door shut behind him and approached the desk.

"How lovely for you."

"Violet." A distinct warning sounded in his voice.

With an exaggerated sigh, she set her pen down and folded her hands on top of her notebook. "Yes, James?"

"Answer my question."

"Why don't you sit down."

"I prefer to stand."

"You're towering, James." She settled back in the chair and gazed up at him. "I really don't like it."

"I really don't care."

"I'm in the library because there's a great deal of activity in the house and I needed a place where I could hear myself think." She glanced around thoughtfully. "Make some notes, jot down ideas, that sort of thing."

"About the library?" Shock widened his eyes. "*My* library?"

"*Our* library."

He sucked in a sharp breath. "You will not touch so much as a footstool in this room."

She ignored him. "The drapes need to be replaced to start with."

"This was Uncle Richard's favorite room." He planted his hands on the edge of the desk and leaned forward, his gaze locking with hers. "You will leave this room alone."

She stood and mimicked his stance, leaning toward him over the desk until her nose was a scant few inches from his. The neckline of her dress dipped, revealing nothing in particular beyond a hint of shadow. A most distracting shadow. "You said I could do as I wished."

"Yes, but I didn't mean—"

"What did you mean?"

"I'm not sure now." What the hell had she done to him? "But I didn't mean you could disrupt my entire house."

"*Our* entire house. And the disruption is just beginning." She dropped back into her—*his*—chair. "Once this floor is finished, I shall move on to the upstairs bedrooms and parlors."

His jaw tightened. "I don't think this is necessary. Any of it."

"I do. And I'm not the only one." A wicked smile curved her lips. "Uncle Richard agreed with me."

James glared. "Uncle Richard would never agree to the chaotic disruption of his household."

She cast him a pitying look. "And yet he did. On more than one occasion right here in this very room."

"Then why wasn't it done before now?" A smug note sounded in his voice. He had her there.

Apparently, she didn't realize it, given the look in her eye. "Because Uncle Richard wanted *me* to take it in hand. He said he wouldn't trust such an undertaking to anyone but me." She rose to her feet. "This is long overdue, James." Her gaze traveled over him. "And quite frankly, the house isn't the only thing that could do with a bit of refurbishment." She studied him with an assessing eye. "When was the last time you had a new suit of clothes?"

"This is new." Indignation rang in his voice. "My tailor finished this suit not more than two months ago."

Her brow arched upward. "Your tailor?"

"And Uncle Richard's, as well." Let her disagree with that.

"Uncle Richard was well past his eightieth year. You are barely thirty." Again, her gaze raked over him. "The style of his apparel suited a man of his advanced years. You might wish to consider a new tailor."

It wasn't enough that she was trying to change his house, now she wanted to change him, as well. "My tailor suited Uncle Richard and he suits me."

"Of course, if you wish to look a bit stiff and stodgy and old-fashioned and far older than your years—" she shrugged "—by all means, go right ahead."

"I beg your pardon."

"I'm only being honest, James. I would think honesty between a husband and wife would be paramount to a successful partnership."

"A what?"

"A partnership." She smiled. "An equal partnership."

"An equal partnership?" This made no sense at all.

"We're not going to get anywhere at all if you keep repeating what I say."

"That doesn't sound like any marriage I've ever heard of."

"Then we shall be unique," she said, as if the matter were closed. "Well, more unique."

"If we are to be equal partners... " He chose his words with care. "Then I should have a say as to how things are managed in this house."

"Goodness, James, management of the household has always fallen to the lady of the house. It is in fact what I have been trained to do."

"Nonetheless—"

She held out her hand to stop him. "However, in the interest of cooperation and partnership, I will limit any changes to the library to those I deem absolutely necessary." She smiled pleasantly. "I suspect you won't even notice."

"I suspect I will," he snapped.

"You did say I had a free hand." A distinct gleam of triumph shone in her eyes.

"You're right, I did." He huffed and started toward the door. Blasted woman thought she had the upper hand. He paused in midstep. Not for long. He turned back to her. "I was wondering how long Mrs. Ryland would be staying with us."

"I really haven't given it any consideration." Suspicion shone in her eyes. "Why?"

"Now that you're residing here permanently, you no longer have need for a companion. And I prefer not to have a woman who detests me living under my roof. I suggest you discharge her."

Her eyes widened. "I will not! I need her assistance. Besides, she's my friend."

"And she may remain your friend." He stifled a satisfied smile. No need to lord his triumph over her. "But you no longer need a companion and I want her out of my house."

"She acts as my secretary, as well."

"She may remain in that position if you wish. However, my secretary does not reside with us, nor shall yours."

Her eyes flashed and he braced himself.

"Very well," she said in a clipped tone. "In the interest of *partnership*, I will abide by your wishes. I concede that you may have a legitimate point and I will admit that you are right. Cleo doesn't like you."

He snorted.

"But I will not turn her out into the street. She'll need some time to find a place to live."

"A week or so should be sufficient I would think." He could agree to be generous. He had, after all, won this round. A minor triumph in the scheme of things, but a triumph nonetheless.

She rose to her feet and cast him a pointed look. "Is there anything else you wish to discuss?"

He frowned. "I still don't see why you have to change anything."

"You wanted a wife, James, and now you have one." She smiled that frighteningly pleasant smile of hers.

"This is not what I had in mind."

"Ah, well, the good with the bad and all that." She picked up her notebook then paused and nodded at the desk. "Oh, I'm selling the desk."

He stared. "Why in God's name would you sell it?"

"For one thing, you don't like it and according to family records I've been perusing, although it was a gift from a member of the royal family generations ago, no one in this family has ever liked it."

"But—"

"Besides, selling it will defray some of the expenses of refurbishment." She stepped toward the door.

"Expenses?" He didn't like the sound of that.

"I certainly can't do what needs to be done without spending a certain amount of money."

"How much money?"

"I have no idea," she said blithely.

"Violet." He adopted his best I-am-the-earl tone.

She ignored it. "You don't want my dearest friend living in your house and I don't want that monstrosity in mine."

"Even so—"

"Partnership, James," she said over her shoulder. "Equal partnership. Give and take."

"I'm doing all the giving!"

"Free hand, remember?" She waved her hand over her head and opened the door. "Oh, this will be fun."

"Fun is not how I would describe it," he called after her even as the door closed in her wake.

Blast it all, the woman was frustrating and annoying and worse yet—in this game of theirs—she was winning. She was as well damnably exciting and every bit as clever as he was. He never would have imagined enjoying doing battle with a woman and yet he was. It was obvious she enjoyed it, as well. A slow smile curved his lips.

He could admit when he was wrong.

This was already fun.

CHAPTER NINE

THE LADIES WERE RIGHT. The Explorers Club ball was a relatively painless way to venture back into society. Violet lay in bed, staring up at the darkened ceiling, trying her best to ignore the rumblings coming from her midsection. It was damnably hard to sleep when one's stomach keep insisting it had not been adequately fed. The refreshment offerings at the Explorers Club had been sadly lacking in appeal, and Violet had been far too apprehensive before last night's ball to eat more than a morsel. Silly as it turned out.

Granted Violet had successfully navigated the salons of Europe and the ballrooms of Brussels and Vienna and Copenhagen and admittedly, the Explorers Club was not at the highest echelons of society. Even so, London was witness to her youth and the scandal of her marriage and a bit of apprehension was to be expected.

Aside from a few awkward moments she refused to dwell on, the evening had gone remarkably well. She encountered several people she knew, all of whom greeted her cordially. No one behaved as if she didn't exist or worse, was a creature of scandal. Of course, she was now Lady Ellsworth, a well-traveled woman of sophistication and not Miss Violet Hagen, who preferred reading and writing bad poetry to social occasions. Now she was rather good at conversing with people she didn't know

and quite enjoyed an innuendo-spiced flirtation. She had
no idea why she'd been even the least bit nervous.

James had quite properly danced with each of Mrs.
Higginbotham's friends and judging by the looks on their
faces, had charmed them with every step. The man certainly did have a way about him. But most of his dances
he saved for her.

Floating around the dance floor to the strains of a
Strauss waltz, with one of James's hands splayed firmly
on her lower back and his other hand clasped around
her own, with the heat of his body close to hers, it was
hard not to be swept back to another time. When she was
twenty-one and dancing with the handsomest, most dashing man in the ballroom. The man who, unbeknownst to
him, held her heart as surely as he held her in his arms.

They had always danced together beautifully, as if
they had been created to dance together. Fated to be together forever. She knew better now. An excellent dance
partner had nothing to do with fate. Or forever.

The very fact that he recalled the things they had discussed during his courtship of Marie was both a revelation and reluctantly endearing. He really wasn't the same
man she had married. She couldn't quite put her finger
on it but there was somehow *more* to the man than there
had been. As if he had been an unformed vessel all those
years ago and now was nearly the shape he was intended
to be. She wasn't sure if that was attributable to maturity or his acceptance of responsibility or even Richard's
death. More likely a combination of all that and probably
more. Regardless, this new James was intriguing and un-
deniably appealing. And a bit terrifying.

And the things he said—that ridiculous claim about
marrying her being the smartest thing he'd ever done.
His ludicrous assertion that he intended to atone for his

vast number of terrible decisions and dreadful mistakes.
And his absurd declaration that he wanted her as his wife
with everything that being his wife meant. It was utter
nonsense, all of it. Still, it was hard to doubt his sincerity. That too was terrifying.

James claimed he was trying to be the perfect husband
and indeed it was impossible to find fault with him. Certainly she wasn't about to throw herself into his arms or,
God forbid, his bed, but they'd had a surprisingly enjoyable evening. By the end of the night, Violet had decided
there was no need to entirely keep her distance. She could
guard her heart and still appreciate his company. Why, in
spite of his declaration about wanting a wife rather than
a friend, perhaps they could be friends after all.

James may have already decided what he wanted but
all Violet wanted was to survive the next three years with
her heart intact.

As well as something to eat. Starvation would not
serve her well. She ignored the voice in the back of her
head that sounded suspiciously like her mother's remind-
ing her that proper ladies did not forage for food in the
middle of the night in—God forbid—the kitchens. She
slipped out of bed, pulled on the red silk kimono robe she
had bought at a fascinating street market on the Mediter-
ranean coast and headed downstairs.

VIOLET PUSHED OPEN the kitchen door and pulled up short.
James sat at the large wooden worktable clad in his dressing gown, a book in one hand and a slice of bread in the
other. In front of him was a wedge of cheese, a crock of
butter, more bread and a plate of cold chicken.

He glanced up at her and nodded at the chair across
the table from him. "Join me."

"Do you always feast at this time of night?" she asked.

"Not always." He smiled. "But it's not altogether un-usual, either."

"Mrs. Clarke doesn't mind?" Violet settled in the chair across from him.

"Who do you think leaves the plates?" He nodded at a convenient stack of plates in the center of the table. "Apparently I inherited the need for something to eat when I can't sleep from Uncle Richard. I discovered that when I wandered down here one night shortly after I came to live with him." A fond smile curved his lips. "We had some of our best talks at this table through the years in the late hours of the night."

She reached for a plate. "What did you talk about?"

"Everything. Nothing." He thought for a moment. "Whatever was on his mind or on mine."

She chuckled and selected a piece of cheese and a slice of chicken. "Richard was good at that. He and I used to have similar discussions in the library when I was here, usually after dinner."

"And what did *you* talk about?"

"Everything. Nothing." She grinned. "The state of the world. My travels. You."

"I see." He considered her a moment. "And how the two of us were wasting our lives not being together no doubt."

"He did raise that subject frequently."

"It was one of his favorites."

But not something she wished to talk about at the moment.

"What are you reading?"

"Pride and Prejudice."

She took a bite of chicken. "Why?"

"Because you once said it was your favorite of Miss

Austen's works. I thought we could discuss it. Share it if you will."

"Why?"

He sighed. "It's going to be a very long three years if you and I are continually at odds."

"Reading a book I like will not prevent that."

"No, but it will give us something to talk about other than your destruction of my home and my mistakes."

She bit back a grin. "Don't forget your terrible decisions, as well."

"I daresay you won't let me."

"Should I?"

He met her gaze and the oddest frisson of something unexpected raced up her spine. "I assure you, I have no intention of forgetting even if I wanted to."

She stared. "You really have grown up, haven't you?"

"So it would appear." He chuckled. "Who would have imagined?" He shook his head. "There comes a time in every man's life when he has to face up to the things he has done. Good and bad. And decide where he goes from there. Mine came a few years ago when Uncle Richard fell ill and I feared we might lose him."

Her eyes widened in surprise. "I never heard about that."

"It's not the sort of thing he would have written you about. Especially as he recovered. Rather quickly in fact," he added wryly. "I now suspect his illness was nothing more than a ploy to shock me into accepting my responsibilities. And it worked."

"I'm beginning to think Richard was a bit more cunning than I had ever suspected. But then he was always determined to do what he thought was best." She broke off a piece of cheese and popped it into her mouth. There was nothing like good English cheddar. She savored the sharp flavor and a tiny moan of satisfaction escaped from her lips.

James's gaze slipped to her mouth and she froze. He cleared his throat. "So did you enjoy our first foray into society?"

"More than I expected to, really." She shook her head. "I don't know why I was hesitant about it. It's not as if I haven't attended social events during my visits."

"Does this mean we can stop our early morning rides in the park?"

"Absolutely not," she said primly. "It's a refreshing way to start the day. I thought you were beginning to enjoy it."

"As much as I hate to admit it, I suppose I am." He paused. "I suspected your reentry into London society might have been difficult for you."

"The Explorers Club ball was scarcely society, but yes, I will admit I was a bit apprehensive."

"I'm sorry I put you in that position."

"You didn't. Uncle Richard did."

"Not really." He shook his head. "The root of it all is my actions. I put you at the center of scandal. I changed the course of your life."

"Well, it hasn't been entirely bad," she admitted. "It was not the life I expected but there's a great deal to be said for being an independent woman traveling the world. It's been a remarkable adventure."

"You don't hate me for it?" The question lingered in his eyes.

"No, I don't." It was on the tip of her tongue to admit she was rather grateful to him, but she bit back the words and changed the subject. She nodded at the book. "So you plan to read books I like in an effort to have something to talk about?"

He nodded. "By my estimate, over the next three years, I can read thirty to sixty books."

"That's a lot of conversation." She reached for a slice of bread.

"I've never been prone to reading." He pushed the crock of butter within her reach. "And these days my reading is limited to the *Times*, financial reports, investment prospectuses, bills of lading, that sort of thing."

"Well, we shall make an educated man out of you yet."

"I am an educated man. At least I did attend school. Cambridge actually. And I did graduate." He grimaced. "Far closer to the bottom of my class than the top, I'm afraid."

She gasped with feigned surprise. "No."

"I did not pay as much attention as one would have hoped." He smiled with obvious chagrin. "So tell me, what do you think of Miss Bennet?"

"We're to begin our discussions now?"

"Why not?"

"Very well." She thought for a moment. "Elizabeth Bennet was strong and independent and stood up for herself when it would have been far easier to do what was expected of her. And she had a father who wished her to be happy regardless of the consequences."

"And does your father wish you to be happy?"

"Honestly, James, I have no idea." She spread more butter than was perhaps necessary on her bread. "I don't know my father well. He was not particularly interested in his children. No doubt because he had daughters rather than sons." She took a bite of bread. "And your father? Did he wish you to be happy?"

"My parents died in a boating accident when I was nine but I would imagine that he did. I have nothing but the fondest memories of both my mother and father." He smiled wistfully. "But that was a long time ago. Richard was as much father as uncle to me after I came to live with him and yes, I think he did wish for me to be happy." His gaze met hers. "He believed my happiness rested with you."

For a long moment their gazes locked. Questions unasked and unanswered lingered in his blue eyes. Questions and determination. She drew a deep breath and turned her attention back to her bread, adopting a lighter tone. "And what do you plan on reading next?"

"I don't know. What would you suggest?"

"I'm not sure how to follow *Pride and Prejudice*. Perhaps something not quite as romantic."

"I like a certain amount of romance," he said in an offhand manner. "The unexpected thrill of the brush of a hand. The pounding of your heart at the whiff of a scent that you know to be hers and hers alone. The moment when your eyes meet hers and awareness arcs between you. On a dance floor or across a crowded room or over a plate of cold chicken."

"Oh." She stared at him. Something fluttered deep inside her. "Indeed." She cleared her throat and pushed back from the table, rising to her feet. "If you'll excuse me. I think I can sleep now."

He smiled, a knowing, satisfied sort of smile. "Sleep well, Violet."

"Good night, James." She nodded and hurriedly took her leave. She was nearly at her door when she realized she hadn't merely left—she had fled. Like a nervous doe. She wasn't nervous of course. She was simply…what? Confused? Intrigued? By this man—this *husband*—who seemed intent on doing whatever was needed to endear himself to her.

Was she supposed to forgive that he didn't want her?

That he wouldn't be trying to work his way into her affections at all if Richard hadn't forced him into this position? If his inheritance wasn't at stake?

No, regardless of how much he had changed, she was not about to let James into her heart. It would be a mistake far greater than any of his because she knew better. There wasn't a doubt in her mind that she was right about this.

The idea that she would fall for him again was ridiculous when one thought about it. She was a woman of the world now. And women of the world did not lose their heads to charming men simply because they knew the perfect thing to say, and had the perfect smile, and made a woman feel as if she were the most perfect creature in the world.

A woman of the world could certainly handle a man like James Branham without losing her head. Or her heart.

She was wrong about one thing, though.

She didn't sleep a wink.

CHAPTER TEN

"WAS THAT YOU-KNOW-WHO I saw you dancing with last night?" Cleo asked in a low tone the moment Violet stepped into the breakfast room. She had slept far later than she usually did, but then it had been a long night filled with annoying thoughts of her husband, his bed creaking in the next room.

"You needn't keep referring to Viscount Welles as you-know-who," Violet said, filling her plate from the still warm offerings on the sideboard.

"I'm trying to be discreet," Cleo said. "One never knows who might be listening. Although Lord Ellsworth left some time ago. Oh, and he mentioned he knew of an agency that assisted in finding flats to let. I ignored him." She paused. "Have you told Lord Welles—"

"No, but I will. He said he would call on me today." Odd but thoughts of Duncan's imminent arrival had all but vanished from her head.

Violet really should have done something about Duncan before now. She'd been the worst sort of coward. She'd realized that when she'd danced with him last night, and realized as well she hadn't been nearly as clear about her feelings as she thought she had.

"Are you going to tell him about the will?"

"We've agreed to limit the number of people who know about the will. I can't even imagine the amount of gossip if the stipulations were to become common knowledge." She shivered. "But I do trust Duncan and I see no other way to explain the…situation."

"The situation being that you and your husband are living under the same roof and appearing to all the world as a happily reunited couple?"

"Yes," Violet said weakly, "that would be the one."

"Humph."

"You really don't think I'm doing the right thing, do you?"

"I think you're risking losing a man who wants to offer you a future for reasons that quite frankly evade me."

"I told you I—"

"Yes, yes, you feel grateful to his lordship." Cleo collected the papers she'd been perusing and stood. "I don't understand it, nor do I think it's a good idea, but all that matters is that you do."

"Duncan is a reasonable man, I'm certain he'll understand."

"Oh, yes, reasonable men always understand when a woman they had hoped to eventually marry decides to spend three years with another man."

"With my *husband*," Violet said firmly. "And I never agreed to anything with Duncan."

"Didn't you?"

"Of course not. I was not free to do so. Admittedly, we have discussed what *might* happen if I were free but we never actually said what *would* happen."

"Semantics, my dear friend." Cleo cast her a pitying look. "Regardless of what you might actually have said, men hear what they want to hear. Viscount Welles included. I do regret that I will not be present to witness this but I have a flat to view. With Mr. Davies." She grinned. "He knows of a flat in a respectable neighborhood and he arranged for me to see it."

Violet's brow rose. "Did he?"

"I mentioned to him last night that I was seeking a new residence and a note arrived first thing this morning regarding an available flat." Cleo shrugged. "It was very thoughtful of him."

"Very thoughtful." Violet studied her friend. "You like him, don't you?"

"He's intelligent and witty and quite nice. As well as charming and dashing and handsome. All that blond hair that always looks the tiniest bit disheveled. And he has the deepest brown eyes I have ever seen, as if they held all sort of wonderfully wicked secrets. I can't imagine why I wouldn't like him."

"Good Lord." Violet widened her eyes. "You more than like him."

"No." Cleo scoffed then grimaced. "Well, possibly." She sighed. "I haven't felt so much as a twinge of attraction for any man since my husband died and that was seven years ago. Quite honestly, I don't know how I feel and it's entirely too soon to feel anything at all. I barely know the man. But…"

"But?"

"But I think perhaps I'd like to. Know him better, that is." She heaved an annoyed sigh. "It's all quite confusing."

"I can see that." Violet chose her words with care. "You've spent the last six years by my side. Sacrificing your own happiness for mine—"

"Don't be silly. I didn't sacrifice anything, least of all happiness. These years have been the most exciting of my life. If it wasn't for you, I never would have traveled the world. Seen things most people never will. Met the most extraordinary people. I wouldn't trade these last six years for anything."

"Even so," Violet said gently, "perhaps it's time to put your needs and wants and desires above mine."

Cleo's brow furrowed. "Are you discharging me?"

"Absolutely not!" Violet paused. "But few men wish their wives to be employed and I would—"

Cleo laughed. "Goodness, Violet, you have me married to the man already. Thus far, we've shared nothing more than a bit of conversation and a few dances. Neither Marcus nor I are ready to march down the aisle."

"So it's Marcus, is it?"

"Yes, it is, and we are simply, I don't know, friends at the moment. As for anything more…" Cleo grinned. "Well, we shall see."

Violet's grin matched her friend's. "Indeed, we shall."

They chatted about last night's ball for a few minutes then Cleo left to meet *Marcus*. No more than a half an hour later, Andrews announced Violet had a caller in the front parlor. This was it then.

Violet checked her appearance in the pier mirror outside the parlor doors, adopted her most welcoming smile and stepped into the room, closing the doors behind her. "Good day, Duncan. How very good…"

Viscount Welles leaned against the fireplace mantel, arms crossed over his chest, looking extraordinarily handsome and more than a little irate.

"According to gossip you and your husband have reconciled your differences."

"What? No polite preliminaries?" There was nothing better than polite preliminaries to diffuse a situation. "No *good day, Violet*? No, *you're looking lovelier than ever, Violet*? You're just going to leap right into it?"

His jaw tensed. "Good day, Violet. You're looking lovelier than ever, Violet."

Of course, it didn't always work. She cast him a brilliant smile. "Much better."

"Gossip has it—"

"Goodness, Duncan, you know better than to believe gossip." She waved off the comment.

"And yet here you are." A grim note sounded in his voice. "Imagine my surprise when I returned to London to learn you and James are living in the same house together, attending social events together, riding in the park early in the morning. *Together*."

She frowned. "How on earth did you know about that?"

"Perhaps you've forgotten what life in London is like. There are few secrets here."

"I suppose I should have expected it." She settled on the sofa and waved him to the nearest chair.

He ignored her and sat down by her side. "Are you and James—"

"No," she said quickly then winced. "It's, well, complicated?"

"Oh?"

"And rather hard to explain."

"Because it's complicated?"

"Oh, good." She beamed. "I knew you would understand."

His brows drew together. "Understand what?"

She drew a deep breath. "You must promise not to reveal what I am about to tell you to anyone."

"Violet, what on earth is going on?" Concern shone in his eyes. "Has James threatened you in some—"

"No, of course not. Don't be silly." She paused. "The threat is not to me. Well, not entirely."

His eyes narrowed.

"Allow me to explain."

"I can hardly wait."

She mustered a weak smile. "As you know, James's Uncle Richard died a few months ago."

Duncan nodded.

"He always thought James and I should be together." She searched for the right words. There didn't seem to be any. "James will not inherit Uncle Richard's property or fortune unless he and I share a residence, appear as a couple and avoid scandal for the next, well, slightly less than three years."

He stared. "Three years?"

"Not quite three years," she said brightly. "Actually, it's two years, ten months, two weeks and five days as of today. More or less."

He ignored her. "And you have agreed to this?"

"There didn't seem to be much of a choice."

"Of course there was a choice." He glared. "You could have said no. You could have told James you have made plans for your life that do not include him. You could have told him you wished to seek a divorce."

She winced. "I suppose I could have."

"For the last year, you haven't wanted to bring up the subject of divorce because you didn't want to upset the old earl. I thought you decided, now that he is gone, there was no longer any reason to put off seeking a divorce."

"I did, however—"

"It's complicated?"

"Yes, it is!" She rose to her feet and paced. "I don't expect you to understand." She paused. "No, actually, I do expect you, of all people, to understand."

He stood. "I am sorry to disappoint you, Violet, but I don't. I know that financially you don't have to do this. Even if you did, I can take care of you."

"Thank you for the generous offer, but I have no need to be taken care of. Nor do I wish to be."

"Yes, I know, " he said with a long-suffering sigh. In spite of all of Duncan's many fine points he simply couldn't comprehend that a woman might well enjoy financial independence and the freedom to make her own decisions. "You've been very clear on that point."

"Men are not the only ones who wish to stand on their own, you know."

He eyed her warily. "Yes, you mention that with unending frequency."

"It can't be said often enough." She paused. "As for James and me." She squared her shoulders and met Duncan's gaze directly. "James did not abandon me when he could have easily done so. I shall not abandon him when it is within my power to save him."

"Because you're in love with him?" The hard tone in his voice matched the look in his eyes.

"Don't be absurd. Love has nothing to do with this." She crossed her arms over her chest. "You and I have been meeting in various parts of the world for nearly two years now. Have I ever once given you any indication I was in love with James?"

"Not that I can recall."

"Why, the very idea that I would be in love with my husband is the silliest thing I've ever heard."

"Methinks thou dost protest too much."

"Oh, for goodness' sake." She rolled her gaze toward the ceiling. "The moment a man thinks he's losing an argument he throws Shakespeare into the conversation as if that alone will prove his point. First of all, the correct quotation is *The lady doth protest too much, methinks*. And secondly, I don't protest too much. I don't protest nearly enough. In love with James? How utterly ridiculous."

"Are you sure?"

"Quite."

"That's something, I suppose." His gaze searched hers. "I have always known my feelings for you are stronger than your feelings for me."

She couldn't deny it even if it seemed rather unkind to admit aloud. "I am very fond of you, Duncan."

"And I have been willing to accept that with the hope that your feelings would grow stronger over time."

"I have never lied to you. I've told you right from the beginning how I felt."

"We made plans, Violet."

"No, Duncan." She shook her head. "What we discussed were possibilities."

"I had hoped they were more than mere possibilities." He sighed. "But you're right. You made me no promises."

"I do consider you a dear friend," she said with affection.

"Yes, well, it's not enough, is it?" He studied her closely.

"I'm afraid not."

"Just because you've agreed—"

"That's not it. Not entirely." She thought for a moment. "James gave me the freedom and the finances to see the world. To become who I've become. Before my marriage I was not the type of girl a man like you paid any attention to whatsoever. It wasn't until we ran into each other a few years ago that you noticed me at all."

He stared at her. "You were indeed shy and soft-spoken but intelligent and quietly lovely. Not at all the kind of girl who would look twice at someone as loud and reckless and foolish as I was."

"What?" She shook her head in confusion. Was she

the only one who remembered the past accurately? Or were everyone else's memories far more exact than hers?

"I was not at all worthy of you then, Violet, and I knew it. But I am now. And if I have to spend the next three years proving it to you, I will," he said.

"I can't ask you to wait for three years," she said slowly.

"You're not." He smiled, stepped closer and took her hand. "I cannot imagine my life without you, Violet, and if I have to wait a lifetime, if only for the merest possibility that you could truly be mine, I will." He raised her hand to his lips and gazed into her eyes. "It seems a small enough price to pay."

"Duncan, I—"

"I have no intention of giving up." He brushed his lips across the back of her hand. "I will fight for you if I have to."

"I don't think that will be necessary," she said weakly and pulled her hand from his. If she were in love with the man, there would be no question of asking him to wait for her. But she wasn't and she doubted she ever would be. Oh, in the back of her mind, she had thought perhaps one day they might have a future together. But it wasn't enough. And it wasn't fair. Duncan deserved better. She drew a deep breath. "I think it's best if we simply part ways now."

His gaze bored into hers. "Is that what you really want?"

"I can't expect you to give up three years of your life on the chance that my feelings might change." She gazed up at him. "This entire situation, my whole life really, it's—"

He smiled. "Complicated?"

"Well, yes." She shook her head. "I'm so very sorry, Duncan. I wouldn't have hurt you for anything in the world."

"My feelings haven't changed." He headed toward the door. "But I do understand the rules now and I agree to play by them."

"What do you mean?" She frowned. "What rules?"

"You and James have to appear as a happy couple with no gossip or scandal. I shall not intrude on that. But I can't imagine there isn't a legal way out of this."

"Uncle Richard was very determined and his solicitors were quite thorough."

"Not as determined as I am." He grinned. "And as long as you're not in love with him—I have a chance. Even if it takes three years."

"I really don't think—"

"I meant it when I said I do not intend to give up." He started to open the door then paused. "Do remember one thing, Violet. I am willing to fight for you. Do you think your husband will ever say the same?" With that, he took his leave.

Violet drew her brows together. Well, that didn't go as she thought it would. But Duncan really did deserve better than someone who was merely fond of him. What on earth did that nonsense about not giving up mean? She'd thought she was rather clear that he should move on with his life.

Even more absurd, Duncan worried that she was in love with her husband. That was the silliest thing he'd said. Once, long ago, she had been smitten with James. But whatever her feelings had been then she was smart enough now not to allow them to reoccur.

"Good morning, Violet." James strode into the parlor.

She summoned a pleasant smile. "Afternoon now, I believe."

"A telegram arrived for you just as I did." He handed her an envelope.

"Thank you." She hesitated for a moment—in her experience telegrams rarely brought good news—then steeled herself, ripped it open and scanned the brief message.

"Was that Welles I saw leaving just now?"

"Lord Welles, yes," she said absently. Surely she was misreading this message.

"What did he want?"

"Just paying a call. Welcoming me back to London, that sort of thing." She sank down onto the sofa. This couldn't possibly be right.

"Didn't he do that last night?"

She shrugged, her gaze fixed on the words that seemed to swim on the page.

"Violet?" Concern sounded in his voice. "Is something wrong?"

She stared at the paper in her hand. According to the dear friend in Paris who managed her fortune, it was gone. All of it. Her investments had failed. A letter would soon follow to explain everything, although it did seem how it had happened was not nearly as important as the very fact that it did.

"Violet!" James's sharp tone caught her attention and she jerked her gaze to his. "What's wrong? Is it bad news?"

"Bad news?" Her money was gone and with it her independence. It was one thing to follow Richard's stipulations because she was doing the right thing out of a sense of gratitude and fairness, and something else altogether to have no options whatsoever. If James lost everything, so would she.

"Are you all right?" James sat on the sofa beside her.

"Yes." She forced a casual tone. "Just some unexpected news. Nothing serious, really."

"Are you sure?" His gaze searched hers. "You seem upset."

"No, really, I'm fine." At once she realized the very fact that abiding by the terms of Richard's will was her choice gave her an escape of sorts should she choose to use it. More importantly, it kept her life in her own hands. Loss of her finances—her independence—tore that away and changed everything. The stakes in the game Richard had conceived had just risen. She had as much to lose now as James.

Six years ago, the decisions regarding her future had been made for her. Now, it seemed it was happening again.

And there was nothing she could do about it.

CHAPTER ELEVEN

VIOLET STARED IN the mirror outside the parlor doors.

For a moment, a young woman—a girl, really—on her way to the engagement party of her friend and the man who made Violet Hagen's heart ache with longing looked back at her. A girl who had long ago learned it was better to keep her opinions to herself, to do what was expected of her and follow all the rules laid down by society and her mother. A girl lacking in self-esteem, who had no idea who she could become. Or who she truly wanted to be.

She shook her head to clear it. At once twenty-one-year old Violet vanished and the Countess of Ellsworth gazed back. Sophisticated, confident, a woman without doubt, who knew who she was. She'd had six weeks since her mother had notified her of her sister's engagement ball, six weeks to prepare for tonight, although she suspected a lifetime would not be enough. Tonight she would face the cream of London society for the first time as Lady Ellsworth. Certainly she had been to a few social events when she had returned to London through the years, although she was always circumspect and rarely stayed long. But she did rather like when men like Evan, who now sought her out, didn't remember that they'd once paid no attention to her at all.

Still, society was one thing, her mother something else altogether. She would have been happy to ignore her oldest daughter's very existence a few months ago. But now

that Violet and James were apparently together, now that
they were *Lord and Lady Ellsworth*, her daughter was no
longer an embarrassment and their presence would add
an extra touch of distinction to the family. Mother had
always been fond of distinction.

The elegant, self-possessed woman in the mirror
raised her chin and adopted a brilliant smile. Tonight
was a test of sorts. Violet Hagen would not have been
up to the challenge. But Lady Ellsworth, a woman of the
world who was as much at home in a castle in Bavaria
or a villa in the south of France as she was in the grand
mansions of Mayfair did not accept failure.

The irony was not lost on her that six years ago another engagement ball had changed her life. It did feel as
though what began then would come full circle tonight.

"You look exquisite." James stepped up behind her and
met her gaze in the mirror. "Absolutely breathtaking."

She started to protest then smiled instead. She'd ordered the gown from the House of Worth in Paris as soon
as she'd known the date of the ball. The famous coutu-
rier had her measurements and it was a simple matter
to write and explain what she wanted. As always, Mr.
Worth had outdone himself. The pale green satin gown,
with its beaded cap sleeves that bared her shoulders, elegant adorned skirt and cleverly draped bustle really was
one of the most flattering things she'd ever worn. The
color brightened her eyes, made her skin somehow look
creamier and highlighted the deep red of her hair. "That's
very nice of you to say."

"I shall be the most fortunate man at the ball with you
on my arm," he said staunchly.

"Goodness, James, one would think you were trying
to turn my head."

He grinned, that vaguely wicked grin of his that promised all sort of wonderfully wicked things. It was becoming harder and harder to ignore that promise.

Odd how far they'd come in a mere six weeks. Scarcely a night went by now that they didn't meet in the kitchen after the rest of the household was in bed, with long chats about nothing and everything. He had finished *Pride and Prejudice* as well as *Wuthering Heights*, which he said was entirely too dark and dire to be at all enjoyable. She had teased him about his lack of literary acumen and had resisted telling him she agreed. She had then given him *King Solomon's Mines*, which he had proclaimed the finest book ever written. Violet was hard-pressed to disagree entirely but, if not the finest, it was certainly the most fun.

She and James continued their early-morning rides and of course, every Wednesday, Effie, Poppy and Gwen joined them for dinner. Occasionally, Cleo and Marcus were present, as well. Cleo's duties as Violet's secretary brought her to the house every day but she had taken the flat Marcus had found for her, conveniently located in the same building where he resided.

Violet would never have imagined in the beginning but they had become quite a convivial group. All three older ladies had fascinating stories to tell about the exploits of their respective husbands and they insisted on hearing all about her years of travel. Occasionally she would catch James staring at her with rapt attention. Which was as gratifying as it was unnerving.

The Explorers Club ball was still the largest affair she and James had attended thus far but they'd been to several smaller social events, a few garden parties, a gallery opening and an exhibit at a small museum among others. She ran into any number of people she had once known and while there was a certain amount of curiosity about her and James—to be expected of course—she was not

treated with anything other than cordiality. It did seem
perhaps that she was the only one still haunted by the
specter of their long-ago scandal. Every public appearance renewed her confidence and bolstered her courage.
Courage she would no doubt need tonight.

"I have something for you," James said with a smile.

Her brow rose. "A gift?"

He nodded.

"Are you trying to bribe me?" she teased.

"Only if it works. Close your eyes."

"Don't be silly."

"If you don't close your eyes…"

"Very well." She sighed and closed her eyes.

A necklace settled around her neck, and he fumbled
with the clasp at the back.

"There." Satisfaction rang in his voice and his hands
rested on her shoulders. They were far warmer than any
man's hands had a right to be and yet goose bumps rose
on her arms and shivered through her. "You may look."

She opened her eyes and sucked in a sharp breath. A
string of perfect emeralds interspersed with diamonds
glittered against her throat.

"Do you like it?"

"Good Lord, James, it's magnificent." She stared at her
reflection. "I've never worn anything quite so exquisite."

"Well, we're off to the engagement ball of the son of a
duke. I thought it wise to make a good impression." James
was well aware of her apprehension about tonight and this
gesture on his part was both thoughtful and rather touch-
ing. "The necklace was my mother's and now it's yours."

"I don't know what to say." She touched the center
emerald.

"She would have wanted you to have it." His gaze
caught hers in the mirror. "You're my wife."

For a long moment their gazes locked, then he cleared his throat and his hands dropped from her shoulders. The strangest sense of loss trickled through her. He handed her a velvet box. "There are earbobs to match."

"Thank you," she murmured and opened the box. Emeralds matching the necklace were encircled by diamonds and sparkled on the velvet lining. "They're perfect."

"As are you."

"Goodness, James, the things you say." She looked in the mirror and replaced the simple gold earbobs she had on with the ones James gave her. "I know you're just trying to be charming. To get on my good side. Work your way into my affections."

"Me?" He adopted an innocent expression. "I would never try to bribe you into liking me."

She widened her eyes and caught his gaze in the mirror. "I do like you."

"Better than you did."

"Better than I have in years."

"I knew eventually you wouldn't be able to resist my dashing good looks and inestimable charm."

"Yes, that's what did it," she said wryly.

It was inevitable, really. Playing the role of happy couple, they would either grow to detest each other—which wouldn't serve either of them well—or they would like each other. And once again be friends. And friends would do. Nothing more of course but friends, yes, being friends was fine.

Violet made a final adjustment to the earbobs, gave a last satisfied nod to the image in the mirror and turned to James. "We should go. We would hate to be late. My mother would never forgive us."

"Then into the fray, Lady Ellsworth." He offered his arm. "Together, we shall bravely face the dragons head-on."

She arched a brow. "Are you calling my mother a dragon?"

"I'm calling everything that we fear or gives us pause a dragon. We all have our own dragons, Violet. To slay or defeat or cause us to flee into the night."

"That's rather philosophical of you." She took his arm. "I didn't know you had it in you."

"Oh, I am a man of many deep and abstract thoughts." He wagged his brows in a mysterious manner. "As well as many secrets. There are all sorts of things hidden inside the dim recesses of my mind. You have barely dipped below the surface of the well of intellectual depth that is James Branham."

She laughed.

"I would be offended, but it does seem pointless." He grinned.

He escorted her out the door and took her hand to help her into the carriage. Abruptly, the thought struck her that there was no one she would rather have by her side tonight than James.

"Oh, but you are absolutely right," she said once she was settled in the carriage.

"Of course I am." He paused. "About?"

"My mother *is* a dragon."

THEY ARRIVED AT the grand London house that had been in Violet's family for generations a few minutes ahead of the start of the ball, but unfortunately a line of carriages had already formed in advance of their arrival. The festivities were well underway by the time Violet and James finally made it in the door.

They paused to be announced by the family butler at the top of the short flight of stairs leading into the ballroom. Wilkens had been with their family for as long as she could remember and tonight was dressed in his finest livery—Mother would allow nothing less.

James squeezed her hand on his arm and spoke quietly. "Are you ready?"

"More than ready," she said with a confidence she didn't quite feel. Violet drew a deep breath and adopted a brilliant smile.

Wilkens gave her a discreet wink before he announced their arrival. Violet bit back a grin. Wilkens had never been fond of Mother.

They descended the stairs to greet her parents together with Caroline, her soon-to-be fiancé, Neville, and Neville's parents, the Duke and Duchess of Trentham.

Father greeted them with a smile that clearly indicated to Violet he would rather be anywhere but here but knew his duty nonetheless. Mother's gaze swept over her older daughter and she nodded with reluctant approval. Apparently Violet had passed muster.

"You're late." Mother's brow furrowed.

"It couldn't be helped, Lady Cranton," James said smoothly before Violet could open her mouth. "We were delayed by the sheer number of carriages waiting to discharge their occupants." He leaned toward her and lowered his voice. "This really is the social event of the season."

Mother beamed. "How kind of you to say, Lord Ellsworth."

Caroline looked stunning as she always did with her striking blue eyes and strawberry-blond hair. She was nearly as tall as her sister but her figure was far more curved. Now in her second season, Caroline was an excellent catch and Neville was a brilliant match. Her sister accepted the attention of one and all as her due even if she seemed vaguely bored. Violet really didn't know her sister at all well given the nearly seven-year difference between them. Perhaps if she had stayed in London... No. She had no regrets about leaving London. But she did regret not knowing her only sibling. Although, even as a child, Caroline had always been her mother's daughter.

They were introduced to Neville, a short, rather chubby chap with kind eyes and a cheery smile who reminded Violet of an eager puppy and who looked at Caroline as if she were the most wonderful creature in the world. Violet couldn't help but wonder if the man knew what he was getting into. The duke was next in line and they chatted with him for a few minutes about Uncle Richard—who apparently had been friends with both the duke and his father—then moved on to greet the duchess.

"My dear girl." The duchess took Violet's hand in hers. "We are so glad to see you at long last back in London and looking so wonderful, as well." She raised a brow as she eyed Violet's dress. "Worth, is it not?"

Violet nodded. "Yes, Your Grace."

"I knew it." She grinned with satisfaction. "I can always tell Mr. Worth's work." She leaned toward Violet in a confidential manner. "My very favorite daughter-in-law has been looking forward to renewing your acquaintance."

"As am I." Pity Violet had no idea who the duchess's daughter-in-law might be. She really should have paid more attention to the comings and goings of society and not just the gossip about James during the years of her absence.

The duchess turned her attention to the next arrival and Violet and James moved into the burgeoning crowd. The ballroom was packed with everyone who was anyone in London society. The gaslights in the massive chandelier that dominated the center of the room sparkled as much as the jewels that adorned every woman's neck. Huge urns of fresh flowers were positioned in every niche and available space, and large palms flanked every doorway. Mother had outdone herself. *Extravagant* was the word that came to mind, perhaps even excessive. It was hard to remember this was a ballroom in London and not a mystical palace of glittering magic and unabashed romance. Interesting as Mother had never been fond of magic or romance, unabashed or otherwise.

Violet and James made their way around the room. He introduced her to any number of people she hadn't met and she renewed her acquaintance with all sorts of people she had known in her youth—none of whom seemed the least bit disapproving about her notable absence in the last six years or her recent reemergence into society. Even Lady Dalrymple, one of her mother's closest friends, a denizen of society and an even bigger gossip than her mother, seemed pleased to see her.

Violet had told herself over and over she had nothing to worry about tonight and now there was actual evidence to support that optimism. With every new person she met and every old acquaintance renewed, her confidence grew and that niggling fear in the back of her mind that she would somehow become quiet, shy Violet Hagen again dimmed. She sent James off to speak to acquaintances without so much as a twinge of doubt. There was no need for him to be by her side every minute. Violet Branham was well up to whatever society might throw her way tonight.

"Violet." A tall, dark-haired woman approached her and took her hands. "I was delighted to hear you were back in London."

Violet stared for a moment. "Jenny Smythe?"

The woman grinned. "Lady Larkfield now. I married one of Neville's brothers."

In those days when Violet had sat endlessly waiting to be asked to dance, Jenny had been sitting right beside her. She was the only person Violet had ever told about her feelings for James and her hopes for happiness in the few days before her wedding. She hadn't seen Jenny since her marriage but the woman in front of her now bore only a vague resemblance to the girl Violet had known. It was remarkable how much believing in one's self and perhaps happiness could change one's demeanor and outer appearance, as well.

"You're the duchess's daughter-in-law?"

Jenny nodded. "One of them, anyway."

"She says you're her favorite."

Jenny laughed. "She says that about all of us. She has three so far. We all get along surprisingly well." Jenny cast a quick look at Caroline and Neville on the dance floor and the vaguest look of unease flashed in her eyes. "Your sister will be the fourth and I'm sure she'll fit right in."

Violet arched a brow. "Are you?"

Jenny frowned. "Not really. But you're her sister and I shouldn't say anything. I do hope she will make dear Neville happy. He's the youngest of the lot and really a jolly sort. He deserves happiness."

"I'm sure Caroline will do her best," Violet said, forcing a note of confidence she didn't feel.

"Goodness, Violet. It's obvious you've changed in all sorts of ways but you never were a good liar," Jenny said and paused. "As you're back, dare I assume that you and James have resolved your differences?"

Violet's gaze drifted to James, engaged in conversation with a small group of gentlemen. She smiled. "You might."

Jenny studied her thoughtfully. "You look happy. Are you?"

The question took her by surprise. "Well, yes, I suppose I am."

"Good." Jenny smiled. "You deserve to be happy, as well."

The old friends chatted for a few more minutes and promised to see each other again soon, then James appeared to claim the next dance.

"I would say your first significant appearance in society is a rousing success." He grinned down at her. "And I was right."

"Were you?"

His gaze locked on hers and his eyes smoldered. "I am the luckiest man here."

"Goodness, James." She wrenched her gaze from his, heat washing up her face. "The things you say."

He chuckled but mercifully didn't pursue the topic.

Violet had just finished dancing with an elderly gentleman when she was approached by a woman she'd managed to avoid for six years. Good Lord, what on earth did she want?

"Violet," Marie said with what appeared to be a genuine smile. "How lovely to see you again."

"And you," Violet said faintly. She wasn't sure what else to say. Coming face-to-face with Marie was yet another test.

Marie wrinkled her nose. "My, this is awkward. To be expected I suppose, given we haven't spoken in what seems like forever."

"Six years," Violet murmured.

"I heard you were back in London. I wanted to call on

you but I didn't know if you would be amenable to that."
Marie shook her head. "I was angry at James, and you
as well, for a very long time."

"Understandable."

"I didn't realize it then but I was marrying James for
all the wrong reasons."

Violet widened her eyes. "Were you?"

"Oh, he was handsome and wealthy and heir to an impressive title, and that seemed more than enough." Marie
drew a deep breath. "Not marrying James was perhaps
the best thing that ever happened to me."

"I'm not sure I understand," Violet said slowly.

"I didn't love him," she said simply. "I daresay you
probably knew that although love didn't seem important
then." Marie chose her words with obvious care. "It took
me some time to realize that he wounded my pride but
certainly not my heart. And to understand as well that I
was wrong. In what I wanted, what I thought would make
me happy." She met Violet's gaze. "And I am happy."

"I heard you had married."

Marie nodded. "His title is not as impressive as James's,
his fortune not as great but—" she smiled "—he holds
my heart."

A weight Violet didn't realize she carried lifted and
she smiled. "How wonderful for you."

"I was not a particularly good friend to you in those
days. Even so, I was hoping now, perhaps, you might see
your way clear to…"

"To be friends?" Violet had known she'd encounter
Marie eventually but she didn't expect to see her tonight
and never anticipated this. She took the other woman's
hand. "One can never have too many friends."

Marie smiled with obvious relief. They talked for a

few minutes more and Violet was struck by the realization that perhaps they really could be friends.

An hour or so into the festivities, Caroline and Neville's engagement was announced with all the pomp and ceremony such an announcement warranted. Mother was in her element.

The ball was by any standard a rousing success. The refreshment tables never emptied, the music never faded and the dance floor was always full. It was an evening full of surprises for Violet, as well. The scandal that had changed her life seemed forgotten or insignificant. Even Marie no longer cared and appeared genuinely interested in friendship. And when she'd danced with her father, he'd offered a sincere apology for not being a better father and told her he was proud of the woman she'd become. A revelation apparently prompted by a talk he'd had with James.

Still, Violet couldn't put Jenny's question out of her head. Was she happy? She certainly wasn't unhappy. She and James had settled into a comfortable companionship—the man was impossible to keep completely at arm's length. And she found she enjoyed his company nearly as much as she once had. No, more perhaps. But a friendship was all it was. And all she would ever allow it to be.

Even so, when she'd circled the dance floor in the arms of her husband, the thought had occurred to her that this was how she had once imagined her life would be. Accepted as a part of society and married to a man who shared her affections. A thought that had vanished the day after her marriage. For now, whatever it was she and James had between them would suffice.

Still, was that happy ending gone forever? And more to the point—did she want it to be?

CHAPTER TWELVE

VIOLET WAS NOTHING short of enchanting.

James could scarcely take his eyes off her, dancing with yet another lucky partner. This new Violet, an enchanting blend of the woman he once knew and the woman she had become, was irresistible. This was the woman he wanted, the woman he was determined to have. It was clear to him that they belonged together. Certainly he had nearly three years to win her heart but three years was a long time and he'd rather not waste any more of it.

"How poor are they that have not patience, Lord Ellsworth."

James's gaze jerked back to the duchess. "Shakespeare?"

"Very good." She considered him for a moment and he resisted the urge to squirm like a child. "You know, when one is a duchess, one expects whomever one is speaking to, to pay a certain amount of attention."

"My apologies, Your Grace. I don't—"

"You were watching your wife." Neville's mother waved off his apology. "You can be forgiven for that." Her gaze shifted back to Violet. "She's turned out quite nicely, don't you think?"

"I do indeed."

"If one cared to look all those years ago, one could see the potential in her. Even you."

"I was something of an idiot in my younger days." No doubt the duchess had known Uncle Richard just as the duke had. One did wonder how often his marriage had been the topic of conversation among people he didn't know. "I didn't realize you knew Violet."

"I didn't. But I have been aware of every young woman who has entered society for the past ten years." She smiled. "I have five sons, you know."

"Of course."

"She has acquired great polish in these years of your separation. And it's obvious, at least to me, she has a kind heart, as well."

He nodded.

"There have been rumors about her through the years as she has traveled abroad. She was a married woman after all, and dalliances are not uncommon, especially when a couple has long been apart. There have been rumors about you, as well. We know the veracity of the gossip about you." She glanced at James. "Do you believe what's been said about her?"

The very idea that Violet had been with other men twisted something inside him. Still, he would be the worst sort of hypocrite to condemn her for it. Aside from his own behavior, he had been the one to let her go. The one to say she could do as she wished. If he wanted to move forward with her, he needed to leave the past—both their pasts—behind them.

"Quite honestly, I don't think it matters."

Her Grace smiled slowly. "Excellent answer. It appears you have grown up after all." She shook her head. "There was a time when the possibility of that seemed extremely remote."

"I'm glad you approve." James chuckled. "Do you know everything about everyone?"

"Yes," the duchess said simply. "I make it my business to know. Being a leader of society is not nearly as easy as you might imagine. I have three daughters-in law who keep me informed as well." She paused. "And I knew your mother."

"Did you?"

The duchess nodded. "We were at school together. She was a good friend and I miss her to this day."

"I had no idea."

"There's no reason you would have. You were very young when she died." Her Grace again turned her attention to Violet. "She would have liked Violet."

"I think so."

"I know so." She watched Violet for a moment. "There has been recent talk about you and your wife, you know. Oh nothing untoward, but speculation about why the two of you appear to have reconciled. Some of them—about money and position—are quite unkind. About you but more so about her."

He should have expected something like this. "Thank you for telling me."

"See that you don't do anything to increase those rumors."

"I shall do my best."

"Well, that will have to do then won't it?" The music stopped and the duchess waved to Violet to join them.

"I was just telling your husband how radiant you are tonight." The duchess beamed. "Why, I daresay there are few gentlemen here who do not want a dance or a word with you."

Violet laughed. "Dear Lord, I hope not. I've scarcely had a moment to breathe all night."

"Alas, Her Grace is right." James sighed dramatically. "I've only managed one dance with you myself." He lowered his voice in a confidential manner. "It's not easy having a wife as brilliant and lovely as Violet."

"Such a wife is to be cherished, Lord Ellsworth. And she does need to know she is cherished." The duchess eyed him thoughtfully. "You would do well to remember that."

"I have no intention of ever forgetting." He smiled at the duchess then turned his smile to Violet. A blush colored her cheeks, probably due to nothing more than the exertion of dancing and the heat in the room. Nonetheless, his heart skipped a beat.

"The two of you make a striking couple." Her Grace smiled smugly. "But then I always thought you would. I do so love it when all is well in the end. When a tale ends with happily ever after."

"I daresay it's not quite the end yet." Violet shrugged in an offhand manner. "Who's to say what will happen next? Uncertainty is part of every breath we take."

"But I assure you, Duchess," James said with a smile, "happily ever after is well worth whatever it may take to get there."

"There you are, Violet." Violet's mother joined them, accompanied by Lady Dalrymple. "And Your Grace," she added as if surprised to see the duchess. James would have wagered otherwise.

"Margaret, Eloise," the duchess said pleasantly. "I must say you have outdone yourself, Margaret." She glanced around the ballroom. "This evening is an unqualified success."

"Thank you, Your Grace." Lady Cranton beamed with pride. "I wanted to mark the engagement of our children with all the splendor it deserves."

"Yes, well, you have certainly accomplished that." The duchess smiled.

It all seemed rather pretentious to James's way of thinking, but then admittedly, what did he know about throwing a ball?

"One does want to make one's mark on the season," Lady Dalrymple proclaimed. "Especially with an engagement. Why, you would hate for it not to be as perfect as possible."

"Perfect, like so many things, is in the eye of the beholder, I believe," the duchess said smoothly.

"Yes, of course, Your Grace. I simply didn't want anything to go wrong. Unlike other similar events in the past." Lady Cranton's lips flattened into a disapproving line.

James could feel Violet tense beside him, but a serene smile remained on her face.

"However, Violet and James have promised to be on their best behavior for this evening," Lady Cranton added.

"I don't recall promising anything of the sort," Violet said with a pleasant smile. "I didn't think it was necessary."

"It's been quite lovely thus far." The duchess's gaze shifted from mother to daughter.

"We wouldn't want a repeat of the last engagement party Violet attended." Lady Dalrymple cast Violet a chastising look.

"Goodness, Eloise, that was a very long time ago," Her Grace said firmly. "And needn't be mentioned tonight."

Violet's mother ignored her. "Promise or not, you wouldn't want to ruin this ball as you did James's engagement party. And his engagement as well for that matter."

Violet froze.

Why in the name of all that's holy was the woman bringing that up now? Hadn't they put that behind them?

Although, perhaps this was his opportunity to come to her rescue. To defend her. To be her knight. Her hero.

"That was entirely my fault, Lady Cranton." He met her gaze directly. "Violet was simply caught up in my own mistake."

"If I recall correctly, it didn't look like it was entirely his fault," Lady Dalrymple said under her breath.

"And yet—" a hard note rang in his voice "—it was."

"Nonetheless, it did appear there was a great deal of enthusiasm on both sides." Lady Dalrymple grimaced. "And then, of course, there was the slap."

"Which I deserved," he added quickly and slanted a glance at Violet, the very picture of calm composure.

"Regardless," the duchess pointed out, "it was a mere kiss. And really insignificant in the scheme of things."

"An engagement was ruined," Lady Dalrymple murmured. "I wouldn't call that insignificant."

"I would call it fortunate." James smiled at Violet who paid him no attention whatsoever.

"Why, if it hadn't been such a dull season," the duchess continued, "I daresay it wouldn't have made any impression at all. It does seem to me, all has turned out well."

"That's very kind of you to say but it was a dreadful scandal." Lady Cranton's eyes narrowed. "The incident wasn't bad enough but after James did the proper thing and agreed to marry her, she fled the country and has been doing God knows what with God knows who ever since!"

"Lady Cranton," James said sharply. Violet hadn't so much as twitched, but she was definitely paler than she had been a moment ago.

His mother-in-law continued without pause. "She does exactly as she pleases. She's entirely too independent to be the least bit respectable. Why, we're lucky, Your Grace, that you have been willing to overlook my oldest daughter's shameful behavior and allow your son to marry my dear Caroline."

The duchess frowned. "Good Lord, Margaret, I do think you're being rather harsh."

Violet's mother raised her chin. "I daresay I haven't been harsh enough. I've welcomed her into my home whenever she's deigned to return to England and I included her tonight, which might well have been a mis—"

"That's quite enough," James said sharply.

Violet laid her hand on his arm. "That's not necessary, James. I am more than capable of speaking for myself."

"It is necessary. It's more than necessary. And it's past time, as well." James aimed a hard look at Lady Cranton. "Your daughter is a woman I am proud and honored to call my wife. Indeed, I consider myself the most fortunate man here. No, in all the world."

"James." Violet's brow furrowed.

He ignored her. "If you cannot treat her with the respect due her, she shall not call on you again and you will not be welcome in our home."

"Then perhaps it's time you took your leave," Lady Cranton snapped.

"It seems to me, Mother, that the strain of the evening may be playing havoc with your sensibilities." Violet lowered her voice and leaned toward her mother, her smile unfailingly perfect. "If we leave now, it will be noticed and remarked upon, thus creating the kind of gossip I'm confident you wish to avoid. And Caroline's perfect evening will indeed be marred. I will not have this evening ruined for her."

Lady Cranton glared. "I daresay—"

"No, Mother, you won't say another word." Violet's

voice was cool and collected, but anger flared in her eyes. The woman really was magnificent. "James and I will stay until an appropriate hour. At that point and not before, we shall take our leave."

"Nicely done, my dear," the duchess murmured.

"Now, if you will all excuse me, I see someone I simply must speak with. It is an excellent party, Mother. You are to be commended." She favored the duchess with a genuine smile. "Your Grace." She turned to the other ladies. "Mother. Lady Dalrymple." She turned and made her way through the crowd in a serene and undisturbed manner.

"That was uncalled for, Margaret." The duchess glared. "I must say I am most disappointed in you."

"With all due respect, Your Grace." Lady Cranton straightened her spine. James wouldn't have thought it possible. "You do not have daughters. You have no idea how difficult an unruly daughter can be." She cast James a scathing look. "And apparently their husbands are no better." She adopted an overly bright smile. "Now, if you will excuse me, there are things I need to attend to. Duchess." She nodded and moved off, her manner nearly as dignified as her daughter's. James did hope it was nothing more than coincidence and not an indication of traits shared by mother and daughter.

Lady Dalrymple's eyes widened and she looked after her friend then back at the duchess. "Your Grace." She bobbed a curtsey and fled.

"Good Lord." The duchess sighed.

"Rethinking your alliance with this family, Duchess?"

"Unfortunately, there's nothing I can do. My poor Neville is head over heels for Caroline. But they aren't married yet," she added, then raised a brow. "You did well to defend Violet."

He tried and failed to resist a smug smile.

"However, it might have been a mistake." She shook her head. "Women who have taken care of themselves don't always appreciate when a man deigns to do it for them."

He frowned in confusion. "That makes absolutely no sense. I would think she would appreciate it. I certainly would."

"For a man who has a certain reputation with women you know absolutely nothing about us."

"I was trying to be, well, her hero."

"Lord save us from men trying to be heroes." The duchess rolled her gaze at the ceiling. "Still, it was sweet in a misguided sort of way."

"Thank you?" Surely the duchess was wrong. Surely Violet would appreciate his coming to her rescue.

"Shouldn't you be going after your wife? Despite an impressive display of civility, I suspect she was somewhat upset."

"Yes, of course."

"And James." The duchess smiled. "I believe you're right. You might well be the most fortunate man here."

"Thank you, Your Grace." He grinned. "I know."

CHAPTER THIRTEEN

VIOLET MADE HER WAY across the ballroom in an unhurried and serene manner, a smile fixed firmly on her lips as if she were concerned with nothing more significant than her next partner. But a multitude of emotions swarmed in her stomach and her head. She needed a moment alone, to breathe deep and wait for the shaking of her hands and the trembling deep inside her to ease.

Violet departed the ballroom as gracefully as she could manage and headed toward the library. With its endless shelves and distinct scents, reminiscent of unknown lands and unimagined adventure, the library had been her favorite room as a child and a sanctuary when she grew older. The broad leather sofa at the far end of the room positioned to face the fireplace was where she had curled up to delve into a newly discovered story. The leaded glass doors opened to a small balcony where she could imagine being the kind of spirited heroine girls in Victoria's England she could only dream about. A sanctuary was certainly what she needed now. The library was blessedly close to the ballroom, as well.

She slipped into the room, closed the door behind her and collapsed against it. Dear Lord, what was wrong with her? One would have thought those dreadful dinners with her family in recent years would have prepared her for Mother's unpleasantness tonight. But this was different. This was in front of everyone who had witnessed her mistakes, her past humiliation. And God help her, it was indeed an engagement party and any observers would surely draw a connection between this party and another six years ago.

No, making her escape was the smartest thing she could do. Even if fleeing made her feel as if it were indeed six years ago and all the confidence and refinement she'd acquired was nothing more than a thin veneer to shatter with a word from her mother.

"Thank goodness it's you," a voice sounded from the far end of the room and Caroline's head appeared above the back of the sofa.

"What are you doing here?" Violet asked.

"Oh…" Caroline patted her hair into place. "Nothing of significance, really."

A muffled masculine laugh sounded from behind the sofa back.

Violet gasped. "You're not alone, are you?"

"My, you are perceptive, sister dear."

"Good God, Caroline, what were you thinking?" Violet rolled her gaze toward the ceiling. She raised her voice. "Come along, Neville. Now that I'm here we can all leave together and no one will be any the wiser."

"One problem with that." A handsome young man popped up beside her sister on the sofa. He grinned with unabashed amusement. Violet remembered that grin. She had fallen in love with that grin. That was James's grin. "I'm not Neville."

Violet glared at her sister. "You do remember this is your engagement party?"

"Don't be silly. Of course I do."

The young man scrambled off the sofa, then helped Caroline to her feet.

"Perhaps you didn't hear me." Violet drew her brows

together. "What are you doing?" Stupid question, really. It was more than obvious what they had been doing.

"Should I leave?" the young man asked Caroline, grabbing his coat off the arm of the sofa and shrugging into it.

"That's probably for the best." Caroline smoothed the wrinkles in her gown.

"Oh, it's definitely for the best," Violet snapped.

He smirked, then took Caroline's hand and raised it to his lips, gazing into her eyes as if she were the only woman in existence. Dear Lord, the man was good. "Until next time."

Caroline giggled.

"There will be no next time!" Violet scowled. "She's about to be married."

He sauntered toward the door, pausing beside Violet. He really was shockingly handsome. "I can overlook that." He flashed her that wicked grin and took his leave.

The moment the door closed behind him she turned to her sister. "Do you have any idea what would have happened had someone else discovered you?"

"It would have been something of a problem, I imagine." Caroline picked a bit of lint off her gown. "It wasn't as if we planned it. This wasn't an arranged liaison." Caroline stepped to the window and inspected her reflection in the dark night. "Everyone does it."

"Everyone most certainly does not!"

"It was passion, Violet. Sheer, impulsive, irresistible passion." She smoothed her hair and adjusted her hairpins. "From what I've heard, you understand passion."

Violet stared. "I beg your pardon."

"Oh, come now, you know exactly what I'm talking about." Caroline's gaze met Violet's in the window. "According to gossip, you're really not in a position to chastise anyone else about amorous adventures."

"I would not believe everything you hear."

"Oh, I would never believe *everything*." She tucked back another errant strand of hair. "But you're scarcely one to talk about improper behavior. Between your husband's reputation and your own, you certainly have no reason to act so superior."

Violet started to deny it, but it seemed pointless. Apparently the price for allowing inaccurate rumors to stand was a sister determined to follow in her own scandalous path. She drew a deep breath. "You don't have to marry Neville if you'd rather not."

Caroline's eyes widened. "Why on earth wouldn't I want to marry Neville?"

"If there's someone else you prefer."

"Don't be silly. Neville is exactly what I want and he is getting exactly what he wants." She turned to face her sister. "I am not an idiot, Violet. Neville will provide me with a grand position in society. I shall provide him with an impressive wife and the heirs he requires. After that my obligation will be fulfilled. Now, not that this little sisterly tête-à-tête hasn't been most enjoyable—" she smiled pleasantly and started toward the door "—but I must return to my fiancé."

"You're not being fair to him, you know."

"My dear sister." Caroline glanced at Violet over her shoulder. "Neville has never been happier." Caroline smirked and left, leaving the library doors half-closed in her wake.

Shock held Violet still for a moment, then she turned on her heel and strode through the door thrown open to the balcony. She leaned on the balustrade, drew in a deep breath and gazed out at the night. She'd really had no idea of her sister's nature. Or that her mother was still so angry at her.

"Are you all right?" James joined her on the balcony.

She wasn't at all happy with him either at the moment. "How much of that did you hear?"

"I reached the door just as Caroline was leaving," he said slowly. "She had a distinctly triumphant look on her face."

Violet shrugged.

James's brow furrowed. "Did she say something to you?"

"She said all sorts of things to me and I said quite a few back to her. I had no idea she was so much like Mother." She frowned. "I can manage my sister. And my mother, as well. There was no need for you to involve yourself."

He hesitated.

She narrowed her eyes. "What is it?"

"You looked as if you needed help."

"I didn't." She turned her gaze back to the gardens.

"I thought you did." He paused. "I still think you did."

"Well, you're wrong," she snapped.

He squared his shoulders. "I was defending you."

"I don't need defending. Nor do I want it. I have taken care of myself quite nicely for the last six years, thank you."

"Yes, but now you're home and—"

"And?"

"And there's no need for you to take care of yourself."

She drew her brows together. "What?"

"It's my responsibility. I'm supposed to take care of you."

Violet cast him a skeptical glance. "A bit late, don't you think."

"I'm trying to make up for that."

"Ah, yes, your effort at amends."

"That's part of it, of course but..." He squared his shoulders. "I'm your husband. I'm supposed to provide for you and protect you."

She scoffed. "Not in this marriage."

"In every marriage," he said firmly. "It's the way things are supposed to be."

"According to whom?"

"Every man I know."

Under other circumstances she might have found his declaration—and probably the entire conversation— rather amusing. Violet was anything but amused at the moment.

"Do you have any idea how your *defense* made me feel?" She shook her head. "As if I couldn't take care of myself. As if I were weak. I didn't like it one bit."

"I was only trying to help." His tone was a bit sharper than before. Surely *he* wasn't annoyed by all this. "I was trying to be your hero."

"Goodness, James." She rolled her gaze toward the heavens. "I stopped believing in heroes quite some time ago."

"Perhaps I can change your mind."

She studied him for a long moment. As much as she hadn't needed or wanted his defense it was rather endearing. She sighed. "Perhaps."

He stared at her. "Do you mean it?"

It was inevitable, really. He was being nothing less than a good friend and the perfect husband. She nodded. "I suppose I do."

"Excellent." James grinned. "I knew I could wear you down."

She raised a brow.

"Not yet, of course," he added quickly, "but eventually."

"Why are you so determined? And why now?" She wasn't at all sure she wanted to hear his answer. She held her breath.

"Not trying to fix things between us years ago was another one of my mistakes. I believe I've admitted that." He met her gaze. "I meant what I said to your mother. The last six years have been entirely my fault beginning with the night I kissed you."

"That was a mistake, James. You thought I was Marie." She waved off his admission. "A mistake on both our parts."

"Do you forgive me, then?"

"Well, yes, for the kiss, I suppose I do."

"Good, because I'd prefer to start our new life together with a certain amount of honesty."

Good Lord, he looked like an errant schoolboy. She bit back a smile. "Honesty is usually a good idea."

"Yes, that's what I thought." He paused. "There's more I need to say. I have in fact been thinking about this for some time."

"I can hardly wait to hear it."

He blew a long breath and met her gaze. "It wasn't a mistake."

She frowned. "What wasn't a mistake?" At once the answer struck her and she sucked in a sharp breath. "The incident?"

"I've always thought of it as *the kiss* but *the incident* is good, too."

"You kissed me *deliberately*?" Surely he didn't just say that. Surely she was mistaken. "Knowing it was me and not Marie?"

He winced. "I'm afraid so."

"But…" She shook her head. "Why?"

"I didn't want to marry her." He grimaced. "I knew

my kissing you would get back to her and she would break it off with me."

She stared in disbelief. "That's the stupidest thing I've ever heard!"

"Yes, well, I realize that now."

"If you didn't want to marry her, you could have said something! Called it off!"

"And I intended to." He paused. "I just wasn't sure how. And then when the opportunity arose, and I saw another way to escape, I seized it." He shrugged in a helpless manner. "Carpe diem and that sort of thing."

"Carpe diem?" Her voice rose. "*Carpe diem?* Did you realize what might happen?"

"When one seizes the day one rarely thinks about—"

"You ruined my reputation!"

"I know and I do ap—"

"You ruined my life!"

"I know that too and I am—"

"You made me the subject of scandal!" She glared. "You made it impossible for me to find a decent match."

"I did marry you," he pointed out as if that made all the difference.

It didn't. "Out of a misplaced sense of obligation!"

"It was the right thing to do," he said staunchly.

"Only to fix a problem you caused in the first place." She shook her head. "You didn't want to marry me."

"I didn't *not* want to marry you. I didn't want to marry anyone." He paused. "You could have said no."

"Could I? Did I really have that choice?"

"Well, I—"

"And then you threw me aside!"

He frowned. "That's not entirely fair."

"Isn't it?" She glared. "*You* decided we would go our

separate ways. *You* decided how we would live our lives. *You* gave me no choice in the matter."

His brow furrowed. "I was trying to do what was best. For both of us."

"For both of us? Hah!" She struggled for a semblance of control then discarded the attempt as futile. "You were trying to have your cake and eat it, too!"

"We've already established I have made a great many mistakes—"

"Dreadful mistakes and terrible decisions!" She crossed her arms over her chest. "So which was this?"

"Both," he snapped.

"Bloody right it was both!" It was still hard to grasp the fact that his ill-fated kiss had been deliberate. "Why me?"

He shook his head in confusion. "Why you what?"

"Why did you kiss *me*? Why not someone else?"

"Because you were, well, Violet."

She stared. "What does that mean?"

He grimaced. "I don't know."

"That poor, quiet Violet could withstand a scandalous kiss? Indeed, it might have made her more attractive to others?"

"No!" He huffed. "I told you I wasn't thinking about the consequences."

"And to think there were moments when I actually felt a twinge of pity for you!" She shook her head. "Forced to marry a woman you didn't want to marry because of a stupid mistake. I never imagined—"

Without warning he pulled her into his arms and pressed his lips to hers. She froze. The touch of his lips on hers, the warmth of his body next to hers, the inevitable sense of rightness and she was swept back to another time, another party, another kiss. God help her, some-

thing inside her melted and like six years ago she kissed
him back. Lost herself in the taste of him, the warm spicy
scent of him, the feel of his body pressed against hers.

At last he raised his head and gazed into her eyes.

"Why did you do that?" She could barely get the words
out.

"I thought I heard somebody in the library."

"There's no one there," she said, her voice annoyingly breathless.

"My mistake, then."

"Yet another one?"

"It wouldn't do to be caught arguing. That would pro-
voke gossip and—"

"And you would lose everything." She pushed out of
his arms and stepped back. "I need to return to the ballroom."

"At least you didn't slap me." He grinned. Brave, stupid man.

"Not yet, but I reserve the right to do so at a later
time." She started for the door. "And you can stop grinning now, James."

"I thought that was rather impressively perfect," he
called after her.

"Yes, well, you always did know how to kiss!" She
swiveled back to face him. "You lied to me, James. For
six years you lied to me."

"Not quite six. And I lied to everyone. Not that that
is an excuse, of course," he added quickly.

"I don't care about everyone. I gave you the benefit of
the doubt. How could I possibly ever trust you again?"
She turned and swept from the room.

The very fact that he had kissed her deliberately, that
he hadn't mistaken her for Marie, put a new light on
everything that had happened between them. And then

he had kissed her again and everything she'd ever felt, everything she'd tried to ignore, flooded through her. How on earth was she going to make it through the next three years? Why hadn't she foreseen the flaw in this entire plan?

She was in love with her husband and always had been.

CHAPTER FOURTEEN

"...AND SO SURELY you can understand why I can't possibly stay in London. With a man I can't trust. With him!" Violet paced the parlor floor, from the fireplace to the door and back, twisting her hands together with every step. "I simply can't do this. It's too much to ask of anyone."

Effie, Gwen and Poppy sat lined up on the sofa, their heads swiveling to follow Violet's pacing, as if they were rapt attendees at a tennis match. No doubt not what they'd expected when they'd stopped by to inquire about last night's ball. Although they did seem to appreciate the tea Andrews served and Mrs. Clarkes's excellent cakes and biscuits.

"We can certainly understand why you're upset," Effie said cautiously, placing another biscuit on her already full plate.

"Oh, I'm far beyond upset. Upset is when one's luggage is late to arrive. Or one's train is delayed. Or when one catches one's heel in one's hem! Oh, no, I am not merely upset. I am furious."

"As anyone would be." Gwen nodded.

"He lied to me. For six years he lied to me." She paused midstep and glared. "Six years!"

"Not quite six," Poppy said helpfully and took a bite of a biscuit.

Violet ignored her. "From the very beginning." For a moment last night, when he had kissed her, she had forgotten the vile deception that had started everything. "Our entire marriage was predicated on a lie." She clenched her teeth. "It was bad enough when I thought it was a mistake."

"One of many mistakes apparently," Gwen noted.

"His life has been filled with terrible decisions and dreadful mistakes." Violet waved indignantly. "And I am apparently at the top of that list!"

"But from what you've said, he does at least acknowledge them." Poppy cast her a tentative smile. "Admitting one's mistakes is the first step toward correcting them and making amends."

"There is no making amends for this. How could there be?" And to think she had actually started to believe all those things he was constantly saying about her—about them. "I had forgiven him, but now, knowing it wasn't a mistake, knowing he deceived me all these years, knowing the truth…how could I possibly forgive him? And then, to add insult to injury…" She sank down on a chair facing the sofa. "He kissed me."

Poppy's eyes widened. "Oh, my."

"How very interesting," Gwen said.

"As if a kiss could make up for six years of lies." Effie scoffed. "I do hope you slapped him again. And with a great deal of fervor."

"Actually, " Violet said with a resigned sigh, "I kissed him back." She was still trying to figure out why she had kissed him back. Why her knees had faltered and the blood had pulsed in her veins and her heart had swelled. Why she had clung to him as if she were a drowning woman clinging to a lifeboat. He had simply taken her by surprise—there was nothing more to it than that. Oh, certainly, it had occurred to her last night that she was in love with him and always had been. Now, in the cold light of day, she dismissed that as utter nonsense.

"I think you can put that completely out of your head." Gwen waved off Violet's confession. "He caught you unawares, that's all. Really, Violet, it was only a mere kiss."

Violet grimaced. "There was nothing mere about that kiss."

Effie's brow rose. "It was an exceptional kiss, then?"

"I'm afraid so." That kiss had invaded her senses, wrapped around her soul and settled somewhere in the vicinity of her heart. The falling sensation in the pit of her stomach and all those feelings she'd once had for James slammed back into her with the ruthlessness of a force of nature. Feelings she'd spent six years denying. She'd convinced herself that what she'd felt was nothing more than a girlish crush and not mad, passionate love. That those feelings would pass with time. And they had. Thinking otherwise was no more than a momentary aberration.

"So James kissed you and you kissed him back," Gwen said slowly, "and it was an extraordinary kiss."

Violet nodded.

"Well, it has been six years," Poppy said, and refilled her teacup.

"And now, because you've discovered that he lied for six years and had the temerity to kiss you, you want to flee to Europe like a frightened fox running from a pack of hounds." Gwen smiled innocently. "Do I have that right?"

"No, you do not." Indignation washed through Violet. "I am not the least bit frightened."

Effie's brow rose, mirroring the skeptical expressions on her friends' faces.

"Very well, I suppose, in some ways, perhaps I am."

Violet paused to choose her words. "Last night, James made me feel all sorts of things I haven't felt in six years."

Poppy's eyes widened. "That certainly changes the story a bit."

"I've never told this to anyone. I never imagined I would."

"You may count on our discretion." Gwen added another spoonful of sugar to her tea.

"And do stop squirming dear." Poppy winced. "You're making us all feel uneasy."

"Sorry." In truth, Violet was entirely too wrought up to sit still. It was all she could do not to bolt this very minute. It made absolutely no sense but she did indeed have an urgent need to flee, fueled by a sleepless night and far too many unanswered questions. It was ridiculous really. By any measure, last night was a rousing personal success. Aside from her mother and Lady Dalrymple, no one cared about the long-ago scandal that had led to her marriage. Regardless, something akin to panic swelled within her. She didn't like it one bit. She needed to leave London and she needed to do so now. Her bags were already being packed and Violet had sent a note to Cleo at her new residence regarding their imminent departure.

She drew a deep breath. "You know why James and I married."

"The accidental deliberate kiss." Poppy frowned. "Or the deliberately accidental kiss."

Gwen cast Poppy a long-suffering look then returned her attention to Violet. "Go on dear."

"I had, well, *feelings* for him then. Feelings that I later told myself were not the least bit, oh, legitimate, I suppose."

"As one tends to do." Effie nodded.

"When he kissed me the first time, I thought he felt

the same way about me, but had just somehow miracu-
lously realized it." She shook her head. "It was foolish of
me, of course. I was wrong. Then after we married, when
he was determined that we lead separate lives, when he
didn't want me—"

"He broke your heart." Poppy cast her a sympathetic
smile.

"The ass," Effie muttered.

"Last night, when he kissed me, I had just had words
with my mother and an unpleasant scene with my sister.
And he had just confessed that the kiss that started all
this was not a mistake as he had always claimed." She
tried to find the right words. There weren't any. "I felt
as if I were twenty-one again. And everything I've become vanished." She frowned. "I'm not sure I'm making any sense. I'm just afraid if I stay here, I'll become
who I once was and—"

"And James will break your heart again," Gwen said
simply.

Violet rubbed her forehead. "Something like that."

"Let me make certain I do in fact understand." Gwen
thought for a moment. "You're afraid of becoming the
girl you once were. The girl who fell in love with James.
The girl whose heart he broke."

Violet nodded.

Effie studied her. "Don't you think the woman you are
now is stronger than the woman you were then?"

Violet widened her eyes. "Without question."

"But that woman worries that the past, including
James, is just too prevalent here," Effie continued, "and
she might not be strong enough?"

"Something else I don't know." Violet looked down
at her hands, clasped together in her lap. She could almost see the ring she'd stopped wearing the day she'd

decided to leave London. "The first year, I would have come back had he only asked. Most of the second year, as well. But that year, when I returned to London, it was obvious he had indeed continued to live as if he wasn't married at all."

"Other women." Poppy nodded in a sage manner.

Violet nodded. "I wasn't thrilled about his behavior but not terribly surprised. James was who he was, after all. Even so, I was angry and disappointed as well. It was time, past time really, that I faced the truth. He didn't want me. He never had." She looked up at the elderly trio. "He probably never would."

Gwen frowned. Poppy sniffed.

"The beast," Effie muttered.

"So I put him out of my head." *And my heart.* "I never saw him whenever I returned to London. In the last few years, Uncle Richard talked about how James had changed, grown up if you will. Richard truly thought James and I belonged together. As much as in some distant portion of my mind that still believes in fairy tales and other such nonsense I wanted to believe Richard, I couldn't." She squared her shoulders. "I have been James's wife for nearly six years. In all that time, he never made any effort to reconcile. He never wrote to me, never followed me, never confronted me and he certainly never fought for me, for my affections. One would think a man who had indeed changed would have wanted to set that part of his life to rights."

"One would think," Poppy murmured.

"Men are idiots, dear," Effie said. "Go on."

"He has said some things in recent weeks that might lead one to believe…"

Violet struggled to gather her thoughts but her mind was a mess of conflicting ideas and emotions. "How do

I know that anything he says now isn't because he'll do whatever he needs to do to keep me abiding by Richard's will?

"And what happens at the end of three years?" She raised her chin. "He didn't want me once, you see. I refuse to go through that again."

"You do realize if you leave, he will lose everything," Gwen pointed out. "As will you."

"Yes, well, that is a consideration." Violet hadn't the vaguest notion what she would do for financial support let alone assist those causes dear to her heart. But at the moment even poverty seemed rather insignificant. She'd exchanged letters about the state of her finances but the explanations she'd received were confusing and made no sense to her. This wasn't the first time she'd considered traveling to Paris to assess the situation in person and determine if she had any financial hope at all. She did fear there was none. "I suppose I could find some way to support myself. Write about my travels or lead tours to various places I've visited. Or possibly open a travel agency. One, I don't know, specifically directed at lady travelers perhaps. You have no idea how difficult travel can be for women."

"What a splendid idea," Poppy said thoughtfully.

"Do not get ahead of yourself, Violet." Gwen thought for a moment. "It seems to me this has all been rather easy for James."

Violet drew her brows together. "What do you mean?"

"James needs you to stay by his side, continue this appearance of a happy marriage. He doesn't have to do much of anything, really, except be charming and thoughtful." Gwen shrugged. "It's not altogether difficult for him."

"You're absolutely right." Effie sat up a bit straighter

and met Violet's gaze. "If James wants his inheritance, and you in the bargain, it seems to me, he should be made to work for it."

Poppy nodded. "To prove he has indeed changed."

"Making him work for it was my idea when this all started. James has never had to work for anything in his life." But James had lulled her into a friendship shadowed by the prospect of something more—love, romance, happily ever after perhaps? And she had fallen for it. Apparently James was not the only one susceptible to terrible decisions and dreadful mistakes.

"Your life was going along quite nicely before Richard died," Gwen said. "A life that was not originally of your choosing. Why should you now be the one inconvenienced because Richard decided to set up this attempt at matchmaking from the grave?"

"Do keep in mind, Violet, that James will not receive his inheritance without you," Poppy added. "You are crucial to this endeavor."

"Regardless of how you may feel at the moment, you are the one in complete control of how this turns out. Therefore it seems to me—" Effie looked at her friends who nodded in agreement "—to us, that if you wish to go to Paris or anywhere else, you should do exactly that."

"And James will have to either follow you or abandon his legacy," Gwen added.

"James has never been good at following," Violet pointed out.

"The James you married, perhaps. This James is different, isn't he?" Poppy asked.

"So it appears." Violet's gaze slid from one woman to the next. "Then you think I should go? To Paris and perhaps to Florence and Athens, as well?"

"It's the only thing to do." Poppy nodded.

"And if you limit your travel to Paris, you can be back in less than a week if you wish," Effie pointed out. "Why, it would scarcely cut into the fourteen-days-a-year limit on time spent apart, but it would give you time to decide if you wish to stay here with James or not. If you can overlook the lie that started all this."

"And the six years since," Poppy added.

Effie continued. "You were thrust into this situation with very little say in the matter the moment we heard the details of Richard's will. And you did say you had things to attend to and places you had planned on being."

"I did and I do." At once, Violet felt like herself again.

"Perhaps leaving for a bit will give you the chance to get your thoughts in order." Gwen offered an encouraging smile.

"And we certainly know how suddenly having a husband around all the time can be trying." Poppy grimaced.

"You should leave for Paris at once," Effie said.

"It wouldn't be at all fair to go without telling him." Violet smiled grimly. "And yet fair doesn't seem particularly appealing at the moment."

"Was it fair of James, or Richard, to put you in this position in the first place?" Gwen asked. "No, it was not."

"James made me the subject of scandal and didn't have the courage to tell me the truth for six years. Without the least bit of regard for my feelings, he changed the course of my life."

"And Richard changed it again," Effie said. "No one consulted you about anything. That, my dear girl, is what's truly unfair."

"Absolutely right." Violet's resolve hardened. If James wanted his inheritance, if he wanted her, he did indeed need to work for it.

Voices sounded outside the parlor and she braced herself.

"Violet." James strode into the room, a rather satisfied smile on his face. As if the fact that he had kissed her and, more significantly, she had kissed him back changed everything between them. She really should have smacked him last night. James turned to the ladies on the sofa. "And how are my three favorite guardian angels today?"

"Goodness, James." Gwen smiled. "You are a scamp."

"Thank you." He grinned. "Has Violet been telling you about her sister's ball?" He shot Violet an admiring glance. She ignored it. "She was a rousing success, and I was the envy of every man there."

"We have no doubt of it." Poppy smiled.

Andrews appeared in the doorway. "Mr. Davies is here, my lord."

Marcus stepped into the room. "James, I need..." He stopped short and nodded cautiously. "Violet, ladies, lovely to see you again."

"You're just in time. I believe I might have interrupted something interesting." James adopted a teasing frown. "Are the four of you plotting something?" He glanced at Marcus. "Conquering the world no doubt."

Marcus chuckled.

"I wouldn't call it plotting exactly," Poppy said brightly.

"Oh, I don't know." Gwen smiled. "I rather like the idea of plotting."

"Plotting it is, then." Effie grinned.

James laughed. "Dare I ask exactly what you've been plotting?"

Violet rose to her feet. Best to get on with it. "I have business I need to see to in Paris. There are, as well, engagements elsewhere I promised to attend. I plan to leave this afternoon."

James stared. "You're going to Paris?"

"I believe that's what she just said," Marcus murmured.

James's brow furrowed. "Surely you're not serious?"

"I have never been more serious," she said pleasantly.

"What kind of business?" Suspicion edged his words.

"None of your concern." She smiled. "You're simply going to have to trust me."

"Why? You don't trust me."

"I have every reason not to trust you," she said sharply.

"If I might have a word," Marcus said. "You do realize being apart for more than fourteen days will violate the terms of the will."

"I am well aware of that." She turned to James. "But I've changed my mind. About abiding by the stipulations of the will, that is."

"What do you mean?" he said slowly.

"Now I want something in return."

Marcus winced.

James studied her cautiously. "What exactly do you want?"

"You keep saying the most charming things. How you want to atone for your mistakes. How marrying me was the best thing you ever did. And so on and so forth." She scoffed. "It's rubbish, James. Complete rubbish."

"It is not." Indignation sounded in his voice.

"You can't make up for six years with a few nice phrases and an emerald necklace."

"You said it was magnificent."

"It is, but that's not the point."

"What is the point?"

"The point is it's time to pay the piper. To prove you mean what you've been saying. And that's what I want." She narrowed her eyes. "You haven't been the least bit inconvenienced by Uncle Richard's will. Your life hasn't changed one iota."

"I wouldn't say that," James said under his breath.

"My life has been completely disrupted. A life, I might point out, that was not of my choosing. There are things I had planned to do before all this happened, people I had intended to see. I have friends, James, as well as obligations. I have made commitments and I intend to honor them." She crossed her arms over her chest. "For six years you have paid no attention to me whatsoever. To where I was, to what I did. Why, you never even summoned up the courage to stay in the same house with me."

"I was only doing what you wanted." He glared. "*You* said you never wanted to see me again."

"And *you* made no effort to change my mind."

"I was abiding by your request!"

"You were a coward."

He sucked in an indignant breath.

"Oh, my," one of the ladies murmured.

Violet shook her head. "You refused to make the best of the situation we found ourselves in. The situation you put us in. *On purpose.* You never fought for me, for us. You never lifted so much as a finger. You didn't make the tiniest attempt at a proper marriage."

"I've admitted that was a mistake."

"Now, you say you've changed. You claim you want your wife. You want me. Now…" She smiled slowly. "I want you to prove it."

"I think last night proved something." A smug note sounded in his voice.

"Goodness, he can't go around kissing her whenever it suits his purposes and think that's all he need do," another of the ladies said with quiet indignation.

"Oh, it was a more than adequate kiss, James, but then you've had a great deal of practice." Violet smirked. Let him be smug about that.

"That's not entirely—"

"I intend to resume my life. The will requires only that we are to be together—it does not stipulate where. It seems to me you have three choices." She ticked the points off on her fingers. "You may accompany me. You may follow me. Or you may begin looking for a position of employment."

"If you only go to Paris," he said slowly, "you could be back in less than fourteen days."

"I could and indeed I might, should I so decide." She met his gaze. "Is that a risk you're willing to take?"

His jaw clenched. "I said I had no desire to travel."

She shrugged. "And I had no desire to marry a man who didn't want to marry me."

"I don't have a choice, do I?"

"More than I had six years ago."

His gaze locked with hers. She refused to so much as flinch. "You said you forgave me for that."

"I forgave you for the mistake. I did not forgive you for the deliberate act." Her voice hardened. "Or the years that followed."

"This is a test, isn't it?"

"You may call it whatever you like."

"I'm not going to Paris today," he said coolly.

"Very well." The oddest wave of disappointment washed through her. But really, what did she expect? "In that case, I have arrangements to make. Mrs. Ryland will accompany me."

It was for the best, really. The longer she stayed here, the more likely all would end in disaster. She would be a fool to think it could possibly be otherwise. She turned to the older women. "Ladies, thank you for your wisdom and your sound advice. I shall see you when I return."

The ladies were right. She needed time to clear her head. Time to decide whether saving James's future was worth the risk to her heart. At the moment, she was entirely too angry to make rational decisions. She nodded at her husband and his friend then took her leave in as serene a manner as she could manage.

One did what one had to do even if it wasn't at all easy. And given the dull ache somewhere in the vicinity of her heart, entirely too late.

CHAPTER FIFTEEN

"WELL, THAT COULD have gone better," Marcus muttered.

"Sarcasm, Mr. Davies," Lady Blodgett reproached, "is not helpful at the moment."

Marcus winced. "Sorry."

Life had indeed been going quite nicely until the moment James walked into the parlor. Certainly Violet was upset about his revelation, but that would pass. She had forgiven him, after all, even if that forgiveness came before she knew the truth of the matter. But last night he had kissed her and she had kissed him back in a most enthusiastic manner. He had felt that kiss right down to his toes, which had nothing to do with the fact that he hadn't kissed anyone for quite some time and everything to do with the woman in his arms, the woman who should always have been in his arms. It had also triggered the most delightful dream last night that no longer seemed entirely far-fetched. He'd been confident that kiss was a turning point as well as a first step toward the future. Apparently, he was wrong.

"Ladies." James eyed the elderly trio. "What do you know about all this?"

"Lady Ellsworth has business to see to in Paris." Mrs. Higginbotham gestured in an unconcerned manner. "Although she did mention something about a party she had planned to attend. A birthday celebration and something of a charitable event, I believe."

"She's risking our future for a party?"

"There was a time…" Marcus said under his breath.

"I would say you're the one risking it," Mrs. Higginbotham pointed out. "You can't expect her to totally upend her life simply to save yours. And you have thus far. It's unreasonable and arrogant of you." She paused. "And your uncle, as well."

"Men." Lady Blodgett huffed.

James aimed a hard look at the ladies. "Does she plan to be back within fourteen days?"

"She didn't say. I had the distinct feeling she hasn't decided." Mrs. Fitzhew-Wellmore's brow furrowed. "But she did mention she might go on to Florence and Athens after Paris. In which case, no. I would think she wouldn't return within fourteen days."

"What are you going to do?" Marcus asked James.

"I don't have much choice, do I?"

"I believe she gave you three choices," Mrs. Fitzhew-Wellmore said.

James thought for a moment. He didn't like this one bit. And there was something about her itinerary—Paris and Florence and Athens—that seemed significant, but he couldn't quite put his finger on it.

"Choice number two, then," James said in a hard tone. "I'm going to follow her."

"Excellent, my lord. So much better than accompanying her, really. This way, your appearance will be a surprise, as if you've had a change of heart. Women do like it when men come to their senses." Mrs. Fitzhew-Wellmore beamed. "We knew you'd do the right thing."

"I've been trying to do the *right thing* since this all began," James said sharply. "I've done my best to be thoughtful and gallant and the perfect bloody husband."

"And it's been hardly any effort at all for you." Lady

Blodgett's voice sharpened. "At some point you are going to have to decide what is more important to you—your inheritance or your wife. And what you are willing to sacrifice to get it."

"You may be right, Lady Blodgett." He glanced at Marcus. "I too have arrangements to make. I can leave tomorrow."

"*We* can leave tomorrow. Mrs. Ryland is going, you'll no doubt need assistance or at least a friendly face. And I have been to Paris more recently than you have. Ladies." Marcus turned to the trio. "Do you intend to go, as well?"

The ladies traded glances. Lady Blodgett sighed. "As much as we would like nothing better, I'm afraid we have…pressing concerns that prohibit our accompanying you."

Mrs. Fitzhew-Wellmore wrinkled her nose. "Financial concerns."

Marcus nodded. "Then as you will not be able to oversee Lord and Lady Ellsworth's adherence to the conditions of the will, might I offer to accompany them as your representative and that of my firm?"

"Excellent idea, Mr. Davies." Mrs. Fitzhew-Wellmore brightened. "We will expect you to keep us apprised of, well, everything."

"Dispatches on a regular basis." Mrs. Higginbotham pinned Marcus with a no-nonsense look. "Telegrams will do."

"Ladies," James said, "Mr. Davies and I have much to discuss. If you'll forgive me, I'll have Andrews see you out."

All three ladies rose to their feet.

Lady Blodgett led the way to the door. "We wish you all the best, my lord."

"Do have a pleasant trip," Mrs. Fitzhew-Wellmore said as she passed by. "Paris is lovely this time of year."

"Women love sacrifice almost as much as they love men admitting they were wrong," Mrs. Higginbotham added. "Try not to muck it up."

James turned the trio over to Andrews and he and Marcus adjourned to the library. James promptly poured them each a glass of whiskey.

"Do you really have arrangements to make or are you simply trying to make a point?"

"Both." He tossed back a healthy swallow. "I'll not do everything she wants at the snap of her fingers. Besides, I can't simply up and leave London on a moment's notice."

"She is the one in control of the situation."

"She has as much to lose as I."

"Not exactly." Marcus sipped his drink. "It appears your wife has money."

"Of course she has money. My money." James huffed. "She's spent it all over Europe for the past six years. She's probably planning how to spend it in Paris even as we speak."

"No, I mean she has her own money. I finally figured it out this morning. From what I've been able to determine, your uncle set up a trust of sorts for her on the day before you were married." Marcus paused. "Do you recall signing something before your wedding that stipulated any property or funds she brought to the marriage would remain hers and hers alone?"

"I signed all sorts of things." He frowned. "Uncle Richard did that?"

"The earl probably meant it to be something for her to fall back on should things between you become difficult in the future."

"You mean if I turned out to be a true scoundrel?" It

was a bothersome thought, although he really couldn't blame Uncle Richard for trying to protect Violet. At least she would not be penniless if they failed to meet the terms of the will.

"A precaution, James, nothing more than that." Marcus offered a supportive smile. "However, it seems that through clever management and investment, that initial amount has become a decent fortune. The account is managed in Paris by a Comte de Viviers."

James drew his brows together. "She never said a word."

Marcus sipped his drink. "Are you going to tell her you know about this?"

"Not for the moment." He considered this new revelation for a moment. "But I do find it interesting."

"Secret funds are always interesting."

"Better than that. This means she didn't have to go along with Uncle's Richard's will. She's doing it because she *wants* to."

"Or because it was your uncle's last wish, and she was very fond of him."

"Or very fond of me." James grinned. "This means there's hope."

"She didn't seem very fond of you a few minutes ago."

James waved off the comment. "A minor misunderstanding. This entire thing—traveling to Paris and wherever else she plans to go—is only because she's annoyed with me."

"My, you are optimistic. She seemed far more than annoyed."

"I kissed her last night." James chuckled. "And she kissed me back."

"You may be overestimating the impact of your kiss." Marcus studied him. "Don't you see an odd parallel here?

It was an ill-advised kiss at another engagement party that started all of this."

"Last night's kiss was not the least bit ill-advised."

"You're sounding a bit smug, you know."

"Marcus, things are looking up. Oh, certainly, Violet is leading me on a chase to Paris and God knows where else. She wants me to prove something to her, work for what I want and I have every intention of doing do. Beyond that, the more time I spend with her, the better she'll know me and the more likely she is to forgive me for the past. See me for who I am now. Maybe even trust me."

"I'm not sure it's a good plan, but it is better than nothing."

"Pack your bags, my friend." James raised his glass. "We're going to Paris."

"Do you think we did the right thing?" Poppy frowned.

"Encouraging Violet to leave London, you mean?" Gwen asked. Poppy nodded. "Well, I'm not sure it was the wrong thing, exactly."

"The woman had already made up her mind," Effie pointed out. "She was simply looking for us to support her decision. Besides, James does need to put forth a certain amount of effort if he wants her for more than his inheritance."

"Do you think he does?" Poppy asked.

"Richard thought he did." Effie thought for a moment. "He certainly has been acting like he does. But Violet needs to know whether or not it is indeed an act to keep her content and adhering to the conditions of the will or something more significant. Being in close quarters, away from London, will no doubt tell her what she needs to know."

"Beyond that, it seems to me they scarcely know each

other at all at this point if indeed they ever did," Gwen said thoughtfully. "My dear Charles used to say there was no better way to get to know a man than by taking him on an expedition."

"Perhaps we should accompany them to Paris?" A wistful note sounded in Poppy's voice.

Effie shook her head. "I do not intend to squander the money I've been allotted for this venture on a trip to Paris." She paused. "No matter how tempting it sounds."

"And it is tempting," Gwen murmured.

"I remember Paris." Poppy sighed. "It's a most romantic city. Something about the French…"

"Romance is certainly called for. Although…" Gwen considered the matter. "I think James may well already be in love with her. Possibly has been for years. There's something in the way he looks at her…"

"Regardless of what Violet says," Effie said, choosing her words with care, "I suspect those feelings she had for James never really vanished."

Poppy's brow furrowed. "Then you do think this is a test on Violet's part?"

"No," Effie said. "I think it's a test for both of them."

Part Two

Paris, Florence, Athens

CHAPTER SIXTEEN

JAMES BRACED HIS hands on the ornate iron railing of the balcony off his room in the Grand Hotel and gazed at the streets of Paris below him, gleaming in the late-afternoon sun. This was not his first stay in the French capital, but his previous visit had been part of a grand tour and his memories were indistinct and blurred by time and over-indulgence. And the revolting tendency of his stomach to rebel at being on water or confined for too long to a train. At the time, he had attributed it to the fact that he and his friends were rarely sober. Today's crossing proved that theory wrong. If he recalled correctly, sleep helped ease his distress. Perhaps he could purchase some sleeping powders to make it through the rest of this trip.

The last time he had visited Europe he had been in the company of a group of friends: like-minded young men who had been far more interested in the entertainments of Paris—and everywhere else—than the cultural and historic offerings. They'd had little interest in enrich-ment of the mind, but it had been a great deal of fun. Fun of any kind was the last thing he expected on this trip.

The optimism he'd felt yesterday had dimmed consid-erably, thanks to an unpleasant channel crossing spent mostly leaning over the railing of the ferry and his real-ization as to the true purpose of Violet's trip. When Mrs. Fitzhew-Wellmore had mentioned Violet might continue on from Paris to Florence and then Athens, something had nagged at the back of his mind. Somewhere during the train trip to Dover, the ferry across the channel and the final train into Paris, the pieces came together and the elusive answer he hadn't quite been able to put his finger on became crystal-clear.

A knock sounded at his door and it opened before he could respond. He glanced over his shoulder. "Aren't you supposed to wait until someone tells you to come in before entering a room?"

"The door was unlocked." Marcus strode into the room. "Somewhat foolish in a hotel. One never knows who might wander in."

"Apparently."

"Feeling better?" Marcus asked.

"Much." Going straight from the ferry to a train had not helped, but another hour and the last lingering effects of mal de mer should be completely gone.

"Well, you're no longer green." Marcus joined him on the balcony. "Is this why you don't like travel?"

"If you spent every minute onboard a ship retching over the railing, would you?" James grimaced. "Lengthy train travel, especially in mountainous areas, is nearly as bad. Sleep is the only thing that helps." He glanced at his friend. "I'd prefer you didn't mention this to anyone. It's rather embarrassing."

"If you insist, but eventually someone might notice." He regarded his friend curiously. "So, are you appreciating the sights of Paris or are you still sulking?"

"I don't sulk," James said in a sharper tone than might be expected from someone who was not sulking.

"My apologies," Marcus said. "Obviously I mistook your constant muttering, disgruntled sighs and snorts of indignation for sulking."

"I simply had a great deal on my mind." James shrugged. "I finally figured out what she's doing."

"Did you?"

"Think about it for a minute." James had stopped by his club yesterday evening and had run into Welles in passing. They'd chatted briefly about nothing in particular but there was a knowing look on his old friend's face when James had mentioned Violet's possible itinerary. He'd paid no attention to it at the time—his mind was far too preoccupied getting his affairs in order. Who knew how long he'd be away and if Violet intended to flit around Europe, he intended to be right by her side. He still wasn't sure what she wanted him to prove, but this was a challenge he did not intend to fail.

It wasn't until he watched the English countryside pass by today on the way to Dover that the answer took shape. At first, he thought the idea was absurd. Now, he was convinced he was right. "What do Paris, Florence and Athens have in common?"

"They're in Europe?" Marcus said cautiously.

"Beyond that." He turned toward his friend. "Consider the rumors that have circulated about Violet in the past six years."

"All right." Marcus thought for a moment. "Sorry, old man, I've got nothing."

"A French count, an Italian sculptor and a Greek poet." James's jaw clenched. "All reputed to be Violet's—" he nearly choked on the word "—lovers."

Marcus snorted. "You can't be serious."

"Oh, but I am." The more he thought about it the more sense it made. "She admitted this trip was a test. What better way to determine if I have indeed changed, if I am willing to leave the past behind, than by flaunting her past in my face. What better way to make me pay for all my mistakes?"

Marcus laughed. "That's the most ludicrous thing I've ever heard."

"Or the most diabolically brilliant."

Marcus shook his head. "Violet does not strike me as the kind of woman who would do something like that."

"Anger does things to a woman, Marcus," James said darkly. "Revenge is the very least of it." He drew a deep breath. "Apparently she's been angry at me for six years. She said I had failed to fight for her. This is her way of giving me the opportunity to do just that."

"Not to throw a bit of rationality into the convoluted case you have so wildly constructed, but Comte de Viviers is the man who manages her fortune."

"And who is more trustworthy to handle finances for a woman than a lover?"

"He was apparently a friend of your uncle's," Marcus said mildly.

"Women love older, rich, titled men." His eyes narrowed. "Especially if they're foreign. Women swoon for men with accents."

"He's not foreign here. We are."

"Maybe I can use that to my advantage."

Marcus laughed. "I think you were right when you said Violet was trying to drive you mad. I believe she's succeeded."

"I can't disagree with you there." He glanced at his friend. "I am ready to fight for her, you know."

"Come to that conclusion, have you?"

"It's been two months. But I think I knew the first day. That's why I had to tell her the truth."

"The truth?" Marcus said slowly. "Yesterday, you were quite confident that you and Violet were going to make a go of this. But you said there had been a minor disagreement. It wasn't minor, was it?"

James drew a deep breath. "I told her that when I kissed her six years ago—"

Marcus nodded. "Thus ending your engagement to Miss Fredericks."

"It wasn't an accident." He grimaced. "I knew full well it was Violet on that terrace."

Marcus stared. "You kissed her deliberately?"

"I'm afraid so."

The solicitor choked back a laugh. "That explains why she's so angry."

"I'm glad you find this amusing."

"It's hard not to."

"Admittedly, it might have been a mistake to tell her the truth, at least now. She might have taken it better if I'd waited another year or two. Or ten."

"Honesty will do you in every time, you know." Marcus grinned then sobered. "Which makes what I need to say now more than a little awkward. I was going over your uncle's will again last night, to see if there were any specific references to Violet's trust—there weren't, by the way. But I stumbled over a clause cleverly hidden in a portion of the will I had not examined as thoroughly as the stipulations."

"Oh?"

"It provides a way to end the conditions of the will." Marcus drew a deep breath. "You would receive everything and you and Violet could resume your lives as you see fit."

James studied his friend. "There's a trick, isn't there?"

"Not really." He shook his head. "But I don't think it's wise to inform you about this clause."

"Why not?"

Marcus drew his brows together. "If things turn out the way you hope they will with Violet and she ever finds out about this, and finds out that you were aware of it, your actions will be suspect. Trust me on this, James."

The idea of getting out from under the stipulations of the will—while appealing—also meant Violet would not be compelled to stay with him. That wouldn't do. If he was going to win her heart, it was obviously going to take longer than he expected. He might well need the entire two years and however many months.

"I do trust you, Marcus," James said at last. "If you think telling me is a mistake, then don't tell me."

"Wise decision." Marcus breathed a sigh of relief. "You still want to stay in her good graces. You do need her, you know."

"I am doing my best." His gaze returned to the streets of Paris. "And not merely for the inheritance."

"So it is love, then?"

"You asked me once before and I wasn't sure of the answer." He met his friend's gaze. "Now I am."

"Yes, I noticed how affectionate the two of you were yesterday."

"A momentary aberration." James waved off the comment.

"You do realize fighting *with* her is not the same thing as fighting *for* her?"

"Oh, I fully intend to fight for her regardless of whether that fight is with a former lover or Violet herself. Once I prove to her whatever it is she wants me to prove we can move on." His resolve hardened. "She wanted me to follow her and I have, which does seem a point in my favor. With any luck, we can now return home."

"One can only hope." Marcus paused. "So, your reluctance to travel, I assume that's due to the little problem you had on the channel crossing."

"Figured that out did you?"

"And if she decides to travel on to Italy and Greece?"

"Then we shall all go to Italy and Greece." Determination rang in his voice, but his stomach lurched.

"I can hardly wait." Marcus braced his hands on the railing and gazed out at the city. "Do you intend to call on her now or wait until tonight?"

Marcus had spoken to Mrs. Ryland before she and Violet left yesterday. It had been obvious for some time that Marcus liked the woman—why, he had managed to find her a flat in the same building he resided in—but James was confident whatever was brewing between them was not significant. A minor flirtation perhaps, nothing more than that. Marcus would confide in him if it was anything serious. If Marcus were truly interested in Mrs. Ryland, James would have to talk some sense into him, save him from himself. How could his closest friend possibly be involved with a woman who detested him? Although she was quite attractive and remarkably efficient. She had given Marcus hotel recommendations, had urged him to telegraph ahead for reservations and provided the name of the hotel manager, although she and Violet were apparently staying at the comte's grand Paris house. And wasn't that convenient? Mrs. Ryland had also told Marcus about a ball for the comte's birthday tonight. There were invitations waiting for them when they arrived at the hotel, for which James was reluctantly grateful. The woman did not like him, but she had been extraordinarily helpful, although James was certain it was more for Marcus's benefit than his own.

"Tonight will do. It's my turn to surprise her. What better place than at a ball."

"Because you and she have such fond memories of the balls you've attended?"

"Because dancing with her is one of the great pleasures of life."

"Tell her, not me." Marcus considered him wryly. "You could have saved us all a great deal of trouble if you had declared yourself to Violet yesterday, unless you have any doubts."

"Oh, I know exactly what I want and how I feel." The blasted woman already had his heart—now he just had to win hers.

Marcus's brow furrowed in confusion. "And?"

"I simply don't see why I can't have it all." He shrugged. "The lady and the legacy."

Marcus snorted back a laugh. "You're playing a dangerous game, my friend."

"A game that requires strategy, outwitting one's opponent and never revealing what you're thinking. Yet another challenge."

"I believe they call that love." Genuine sympathy shone in Marcus's eyes. "You do realize you might lose everything."

"I've always been good with the turn of a card or the roll of the dice, especially when the stakes are high. The stakes have never been higher." Determination edged his words. "And I intend to win it all."

IT DID SEEM to James if one was going to volunteer to accompany someone on a trip to Paris, one might have made clear one's knowledge of the language was minimal.

Marcus's schoolboy French was no better than James's and James was well aware his was practically nonexistent. Thanks to their lack of prowess with the language, an incomprehensible map and carriage drivers with a dislike of anyone English, by the time they reached the comte's grand mansion in a fashionable area of equally grand houses just off the Champs-Élysées the comte's birthday ball was well underway. They were announced at the entrance to the ballroom, but the crowd was such that James was certain no one heard their names. Or cared.

"Now what?" Marcus surveyed the gathering.

"Now, I'm going to find my wife." James adjusted his cuffs. "I would like to meet the comte, as well."

"You're not going to do anything foolish, are you?"

"You mean like demand she return home at once?" James shook his head. "I'm not that stupid."

"Good. You do need to watch your step."

"I am well aware of that." If they were at home, James could simply ask someone if they'd seen Violet. This would take a bit more effort. Still, a charming manner and equally charming smile knew no language barriers.

"As I have no desire to witness your happy reunion, I believe I shall leave you to it." Marcus nodded and wandered deeper into the throng, no doubt to find Mrs. Ryland.

James scanned the milling multitude. It wasn't easy, the room was packed with celebrants. It was apparent from the distinguished appearance of the gentlemen present, the elegant clothes and the sparkling jewels adorning every lady in the room that this was the very cream of Paris society. He adopted his most engaging smile and made his way through the crowd, keeping to the perimeter of the overflowing dance floor, murmuring a polite *bon soir* and nodding in feigned greeting as he went. He finally spotted Violet moving from one small cluster of guests to another. His heart sped up. He hadn't realized how much he'd missed her. If he missed her this much after a single day, how would he feel if he lost her forever? His stomach twisted at the thought.

She moved with grace and elegance, completely at ease. As if she belonged here. It did appear she was more at home in a ballroom in Paris than she had been in London. Without warning, the thought struck him—could she possibly be happy with him? And worse—was he worthy of her? He pushed aside the disquieting notion.

Violet greeted an elderly gentleman on the far side of the ballroom and began what appeared to be a serious discussion, judging by the stiff lines of her posture. This was the Comte de Viviers, no doubt. He was definitely a contemporary in age of Richard's, even if he did strike James as being a bit more lively than his uncle had been. But then he was French and the French were well-known for their carefree ways, which probably did indeed make a difference in a man's waning years.

"Pardonnez moi." An elegant older woman stepped to his side. *"Êtes-vous Lord Ellsworth? J'ai voulu vous rencontrer depuis longtemps, mais je ne savais pas que vous étiez à Paris."*

At once he regretted the lack of attention he'd paid in his youth when earnest instructors had tried and failed to teach him French. Or any other language, for that matter. Aside from his name, he had no idea what she said. He shook his head in apology. "I am sorry, but I'm afraid my French is limited to *la plume de ma tante est bleue.*"

The lady's brows drew together. "Why would the pen of your lady be blue?" she said in accented English.

"I have no idea." He grinned. "But that's the only phrase I can remember from my attempt to learn French as a boy."

"A rather worthless phrase though, is it not?" Amusement gleamed in her eyes. She was a handsome woman, obviously quite striking in her younger days, now somewhere in her sixties or seventies, he thought. It was really impossible to tell.

"It is indeed." He chuckled. "Unless of course I was attempting to find my aunt's pen, in which case knowing the color would be of benefit."

"You are amusing." She laughed. "And your apology is accepted. You are the Earl of Ellsworth, no?"

"I am," he said cautiously.

"There is no need to be suspicious. I heard your name announced."

"Oh, I wasn't—"

Her brow rose.

He smiled wryly. "Again, my apologies."

"It is difficult when one doesn't understand anything everyone around you is saying. When you are a—what is the term?" She thought for a minute. "Ah, yes, a fish out of the water."

"You have no idea."

"Do not be a goose, *certainement* I do." She smiled. "We have all, on occasion, felt like fish out of the water, flopping around in desperation. It is only natural."

"I suppose it is." He studied her. "You don't strike me as the kind of woman who would ever feel out of place."

"What a charming thing to say. But I am French. French women never allow our moments of uncertainty to show." She lowered her voice and leaned closer in a confidential manner. "We cover them with loud voices and the occasional flinging of pottery."

He chuckled. "Even so, I suspect those moments are few and far between."

"You are a charming devil, but then I expected nothing less."

Expected? He drew his brows together. "I'm afraid you have me at a disadvantage."

"How delightful of me." Her eyes sparkled with amusement.

"You seem to know me, but I don't know you."

"Mystery is part of the fun of a chance encounter, is it not? Ah, but you have nothing to drink. That will not do." She peered around him, nodded to someone and a moment later a waiter in a powdered wig and ornate livery appeared with a tray of champagne. James took a glass and handed one to her.

"Merci." She took a sip. "There is nothing better than excellent champagne on a fine spring evening."

"In any language." He grinned and took a sip. It was indeed excellent. His gaze strayed to Violet still talking to the comte.

"I see you found your wife."

He frowned. "How did you know I was looking for my wife?"

"A man has a certain look upon his face when he is looking for something." She smiled in a knowing manner. "And another when he has found it."

"Yes, well—"

"I heard your name announced, remember? And you did not arrive with her." She shrugged. "It was a simple observation. Nothing more than that."

"Of course." He did need to be less suspicious. It probably had something to do with that fish out of water feeling. "So, do you know the comte well?"

She sipped her wine. "I was once his mistress."

"Were you?"

"A very long time ago. We were quite young then." Her gaze settled on the comte. "He was one of those men who feared the confines of marriage but could not resist the lure of love." A serene smile curved her lips. "Love, my lord, is usually irresistible."

"Yes, I suppose it is." He blew a long breath. "My wife and I are, well, we have been, oh, estranged is the right way to put it."

"Yes, I know."

"You do?"

"I have known her since her first trip to Paris. She is a lovely woman. Very kind and very smart. She never speaks of you." She slanted him a shrewd smile. "But she never said you were dead, either."

"That's something, I suppose." James braced himself. "So she and the comte are close?"

"Very."

His stomach twisted. "I see."

"He thinks of her as one would a daughter."

"A daughter?" He brightened.

"Or perhaps a niece." She nodded in the direction of Violet and the comte. "Gerard was an old friend of your uncle's. When she first came to France, she arrived with a letter of introduction from him. She stayed, oh, six months or so if I recall. Gerard has welcomed her as family ever since."

He sipped his wine and tried not to grin. He'd never been so pleased to be wrong before.

She glanced at him. "You thought it was something else, did you not? Something of an *affaire d'amour*, perhaps?"

"No, of course not." He scoffed.

She cast him a skeptical look.

"Well, there have been rumors," he said weakly.

"And you did not know her well enough to know whether they were true or not?"

"I thought I did once but..." Who was this woman anyway? He frowned. "I say, you seem to know a great deal about Violet and me. I thought she never spoke of me."

"She did not, until her arrival yesterday. But Gerard and your uncle corresponded regularly. You would be surprised at how much I know."

He chuckled. "I don't even know your name and yet I daresay at this point, that would not surprise me."

"Julienne."

"What?"

"My name. I am Julienne."

"James." He raised his glass to her. "It is a pleasure to meet you, Julienne."

She regarded him with interest. "She does not know you are here, does she?"

"I intended to surprise her."

"And catch her unawares if indeed she was engaged in pursuits of an intimate nature?"

"Nothing of the sort," he said indignantly. He could honestly say the thought hadn't crossed his mind. "I had intended it as a surprise. A good surprise. Proof, I suppose, of my intentions."

"And your intentions are to win her heart?"

He stared. "Why would you say that?"

That knowing smile again creased her lips. "I am French."

"And you know when a man is looking for something?"

"Exactement." She considered him thoughtfully. "And are you up to the task of winning her heart?"

"I don't know." His tone hardened. "But I don't intend to fail."

"There is something about determination in a man that can be most appealing. That will serve you well."

She nodded in Violet's direction. "Come, I will introduce you to the comte."

He hesitated. "You and the comte are still friends, then?"

"But of course." She took his arm and they started toward Violet and the comte. "There comes a time in every man's life when he must make choices. Decide what is more important to him. What he cannot live without. Do you understand?"

James nodded.

"In Gerard's case, it was his freedom or me."

"I can't imagine any man choosing anything over you," he said staunchly.

"My dear Lord Ellsworth, you are so very gallant." She chuckled. "But you misunderstand. He did choose me."

"You said you used to be his mistress."

"And indeed I was. Now, however—" a satisfied note sounded in her voice "—I am his wife."

CHAPTER SEVENTEEN

"I HAVE BEEN trying ever since my arrival for a private word with you." In spite of her best efforts, frustration rang in Violet's voice. Frustration that went far beyond concern about her finances. She refused to dwell on James's decision not to accompany her, or his six-year lie or his kiss. At least not right now, although none of it was ever far from her mind. Or her heart. Best to deal with one problem at a time. There was, however, something rather gratifying about being frustrated while speaking French. As if the language itself was conducive to expressing frustration. "I'm beginning to think you're avoiding speaking with me."

"On the contrary, my dear Violet." The comte smiled. "You told us all about the circumstances you find your-self in upon your arrival yesterday. And we had a lively discussion at dinner last night."

"It was late and there were twenty other people there."

"It is my birthday." He shook his head in a chastising manner. "Surely you do not begrudge me the company of my friends on my birthday."

"Of course not, but—"

"It is not every day a man reaches the grand age of eighty-one." He heaved an overly dramatic sigh. "I should be allowed to enjoy myself without having to talk of se-rious matters."

"From what I've heard, you've thrown a grand birthday ball every year since you turned sixty."

"Fifty." He grinned in an unrepentant manner. "One never knows which birthday will be one's last."

"You are entirely too stubborn to let this birthday be your last," she teased. "We marked your birthday last night and again today—when exactly is your birthday?"

He chuckled. "Does it matter?"

"I suppose not." She smiled reluctantly. The man really was a dear, in many ways the French version of Uncle Richard. Still, there were things she needed to know. "But we do need to talk about my trust."

"I wrote to you, did I not?"

"Well, yes, but it made no sense."

"It is most confusing." He spread his hands in a gesture of helplessness. Even at his advanced age, the Comte de Viviers was the least helpless man she had ever met. "Government regulations. Laws regarding finance." He shook his head in a mournful manner. "What can you do?"

"You wrote that my money is gone. All of it."

"Today, yes." His eyes twinkled. "But tomorrow, we shall see."

"So there's hope?" she said slowly.

"There is always hope, my delightful flower. Finances are like love." He raised a shoulder in a casual shrug. "They ebb and flow."

"What utter nonsense. Numbers are numbers. They do not ebb and flow."

"Perhaps not in England. Such a stuffy country." He shuddered. "But this is France. Today your money is gone. Tomorrow is yet to be determined."

Any hope she'd felt a moment ago vanished, and she huffed. "I've never known you to be quite so annoying."

He chuckled. "Then you have not paid attention."

"About so many things," she said under her breath.

It was pointless to argue. For good or ill, she'd followed Uncle Richard's advice and turned the trust he'd provided for her over to the comte on her first visit to France. He'd said his old friend was brilliant at managing money and had in fact built his fortune from the pittance his father had escaped to England with during the revolution.

Regardless of the current state of her finances, she could not regret putting the management of her funds in the comte's hands. While her upbringing had prepared her to be an excellent hostess and wife, her education regarding anything of a financial nature beyond basic household management had been sadly lacking. Women were not expected to manage their own funds, after all. She'd never given her deficient education any particular thought before. Rather stupid, as it turned out.

Although it might have made no real difference. Violet had no particular head for numbers. In the years of their travels, Cleo—who was not hindered by the elite education Violet had received—handled their funds and was indeed excellent at it. She hadn't told Cleo about her financial problems yet. Perhaps Cleo could figure out what had happened to her money.

"I assume there are account statements? Records of some sort?"

"Of course. I send you an accounting every year."

"Yes, I know." She did wish she'd done more than merely glance at them in passing but they made no sense to her. Nor did she need to pay more attention. The allowance and traveling expenses she'd received from James were more than sufficient for her needs. Her trust was a reserve against an uncertain future. "I am simply trying to understand—"

He gasped in a show of apparent dismay. "You do not trust me, dear Violet? You think I have absconded with your money?"

"Absolutely not," she said quickly. "My apologies if I allowed you to think, even for a moment, that I did not trust you. I have always trusted you and I always will. But I'm terribly confused and I just don't understand." She sighed. "It's time, past time really, that I paid more attention to such matters."

He reached out and patted her hand. "I shall provide you whatever papers you deem necessary before you leave Paris. My heart would shatter if you thought me unworthy of your trust."

"I don't. Not for a moment. I didn't mean. Oh, I am sorry." Good Lord, she was sputtering. She never sputtered. Nor did she ever lose her composure. No doubt this could be blamed on James. Nothing about her had been the same since Uncle Richard had planted her husband back in her life.

"A misunderstanding. Nothing more than that." He waved off her comment and his gaze slipped to a point behind her. "Ah, I see we have a newcomer. Looking for you, no doubt."

She turned and caught her breath. *James?* Her husband and the comtesse were making their way toward them. The man had actually followed her to France. Her heart fluttered. Blasted heart. No doubt his presence had more to do with his inheritance than anything else.

"He is not as handsome as I remember."

"Nonsense." James had any number of flaws, but his appearance was not one of them. "He is one of the most attractive men I've ever met."

"You defend him." Gerard raised a brow. "How very interesting."

"Not at all." She shrugged. "Simply a statement of fact." She drew her brows together. "What do you mean— as you remember? I thought you hadn't met James."

"Only once and so briefly I would be astonished if he remembered." He met her gaze. "Six years ago, Julienne and I were among those in attendance at his engagement ball."

Surprise widened her eyes. "I didn't see you."

He chuckled. "There were a great many people there."

She shook her head. "You never said a word."

"What would be the point?" He shrugged. "It would only have made you uncomfortable."

"Perhaps." There was no perhaps about it. If Violet had known Gerard and Julienne had been witness to her humiliation, she would have been entirely too self-conscious to reside with them or stay in Paris at all, for that matter. But they'd welcomed her, and Cleo as well, into their lives, providing a refuge after she'd fled London.

"Richard sent you to me."

"To manage my finances," she said slowly.

"To be of help with your finances and anything else you needed," he said gently.

And the comte and comtesse had indeed been a great help. By the time she left Paris she'd been well on her way to becoming the woman she was now. They had guided her through endless social events, encouraging her to savor the charm of life in the French capital, urging her to speak her mind and stand up for herself. Gerard instilled in her a greater appreciation of music and art and history. Julienne subtly instructed her in the fine arts of flirtation and conversation, and how to balance being true to herself with making others feel important.

"Were you ever going to tell me this?"

"I did not keep it from you, my dear Violet. You never

asked and I never thought to mention it." He smiled. "Was it necessary to know Richard guided you to us?"

"No." She shook her head. Richard's hand in her life had been far greater than she knew. She wasn't sure whether to be grateful or annoyed. Regardless, it scarcely mattered now. She returned the older man's smile. "I suppose it wasn't."

"Look who has come to join us," the comtesse said in French. "My dear, I think you have misjudged him."

"Oh, I doubt it," Violet replied in French. She turned to James. "What are you doing here?"

"I have no idea what you just said." He took her hand and raised it to his lips, his gaze locking with hers. "But it sounded delightful."

A shiver ran through her at his touch. "What do you mean you have no idea?"

The comtesse leaned toward Violet. "He does not speak French." She cast James an approving look. "Other than that, I find him quite charming."

Violet switched to English. "You don't speak French?"

"Aside from one completely useless phrase, I'm afraid not." James grimaced. "The price of a misspent youth."

"Then it is fortunate we speak English, although I have always found it an awkward language." Gerard frowned as if the difficulties of the English language could be laid squarely at James's feet.

"I shall have speak to the queen about that," James said with a smile.

Violet resisted the urge to roll her eyes at the ceiling.

"Ah, very amusing, Lord Ellsworth." The comte chuckled. "Unless you really do know your Queen Victoria, although I doubt even she can do anything about your language."

"I don't believe her authority extends to syntax, my lord."

"Pity." Gerard studied James for a moment. "For more than fifty years, your uncle and I corresponded regularly. He found you most amusing."

James grinned. "I know."

"While it scarcely seems necessary," Violet began, "allow me to introduce you. This is my husband, the Earl of Ellsworth. James, this is the Comte de Viviers."

"I have always wanted to meet—" James's glance slipped to Violet and back "—a French count."

A French count? Of course, she realized, the rumors.

"Thus showing a complete lack of ambition," Gerard said coolly.

Violet winced to herself. She should have known the comte might not have the best opinion of James.

"I have not always been the man my uncle wished me to be." James met the comte's gaze directly.

The comte's gaze hardened. "And are you now?"

"I'm not sure a man can ever live up to the expectations set for him." James's words were measured and unquestionably sincere. "He can only try."

"Très bon," Julienne murmured.

Very good indeed.

The comte considered him for a long moment. Violet would have been hard-pressed not to squirm under such scrutiny but James didn't so much as flinch. His demeanor was both impressive and admirable. An unexpected sense of pride surged through her. This was a man a woman could be proud of. Who would have ever imagined such a thing.

At last Gerard nodded. "Perhaps you will do."

"Thank you, sir."

"I assume you are here to speak to your wife."

"I intend to dance with her first." James turned to Violet. "If she would do me the honor."

"How could I possibly say no?" Although she would have much preferred not to dance with him. Or talk to him. Or do anything but scream all the things she'd been thinking since she walked out of the parlor yesterday. A waltz began, and he took her in his arms, entirely too close for propriety, at least in England. She tried to put a bit more distance between them, but he held her firmly and she surrendered. "Why are you here?"

"You asked me to come."

"You said no."

"On the contrary, I said I couldn't come *yesterday*," he said smoothly, the tiniest gleam of satisfaction in his eyes. "I do have responsibilities, you know. I simply can't drop everything and dash off to Paris. I gave up acting on impulse some time ago. Arrangements needed to be made and so I made them." He shrugged. "It put me no more than a day behind you."

She narrowed her eyes. "What are you up to, James?"

"You wound me deeply, Violet." He sighed. "I am here because you are here and I cannot bear even a day without you."

She raised a disbelieving brow.

"You wanted me to follow you and so I did." He grinned and led her through a turn.

"I don't trust you."

"Nor should you, at least at the moment. But I have every intention of earning your trust. And your forgiveness."

"Oh?"

"I cannot change the past, Violet, I can only atone for it." He smiled and pulled her tighter against him, leaning close to murmur into her ear. "Regardless, you did not win this round, my dear."

She nearly stumbled at his words. "What are you talking about?"

"This game we are now playing," he said in an off-hand manner, as if he were commenting on nothing more important than the weather. "Your escapade across Europe. My having to prove something."

A game? He thought this was a game? This wasn't a game—the rest of their lives were at stake.

James executed a complicated step, and she followed him without pause. Still, Violet had always rather liked games and she was quite good at them. Exceptionally good, really. And hadn't Uncle Richard helped her hone her skills at chess? She was rather more competitive than was appropriate for a woman. Yet another trait she didn't discover until after her marriage. If a game was what James wanted, she was more than willing to play, but by her rules. "I didn't realize this was a game."

"Of course you did." He chuckled. "And so I give up."

"You said you won this round."

"Ah, but in surrender, I win. You wanted to go to Paris. I did not and yet here I am." The music came to an end and they slowed to a stop. He gazed down at her, his smile entirely too smug. "So I shall be by your side every minute. In Paris and wherever else you wish to go."

"Wherever?" She tilted her head and considered him. "You said you had no desire to travel."

"I find traveling inconvenient and uncomfortable. However, as I have very little experience with it, I have reconsidered. I admit that I might possibly be wrong." Something that looked annoyingly like triumph shone in his eyes. "I can now see there might be certain benefits. Educational opportunities, the broadening of one's horizons, that sort of thing. And you would be the first to say my horizons could use broadening."

"Indeed." Apparently, the game had begun. "My, this is a change of heart."

"Atonement is not easy."

"Nor should it be." She smiled pleasantly. "Although I should tell you I had nearly decided to return to England once my business here was concluded."

"Excellent." He grinned with obvious relief. "Then we can return home tomorrow."

"Don't be silly." She scoffed. "My concern was about the stipulation that we not be apart for more than fourteen days. I left without giving it due consideration. It was quite thoughtless on my part. But now that you've joined me—" she beamed "—I see no reason why we can't continue on."

"Continue on?" he said slowly.

"Goodness, James, surely you didn't think your vow to be by my side every minute would make me want to scurry home to England?"

"No, not for a moment."

"Unless you didn't mean it." She widened her eyes in an innocent manner. "Unless you were simply grasping at straws in yet another one of those carpe diem moments?"

"I meant every word I said," he said staunchly.

Traveling on to Italy and Greece really was an excellent idea. Since his revelation about the incident, it felt very much as if they were starting from the beginning. Being away from London would be a reprieve of sorts, and give them both time to reconcile their differences or decide what they wanted beyond the next three years. Was she willing to give up the life of adventure and freedom she'd had since her marriage and remain in England, with James, for the rest of her life? Was he interested only in his inheritance or was she what he really wanted?

"You mentioned Florence and Athens to Mrs. Higginbotham and her friends."

She nodded, took his arm, and they moved off the

dance floor. "Did you visit Italy and Greece on that grand tour of yours?"

"We did not travel to Greece but we did spend some time in Rome as well as Florence. However, it was a long time ago," he added quickly. "I barely remember it at all."

From what she knew about the grand tours of young men, the spirits consumed and James's frolic-filled past, she wasn't at all surprised. "Then this will be enjoyable for you. The only thing better than one's first visit to Florence is returning. As for Athens..." She heaved a heartfelt sigh. "One can almost feel the presence of the ancients in the very air one breathes."

"Sounds delightful." The look in his eye belied his words. The man really wasn't fond of travel.

"And when the moon lights the marble of the Parthenon, it's quite the most romantic thing I've ever seen."

"Is it?" he said thoughtfully, then smiled. "I can't wait to see it."

She wasn't sure she liked that decidedly wicked smile. Nonetheless, she returned it. "And I can't wait to show it to you."

"When do we leave?"

"I shall speak to Cleo about making arrangements. I have an errand to see to in the morning but, depending on the train schedules, we can probably be on our way by early evening." It would take at least two days by train to reach Florence from Paris. Violet would have to check with Cleo, but by her calculations, they would reach Florence with a day or two to spare.

"I thought perhaps we could stay another day and you could show me Paris."

Her eyes widened with surprise. "You wish to see Paris?"

"Not especially. I was here once before but I recall lit-

tle of the important sights. I thought you'd like to point
out how well traveled and knowledgeable you are and
how ignorant and provincial I am."

"Oh, well, when you put it that way." She smiled.
"That does sound like fun, but we only have the afternoon. There is a gathering in Florence I promised to attend and we do need to be on our way. However, I would
be happy to show you how ignorant and provincial you
are in Florence."

"Florence it is then. One more thing." He placed his
hand over hers still on his arm. "Will we be staying here
tonight or will you be joining me at my hotel?"

She tugged at her hand, but he held it fast. "I have no
intention of staying anywhere but here."

"Very well." He nodded. "Then I shall join you."

"Why would you join me?"

"Fourteen days, remember?" He frowned. "Or fourteen nights, I suppose. Regardless, we have already
squandered one of them. I should hate to lose any more."

He did have a point. Even so, she was willing to *squander* another night. "I hadn't planned—"

"Perhaps you misunderstood when I said I intended
to spend every minute with you." He smiled in an overly
agreeable manner. "If you prefer to stay here, I'm certain the comtesse can find a room for me. She seemed
to like me."

"She likes everyone," Violet said sharply. The last
thing she wanted right now was to be under the same
roof with her husband. His unexpected appearance gave
her a great deal to think about. She forced a note of calm.
"There are numerous guests staying here, relations and
friends. I daresay there are no available rooms."

"Then I shall have to sleep on the floor outside your
room. Surely there's a spare blanket to be found."

She yanked her hand free. "You wouldn't."

"Oh, but I would." A hard note colored his words "Every minute, Violet."

"If you expect me to share your hotel room—"

"Suite. My hotel suite." He shrugged in surrender. "It has two bedrooms."

"Confident, weren't you?"

He smirked. "Yes."

"And Cleo?"

"I arranged a room for her, as well."

"How thoughtful of you."

"*Thoughtful* is one of my best qualities." He wagged his brows at her, and she resisted the urge to laugh. Admittedly, he was amusing, but amusing was not nearly enough.

"Yes, well, we shall see."

She ignored the look in his eyes. As if once more he had won. What a dear, sweet, stupid man. She hadn't even begun to play.

VIOLET WAS RIGHT. It was impossible to think clearly knowing James was in the next room. And just as impossible to sleep. Despite the lateness of the hour when they arrived at the Grand Hotel, she had done nothing but toss and turn since she'd climbed into bed. Of course she'd done nothing but toss and turn last night, as well. Apparently, a complete lack of sleep was the price to pay for having anything whatsoever to do with James Branham.

Last night, she had indeed decided to return to London and adhere to the time limitations decreed by the will. At least for now. Her reasons for agreeing to abide by the stipulations in the first place hadn't changed. Still, knowing the kiss that had changed both their lives forever wasn't a mistake, it was difficult to feel grateful for the life James had given her. Certainly, if he hadn't kissed her, hadn't been forced to marry her and then sent her off to lead her own life, she wouldn't have become the woman she was now. Even so, she couldn't help but wonder what might have happened if James had made any effort at a real marriage. Or if he hadn't kissed her at all, for that matter.

Would she now be happily wed, with a husband who cared for her, and a house full of children? Or would she be alone, the spinster sister of the incomparable Caroline? The unmarried subject of pity and comments behind gloved hands. *Wasn't it curious how one sister was so lovely and delightful and the other, well, the other was well-read.*

Forgiving James for a mistake was one thing. Forgiving him for a deliberate act was something else altogether. If he truly wanted her forgiveness, he was going to have to work for it even if it meant forcing him to visit every country on earth.

Thankfully, James's hotel bed did not creak even though she found herself listening for it. At long last, her eyes drifted closed.

A knock sounded at the door to the suite's parlor. Another minute and she would have been fast asleep. Violet threw back the covers and pulled on her robe.

She moved to the door and flung it open. "Yes?"

James froze, his hand fisted as if he were preparing to knock again. "Good. You're awake."

"I wasn't until a moment ago," she lied. "What do you want?"

"I can't sleep." His hair was slightly tousled and he had the endearing look of a little boy. He wore his deep blue dressing gown, the one that perfectly matched his eyes, over silk pajama trousers. With the dressing gown belted it was impossible to tell if he wore the shirt, as well. Not that she cared, of course.

"Perhaps you're not trying hard enough."

"You can't sleep, either," he said with a knowing smile. "Your bed creaks, I heard it."

"My bed does not creak." Although it did a bit.

He ignored her. "You don't look like someone who was sleeping soundly."

"Why, thank you."

He frowned. "Was that a compliment?"

"Yes. Now, good night." She started to close the door, but he stopped it with his slipper-clad foot.

"I can't sleep."

"Yes, I know, you said that." She sighed. "Apparently you think I can do something about your failure to sleep. What is it you want me to do?"

Surprise flashed in his eyes then he grinned.

Heat washed up her cheeks. She ignored it and raised a brow. "Really, James? You expect me to join you in your bed simply so that you can get a good night's sleep?"

"I can't think of a better way and it's an excellent idea, but…" He chuckled. "That hadn't occurred to me until a moment ago."

"I'm not sure whether to be offended that it didn't occur to you sooner or offended that it ultimately did," she said without thinking, noting what might have been the merest hint of disappointment. She shoved it aside.

"Actually, there's a chess set in the parlor and I was wondering if you played."

"Of course I play." She stepped past him and moved into the parlor, where the board was already set up on a small round dining table. "But no more than two games, perhaps three if we each win one." She sat down at the table. "Although I daresay that won't be necessary."

He grinned and sat down. "You expect to win, do you?"

She smiled.

"What shall we play for?"

"Satisfaction." She nodded at the board. "You may be white."

"And move first?" His brow rose. "You're willing to give me that advantage?"

"I don't consider it an advantage."

"Very well, then." He moved his queen's pawn, a fairly expected opening move.

She mirrored his move with her own. "I can't show you the entire city in an afternoon, you know. Visitors take weeks to see all there is to see in Paris."

"I don't expect you to." He moved another pawn.

"Is there anything you particularly want to see?" She countered with her king's pawn.

"Nothing comes to mind." He moved his knight. "Show me what you think I should see. Something to make me less ignorant and provincial, perhaps."

"Not possible," she murmured, her gaze on the board. "That's rather courageous of you, putting yourself in my hands."

"Indeed it is." He paused. "I can be courageous."

"Are we back to that hero nonsense again?" She moved a rook.

"Only if it's working." He moved another pawn. "Is it?"

"No."

"But I don't think you're as angry with me now as you were yesterday."

"You're wrong." She studied the board. "Did you bring your valet along?"

"No."

"Why not?" She moved her knight. "I thought every gentleman traveled with a valet."

"I get the distinct impression you are baiting me. Waiting for me to say the wrong thing so you can point out how very wrong I am."

"Nonsense." Although he wasn't entirely wrong.

"I did not bring my valet because you did not bring your maid." He moved his bishop. At once she realized his strategy and bit back a grin.

"I prefer not to travel with an entourage. It's much less cumbersome and expensive that way. Besides, most good hotels provide maid and valet services."

"And it's easier to be alone." He shot her a quick smile. It wasn't the least bit wicked but something rather genuine and appealing. She ignored it.

The first game was quickly played and she won with hardly any effort. Apparently James was not paying as close attention as he should because the second game was much slower and more thoughtful and the man played well. For a moment she even thought she might lose. Until she noticed he was playing exactly as Uncle Richard had played and was able to keep ahead of him.

James was a very good player. But then so was she. She'd had no doubt she'd beat him tonight. As for the larger game they were playing—simply by following her to Paris he had indeed won this round and taken her by surprise. Admittedly, it was perhaps a nice surprise even if his motives were in doubt.

Now, it was her turn to surprise him.

CHAPTER EIGHTEEN

THIS WASN'T AT all what he'd expected. He'd assumed Violet's errand was more in the manner of a stop at a milliner's or a consultation at one of the city's celebrated fashion houses. Instead, their carriage pulled up in front of an ancient gray stone edifice on the outskirts of the city in an area that was just one side of respectable. He wasn't entirely sure which side. The building had the distinct look of a school, large but not grand enough to be a manor.

"You seem less angry today," he said and helped her out of the carriage.

"I'm not," she said. "But it serves no purpose to be less than civil to you."

"I thought I was wearing you down."

"You're not. And you needn't keep asking me if I'm less angry than I was the day before. I don't foresee my anger diminishing in the near future."

He stifled a grin. She could deny it all she wanted but there was the tiniest crack in the armor she'd erected against him. "My mistake then."

"One of many." She paused and surveyed the house. "I thought you'd like to see where some of your money goes."

"I thought it all went for travel and fashionable gowns and whatever else women spend money on."

"Not all." She surveyed the area with a satisfied smile. "And it did seem wrong not to share your generosity."

"You're quite welcome." He looked around. "What is this place?"

"A sanctuary, James." Violet started toward the door. "A haven, if you will."

"A haven from what?" He trailed behind her.

She glanced over her shoulder at him. "The inequities of life."

"I have no idea what that means." He followed her up the stairs.

"This is a place for women who have been abandoned by men—fathers or husbands." She shot him a pointed look, which wasn't the least bit fair. "They live here as long as they need to and learn skills necessary to support themselves. So they can earn a decent living when they leave."

He frowned. "I did not abandon you."

"Semantics, James. Abandoned, discarded." She shrugged. "In the end, they are much the same."

"Tell me something, Violet. Are you angry about the first kiss or the second, or that I never fought for you?"

"Or the fact that you lied to me for six years?"

"That, too."

Her eyes narrowed. "All of it."

"Although I should point out, I didn't lie to you for six years. I lied once and simply never acknowledged it."

"Oh, that is a distinction." Sarcasm edged her voice. "I shall bear it in mind."

Apparently, this was the reward one received for being honest. For confession. It might well be good for the soul, but that was the extent of it. He would keep that in mind the next time he decided to reveal secrets best kept to himself.

The door opened and a short, dark-haired woman stepped out to meet them. She was older than he, in her fifties perhaps but, as with the comtesse, it was impossible to guess her age. Obviously there was something timeless about French women. She was surprisingly lovely and moved with a grace and bearing at odds with her simple attire. The lady greeted Violet with open arms and the women broke into excited chatter—in French, of course.

James adopted a polite smile and stood by, feeling like the idiot he no doubt appeared.

"In English, please, Marceline," Violet said at last and nodded in James's direction. "I have a friend with me today."

"So I see." Marceline smiled and inclined her head toward Violet. "This is not the same friend you've brought before."

"No. This is Lord Ellsworth," Violet said smoothly, failing to mention he was her husband. What other *friends* had she brought here? "James, allow me to introduce you to Madame Gagnon."

"Madame." James nodded a bow.

"Welcome to Maison d'Espoir, my lord." Madame Gagnon peered around them. "Mrs. Ryland is not with you?"

"Not today," Violet said. "She is seeing the sights of Paris today."

Marcus had been eager to have Mrs. Ryland show him around the city, even though the man had visited just last year. It struck James that his friend wanted to be alone with Mrs. Ryland every bit as much as James wished to be alone with Violet. He did need to have a serious talk with Marcus about that woman.

"Marceline is a cousin of the comtesse's." Violet waved at their surroundings. "All this is her doing."

"Is it?" His brow rose. "She started this?"

"Indeed she did, but it is a very long story. Madame Branham will tell you all about it when you leave." Madame Gagnon took his arm. "But now, would you like to see our humble enterprise?"

"Very much." He nodded.

"Excellent." Madame's eyes twinkled. "And when we are done, you will no doubt wish to contribute to our efforts."

Violet grinned.

He chuckled. "A tour for a donation?"

"Not at all." Madame shrugged. "The tour is free. But, should you wish to donate, I will be happy to take your money." Her smile faded. "It is not easy to do what we are trying to do here. No one really cares, you see. Funds make it possible, but there is never enough. Violet is a great help and Julienne does what she can."

James nodded.

"And last night's ball always raises a substantial amount," Madame added.

James pulled his brows together. "I thought it was in celebration of the comte's birthday."

"And what better way to celebrate one's birthday and one's own good fortune than by asking one's friends to give to others rather than give to you? Gerard has requested donations for us instead of gifts for himself since we first opened our doors."

"Very generous of him," James said.

"He is a good man." Madame paused. "One would think it easy to be generous when one has so much yet I know of many with wealth who resent giving it to those who desperately need it."

"But if one throws a grand celebration that is both exclusive and fashionable, and it becomes the high point of the season, no one seems at all hesitant to contribute to a worthy cause to win a coveted invitation." Violet and Madame exchanged grins. "It's really quite brilliant."

"Indeed it is," James said with a smile and made a note to check with his accountants as to what charities Uncle Richard had supported that James now supported. It was embarrassing to realize he had no idea. Worse, it hadn't even occurred to him to check. There was simply a regular notation in reference to charitable donations on the accounting books he looked at every month.

"Now then, my lord," Madame Gagnon began, "on this floor we have mostly schoolrooms to learn a trade…"

She led him past one classroom after another, most filled with women of all ages. He noted some barely in their teens and others older than Madame. In one room they were learning millinery skills, in the next fine dressmaking, in another students were engaged in bookbinding and in one women practiced illustration. On the upper floors were private living quarters as well as classrooms dedicated to teaching reading and writing, mathematical and accounting skills. Madame explained they also had programs to train nurses and teachers. She pointed out with pride some of their past residents now owned shops of their own and nearly all the women trained here had gone on to paying positions, including a fair number who had found employment in the fashion houses of Paris.

"And this is a private concern?" James asked when the tour was concluded. "You receive no help from the government or the church?"

"The government is run by men who have no interest in what happens to women." Disdain sounded in Madame's voice. "As for the church…" Madame wrinkled her nose. "There are many charitable endeavors that are run by the church. And while they are most worthwhile, there are strict requirements as to the practice of religion.

"Here, we are unique. We don't care how you choose to pray or if indeed you do pray. We have rules regarding comportment, attendance and behavior that are necessary when you have dozens of women living together, but we do not require obedience to the rules of Rome. We believe God helps those who help themselves. We make it possible for our women to help themselves." She smiled. "There is, however, a church a short distance from here, and most of our residents, including myself, are there every Sunday. One does like to err on the side of caution."

James laughed. They chatted for a few more minutes then returned to the carriage, but not before James promised a sizable contribution—not merely to impress Violet, although he wouldn't mind that, and not to ease a somewhat guilty conscience about his own charitable giving—but because Maison d'Espoir was indeed unique and helping a problem he had never paid any attention. A problem obviously close to Violet's heart. It struck him that his wife, and nearly every woman he knew, was no more than a step or two away from financial disaster. The loss of a husband or a father could see them on the streets. No doubt why Uncle Richard had thought it necessary to arrange a trust for Violet.

Violet gave the directions to the driver, and they headed back to the hotel.

"That was…" James began.

"Yes?" Violet studied him closely.

"Rather remarkable."

"I think so." She smiled. "I don't believe there's anything like it anywhere."

"Your friends saw a great need and instead of ignoring it, did something about it." He nodded. "Most admirable."

"Maison d'Espoir opened its doors more than twenty years ago. It has helped a great many women through the years."

"Madame said you would tell me how it began."

Her brow rose. "Are you really interested?"

"Yes, I am."

"Very well." She paused to gather her thoughts. "When the comtesse was quite young, her father died and she was forced to wed a much older man. She was far too young to marry, really, but she had no other choice. Even though her parents were of noble birth, her father left little with which to support his family. The marriage was brief, only a few years if I remember the story correctly, and then he died, leaving Julienne a considerable fortune."

"So she started this to help women in her situation?"

"Not then, but she did support her mother and her brothers and sisters. A few years later, she met the comte and eventually they married."

"And then she started this place?"

"No." She shook her head. "It wasn't until Marceline's husband died—"

"Leaving her penniless?"

"Would you let me tell the story?" She huffed.

"You could tell it a little faster."

"I shall do my best." She thought for a moment. "Where was I? Oh, yes. Marceline was left enough to live quite well on. As I understand it, it was a chance conversation between the two women, reflecting upon their respective circumstances and how but for the grace of God it all could have been so much worse for both of them. And how truly dreadful life was for some women who, through no fault of their own, were in the position of not knowing how to feed themselves, or worse, their children."

"And?" he prompted.

"And they decided someone should do something. But the government didn't care and the church was entirely too restrictive, so they started Maison d'Espoir."

"*Maison* is *house*, I think. House of?"

"Hope." Violet shook her head. "Hope is in short supply for women who find themselves penniless, without family to fall back on. You've seen women in London, in places like Whitechapel. Do you think they do what they do because they want to? Because they have other choices? They have no hope, James. No possibility of a better life.

"This place gives women a place to stay, to learn some sort of skill that will lead to a respectable job. For most of them that begins with learning to read and write. Frequently, they come with children and their children are taught, as well."

"I can see why you support it."

"Actually, you support it."

"You spend your allowance on this," he said slowly, although he had already surmised as much.

"Not all of it. I do like fashionable clothes and nice places to stay." She shrugged. "But I do what I can. You've been quite generous. It's not a dreadful sacrifice to cut corners where possible. Besides, it's rather fun to travel without accoutrements all the time. There's far more freedom and independence when one isn't dragging around an entourage and a mountain of luggage. It makes everything so much more of an adventure."

"I see." At once her comments about expenses made sense. "So was this yet another test? Bringing me here?"

She looked at him in surprise then smiled. "I suppose it depends."

"On?"

"How well you do." She turned to watch the streets passing by the carriage, apparently lost in her own thoughts.

As was James. He'd never paid attention to what Violet did with her allowance. It was hers to do with as she pleased. That it pleased her to help others should have come as no surprise and yet it did. A reflection no doubt of his own lack of awareness about the needs of those less fortunate. He would have to do something about that when he returned home, hopefully with Violet's help.

There was a note from Mrs. Ryland at the front desk when they arrived at the hotel.

"Cleo has booked us on the night train to Milan." Violet scanned the note. "Excellent, as we'll then cross the Alps during daylight."

"We will?" His stomach lurched at the thought.

"Oh, you always want to travel through the Alps by daylight. The scenery is breathtaking. Besides, it's much safer."

"Is it?"

"Without question. I can't tell you the stories I've heard from passengers who have been forced to disembark in the middle of nowhere because of avalanches or heavy snowfall. We really should have no problems at this time of year, but one never knows," Violet said absently, her gaze still on Mrs. Ryland's note. "From Milan, we'll take trains to Bologna and on to Florence. Barring any unforeseen difficulties, we should be there in two days." She refolded the note and glanced at him. "Did you still wish to see something of Paris?"

"Absolutely." He had no particular desire to see Paris, but anything that kept Violet by his side was worthwhile.

"I can't think of anything I can show you in the time we have. We could go to the Louvre, of course, but we probably couldn't see more than one gallery if that."

Good. He wasn't overly fond of old art. "Then show me just one sight. Your favorite, perhaps."

"A favorite? In Paris? Impossible." She thought for a moment then smiled. "But I do know just the thing." She took his arm and led him back through the doors to the street. "And I shall show you a bit of Paris on the way."

"Where are we going?" He nodded to the doorman who hailed an open-air carriage. Apparently there were some things that needed no translation.

Violet gave the driver directions and James helped her into the vehicle. "We're going to the most popular spot in Paris."

He'd seen any number of places on his only visit to Paris that were extremely popular but he couldn't imagine Violet taking him to one of those. Still… "Scandalous, is it?"

"I'd never take you anywhere scandalous, James. You would enjoy it entirely too much." A prim note sounded in her voice.

"Not scandalous then?" He adopted a forlorn expression.

"Not really, although it has been the center of controversy."

"That will have to do, I suppose." He sighed. "But I am disappointed."

"I daresay the last thing you need is a visit to anything remotely scandalous."

"I don't know." He grinned. "A little scandal on occasion is probably good for the soul."

"I doubt your soul could handle any more scandal."

"Bloody hell, Violet." He drew his brows together. "I haven't done anything the least bit untoward for the last two or three years."

"I know." She waved at the building next to the hotel

when they pulled away from the curb. "That's the Palais Garnier, the Paris Opera House. The inside is even grander than the outside. The marble staircase is quite extraordinary."

He ignored her. "What do you mean—you know?"

"Aside from the fact that Uncle Richard made it a point to continually mention your reformation, the gossip about you has been considerably less in recent years. Practically nonexistent. Why, your name hasn't been linked with another woman's in quite some time." She nodded toward a building resembling a Greek temple. "That is La Madeleine, a Roman Catholic church. Construction on it began under Louis XV, I believe, but the design changed and building was stopped by the revolution. It wasn't completed until oh, some fifty years ago."

"Doesn't that tell you anything?"

"Well, yes." She shrugged. "I suppose it tells me revolutions are not conducive to building projects."

"No." He huffed. "About *me*."

"Probably." She glanced around. "This is the Place de la Concorde."

"I've become almost dull, you know."

"I doubt that." She frowned. "Now, do you want to hear about the sights of Paris or not?"

Not! "Do go on."

"As I was saying, this is the Place de la Concorde."

On their left was a large rectangular square with fountains and statues and everything one expected to see in a large square. Not especially interesting.

"The obelisk was a gift from Egypt—"

"As was the one in London," he said pointedly. "It's been my experience that if you've seen one obelisk, there's no need to see any more."

She ignored him. "The fountains are two of the loveliest in Paris, the allegorical figures—gods, goddesses and nymphs—on one denoting rivers, the other the seas." She waved to one side. "From here you can see the Tuileries Gardens and the Louvre in that direction—" she gestured in the opposite direction "—and to the west, you can see the Arc de Triomphe de l'étoile."

The massive structure loomed against the afternoon sun. "It's rather hard to miss."

"It's said to be the largest such arch in the world. Napoléon's work, of course."

"Well, you know what they say about men who erect enormous monuments to their triumphs."

"No." The corners of her lips twitched and a distinct challenge shone in her eyes. "What do they say?"

"They say such men are trying to make up for a physical lack of some sort."

"Yes, well, he was short, wasn't he?"

"Apparently." He choked back a laugh. "I'm certain that's what it was."

"Keep in mind, James." She met his gaze directly. "Just as you are not the same man you were, I am not the same woman I was."

"I am well aware of that."

She turned her attention back to the square. "It is lovely but even the fountains and the statues and the charming views cannot negate the history of the place."

Oh, good, history. He winced. "History is yet another area where I am deficient."

"During the revolution, this is where the guillotine was," she said in a manner entirely too casual for the topic. "This particular obelisk marks the spot where it stood. More than a thousand people lost their lives here. Most of them for little more than the misfortune to be born of noble families."

"Scarcely a hundred years ago," he murmured. Entirely too close in time for comfort. It was no doubt only in his mind but it did seem the sky darkened for a moment. A chill crawled up his back.

They turned onto an avenue bordering the Seine. Violet nodded toward the river. "A fair number of unidentified bodies are found in the Seine every year. They end up at the Paris morgue. The morgue has long been one of the most popular sights in Paris."

"Is that where we're going?" He really had no desire to see the dead of Paris.

"No." Her brow furrowed. "Do you want to?"

"Not especially." He paused. "Do you?"

"No." She shivered. "I went once and it was quite enough, thank you. There's something terribly sad about seeing a body no one cares enough about to claim." She grimaced. "And even sadder to see how many people delight in viewing those poor souls." The carriage slowed to a stop. "Oh, good, we're here."

"Are we?" He helped her out of the carriage. They were standing in front of a grand drive leading to a large curved front building with towers and wings on either side. The architectural style was not apparent—it struck him as a mix of far east and perhaps Moorish elements. "This is the most popular spot in Paris?"

"No." She adjusted her parasol. "This is Le Trocadero, a concert hall. It was built for an exposition. Parisians are quite fond of expositions and world fairs. There's another planned for next year." She turned toward the river. "That's what I wanted to show you."

On the other side of the Seine, a massive iron structure was under construction. It looked like a giant, unfinished skeleton of some prehistoric beast supported by wooden scaffolding.

"Do you know what that is?" An innocent note sounded in her voice. Another test, no doubt.

"Of course, I know what it is." He scoffed. "That's Monsieur Eiffel's tower. Or the base of it anyway."

"Very good, James."

"I'm not completely uninformed, you know. Even at home I've seen pictures recounting the structure's progress." He nodded toward the construction. Above the four-legged square base of the tower, arms of lattice-like iron reached toward the sky. "They completed the first level two months ago, if I recall correctly. Now they're on the second stage and it appears already halfway finished."

She stared at him. "How do you know that?"

"A man less sure of himself than I would take offense at the doubt in your voice," he said mildly.

Her eyes shone with amusement. "Fortunately, you have no lack of confidence."

"Indeed." He studied the structure for several minutes. What had been built so far was remarkable. The finished tower truly would be a modern marvel. "I've always been fond of architecture and engineering. I find it fascinating. I would have pursued the study of architecture in school but that would have required, oh, what's the word?"

"Effort?" she suggested.

"Exactly." He smiled. "Besides, my future was laid out for me when I became Uncle Richard's heir. I didn't see the point of studying anything that I would never use."

"Do you regret that?"

"I've never really thought about it." He considered the idea for a moment. "I rather like the management of property and business interests. I never expected to, but I seem to have some sort of knack for it." He glanced at her, then returned his gaze to the tower. "I have a fair number of regrets, but no, that is not one of them."

"I see."

"Are you now going to ask me about my regrets?"

"I can well imagine with all those terrible decisions and dreadful mistakes you've made."

"Admitting them doesn't mean I regret them all." He chuckled and changed the subject, nodding at the tower. "From what I've read, there was considerable debate over the design."

She nodded. "Some people absolutely hate it. But I think it's going to be grand. Higher than the pyramids and they're magnificent."

He raised his brow. "You've been to the pyramids?"

"I have." She nodded. "I've even climbed to the top of the Great Pyramid." Her chin lifted and she gazed at the metal structure. "You miss a great deal when you don't climb to the top."

"I shall remember that. Perhaps we can come back when it's finished," he added in an offhand manner.

"I would like to see the view from the top." She cast the structure a wistful look then turned to him. "We should return to the hotel. We leave in a few hours."

He signaled for a cab and a few minutes later they were on their way. Violet gazed at the passing scenery, unexpectedly quiet.

"Aren't you going to point out the sights on our way back?" he teased.

"They're the same ones we saw on the way here." She sighed. "Sometimes I find myself forgetting how angry I am at you."

He grinned. "Then my plan is working."

"And what plan would that be?"

"My plan to work my way into your affections so you will then forgive me for everything. And you must admit, we have had a nice day together."

"I shall have to correct that tomorrow," she said in a lofty manner, but the corners of her mouth quirked, as if she were holding back a smile.

It wasn't much, but it did seem a solid step forward. And for today, it was enough.

CHAPTER NINETEEN

OF ALL THE places in the world she'd been fortunate enough to visit, Florence had laid claim to her heart. While some ancient buildings in the heart of the city had been razed in recent years to provide new squares and wider boulevards in the manner of Paris or Vienna, most of Florence was like a step back in time. Narrow, winding streets promised ancient mysteries and lingering magic. Certainly in London there were narrow passage-ways every bit as old, but there was something different here. Here, it seemed the veil between the past and the present dimmed, fading to nothing more than a state of mind. Walking the same streets once trod by Da Vinci and Michelangelo, by Dante and Botticelli, Violet could feel the vitality of life in the Renaissance when Florence was a city-state at the height of its glory. Here, it was hard to remember the twentieth century was fast approaching.

History and art and music pulsed in the very air around her in Florence. A silly, fanciful notion of course, but one that had claimed her on her first visit and never left. There were those in the world who believed one's soul continued after death to be reborn over and over through the ages. If she believed in such things, Violet would have said Florence was the home of her soul.

James had insisted he and Marcus would collect their luggage and meet them at the pensione that was their favorite place to stay in Florence. Violet preferred to keep their group together as neither James nor Marcus had mentioned knowing the languag, but James was not at all his usual self. Indeed, he hadn't been his usual self for much of the journey from Paris. Violet gave them the address, then she and Cleo hailed a cab and went on ahead to the Palazzo Enpoli, near the cathedral.

"I did send a telegram, but there's no guarantee Lady Fenton will have rooms available," Cleo said.

"We shall have to take our chances." Violet surveyed the passing scenery, the red-tile-roofed buildings, natives going about their daily business, carts filled with produce and goods for the markets, tourists strolling with guidebooks in hand. "It simply makes it that much more of an adventure."

"You do realize there are times when your definition of adventure and mine are completely at odds," Cleo said wryly.

Violet laughed.

"At this time of year, I'd be shocked if she had more than one vacant room. So I also sent a telegram to the Hotel dei Pucci requesting a room." Cleo paused. "Marcus and I will stay there."

Violet raised a brow. "You requested just one room?"

Cleo nodded.

"I see." Violet shouldn't have been the least bit shocked and yet she was. But Cleo was a widow, after all, nearing thirty and certainly smart enough to know what she was doing. It had been clear from the moment they met that she and Marcus were attracted to one another. Even so... "Are you certain you wish to do this?"

"Dear Lord, yes."

"I really don't think that kind of enthusiasm is, well, seemly, is it?" Violet knew how prudish she sounded but she couldn't help herself. This was not at all like Cleo, who was usually far more concerned with propriety than Violet. Which did seem to indicate Cleo's feelings for Marcus were more serious than Violet had suspected.

"Oh, I think enthusiasm is appropriate." Cleo drew a deep breath and released it all at once. "Marcus and I were wed a few days before we left for Paris."

Shock widened Violet's eyes.

"Surprised?"

"Good God, Cleo, how could you?"

Cleo's brow furrowed. "You don't like him?"

"Oh, no, I like him. He seems like a fine man. He's most amusing and obviously intelligent and rather dashing, as well. It's just that…" Violet grinned. "You didn't invite me."

Cleo laughed with relief. "We didn't invite anyone. It was a civil ceremony at a registrar's office. We didn't want any fuss."

"Why didn't you tell me?"

"We haven't even told our families. Although I daresay my mother will be thrilled that I married anyone, let alone a man with a good future and respectable family. We really haven't had time to tell anyone—your fault entirely." She met Violet's gaze pointedly. "You found out James lied to you and then we were off to Paris and now we're on to Italy and Greece."

"Well, yes, things have happened rather quickly, haven't they?" She studied her friend. "Are you certain about this?"

"It's too late if I'm not." Cleo smiled. "But yes, I am. He's really quite wonderful."

Violet frowned. "Does James know?"

"Marcus intends to tell him when the right moment presents itself." She shrugged. "He doesn't like me, you know."

"Nonsense." Still, she was hard-pressed to deny it.

"It doesn't matter." Cleo grinned. "I don't especially like him, either."

"Well, the two of you are going to have to work out your differences," Violet said firmly. "You are my dearest friend and James has no closer friend than Marcus. It won't do for you and my husband to be at odds with each other."

Cleo's eyes widened. "You called him your husband."

"Well, he is," Violet said uneasily. "And I've called him that before."

"Rarely and certainly not with that same tone in your voice." Disbelief rang in Cleo's voice. "Have you forgiven him?"

"No." Violet scoffed. "Of course not."

Doubt shaded Cleo's eyes.

"I have not forgiven him," Violet said in a firm tone, ignoring that she was starting to like him again. Blasted man.

"I just want you to be as happy with James as I am with Marcus." Cleo shook her head. "And I'm not sure, after everything that has happened between you, everything he's done, he can make you happy."

"Are you sure Marcus can make you happy?"

"Yes," Cleo said without so much as a moment of hesitation.

"Good." Violet smiled and pushed aside the disquieting question of whether James could make her happy. Or whether she could make him happy, for that matter. "Between his blond hair and yours, no doubt you'll have dozens of little fair-haired children."

"Dozens?" Cleo laughed. "Neither of us want dozens but a few would be nice."

They pulled up in front of Palazzo Enpoli, a square-shaped, gray stone block building—unimpressive in outer appearance to Violet's eye, as many palazzos here were. Double arched windows marked the first and second floors. Three tall arched openings that originally led to the courtyard and were now closed off by raised wooden panels were evenly spaced on the ground level, the door unobtrusive in the center archway.

Before they reached the entry, the massive wood door creaked open.

"Violet!" Lady Fenton, Penelope, swept out of the doorway and threw her arms around Violet. "What a wonderful surprise. And Cleo." Penelope greeted Cleo just as exuberantly. She had never treated Cleo as anything less than a friend. "I am so delighted to see the two of you. Violet, your letter last month said you were forgoing travel for a while. How wonderful that you changed your mind." She peered around them. "Where are your bags?"

"They should be here any minute," Cleo said.

Penelope hooked her arms through her friends' elbows—not easy as she was considerably shorter than both women—and led them into the palazzo, through the columns marking the large courtyard. "I can't tell you how horribly dull Florence has been of late."

Penelope was American by birth, the daughter of a wealthy diplomat. Some five years older than Violet, she had met and married Lord Fenton on her first trip to London. Unfortunately, the marriage lasted only a few years before his lordship succumbed to a bout of influenza. Penelope had no desire to return to America, and England held no particular appeal, so she'd wandered Europe for a year or so until she'd found herself in Florence. She'd fallen in love with the city just as Violet had and when the opportunity arose to purchase the Palazzo Enpoli, she didn't hesitate. She let suites in the palazzo

not because she needed the money—although she often
confided upkeep on a sixteenth-century building was
an endless drain on her finances—but because she enjoyed the company. Penelope wasn't at all fond of being
alone. Her guests were always by referral and her home
was rarely empty.

"Now that you're here, life will be much more interesting." Penelope led them to a table in the back of the
courtyard where Tomasia, Penelope's cook, greeted Violet and Cleo with effusive Italian and motherly hugs.

A buxom older woman with a smile that clearly said
she would treat you as one of her children whether or
not you wanted to be so treated, the cook offered them
glasses of something citrusy and delightful accompanied
by plates of pastries. Refusal was pointless and would
only result in a well-meaning lecture in Italian about how
impossible it was for a thin woman to find a good husband. Violet and Cleo adored her.

"In spite of your letter, I had hoped you would be
here—given tomorrow's unveiling. I've had a sneak peek
and this new sculpture is really Rinaldo's masterpiece."
Penelope's brow furrowed in confusion then her eyes
widened. "Oh, my, that's why…"

"Why what?" Cleo asked.

"Nothing important." Penelope waved off the question.
"You know how my mind wanders." She hesitated. "The
sculpture might be somewhat different than you expect."

"It's still the goddess Minerva, isn't it?" Violet asked.

"Yes, of course. The commission was specific regarding the subject of the work. And you know the Italians—
anything else would be tantamount to sacrilege." She
smiled. "I do think you'll love it."

Penelope was a patron of the arts, when she liked the
art in question. And she did like the work of Rinaldo Laz-

zari. Penelope had taken an interest in his work and now provided financial support for the artist, as did Violet.

"Unfortunately, since I hadn't heard from you, I assumed you weren't coming. I'm afraid I only have one room, so you'll have to share. However, it's the enormous suite on the top floor."

"We do have two others in our party, as well," Violet said.

"But I took the precaution of telegraphing for a room at the Hotel dei Pucci," Cleo added quickly. "So we will be fine."

"Are you sure?" Penelope asked. "I can have one of the parlors made up for you."

"Actually, we're traveling with Lord Ellsworth and his friend Mr. Davies," Violet said.

"Lord Ellsworth?" Penelope frowned. "Your husband's uncle Richard?" Penelope knew everything about Violet and James and had from Violet's first visit five years ago. Perhaps because Penelope was American and had a unique view of English aristocracy it had been remarkably easy for Violet to pour out the story of her marriage, helped by a significant amount of local wine.

"No, I'm afraid Uncle Richard died a few months ago."

"Then Lord Ellsworth is—" Penelope gasped and her eyes widened "—the husband?"

"James." Violet nodded. "Yes, the husband."

"You're traveling with the husband?" Penelope shot Cleo a disbelieving look. Cleo shrugged. "What on earth does this mean? How did it happen? Have the two of you reconciled?"

"No." Violet shook her head and paused. As much as she'd love to tell Penelope the truth about her current situation, the American had a difficult time keeping things to herself. And there were far too many English living in Florence to risk talk that would inevitably get back to London. She smiled weakly. "I mean yes. It's very new and rather complicated and..."

Penelope held up a hand to stop her. "No need to go into details. Well, not now. I understand completely. It's always complicated between a man and a woman. It probably wouldn't be any fun if it wasn't. Oh, and speaking of complications between men and women, do you remember that American writer who was here on your last visit? Well, as it turns out..."

The ladies chatted for another few minutes, catching up on all sorts of inconsequential matters—what mutual acquaintances were in Florence at the moment and the latest gossip. Penelope made it a point to know everything of interest when it came to the English and American communities in Florence.

The massive iron door knocker clanged and echoed through the courtyard, the door opened promptly by Penelope's majordomo. James and Marcus stepped inside, Marcus reading aloud from a small book he held in one hand—obviously an Italian language phrase book.

"These must be your companions now." Penelope considered the newcomers. The majordomo waited until Marcus had finished his attempt at Italian then addressed him in nearly flawless English. "Which one is yours?"

"The dark-haired one, on the right," Violet said.

"So this is the husband," Penelope said under her breath. "You never mentioned how dashing he is."

"Didn't I?"

"No, you certainly did not." Penelope considered James with an appreciative smile. It was surprisingly annoying.

"He has an attitude to match," Cleo muttered.

"They usually do when they look like that. And the other one is the friend?"

"Mr. Davies is his lordship's solicitor," Cleo said.

There must have been something in her voice. Penelope cast Cleo a curious look. "And he's yours?"

Cleo hesitated, then grinned. "Yes, he is."

"But it's something of a secret at the moment," Violet added.

"I won't say a word," Penelope promised and crossed to the entry to greet the newcomers.

Cleo leaned close to Violet and spoke quietly into her ear. "Please don't say anything to his lordship about Marcus and me."

"Of course not." Violet patted her friend's arm. "It's not my secret to tell. And do try to like him at least a little. He and I will be together for the next three years." *At least.* The thought popped unbidden into her head. She ignored it.

"The only reason I don't like him is because he's treated you disgracefully."

"That was a long time ago, Cleo." Violet's gaze settled on her husband.

"And then he continued to let you believe a lie for six years."

"I'm well aware of what he's done. But he is trying to make amends."

"I shall make an effort to like him, but it won't be easy." Cleo's brow furrowed. "Do be careful."

"I assure you, there's nothing to be careful about. I have not forgiven him for six years of deceit." Violet's gaze settled on her husband and she frowned. "Is it my imagination or does he still look rather pale?"

"He did say he'd eaten something that didn't agree with him," Cleo pointed out.

"And then spent most of the trip alone in his sleeping car." In fact, Violet hadn't seen much of James at all during the two days it had taken them to get to Florence. The first morning of the trip, as the train had wound its way through the Alps, James had appeared briefly, then abruptly took his leave, Marcus later explaining James was still suffering from whatever it was he had eaten. Fortunately, none of the others were affected. James had of course joined them when they changed trains but then had disappeared into a sleeping car for much of the rest of the trip. According to Marcus, James slept most of the time, which would serve him well.

It wasn't uncommon for those who did not travel frequently to experience any number of stomach problems due mostly to unfamiliar foods. Why, both Violet and Cleo had had their share of difficulties through the years. And even if she was still furious with him she couldn't help but feel bad for the poor man. Sleep really was the best thing for him.

"I was just telling your husband how sorry I am that I don't have accommodations for all of you." Penelope and the gentlemen joined Violet and Cleo. "Violet, your bags and Lord Ellsworth's are being brought to your room."

"Lady Fenton only has one room, but I have arranged for accommodations for Mr. Davies and myself at a nearby hotel," Cleo explained to James.

"Lady Fenton." James frowned. "Are you sure there's nothing you can do?"

"Not to worry, James," Marcus said quickly. "Mrs. Ryland and I will be fine at a hotel. Shall we join you for dinner?"

It might have been a trick of the late-afternoon light slanting into the courtyard from widows near the ceiling, but it did seem James turned the tiniest bit green at the thought of dinner.

"Actually, I was thinking of forgoing dinner and retiring early tonight," Violet said quickly, glancing at James. She wasn't the least bit tired, but he obviously needed rest. "We've been traveling for two nights and nearly two full days. It's been terribly tiring and I never sleep well on a train."

"Of course, if that's what *you* want, I have no objections." Relief flashed through his eyes so quickly she might have been mistaken, but he did look a shade better than he had a moment ago.

Cleo and Marcus took their leave and Penelope showed them to the grand suite on the top floor. Violet and Cleo usually had private rooms here adjoining a small sitting room. This was one large room, magnificent with painted murals, ancient beamed wooden ceilings and inlaid wooden floors. There was a sitting area with a sofa and matching chairs—quite lovely and probably at least a hundred years old. An ornate painted dressing screen in the corner of the room could be unfolded to hide a shaving stand with a pitcher and provide a modicum of privacy for changing. The bed seemed small in the huge room, but was in fact massive with dark wood and intricately carved head and footboards. Carved posts held up a canopy draped with deep red silk. It was straight out of a sixteenth-century painting by Raphael. All it needed was naked, romping courtesans to complete the picture.

Two of Penelope's wonderfully efficient maids finished unpacking their bags and immediately disappeared.

"I'll have Tomasia prepare a light supper whenever you wish." Penelope glanced around the room with a critical eye then nodded with satisfaction. "I do hope we can have a long chat later. I'm dying to hear all about…" She slanted a quick glance at James. "London. Yes, that's it. I haven't been to London in years. You know how quickly things change in London."

"Indeed I do." James considered her thoughtfully. "You're not English, are you?"

"Only by marriage. Well, I have other matters to attend to and guests, of course. I shall see you both later." She cast them a brilliant smile and took her leave. Penelope always had a dozen things going on at any one time. Aside from her guests, she frequently hosted receptions for visitors from England or America and held weekly salons for debate and discussion on topics ranging from art to literature to politics for those countrymen now living in Florence.

"American?" James asked.

Violet nodded. "She married Lord Fenton a dozen years ago or so. Unfortunately, he died and she had no real attachment to London so she decided to travel and ended up here."

"Then when she said she wanted to hear about London what she meant was that she really wanted to hear about you and me?"

"Of course that's what she meant. Naturally she's curious about the two of us being together."

"She knows everything about us?"

"Everything up until a few months ago, yes." Violet paused. "She's become quite a good friend and while I do adore her, she can't keep a secret to save her soul. If I told her you and I were together because of the terms of Uncle Richard's will, it would only be a matter of time before everyone in London knew. Florence has a large community of English and Americans."

"So…" James aimed a pointed look at the bed and grinned.

"Don't even think about it." Violet nodded at the sofa. "That's where you'll sleep."

"I never thought otherwise," he said in a firm tone, but laughter shone in his eyes.

Violet pulled a few blankets and a pillow from a chest at the foot of the bed and dropped them on the sofa. "I'm sure you'll be quite comfortable."

"No doubt." His smile faded. "Quite frankly, Violet, while it's entirely too early to retire for the night, I wouldn't mind lying down for a bit."

"I think that's an excellent idea." She studied him for a moment. "You look better than you did, but you still don't look at all well."

"The price one pays for travel," he muttered, and moved toward the sofa.

"Adventure always has a price, James. Eating something that disagrees with you is a common problem." She frowned. "Although I would think you would have felt better by now. I wonder if you might have a touch of food poisoning."

"No doubt." He sat down on the sofa.

It was obvious that the delicate antique, with its carved walnut back and cabriole legs, while long enough was entirely too narrow for comfort. If he'd been feeling up to snuff, she wouldn't have given his well-being a second thought. As it was, a distinct sense of guilt washed through her. Poor man was hiding it, but it was obvious he still hadn't quite recovered.

"I'm going to find Penelope for that chat she wanted." She waved at the bed. "Why don't you rest on the bed until I return."

"Are you sure?" Hope sounded in his voice.

She nodded. "I am."

"Thank you." The man fairly bounded across the

room. Maybe he wasn't feeling as bad as he looked. He collapsed onto the bed and groaned. "Thank God, it's not moving."

Violet rested the urge to smile and left the room, closing the door softly behind her. She found Penelope in the main parlor with some of her guests—two fashionably dressed sisters from Yorkshire and a recently wed couple from America. The sisters were some twenty years older than Violet, ordinary in appearance and distantly related to Penelope's late husband. They were on their first trip beyond England and were staying a full month in Florence. The Americans were off to Rome in a few days. The guests were all quite pleasant and well-read and Violet soon found herself immersed in a discussion of whether Italy's greatest contribution to history had been the Roman empire or the Renaissance.

Violet returned to her room to check on James an hour and a half later. He was sleeping soundly so she rejoined Penelope and they shared a light supper and rather more wine than was perhaps wise. Violet hadn't been to Florence for over a year and they had a great deal to catch up on. There was nothing like chatting with female friends about everything and nothing—although she did manage to keep the conversation away from James. The only thing missing tonight was Cleo. Violet was going to have to get used to Cleo's absence. As pleasant as Marcus seemed, Violet suspected he wouldn't want his wife to be employed. She could hire another secretary fairly easily, but it would be impossible to replace her friend.

It was late in the night when she finally returned to the room. James's clothes were strewn across the floor and he was snoring softly, one naked arm hanging off the bed. Which did make one wonder what, if anything, the man slept in. For a moment, she was tempted to pick up the covers and find out. The influence of the wine no doubt. What harm would a quick peek do? She was his wife, after all. Still, that would be a dreadful invasion of his privacy. And rude. She did try never to be rude. Worse, he could possibly wake up. And then…

She drew a steadying breath and shoved the thought aside. So much for him taking the sofa. She didn't have the heart to wake him. The man was obviously exhausted. Besides, he looked so sweet and rumpled and charming. Almost like a child. This was probably what his children would look like. She discarded that thought, as well.

The sofa would have to do for tonight. She managed to disrobe and don her nightgown without waking him. She plumped the pillow, then settled on the sofa and pulled the blanket over her. Immediately, she realized this was perhaps the most uncomfortable sofa in the world. It might well have been delightful when it was newly made a few hundred years ago. What stuffing was left in it was obviously original. She tried to roll over, but the sofa was too narrow. She shifted to her side in an effort to find a modicum of comfort. And failed. She'd never before realized how one could overlook a lack of comfort when one was properly seated on the edge of a sofa cushioned by layers of clothing and a bustle. It was an entirely different matter when one was trying to sleep.

Violet's gaze drifted to the enormous bed. Even if the sofa had been more accommodating, James's snoring probably would have kept her awake. Although really, it wasn't that bad, not nearly as annoying as the constant creak of his bed at home. Until tonight, they hadn't slept in the same room together since their wedding night.

That night hadn't been as awkward as she had expected. Rather nice really. James had been thoughtful and passionate and skilled. Or so she had assumed, given his reputed experience with women. In subsequent years, in discussions with Cleo and Penelope and other women far more experienced with the nature of that which transpired between a man and a woman, she discovered that her one intimate experience with James might have been remarkable only in that it was her first experience. She'd been tempted through the years to join various men—including Duncan—in their beds. She'd certainly had numerous opportunities and more than a few invitations. It wasn't that it had seemed wrong exactly, in a moral sense. It was simply that with no other man had it seemed particularly right.

She shifted onto her back and stared at the ancient wood-beamed ceiling, deeply shadowed in the faint starlight that drifted in from the open windows. She really was tired, but sleep evaded her and her thoughts returned to an annoying idea that had popped into her head somewhere between Paris and Florence and refused to leave.

James wasn't the only one who had made terrible decisions and dreadful mistakes in the past six years. Violet certainly could have confronted him on one of her visits to England. Barring that—she could have written to him. It struck her that even as he had never confessed about *the incident*, she had never told him of her feelings. He'd never fought for her—for them—but then neither had she. Was she so afraid that he would break her heart or was it a matter of pride? Still, there was no going back even if she had no idea what going forward meant.

Violet stared at the ceiling for what seemed like hours. Surely the sun would rise soon and put an end to her torture. But only stars shone through the windows.

This was absurd. Enough was enough. James had been sleeping all evening and most of the night. Surely he must feel better by now. And he had agreed to take the sofa, after all. He was only in the bed because she was being considerate. James was simply going to have to move. She threw off the blanket and made her way to the bed. The covers were hanging low on his back—a rather nicely sculpted back from what she could see. She resisted the odd impulse to run her fingers along the dip of his spine, feel the heat of his skin under her touch. Apparently, the man was indeed sleeping in nothing at all. Fortunately, she was entirely too weary to care.

"James," she said softly.

There was no response.

"James," she said again a bit louder and poked him.

Nothing.

She shoved him and raised her voice. "James, wake up."

He snorted and repositioned himself, but did not wake.

Good Lord, the man was dead to the world. He wouldn't have noticed if a herd of elephants thundered through the room. Or if the building collapsed around his head.

And he certainly wouldn't notice if he wasn't alone in the bed.

If she wasn't so tired, and had had one less glass of wine, she'd discard the idea immediately. But at the moment it had a great deal of appeal. Oh, certainly, she didn't trust him in general, but he would never take advantage of her. Especially if she were up and out of bed before he woke. Yes, that was exactly what she would do. One might consider it another test of sorts. For both of them.

She pulled a few more pillows from the chest and created a barrier in the middle of the bed. Not that she thought for a moment that James would attempt anything untoward. The pillows were simply a precaution against her rolling over and wrapping herself around him in her sleep. And really, should either of them want something more than sleep, the pillows would not prohibit that. Regardless, it would do. She carefully lay down on her side of the bed and stifled a moan of delight. The bed was harder than she was used to and the mattress rather lumpy. Nonetheless, it felt like heaven.

Her eyes drifted closed, his faint snores oddly comforting. And in her last conscious thought before sleep at last claimed her, the most unexpected idea drifted through her mind.

She could become accustomed to this.

CHAPTER TWENTY

VIOLET OPENED HER eyes and found herself staring into James's amusement-filled gaze.

"Bloody hell," she muttered.

"And good morning to you, too." James lay on his side, propped on one elbow, grinning down at her.

She pulled the covers up to her neck. "You're awake."

"As are you."

"I intended to wake up before you."

"And yet, here you are." He shook his head in feigned puzzlement. "I distinctly recall lying down on this bed last night by myself. Imagine my delight to wake up and find I was not alone."

She raised a brow. "Delight?"

"Absolutely." His grin widened, decidedly smug and more than a little wicked. And nearly impossible to ignore.

She sat up and nodded at the sofa. "You were supposed to sleep over there."

"I tried it." He shuddered.

"Are you feeling better?" His color had returned and he did look his normal self.

"Much. Refreshed and invigorated." He drew a deep breath. "It must be the air here."

"As well as a great deal of sleep."

"And how are you on this fine morning?" he asked

politely, as if they had run into each other on the street
and not across a barrier of pillows.

"Quite well, thank you." She frowned. "Are you going
to get up?"

"I was considering it." He glanced at the row of pillows. "Is this to protect you or me?"

"You?"

"In the event you decided to seduce me in the middle
of the night."

She laughed. "I assure you, you're quite safe."

"Pity." He heaved an exaggerated sigh.

She'd never imagined the appeal of a man still in his
bed. With his hair disheveled and his jaw darkly shadowed, coupled with that knowing smile of his, he looked
almost irresistible. Not to her, of course.

His expression sobered. "I do hope you know I would
never take advantage of you."

"I do know." Her gaze caught his and for a long moment they looked at each other. With very little effort, he
could lean across the pillow and press his lips to hers. Or
sweep the pillows aside and take her in his arms. Or—

"However—" his wicked grin was back and the moment lost "—should you ever wish to be taken advantage
of, all you need to do is ask."

"I shall keep that in mind." She suppressed a grin of
her own. "Now then, are you getting out of bed or not?"

"I thought I'd let you go first."

"Why?"

"Because I am a gentleman," he said in a lofty manner.

She narrowed her eyes. "You don't have anything on,
do you?"

"Not a stitch."

"Do you always sleep sans clothing?"

"No, but last night…" He ran his hand through his

hair. "Honestly, Violet, I don't remember much of anything from the time you left." His brows drew together. "I did have vague dreams about disrobing and climbing into bed and another about wrapping my arms around a buxom, incredibly soft woman."

She gasped in feigned outrage. "You tried to seduce the pillows!"

"Don't be absurd." He scoffed. "I believe the pillows tried to seduce me."

"Naughty pillows." She grinned. "We really do need to get up."

"I thought I was being polite, offering to let you go first. Thus alleviating any embarrassment you might feel at the sight of my naked body."

"Oh, I daresay I wouldn't be the least bit embarrassed," she lied. She'd never seen a naked man aside from one carved in marble. The night they'd spent together was completely in the dark.

"Then it's possible I would."

"Really?"

"Probably not." His gaze traveled over her. "From what I can see you seem to be wearing an extraordinarily voluminous garment. I daresay that wouldn't cause embarrassment for anyone."

"It does have a lot of fabric." She glanced down at her nightgown. "But it is rather sheer."

"Is it?" His eyes widened innocently.

"We can play this game all day, James, but I for one am eager to be off. We have things to do." She adopted her best no-nonsense manner. "I'm going to gather my clothes and take them down the hall to the lavatory. I shall dress there. You may dress while I'm gone."

"Very well." He nodded in agreement, but the look in his eyes was entirely too amused.

She started to throw off the covers then stopped and looked at him. "You may now indeed do the gentlemanly thing and close your eyes."

"That would be the gentlemanly thing. But..." He shook his head. "Where would be the fun in that?"

"Good Lord, James." Violet flung off the blankets, slipped out of bed and stepped to the wardrobe. She knew full well he watched her every step and realized too late there was probably a better route to the wardrobe that did not include walking in front of the windows.

"My, that is sheer," James murmured.

"And are you embarrassed?"

"Yes." He nodded firmly. "Never so much as I am at this very moment."

She grabbed her kimono and pulled it on. There, that provided at least a modicum of decorum.

"If you did decide to seduce me, might I suggest you wear something else?" he said.

"You don't like my robe?" It had perhaps seen better days, but it was brightly colored and unique and she quite liked it. "It's comfortable and extremely practical."

"Oh, I like it. It's rather exotic. I simply think it would look better off than on."

"Yet another dream, James." Good Lord, the man was incorrigible.

He laughed.

It was all she could do to select something to wear knowing he was watching her. It was unnerving. And annoying. Heat washed up her cheeks.

She grabbed her blue-and-white-striped walking dress and her undergarments, hurried across the room and opened the door.

"If you need any help, I would be happy to lend my assistance."

"Your offer is most appreciated, but I can manage." She stepped through the door. "I am eager to be off, we only have today."

"What?" Genuine distress sounded in his voice. "I was under the impression that we were staying for a few days, possibly a week or more."

"I don't know where you got that idea. But I would be happy to discuss it when I'm dressed."

"Perhaps it occurred to me since getting here in the first place required a long and arduous journey," he said sharply.

"Nonsense. We made excellent time and it was hardly arduous." She closed the door and missed his next comment. Probably for the best. Fortunately, the lavatory was unoccupied. Violet stepped into the large room and locked the door behind her.

When Penelope bought the palazzo she was determined to bring it into this century without losing the charm of its past. Although there were lavatories original to the building, Penelope had installed modern conveniences. She had spared no expense and while the walls in the lavatories boasted centuries-old frescoes—some designed to look like swagged drapery and ornate tiles— the fixtures were thoroughly up-to-date.

One of the most important lessons Violet and Cleo had learned in their years of travel was how to dress for the day without the assistance of a maid. They had learned as well the necessity of speed when one was sharing facilities at a hotel or pensione with strangers. In no time at all, Violet was ready for the day.

She returned to the room and glanced around. James was nowhere in sight. "James?"

"Behind the screen. Shaving."

"I thought gentlemen went to a barber for that." She

absently picked up his clothes still on the floor from last night and tossed them on the bed. "Or had their valets shave them."

"I didn't bring my valet, remember. And I'm perfectly capable of shaving myself. I've never been fond of allowing anyone to put a blade to my throat."

"Understandable."

"Now then, what did you mean?" He stepped out from behind the screen, fastening the cuffs on his shirt. "Why do we only have today? I thought you were going to show me the sights of Florence. Make me view endless galleries of boring old paintings and traipse through countless churches and whatever else there is to see."

She raised a brow. "You don't like Renaissance art?"

"I don't dislike it, I suppose, but there are entirely too many Madonnas and children for me. In fact, I'm not really fond of anything created more than a century ago." He shrugged. "I much prefer art that is more contemporary—like that of Manet and Constable and Turner."

"Then it's fortunate for you that I intended to forgo the Uffizi. Although it is one of the finest collections of art in the world," she added in a vaguely chastising manner.

"Aren't they all," he muttered.

She choked back a laugh. "But I enjoy Florence entirely too much to race from one sight to another. I much prefer to meander around the city and see what might present itself."

"I never suspected you to be a meandering sort." He considered her curiously. "I thought you were more a guidebook in one hand, sturdy parasol in the other kind of woman."

Admittedly, on her first visits to Paris and Florence and everywhere else, she did indeed have a guidebook in one hand and a parasol in the other. "I imagine there are all sorts of things about me you never suspected."

"So it would appear."

"I do intend to take you to see Michelangelo's masterpiece. I always make a point to stop by the Accademia to visit the *David*."

"David?" he asked in an offhand manner.

She grinned. "Are you jealous?"

"Of course not."

"You sounded jealous."

"You misheard."

She'd wager a great deal she hadn't. "You do realize I'm talking about a statue."

"I knew that."

Violet doubted it.

"Accademia, Michelangelo, *David*—I knew exactly what you were talking about." Indignation she didn't quite believe sounded in his voice. "I'm not entirely lacking in culture."

"I didn't think that for a moment," she said lightly. "Well, not entirely. I should warn you, there will be paintings in the Accademia, but I promise I won't force you to linger."

"Most appreciated."

"And we have the unveiling of a new work of art to attend this afternoon."

"Oh, that does sound like fun," he said under his breath. "Are you sure we can't stay another day? A nice relaxing day of meandering?" A tempting note sounded in his voice. "Doesn't that sound enjoyable?"

"As much as it pains me to cut any visit to Florence short, there's a gathering in Greece I attend every year. I hadn't planned on going at all this year, given Uncle Richard's death, but plans change." She cast him a pointed look. "This is not a simply for pleasure trip. Obligations, James. Tomorrow, we're off to Athens."

"And how do we get to Athens?" he asked slowly.

"We take the train to Brindisi—that's a full day's trip. Then we'll take a steamer to Athens."

"And that will take…?"

"Excepting any weather problems…" She thought for a moment. "About two and a half days."

"So we'll be at sea for two and a half days," he said slowly.

"It scarcely feels like it, really," she said blithely. "We're frequently in sight of land."

"Oh, well, yes, that makes all the difference." He didn't sound especially convinced.

"You must be famished." She shook her head. "You hardly ate anything yesterday. Penelope's cook always has the most wonderful breakfasts."

"You're right—I'm starving." He waved toward the door. "Shall we?"

"At least we can agree on that." She smiled. "I'm hungry, too."

They made their way to Penelope's breakfast room on the first floor. With its bright colors and cheerful fabrics, it might have seemed at odds with the ancient decor in the rest of the palazzo and yet it had always struck Violet as being rather perfect.

The sisters Violet had met last night—Miss Emma and Miss Nancy Green—were seated at the large table and Violet introduced them to James.

"A pleasure, Miss Green." James took Emma's hand and raised it to his lips, his gaze never leaving hers. "I can't tell you how delightful it is to meet the flower of English womanhood here in the heart of Italy."

"Oh." Emma's eyes widened and she blushed. "Thank you, my lord."

Nancy, who looked a few years younger than her sister, held out her hand the moment James released Emma's. He took it without hesitation. "And yet another Miss Green." He brought her hand to his lips and gazed into her eyes. "How is it possible for two such enchanting creatures to belong to the same family?"

Nancy giggled.

Good Lord.

Violet excused herself and went to the sideboard to peruse this morning's breakfast offering. Tomasia was replenishing platters and greeted her with a broad smile and a few subtle, admiring glances at James. The cook had, as always, outdone herself with a sausage-and-cheese-laden frittata, thinly sliced cold meats, pastries, an assortment of breads, cheeses and fresh fruits. Violet filled her plate with more than she could possibly eat and returned to the table.

Apparently, she'd been gone long enough for James to work his questionable magic and both ladies gazed at him as if he were the most remarkable creature ever to set foot on the earth. Violet had forgotten how truly charming the man could be.

"The ladies were just telling me that this is their first visit to Florence," James said.

"Oh, my, yes." Nancy nodded eagerly. "Our first trip anywhere, really."

"Well, we have been to London," Emma pointed out. "Several times, in fact." She frowned. "It's extremely crowded and the traffic is rather intimidating." She brightened. "Still, we do like London."

"But Paris." Nancy heaved the heartfelt sigh of a true romantic. "Paris was everything we expected it to be."

Tomasia set a huge plate of food in front of James. He cast her a grateful smile. She grinned in return and a

blush washed up her face. Violet's mouth dropped open
in shock. Tomasia never served anyone. James caught
Violet's gaze and winked. The man really had no shame.

"Emma and Nancy are on a sort of independent grand
tour," James said between bites.

"Indeed we are." Emma nodded. "We recently came
into a great deal of money, more than enough to travel,
so we thought 'why not?'"

"Father died, you see." Nancy leaned closer in a confidential manner. "We had no idea he was, well, rich. He
certainly never acted rich."

"Father was something of a miser." Emma shrugged.
"But we never went without and he was a dear in his
own selfish way. We're sure he would have wanted us to
enjoy his money."

"Father considered travel frivolous. *Why, there's nothing worth seeing in the world one can't see right here in
England,* he used to say." Nancy grinned. "So it was the
first thing we did."

"Not the first thing." Emma's grin matched her sister's.
"First—we ordered entirely new wardrobes."

"And might I say, I've never seen two ladies quite so
fashionably attired," James said gallantly.

Nancy giggled. Again.

"And you're planning a month here in Florence?" Violet asked before James could say something else annoying.

"We only arrived yesterday morning." Emma patted
the familiar red cover of a Baedeker's guide by her plate.
"We intend to see everything there is to see."

"You do plan to go to the Uffizi, I hope." James adopted a stern manner. "It's one of the finest art muse-
ums in the world."

"Yes, of course." Nancy nodded. "We're students of

art, always have been. We intend to spend the entire day there."

"But today we plan to see the *David* sculpture. You know, the one by Michelangelo," Emma said in an aside to Violet.

"Oh, yes, that one." Violet nodded. "It really is remarkable."

"What a startling coincidence, ladies." James's eyes widened in feigned astonishment. What was he up to? "Lady Ellsworth and I were planning on visiting that very sculpture right after breakfast." He smiled. "Why don't you join us?" He turned to Violet. "Unless you can think of any reason why not?"

Violet shook head. "Not one."

"Are you certain?" Hope shone in Emma's eyes. "We would hate to be a bother."

"Nonsense," Violet said, surprised to note she would rather be alone with James. And *David*, of course. "There is nothing more enjoyable than to see the sights with newly found friends."

"According to my guidebook…" Emma picked up the small book and proceed to read. "*David*, also known as *Il Gigante*, was shaped by the youthful artist in 1503 to 1504…"

Violet had heard all this before. Far more fascinating than the details dispensed by Emma was the attention paid to her—and her sister—by James. He listened with what appeared to be rapt attention, occasionally asking a surprisingly pertinent question of one or both of the sisters and was equally attentive to both women. He joked, he teased, he laughed and he flashed that wicked grin. He did nothing the least bit improper or untoward, nothing even overtly flirtatious, yet one could see the ladies bloom under his attentions.

A quarter of an hour later they were on their way. The moment they were out the door, James offered his arms to the sisters. Emma took his right side, using her free hand to hold her open *Baedeker's*, a bag over her arm with their sketching pads. Nancy took his left, holding her parasol over them both. They were quite the jaunty trio. Violet trailed behind them.

Apparently neither sister had ever considered that not every thought they had was worth saying aloud. James didn't appear at all bothered by their incessant chatter even while it made Violet's teeth clench. But there was something to be said for walking to the rear of a group. No one expected you to respond to a comment. Of course, no one directed a comment at you, either. Now she knew how the extra wheel on a carriage felt.

She shouldn't be the least bit annoyed by the attention James paid the sisters. He really couldn't help himself. Charm was practically second nature to him. And he didn't merely acknowledge their remarks—he responded with questions and observations and his own opinions. The ladies hung on every word he said and gazed at him as if he were the most wonderful man in the world. It struck her that perhaps today, for them, he was. James had turned this excursion with strangers into something more than a bit of sightseeing. The Green sisters would no doubt remember this time spent in the company of the delightful Lord Ellsworth for the rest of their days. In hindsight, it would be one of the brightest spots of their trip. It was kind of James and considerate and, well, nice.

Her steps slowed. Hadn't he been nice to her all those years ago? Hadn't he paid attention to her when no one else had? Hadn't he listened to what she had to say? James Branham was a truly nice man. Then and now.

Why hadn't she noticed?

Even when they reached the Accademia and Emma felt compelled by the magic of her *Baedeker's* to announce that the art displayed here was an important collection not for the casual observer, but for students of the development of Italian art from the fourteenth to sixteenth centuries, James gave her his full attention. Why, the man even went so far as to inquire as to the importance of several works on the walls of the gallery leading to the Cupola Saloon, the current residence of *David*. Such inquiries sent both sisters sitting down on a marble bench and frantically paging through the guidebook in an effort to be the first to answer James's question.

With the ladies occupied, Violet sidled up beside James. "You just couldn't resist, could you?"

"Resist what?" he asked absently, his gaze fixed on the Fra Angelico work in front of him of a Madonna with saints and angels.

"Flirting with them."

"Was I flirting?" He glanced at her with astonishment.

"Yes, James, you were."

He narrowed his eyes. "Are you sure?"

She bit her lip to keep from laughing. "There's not a doubt in my mind."

"Thank God." He breathed a sigh of relief. "I thought I'd forgotten how."

She took his arm, and they strolled down the gallery toward the famous statue. "Utter nonsense. I can't imagine such a thing."

"I haven't flirted in quite some time." He grinned. "It's good to know I haven't lost all my skills."

"It's a gift, dear." She patted his arm.

"Be careful, Violet." He smiled. "You're sounding very much like a wife."

She smiled and nodded at *David* growing larger with every step. "You really don't remember seeing this?"

"I'm not sure I did." He shrugged. "Cultural enrichment was really not the goal on my grand tour."

They reached the saloon and stepped aside. Nancy and Emma joined them a moment later.

"Well?" Violet leaned close to James. "What do you think?"

"He certainly is big." James gazed up at the marble statue.

"Ladies?" Violet glanced to her other side. Both sisters gazed upward as if entranced.

"Oh, my." Nancy's mouth had dropped open and she stared with the appreciation of a true student of art. "Magnificent."

"He really is a masterpiece." Emma reluctantly tore her gaze away from the statue, pulled two sketch pads from her bag and handed one to her sister. "We'll only be a minute," she said with a dismissive smile.

"Take all the time necessary," James said. "Shall we circle around him?"

"You will want to see every angle." They moved toward the back of the statue.

"Did you know Michelangelo carved this from a single block of marble?" James said in an offhand manner. "A block that was abandoned by another artist because of a flaw?"

"I did know that. I'm surprised you did."

"Even when you're not paying attention to anyone trying to educate you, something does permeate on occasion. And I looked at Emma's guidebook," he added.

She laughed.

"Do you want to hear more?"

"No, but thank you." She turned her gaze back to the

statue. "I come here every time I come to Florence and I do try to come every year. There's something about this statue, the way it seems you could reach out and touch it and feel the blood pulse in his veins."

"His head and hands seem overly large to me. Somewhat out of proportion, don't you think?"

She nodded. "The statue was originally intended to be placed high on the cathedral, where he'd be viewed from below. If you're looking up at him from a great distance, his proportions would probably appear accurate. It was decided not to place him on the cathedral when he was finished because he was pronounced too perfect to be so far away." She ran her gaze over the white marble, from the curls on *David*'s head, past the piercing eyes and down the length of the muscular figure, to the stump he leaned against that was originally covered in gold leaf. "Such a magnificent talent. Michelangelo was only twenty-six when he sculpted this."

"I'm well past twenty-six and I haven't done much of anything," James said wryly.

"Don't be absurd." She cast him a chastising glance. "You managed all of Uncle Richard's property. You handled his investments and business interests. And Uncle Richard said you did it quite well." She turned her gaze back to the statue. "Talent comes in all shapes and sizes, James."

He chuckled. "My, that was profound."

"I read a lot." She tugged at his arm. "Come along. Let's see how the ladies are faring."

They continued around the statue until they reached the sisters. Emma and Nancy were comparing their drawings side by side.

"May I look?" Violet asked, circling around behind them.

"Yes, of course," Nancy said.

"We would love your opinion," Emma added.

For a moment, Violet wasn't sure what to say.

Good Lord.

The sisters were both quite skilled and drew exactly what they saw in terms of proportion and perspective. As they were standing very close, very nearly under *David*'s marble intimate regions, the feature that was most prominent was that which was, well, most prominent.

"You know the copy in South Kensington has a fig leaf to cover it whenever the Queen visits," Nancy said in an aside to Emma.

"Seems a shame, doesn't it?" Emma murmured.

"Well done, ladies," Violet said with quiet enthusiasm. The last thing she wanted was to burst some other woman's bubble. Nor did she relish the idea of the sisters returning home to sing the praises of the charming Lord Ellsworth while noting how unpleasant Lady Ellsworth was. "Will you be hanging these at home?"

The sister's gazes met and they each sucked in a sharp breath of excitement.

Nancy grinned. "I know just the perfect place."

"What an excellent idea." Emma beamed.

"May I see?" James asked politely.

The ladies turned their sketch pads toward him, their faces glowing with pride. His eyes widened.

"Excellent job, ladies," he said slowly, glancing from the sketches to the larger than life statue. "I don't think I've ever seen a drawing quite so…" He cleared his throat. "Realistic."

"Thank you, my lord," Nancy said with a brilliant smile.

They continued to work their way along the gallery, Violet and James parting company with the sisters as soon as they left the Accademia. Emma and Nancy were off to see a number of churches on their schedule today, including Il Duomo, the grand cathedral that was the heart of Florence.

"Did you see what they drew?" James asked as they casually strolled in the general direction of the market.

"I did."

"You encouraged them to hang their drawings in their home," he said mildly.

"That was not my intention."

He snorted with amusement. "I can well imagine the reactions of their Yorkshire neighbors when they see the sisters's depictions of Michelangelo's impressive work."

"Well, they were well drawn," she said weakly.

He chuckled. "Indeed they were."

"I was simply trying to be supportive." She eyed him pointedly. "You could have said something."

"I think anything I said would have been embarrassing." He winced. "For all of us."

"No doubt."

"I was under the distinct impression that they were maiden ladies who lived in the country."

"I believe they are."

"And to draw with such speed and accuracy. Every detail was perfect."

"They did seem to be accurate…"

"It does make one wonder."

She groaned. "Don't say it James."

"Don't say what?" His eyes widened innocently. "I was simply curious. I mean, one does wonder." He grinned. "Where did they learn to draw?"

CHAPTER TWENTY-ONE

IT REALLY WAS a grand day.

The sun was shining, Florence was a feast for the senses and Violet was starting to like him again. Maybe even more than like him. Oh, she was subtle enough about it, but James could tell. It was in the way she looked at him when she thought he wasn't looking. The way she held on to his arm when they wandered the streets of the city. The way she fought against smiling at his comments and the way she teased him.

They'd spent much of the day thus far doing exactly what she liked to do in Florence—meandering without a particular destination in mind. And, whether it was deliberate or not, she managed in the process to show him a great deal of Florence.

"I don't agree with him, you know," he said abruptly. He and Violet were rubbing the snout of a three-hundred-year-old bronze boar displayed on the edge of a covered market offering woolen goods and leatherwork. Rubbing the nose was said to bring good luck and while it did seem silly, one could always use a little more luck.

"With who?" She drew her brows together. "The pig?"

"No, Mr. Green."

Her brow furrowed in confusion. "Who is Mr. Green?"

"Emma and Nancy's father." He shook his head mournfully. "You weren't paying attention."

"Of course I was." The corners of her lips quirked

up just a bit as if she were trying not to smile. That was a point for his side in this game they played. "Disagree with him about what?"

"I think there's much worth seeing in the world outside of England." He smiled. "Thank you for showing me a part of it."

"Goodness, James, I've scarcely shown you anything at all. There was no time in Paris and not substantially more here." She drew a deep breath. "I should thank you as well for making it possible for me to see the world."

"It was the least I could do." He paused. "I am sorry, you know. About the incident."

"Yes, I know."

"Have you forgiven me?"

"Don't be silly. Of course not." The smile in her eyes belied her words. It was indeed a very good day.

Late in the afternoon, they returned briefly to Lady Fenton's as Violet insisted this unveiling was an important event and she wanted to be properly attired. It simply would not do to wear the same thing she'd worn all day. She pointed out he could probably use some freshening up, as well. They missed Marcus and Mrs. Ryland, who had stopped by earlier in the day but left a note saying they would join them at the unveiling. Lady Fenton said she had a number of things to attend to before the event but she too would see them there. It did seem a great deal of fuss about a new painting in a city filled with masterpieces but it scarcely mattered. If Violet wanted to attend the debut of a new work of art, he would happily be by her side.

The unveiling was in a gallery not far from Lady Fenton's, no more than a leisurely walk. They paused in the Piazza della Signoria to admire the Palazzo Vecchio, a castle-like building with a tall, narrow clock tower, the seat of political power in Florence since the fourteenth century. An empty spot near the front entry marked where the statue of *David* had stood until moved to the Accademia some fifteen years ago. James really had looked at Emma's guidebook.

Next to the palazzo was the Loggia dei Lanzi, a huge public gallery dating back five hundred years. Some three or four stories high, the building was open on three sides. Massive columns framed three arches in the front and one on each end. The interior soared to vaulted ceilings, echoing the lines of the arches. It really was remarkable. Violet explained it was originally built for public meetings, ceremonies and the like but was now primarily for the display of some of Florence's greatest sculptures.

"Do you know who designed it?" he asked.

"Not offhand. I could look at Miss Green's guidebook if you'd like." She nodded toward the gallery. "There have been sculptures here for the last three hundred years."

While he could admire the skill of the creators of the assorted works, it did seem to him that they all looked very much alike—naked warriors in death throes or triumph, the fall of comrades, the kidnapping of women, that sort of thing. And, aside from a couple of bronzes, they were all white marble.

"Are all the statues in Florence naked?" he asked casually.

"Not all. There's a bit of draping here and there." Violet pointed to a sculpture of four figures entwined, depicting some ancient legend. "That figure even has a helmet on." She glanced at him. "I thought you liked nudity."

"It rather depends on who is nude," he said mildly.

"Stop it, James." She huffed. "This is neither the time nor the place."

"Rubbish, Violet." He shot her a grin, and she blushed,

which obviously annoyed her. There was nothing more enjoyable than making Violet blush. "It's always the time."

She ignored him. "That particular sculpture was only carved some twenty years ago. Even today, Florence has a thriving art community. That work was a commission and it made the artist's reputation and his fortune."

"It's very nice."

"You don't like sculpture, either?"

"I am a peasant, aren't I?"

"No." She sighed. "You're a man of privilege who has ignored the opportunities of his position."

It wasn't a rousing endorsement, but it could have been so much worse.

"The gallery is in this direction." They turned onto a narrow street off the piazza. "Lady Fenton is a patron of artists she likes and she's quite fond of Rinaldo Lazzari—the artist whose work is being unveiled."

James had never heard of him but it would have been shocking if he had.

"He's quite good. He won the commission for this work. If it's well received, it will lead to additional commissions and the sale of other of his works. Even in Florence, it's not easy to be an artist. Penelope contributes to his support." She paused. "As do I."

"I see." Yet another cause of hers. He wasn't entirely sure how he felt about that. It was one thing to give to women in need, quite another to support struggling artists. Still, while he supplied her allowance, there were no restrictions on how she spent her funds.

Violet stopped in front of a building similar in appearance to Lady Fenton's palazzo.

"We're a bit early, but we should go in. The gallery is on the ground floor." A warning note sounded in her voice. "A lot of these people are good friends, James. I expect you to use that considerable charm of yours. As you did in Paris."

He chuckled. "I do know how to behave in polite company, Violet."

"Of course you do." She reached out and straightened his tie. "I'm not quite sure why I'm nervous about this but I am. Introducing you to my friends as my husband—"

"Which I am."

"Letting people think we're reconciled."

"Well, we're not at war." He caught her hand, pulled it to his lips and placing a kiss in her palm. He gazed into her eyes. "Are we?"

Her eyes widened slightly as if just realizing—or perhaps accepting—it herself. "No, I suppose we're not."

"I promise to be on my very best behavior."

"Good. This could be awkward," she added more to herself than to him and turned to the door, speaking a few words of Italian to the doorman, who promptly allowed them to enter. They stepped into an open colonnade surrounding a courtyard. Fashionably dressed and obviously wealthy art lovers chatted in small clusters scattered throughout the courtyard. Liveried waiters carrying trays of champagne and delicate finger foods wound their way through the rapidly filling area.

"How many languages do you speak?" he asked.

"Several," she said absently, scanning the gathering. "And you?"

"One." He paused. "I do know a few words of Latin."

Her brow rose. "Carpe diem?"

"That would be it." He glanced around. There were no paintings on the walls, only a large, fabric-covered *something* in the center of the courtyard. At once he re-

alized his mistake. "I thought this was the unveiling of
a painting."

"Why would you think that?"

"I don't know," he said in a sharper tone than he had
intended. "This is for a sculpture, isn't it?"

She met his gaze and smiled pleasantly. "Why, yes,
James, it is."

"Violetta!" A voice called and they turned. A man
about James's age and height standing near the covered
sculpture said a few words to his companions then hurried toward them, a broad smile on his face.

"Rinaldo!" A brilliant smile creased Violet's lips, and
she moved toward him, James right at her heel.

"Violetta!" The Italian pulled her into his arms and
off her feet. Violet laughed and responded. In Italian.

"I beg your pardon," James said without thinking and
stepped forward. They ignored him.

Rinaldo set her on her feet and she stepped back, but
her hands remained in his. They immediately burst into
an animated discussion. Again, in Italian.

Oh, he didn't like this one bit. Not least of all because
he didn't understand a single word. Regardless, there was
nothing he could do that wouldn't cause undue attention.
And he did promise to be on his best behavior. He was
fairly certain the indignant ravings of a jealous husband
did not fall under the category of best behavior.

Jealous husband?

Well... Yes. He squared his shoulders. That was exactly what he was. And what man wouldn't be to see his
wife greeted with unabashed affection by a stranger?
A male stranger—one of her *friends* no doubt—and a
shockingly attractive friend at that. In fact, the Italian
bore a distinct resemblance to the statue of *David* with
dark curly hair and a long, somewhat flat nose, broad

shoulders, a muscular physique and large hands. James refused to even speculate on what other features this *Rinaldo* shared with *David*.

James forced an unconcerned expression as if it was every day his wife was greeted with unbridled enthusiasm by an entirely too handsome Italian. Although being completely ignored was annoying and unquestionably rude. Violet hated to be rude. The least he could do was stop her. He cleared his throat.

Violet leaned closer to the Italian and said something obviously amusing as the man laughed in response. Finally she turned to James.

"James, this is my dear friend, Signore Lazzari," she said in English. "Rinaldo, allow me to introduce my husband, Lord Ellsworth."

Rinaldo Lazzari? This was the artist? This was the *Italian sculptor*?

Lazzari frowned. "This is the husband? *Quindi voi due avete riconciliato le vostre differenze?*" he said to Violet.

She hesitated then cast him a brilliant smile. *"Sì."*

"Meraviglioso!" He grabbed James by the shoulders and before James could say a word, kissed him on both cheeks. "I am so pleased to meet you at last," he said in heavily accented English. "And you have come to see my masterpiece."

"I look forward to it," James said slowly.

"Rinaldo's commission was to create a sculpture of Minerva—goddess of the arts, industry, commerce and war," Violet explained. "His work will represent Florence at an exhibit in connection with next year's world exposition in Paris."

"I hope you will not be disappointed," Lazzari said with a smile that clearly said such disappointment was impossible. And Violet thought James was arrogant. The artist turned his attention back to Violet. "We understood you would not be here. Francesca will be so pleased. Tonight we celebrate. You will join us, no?"

She shot a quick glance at James, then beamed at the artist. "We would be delighted."

James was fairly certain he wouldn't be the least bit delighted, but he smiled cordially nonetheless.

"Eccellente!" Lazzari clapped James on the back. *"Scusa, per favore*, I should speak to the others." He flashed Violet a knowing grin. "It is true that the artist who conveys as much charm as talent gets many more commissions, no?"

She laughed. Lazzari nodded at James then moved off to greet other guests.

"Was that necessary?" James asked the moment Lazzari was out of hearing. "The way he greeted you was a bit excessive, wasn't it?"

"The man's Italian, James." She waved off the question. "An overabundance of enthusiasm is to be expected."

"I'd prefer he be somewhat less enthusiastic when it comes to my wife."

"Rinaldo has always been enthusiastic, especially when it comes to women." Her gaze returned to the covered sculpture. "And I have always been your wife."

"What did he say to you?" James's brow furrowed. "When you introduced us."

"If you want to know what people are saying, perhaps you need to learn the language."

"Perhaps. However, at the moment—"

"He asked if we had reconciled. I said yes."

"I do understand *yes* in any number of languages, but thank you for the translation." He narrowed his eyes. "Lazzari is the artist, isn't he? *The* Italian sculptor?"

"He's *an* Italian sculptor." She waved off his question. "I'm not sure you can call him *the* Italian sculptor. There are any number of Italian sculptors. Why, you can hardly throw a chisel, or a brush for that matter, without hitting an artist of some kind in Florence."

He scowled. "You know what I'm asking."

"Of course I do." She peered around him. "Oh, good, I was wondering when they'd arrive."

"Violet!"

"Not now, James." She waved to someone behind him.

He clenched his teeth. "You're changing the subject."

"Am I really?" She smiled in an innocent manner. "I can't imagine why." Violet stepped forward to greet Marcus and Mrs. Ryland. A moment later, she pointed out Lady Fenton speaking to people they hadn't seen since their last visit and insisted they simply had to say hello. She took Mrs. Ryland's arm and steered her toward a group on the far side of the courtyard.

"And good day to you, too." Marcus grabbed two glasses from a passing waiter and handed one to James. "What was that all about?"

"She was making her escape," James said darkly and sipped his champagne.

"From?"

"Me."

"Dare I ask why?"

"She's avoiding my questions." He grit his teeth. "About the Italian sculptor."

Marcus's brow furrowed. "The Italian—" He expression cleared. "Ah, yes, *the* Italian sculptor. The subject of rumors about her." He paused. "From what Cleo has said, Florence is full of sculptors and artists and writers—foreign and Italian. Are you sure this sculptor is *the* sculptor?"

"Given the way he greeted her, they are exceptionally close."

Marcus studied him curiously. "Jealous?"

"Apparently."

Marcus grinned. "I've never seen that before."

"I've never felt this way before." He sipped his champagne, his gaze never leaving Violet. "And she is my wife."

"I thought you said you had agreed to leave the past behind."

"More or less."

"Then what difference does it make if that is *the* sculptor or not?"

"I really hate it when you make sense."

Marcus chuckled. "It's my job."

"You're right." As much as he did hate to admit it. "If I expect her to forgive me, I need to forgive her."

"Of course in your case, there is much to forgive," Marcus said mildly. "In her case, I'm not so sure."

"Neither am I." He drew a deep breath. It didn't help. "The thing to do is ignore it." Not bloody likely. "It was my idea to put the past behind us." Of course, it was his past he was concerned about. In spite of the rumors, he really wasn't sure there was any particular untoward behavior in Violet's past. "It's the sort of thing one does with a…" He closed his eyes and prayed for tolerance. "Partner, an equal partner."

Marcus coughed, a failed attempt to hide his amusement.

"Are you enjoying Florence?" James asked, preferring to talk about anything else. "Is the delightful Mrs. Ryland showing you the sights of the city?"

"She is delightful and I like her. I like her a lot." Marcus met his gaze firmly. "Learn to like her, James. She's

your wife's dearest friend." His gaze drifted to Mrs. Ryland and Violet. "And I plan on having her in my life for
a long time."

James frowned. "That sounds serious."

Marcus smiled. "I understand we're heading to Greece
tomorrow."

One more person changing the subject. Did everyone
have secrets but him? "Unfortunately. I was hoping for
a few more days to recover. And I rather like Florence."

"As do I. I always have." Marcus nodded. "Are you
going to take those sleeping powders again?"

"It's that or travel with my head in a bucket."

"Ah, well, obvious choice then."

A distinguished-looking gentleman announced something in Italian and the crowd gathered around the sculpture. James traded his empty glass to a waiter for a new
one. Violet and Mrs. Ryland appeared out of the milling
assembly to join them.

Once the group quieted, the gentleman who had called
them to order began speaking. Obviously this was a
speech about how talented and extraordinary Lazzari
was, given the way the speaker gestured at him and the
way the sculptor smiled modestly.

"Do you want me to translate for you?" Violet said in
an aside to James.

"Is it interesting?"

"Not particularly."

"Then I am blissful in my ignorance."

She choked back a laugh and returned her attention to
the speaker still extolling Lazzari's talents.

That James made Violet laugh was certainly to his
credit. Regardless of what else might have passed between them, he'd wager the Italian didn't make her laugh.
It was entirely possible that Lazzari wasn't *the* sculptor.

And possible as well that the rumors about Violet had little or no basis in fact. Indeed, there might not be a sculptor at all. At least not one who was a lover. And James had, after all, been wrong about the count.

It scarcely mattered, really. If he wanted her to overlook his past, he had to overlook hers. No matter how difficult it might be.

After an endlessly long speech—which might not have seemed so endless if he understood the language although he doubted it—the speaker signaled to Lazzari. The artist stepped up and said a few words—no doubt how pleased he was to have received this commission and how he did hope he lived up to expectations and so on and so forth. Then, with a grand flourish, he yanked the cover off the sculpture.

The crowd gasped in appreciation then applauded.

James stared.

Marcus cleared his throat.

"Oh, dear," Mrs. Ryland said under her breath.

"Oh, my," Violet murmured.

Carved out of white marble, the statue was twice as big as life, depicting the goddess reclining on a chaise, propped up on one elbow. A book dangled from one hand, a helmet was nestled by her feet. Her hair fell in waves over her shoulders and curled over her naked breasts. The position of her legs served to conceal some of her more intimate areas. She rested on a bed of carved drapery. Even with his limited knowledge of all things artistic, he could see this was a magnificent work.

The face was especially exquisite. But then why wouldn't it be?

It was Violet's face.

"I can see why you might be nervous about this."

James gestured at the statue. "Why, you might think this would be awkward."

"It's really rather unexpected."

He glanced at her. "You didn't know about this?"

"I knew it was a possibility," she said in an offhand manner. "Goodness, James. I posed for it."

CHAPTER TWENTY-TWO

"YOU WHAT?" SOMETHING AKIN to horror shone in James's eyes.

Violet couldn't help herself. One look at his face and she burst into laughter.

"This is not amusing." Indignation rang in his voice.

"Oh, come now." She choked back another laugh. "It's a little amusing."

He glared. "This is you!"

"Not all of it." She studied the statue.

He waved at the sculpture. "It's your face!"

"It does bear a resemblance, I suppose."

"It bears more than a resemblance." His gaze shifted between her and the sculpture. "And what of the rest of it? Is it you?" Dear Lord, the man was actually comparing her figure to the statue's.

"He did make some alterations," she said thoughtfully. "Improvements, really."

"Improvements?" He could barely choke out the word.

She pointed at various spots on the marble figure. "There, the bosom. It's a bit larger than mine. And the hips, as well. Don't you agree, Cleo?"

"It's rather hard to tell." Cleo shrugged.

"That's what I thought." Violet sighed. "So, as to your question James, about whether the rest of the statue is me or not, I can't say." She smiled. "I really don't know."

"How can you not know if this is you or not?" He ground out the words.

Oh, this was fun. "Good Lord, James. I never imagined you would be quite this stuffy."

"I think a certain amount of stuffiness is to be expected. That—" he waved at the statue "—is my wife!"

"Immortalized in stone." She grinned. "I would think you'd be proud."

"Proud?" His eyebrows shot upward. "*Proud?* You're naked!"

"No, James, I am quite properly clothed." She nodded at the sculpture. "She's naked."

He grit his teeth. "This is another test isn't it?"

It wasn't, but there was no need to tell James that. In fact, she was nearly as surprised as he to see her own face staring out at her. It had been several years since she'd posed for Rinaldo. While she knew it was a possibility, that he chose to use her likeness for Minerva was unexpected and extremely flattering. She shrugged. "Not necessarily, unless of course you wish to turn it into a test."

"It really is a remarkable work," Cleo said.

"The man has a great deal of talent," Marcus added, obviously in an effort to distract his friend from his indignant outrage. "Although wasn't Minerva the goddess of war?"

"As well as art, industry, commerce and wisdom." Penelope stepped up beside them. "She was quite busy as goddesses went."

"Of course." Marcus nodded. "But one would think a goddess of war and everything else would be depicted with a sword and shield and probably clothes."

Oh, yes, drawing further attention to the nudity was certainly the way to distract James.

"Poetic license if you will, Mr. Davies. I've never met

an artist who didn't take certain liberties," Penelope said. "Unless of course, the work in question was a portrait and even then we do hope the artist will make some, oh, improvements. If we want the unvarnished truth we might as well have a photograph taken."

"Might I point out nearly every classic sculpture of a male warrior or god is usually sans clothing," Cleo said.

Penelope turned to Violet. "Imagine my surprise when I saw your face on Rinaldo's work."

"She posed for him," James said through gritted teeth.

"Of course she did. Some time ago if I recall." Penelope's eyes widened. "And why wouldn't she? He's quite talented and it really is an honor that he chose to use her face for that of a goddess. Goodness, my lord, we've all posed for him."

Marcus cast a questioning glance at Cleo. She smiled in a noncommittal manner.

Penelope nodded at Minerva. "In fact, I'm fairly certain those are my feet."

"Why you?" James said to Violet.

She frowned. "What do you mean—why me?"

"Well, well, you two have indeed reconciled. You sound exactly like a husband and wife." Penelope took Cleo's arm. "Oh, look, dear, isn't that the ambassador? We really should say hello." She glanced at Marcus. "Come along, Mr. Davies."

"What ambassador?" Marcus asked, following after the ladies.

"It doesn't matter, it's just an excuse," Penelope said, and the trio made its way through the crowd.

"Why did he choose to use *your* face?" James crossed his arms over his chest.

"Why not my face?" she said slowly.

"It seems to me a man might want to immortalize a

woman he had certain feelings for. A woman he was in-
timately involved with."

It was obvious James thought Rinaldo was her lover.
And just as obvious that it bothered him. "You're jealous."

He ignored her. "You're a married woman."

"Oh, I don't think you of all people can use that particular argument." She narrowed her eyes. "Why not me?"

"Because I don't like it!" He huffed then paused. "Actually, I do like it. It's quite good. What I don't like is
that it's you. And whether or not anything from the neck
down—"

"I do like to think of myself as inspiration."

"—is you or Lady Fenton or Mrs. Ryland or God
knows how many others, everyone who sees this is going
to think it's all you."

"Perhaps." He was right, of course. Not that it mattered. When she'd posed for the artist she was discreetly
draped in yards of sheeting, something reminiscent of an
ancient toga. And Rinaldo's wife was present, as well.

"I have no desire to share you—even in marble—with
the rest of the world."

She stared at him for a moment then smiled. "That's
rather sweet of you."

"I did not say it to be sweet." He grabbed a bite-sized
pastry off the tray of a passing waiter.

"Then it was just the jealousy speaking?"

"Yes!" He popped the hors d'oeuvre in his mouth, no
doubt to keep from having to say more.

She gazed into his eyes. "You were the one who
wanted to put the past behind us. You promised not to
throw my affairs in my face if I didn't throw your affairs in yours."

"Yes, well, that's proving a bit more difficult than I imagined," he said sharply.

She wanted to laugh with sheer delight. The man really did have feelings for her. Feelings serious enough to warrant jealousy. Feelings that had nothing to do with his inheritance. And wasn't that…wonderful.

"Come along, James. There are all sorts of people here I want to introduce you to." She took his arm. "As my husband."

He glared at her. "Won't that be awkward?"

"Oh, it will definitely be awkward." She smiled. "But worth it, I think. After all, I'll be introducing you that way for at least the next three years."

"At least?" A slow grin spread across his face.

"Don't be smug, James," she said coolly. "You haven't won anything."

He glanced back at the goddess and then looked at Violet's hips. "I don't think you need any improvement."

And that was rather wonderful, as well.

James was as good as his word. No one could have asked for a more charming, thoughtful companion. The perfect husband. It was easy to forget she was still angry with him. Indeed, it was becoming more and more difficult to remain angry with him. In truth, and Violet wasn't sure how or when it had happened, but her anger had nearly faded away altogether. Perhaps she had forgiven him at that. He was at once an entirely different man than he had been six years ago and yet there were moments when he was very much the same.

When the reception drew to a close, Violet and James took a carriage to Rinaldo's family home on the outskirts of the city. Cleo and Marcus begged off, saying they wished to retire early given tomorrow's travel. It was all Violet could do not to laugh at the innocent looks on their respective faces. James apparently still did not know about the couple's marriage.

The house was near one of the last remaining sections of the ancient wall that had once surrounded the city. Rinaldo's house had been his family's home for generations. A large outbuilding on the property had been turned into his studio. The house was already crowded with friends and relatives when they arrived.

"There's someone I want you to meet." Violet scanned the gathering. "I didn't have the chance to introduce you earlier." She took his arm and guided him through the crowd.

"Another friend? Another sculptor perhaps?" James asked innocently.

"I should smack you for that," she murmured.

"Oh, would you?"

She ignored him and caught the eye of her friend who waved them closer. "James, allow me to introduce you to Signora Lazzari. Francesca, this is my husband, Lord Ellsworth."

"Ah, *il marito*." Francesca was significantly shorter than James and yet still managed to kiss him on both cheeks with an enthusiasm nearly as great as her husband's greeting of Violet. Apparently, James had no particular objection to a wholehearted welcome when it came to a lovely Italian woman. "Welcome to my home, my lord."

"This is your home?" James asked.

"*Sì.* And the rest of my family, of course." Francesca beamed. "I am so sorry I did not meet you at the unveiling. I left immediately after Minerva was revealed." She looked around with satisfaction. "But as you can see, I had much to do here. Violetta, did he meet Rinaldo?"

Violet nodded. "He did."

"And Signore Lazzari is your husband?" James said slowly.

"He is." Francesca's pride-filled gaze shifted to Rinaldo, engaged in animated conversation on the other side of the room. "It is so much more convenient that way, for the children, you understand?"

James nodded.

"They have…" Violet looked at her friend. "Is it still five?"

"Sì." A firm note sounded in Francesca's voice. "And five it will remain."

"Francesca and I attended the same school in England, although she was older and we didn't know each other then." Violet smiled. "We met again on my first trip to Florence."

"And have been friends ever since." Francesca's gaze skimmed over the gathering. "Violetta has been here many times. We consider her our English cousin and we celebrate her visits with food and wine and music."

Violet laughed. "The Lazzari family wastes no opportunity to celebrate."

The first time Violet had visited Francesca and Rinaldo's home it had been a bit overwhelming. Especially when compared to Violet's own reserved and very English family. Even when she was a child, family gatherings were restrained and proper and obligatory. She would wager every person at the Lazzari house tonight was here because they wanted to be nowhere else. There was a joy to be found in the presence of this family and their friends that warmed Violet's soul. She never left without promising to return and she always meant that promise.

Francesca caught sight of something and frowned. *"Mannaggia."* She sighed and held up a finger. *"Un mo-*

mento. Scusami." With that she hurried off to see to whatever crisis had arisen. A not-infrequent occurrence in Violet's experience.

Someone passing by paused long enough to hand Violet and James each a glass of wine. James gratefully threw back half the glass.

Violet choked back a laugh. "Not what you expected?"

"Not exactly." He smiled. "So Lazzari's wife is a friend of yours?" he asked in an offhand manner.

"Indeed she is." Violet took a sip of the deep red wine that spoke to her of sun-drenched days and warm breezes and star-filled nights.

"A good friend apparently."

"Very good." Perhaps it was time to put the man out of his misery. "By the way, I would never be involved with the husband of a friend. Or anyone else's husband for that matter."

"I know." He nodded. "Or rather I should have known. I suppose I expected you to be as…disreputable as I was. Or used to be." He blew a long breath. "If one was strictly catering to one's own desires, one could ignore things like responsibilities and regrets. And guilt."

Violet wasn't sure what to say. She'd never expected this kind of confession, especially not here and now. Nor was she entirely sure what it meant. But it was most intriguing.

"So." James took another sip. "You're a member of the family, are you?"

"Yes, and extremely proud to be considered family." She glanced around the crowded room. "These people are welcoming and honest and very kind. They aren't worried about propriety or position or—"

"Or titles or wealth." James considered the gathering. "They are rather free-spirited, aren't they? Happy as well, it appears. And unconcerned about showing their happiness."

"Every time I visit, I can't help comparing my family with this one." She snorted. "Can you imagine my mother here? Or my sister for that matter."

"Until tonight I couldn't imagine you here."

"Oh?"

"Well, everyone is having a great deal of fun."

"I have fun." She drew her brows together. "I frequently have a considerable amount of fun."

"I stand corrected." He chuckled. "The Violet I knew six years ago would have been uncomfortable with all this. *Violetta* is completely at ease."

"One of the benefits of years of travel, James." She took a sip of wine. "I've met some of the nicest people in the most interesting places. One needs to be open to new experiences when one wanders the world. And in the process, one discovers different from what one is accustomed to—while it might be momentarily awkward—is not necessarily bad. It's simply…different."

His gaze wandered over the gathering, a faint pensive note in his voice. "This is not our world, Violet."

"Do be careful, James. You're sounding philosophical again." She sipped her wine. "It didn't used to be Francesca's world, either. She was orphaned at an early age, the only child of parents descended from prominent Florentine families. She was sent to England to school, her family's fortune and her future left in the hands of an untrustworthy guardian. When she finished school and returned to Florence, the guardian claimed the fortune left by her parents had been spent on her education and there was nothing left."

James winced.

"Fortunately, her parents had friends, one couple in

particular who took her in and gave her a home." She
looked around. "They're probably here somewhere. He
was an art dealer and, as Francesca speaks several languages, she proved helpful in his dealings with foreign
clients. It was through him that she met Rinaldo."

"And lived happily ever after." He grinned.

"Now, Lord Ellsworth." Francesca appeared beside
them. "I would be the most awful of hosts if I did not introduce you to the rest of Violetta's family."

"I would be honored," James said with a smile and offered his arm. "And please call me James."

"Oh, I could never call you James, my lord. I was
taught that would be highly improper," Francesca said,
then smiled. "But James is Giacomo in my country."

"Then Giacomo it is." He leaned toward Violet and
lowered his voice. "Wasn't Casanova's first name Giacomo?"

"However, as Shakespeare pointed out..." She smiled
innocently. "What's in a name?"

He snorted back a laugh then turned his attention to
Francesca, and the two of them circled the room, barely
taking more than a few steps between introductions. Violet started behind, them then encountered one person
after another she'd met before, everyone greeting her as
if she truly were a member of the family. Violet noticed
Francesca introduce James to her mother-in-law, who
promptly pulled him into the dancing. While a look of
apprehension did flash across his face, he didn't hesitate
for so much as a moment. Good man. The thought pulled
her up short. Dear Lord, she was proud of him.

When the opportunity arose, Violet stepped out of the
flow of celebrants to take a deep breath and observe the
festivities. No less than a hundred people filled the house,
spilled onto the loggia and tumbled into the garden. Chil-

dren darted about, laughing and calling to one another and doing all those things children tend to do when adults are paying no attention. Endless platters of food covered the tables, wine flowed without pause, music and laughter filled the air and from oldest to youngest, everyone danced.

It was a far cry from the ballrooms in Mayfair.

"You are happy, my dear friend." Rinaldo joined her and refilled her glass.

"I've never been especially unhappy." She glanced at him. "So yes, I suppose I am."

"No, you are different this year, Violetta. There is an air about you. A reason now for your happiness, perhaps?" Rinaldo nodded toward James, now dancing with one of the sculptor's aunts.

"James? No." Her gaze lingered on her husband. "It is possible, I suppose. But no, surely not."

He raised a skeptical brow.

"Perhaps." She frowned. "Oh, I don't know. One minute I'm certain as to how I feel about him and the next minute I'm not."

"Ah, confusion, a sure sign."

"Well, that's something." She laughed. "A sure sign of what?"

He smiled and considered James thoughtfully. "He wears the look of a man in love."

"Does he?" Her immediate impulse was to deny it. Without warning, she realized she didn't want to. She wanted James to be in love with her. After all, no matter how hard she tried to ignore it or deny it, she was in love with him.

"Come, Violetta." Rinaldo shook his head. "Love is a great happiness. One of so many we have to celebrate tonight." Without warning, he whisked her, laughing, into the swirl of dancers.

Violet danced with one partner after another even though she was unfamiliar with most of the steps and the term *partner* was decidedly loose—none of which mattered in the least. She'd always had a grand time at these gatherings of the Lazzari family, but tonight it was different. Tonight, James with her.

She tried to ignore Rinaldo's charge that James was in love with her. If true, she really did mean more to him than simply the path to his inheritance. Certainly, he had been rather wonderful these past few months. He needed her to abide by the terms of the will, after all. She had reconciled herself to spending three years in a cordial, perhaps even friendly, relationship. But even before they had left England, before she'd known the truth about that long-ago kiss, hadn't things between them changed? Evolved, perhaps? Hadn't they been on their way to… what? A future together? Happily ever after? She wasn't entirely sure she was ready to find out. She firmly set any thought of James's feelings aside and enjoyed the festivities. After all, who knew when she'd be back.

Eventually, Violet found herself in James's arms.

"You are having an exceptionally good time," he said with a smile. "I don't believe I've ever seen you quite so carefree."

"Until two months ago, you hadn't seen me for six years. For all you know, I am frequently carefree." She smirked. "And lighthearted, as well."

"My apologies, Lady Ellsworth." He adopted a serious expression. "I didn't mean to imply that you were too somber, too serious and entirely too proper."

"Apology accepted, my lord," she said in a lofty manner, then smiled. "And yes—I am having a splendid time. I always do. Are you?"

"I can't remember when I've had such an enjoyable evening." He grinned. "Aside from the fact that I have no idea what anyone is saying, of course."

"It adds to the adventure, James."

He chuckled. "Yes, I suppose it does." He paused. "I am wondering about one phrase that I keep hearing over and over."

"And that is?"

"Every time I'm introduced to someone they say in a distinctly knowing manner, 'ah, *il marito*.' Now I've been assuming that translates to '*ah, what a handsome, dashing devil the Englishman is, and isn't Violetta a lucky woman.*'"

She laughed.

"But I suspect that might not be entirely accurate."

"Not entirely." She grinned "*Il marito* means 'the husband.'"

"That explains it, then."

"I suspect some of them didn't believe I actually had a husband. That I simply claimed to have a husband to avoid would-be suitors."

"And have there been many would-be suitors?" he asked as if it was of no importance. But she suspected it was.

"Dozens," she said blithely. "Far too many to mention."

"I was wrong about the count and the Italian sculptor." He gazed into her eyes, abruptly serious. "Am I wrong about the Greek poet, as well?"

"Come now, James." She forced a light laugh. "You don't expect me to reveal all my secrets, do you?"

"No, of course not. Where would be the fun in that?"

He pulled her closer against him. "I'd much rather charm
your secrets out of you."

She laughed.

He wagged his brows. "I can see it's already working."

"You're very good at charm."

"I know." He grinned that wonderfully wicked grin
of his, and something inside her fluttered.

"Goodness, James, you really are arrogant."

"I know that, too."

Violet shook her head in mock dismay but smiled
nonetheless. The man was hopeless. And nearly irresistible. Then why was she so resistant? She had no idea
where that had come from and steadfastly ignored the
question. She glanced around the room. "You said this
wasn't our world. You're right, of course. But it is a delightful world to visit."

"And a visit is never enough." He smiled into her eyes.
"So tonight, we leave Violet and James behind. Tonight,
we're Violetta and Giacomo."

She grinned. "Oh, Giacomo, you do say the most enchanting things."

They laughed and danced, ate and drank and celebrated
Rinaldo's success until the wee hours then regretfully
made their way back to Penelope's. The stars shimmered
overhead. Lamps cast pools of light on cobblestone streets.
Florence at night was even more magical than during
the day.

"Will you be sleeping on the sofa tonight?" Violet adopted an unconcerned tone, as if his answer was of no
importance whatsoever.

"No, will you?"

"I tried last night," she said lightly. "I didn't like it
at all."

He nodded. "Understandable. I don't think it was originally designed to be a sofa but something more akin to a Renaissance torture device, no doubt invented for the Medicis themselves." He paused. "Shall I get the pillows?"

She hesitated, although there was no need for hesitation. She was certainly not about to share a bed with him without a barrier—regardless of how insubstantial—between them. Even if she wasn't entirely sure she really wanted to. She nodded. "Yes. Of course. Absolutely."

He grinned that wicked grin of his that at the moment said he knew exactly what she was thinking. "Very well."

"Then I'll change in the lavatory." She grabbed her nightclothes and edged toward the door. "Easier, I think and, well, less…"

"Awkward?" he asked pleasantly.

She smiled weakly and practically scurried out of the room. What on earth was wrong with her? Certainly they'd had a delightful evening. One might even call it romantic. But while she was willing to share his bed as a practical matter, she wasn't ready to sleep with him in an intimate sense. It would take far more than a wonderful evening for her to allow herself to be seduced.

Or for her to seduce him? The thought popped into her head and refused to leave. She tried to ignore it, but it did strike her as not nearly as far-fetched an idea as she would have thought. She certainly could seduce him if she wanted to. James wouldn't be the least bit reluctant. Why she wasn't dismissing the idea altogether was both annoying and oddly intriguing.

Even when she returned to their room, the idea lingered. James was in bed, apparently already asleep, the pillow wall in place. She wasn't quite sure if she was relieved or disappointed. No, she was definitely relieved. Making love with James would be an irrevocable step. It would be the crossing of a line she was not quite ready to cross.

She lay in bed for a long time listening to him breathe. Wondering if he dreamed and if he did, did he dream of her. Resisting the urge to reach out and touch him. Ignoring an aching need that simmered just beneath the surface when his hand would brush hers or when he took her in his arms to dance or when he shared the same bed. Good Lord, what was happening to her?

It was impossible to sleep with a dozen different questions crowding her mind, demanding answers that she didn't have.

Had she put the past behind them? Could she? She'd been justifiably angry when he confessed the truth about their ill-fated kiss. But if one thought about it—he had actually only lied once. He simply hadn't corrected it for six years.

What did she want? Was the love she felt for him enough? And more importantly—could she trust him? With her future? With her heart?

And did she have the courage to take the risk?

CHAPTER TWENTY-THREE

IF JAMES HAD thought the trip from Paris to Florence was grueling, it paled in comparison with the journey to Greece. From Florence, it took a full twenty-four hours and three separate trains to reach Brindisi on the western Italian coast. He found train travel not as difficult in Italy as there were no Alps to traverse, and mountains, for the most part, stayed in the distance. Still, he only joined the others occasionally, preferring to remain alone in the sleeping car he was forced to share with Marcus. Marcus wasn't especially pleased by the arrangement, either. Violet seemed oddly preoccupied whenever he ventured out of his car and Marcus spent most of his time elsewhere on the train with Mrs. Ryland. If she was important to Marcus, and it was becoming painfully obvious that she was, and she was certainly important to Violet, James needed to make an effort to be as cordial to her as possible, perhaps even cultivate her friendship. After all, they both cared for the same people.

His stomach had almost settled back into its usual place when they boarded a midnight steamer at Brindisi. Fortunately, he had his own quarters and a good supply of sleeping powders. Even better, the trek to Florence had shown him how much of the stuff to use. He had no desire to sleep through their first night in Athens. Although, by the time they reached Pireaus, the port for Athens, he had made any number of promises to the

Almighty about regular church attendance and avoiding even the most minor of sins and the like. Although
it did seem he was becoming somewhat accustomed to
the sway of a train or the roll of a ship as he arrived in
Greece in considerably better physical disposition than he
expected. Regardless, he was not sure what their return
route to England would be, but he absolutely refused to
set foot on anything other than a ferry to cross the English Channel ever again.

"Marcus said you again ate something that disagreed
with you," Violet said when their party was once more
on solid ground. Genuine concern shown in her eyes.
And didn't that make it all worth it.

She insisted it was far more convenient and less expensive to hire a carriage for the drive to Athens rather than
take the train, and he had no desire to argue the point. He
was feeling almost his normal self, so why tempt fate? He
did realize at some point he would have to confess his
problems with lengthy train trips or anything on water,
but he'd prefer to avoid that revelation as long as possible. Ridiculous male pride, no doubt. After all, what man
wanted to look weak in the eyes of the woman he loved?

And he did love her. More and more with every passing day, every new conversation and every new adventure. She was kind and generous, smart and funny. And
sleeping next to her with nothing but a blockade of pillows between them was surely a new kind of hell. The
woman made him ache with something that went far
beyond mere desire.

He'd pretended to be asleep when she returned to their
room in Florence. It seemed the smartest thing to do.
While she was certainly starting to like him again—
perhaps even trust him—he didn't want to push too hard.
A little self-denial was a small price to pay for a future

together. Admittedly, the price seemed entirely too steep when he was lying in bed mere inches from her. But winning Violet's trust and her heart required patience. Even if it killed him.

The drive to Athens was uneventful and uninteresting. Midway to the city they stopped at a tavern to stretch their legs. Violet urged him to try some of the local offerings, saying the only way to become accustomed to foods of another country was to try them. Whether her advice was sound or not, he did sample *loukoumia*—similar to Turkish Delight—and a drink called *masticha*. He still wasn't sure if he liked it or not although it was shockingly potent. Both Violet and Mrs. Ryland drank it without so much as a moment of hesitation. James didn't know if he was appalled or proud.

James wasn't sure what he had expected on the drive to Athens. A landscape littered with the remains of ancient Greece, no doubt. While there were mountains at a distance, and the occasional hill here and there, Athens itself was situated on a plain. The scenery was green and lush but not particularly striking—vineyards and olive groves for the most part—until they passed a hill that had blocked their view and abruptly revealed an ancient temple on a low rise. And behind it, high on another hill, sat the Acropolis. Regardless of how many paintings or photographs one had seen, it was impossible to prepare oneself for the sheer majesty of the ancient complex.

"You're impressed, aren't you?" Violet asked with a smug smile.

"It takes one's breath away. Besides—" he chuckled "—you would have been disappointed if I had said no."

"Indeed I would have." She nodded toward the temple. "That's the Temple of Theseus. It was used as a church for hundreds of years, which is why it's so well preserved.

Theseus was a legendary king of Athens and a great hero.
It's believed he's buried in the temple."

"Did you learn all this in school?"

"While I would love to say yes and point out all you
might know had you applied yourself to your studies, I
can't." She shrugged and her gaze returned to the Acropolis. "Nearly everything I know about places like this is
because I have been fortunate enough to see them for myself. Which makes me want to learn more about them."

He nodded. "Apparently it's contagious. Tell me more."

"Oh, good." She grinned. "I do like telling you what
you don't know."

He laughed. He had the woman teasing him now. That
was a very good sign.

"Athens is celebrated as the birthplace of western civ-
ilization," Violet began. "The Parthenon is perhaps the
best known…"

By the time they reached the hotel, James had been
nicely versed on the Acropolis, the Parthenon and the
more important sights of Athens. Admittedly, there were
moments when his mind strayed from what Violet was
saying to the way the sunlight glinted off the reddish-gold
strands of her hair that had escaped from her hat. Or the
way her green eyes glowed with passion for her subject,
and he wondered how they'd look when filled with passion of another sort. Or the way she'd bite her lip when
considering a point and he would recall how delightful
those lips had felt pressed against his own.

Mrs. Ryland had wired ahead for rooms at the Grand
Hotel d'Angleterre. They'd no sooner checked in than
Violet was greeted with unbridled enthusiasm by a small
group of English-speaking acquaintances—chattering ladies and overeager gentlemen. All of them talking about
how grand it was to be back in Athens and surely the

great poet was with them in spirit and wasn't it all terribly exciting. It didn't seem the least bit exciting to James, nor did it make any sense to him, but at the moment, he didn't care to find out who they were or what they were going on and on about. He slipped away—although he wasn't entirely sure Violet noticed—and escaped to their accommodations. He and Violet had a suite on the top floor with a view of the Acropolis. Fortunately, there was only one bedroom. Unfortunately, there was a relatively comfortable sofa.

Violet arrived a half an hour later, her eyes bright with exhilaration. "Goodness, James, where did you disappear to? One moment you were there and the next you had vanished. I would have introduced you. Oh, well. You'll meet everyone later." She paused at the opened doors to the balcony. "Splendid view, don't you think?"

He leaned against the doorjamb and crossed his arms over his chest. "As if we're being looked down upon by the gods themselves."

Her brow rose. "Sarcasm, James?"

"Not at all." He shrugged. "Just an observation."

"There's nothing like being able to gaze at one of the most remarkable ancient sights in the world to remind you of how far mankind has come." She pulled off her hat and gloves and tossed them onto a chair.

"Who were the people in the lobby?" He wasn't sure he was going to like the answer, but they probably had something to do with why they were in Athens.

"Let's see. There was Lady Knowles and Mrs. Hartley—they're from Kent." She glanced around the room. "Did the maids unpack?"

He nodded.

"And how are you feeling?"

"Quite well, thank you." Any residual queasiness had

vanished and he did indeed feel ready for whatever Violet and Athens had in store.

"Good." She smiled and stepped into the bedroom, stopping before the wardrobe. She opened the doors and continued. "Mrs. Baldwin and her sister Miss Thorpe were in the lobby. They're from somewhere in Derby if I recall. Then there was Mr. Metcalf, Mr. Irvine and Mr. Baines—all of whom teach at a boarding school, I forget where. And who else was there? Oh, yes, there was—"

"Let me rephrase that." He adopted a pleasant tone. "I don't mean who are they individually. I mean who are they as a group. At least I assume they're a group."

"In a manner of speaking." She rummaged in the wardrobe.

"Why exactly are we in Athens?" he said slowly, something he should have asked before now. "We were in Paris for a birthday celebration, in Florence for the unveiling of a statue, so I assume we are in Athens for something in particular."

"Indeed we are." She pulled a pair of well-worn, exceptionally sturdy walking shoes from the wardrobe as well as a hat far simpler than the one she'd had on and returned to the parlor. "I was afraid I had forgotten these." She smiled in triumph and settled on the sofa. "I wasn't sure I was going on to Greece when we left London."

"Those may be the ugliest shoes I have ever seen."

"Aren't they, though? They're also practical and comfortable and, I suspect, indestructible. They've seen me through many an adventure. I adore them." She slipped off the short boots she had on.

Silly how the flash of a stockinged ankle could bring to mind all sort of delightfully wicked things. Sliding his hand along the long length of her leg. Untying her garters—

"Stop it, James," she said mildly.

"Stop what?" He widened his eyes in feigned innocence.

"Whatever it is you're thinking."

"Not as easy as it sounds," he murmured then drew a steadying breath. "Back to my original question. Why are we here?"

"Do you remember that I once wrote poetry?" She pulled on one of the shoes. Apparently there was nothing like seeing a shapely ankle imprisoned by an ugly shoe to quell a man's desire.

"Vaguely, as I don't believe you ever let me read your poems."

"Yes, well, there was a reason for that." She grimaced. "They were quite dreadful. I did fancy myself a sort of Lady Byron."

He winced. He'd never been fond of Byron.

"I was in Vienna a few years ago when someone I met somewhere said something about a society dedicated to the appreciation of the life and works of Lord Byron. They mentioned it meets every year in Athens so obviously I had to come." She slipped on the second shoe and tied it.

"It doesn't seem the least bit obvious to me." His brow furrowed. "Shouldn't this society meet in England?"

"Lord Byron died in Greece. In the war for independence. He's a national hero here." Indignation flashed in her eyes. "I'm shocked you didn't know that."

"Of course I knew that." It did sound vaguely familiar.

"So Cleo and I decided to join the society and now we come every year. This is our third, I believe."

"To talk about Lord Byron?"

"Well, yes, in part. We do discuss his life, the places he visited, the adventures he had."

"All extremely scandalous I believe," he noted. "If I recall correctly, wasn't he denied burial at Westminster Abbey because of his dissolute behavior?"

"A dreadful miscarriage of justice. The man was brilliant, one of England's greatest poets." Her brow furrowed with indignation. "He should have taken his place at Westminster with Chaucer and Sheridan and Mr. Dickens. At the very least he should have some sort of memorial in the abbey as do Shakespeare and Milton and Jane Austen."

"It is rather a shame when a man's past—his terrible decisions and dreadful mistakes—are held against him even in death." He smiled pleasantly.

"Yes, well, death does stifle one's abilities to reform." She met his gaze pointedly. "Fortunately, as you are feeling much better, there's certainly time for redemption. Perhaps if Lord Byron had lived longer he too would have shown remorse."

"Entirely possible." Although, given what he could recall about Byron's life, he doubted remorse was in the man's nature.

"Discussion of his life is really a minor part of the gathering here. I've always had the distinct impression that regardless of how much society members appreciate his work, the impropriety of his life makes some of them…" She thought for a moment. "Oh, uncomfortable, I would say."

"Imagine that." It was all he could do not to laugh aloud. Those society members he'd seen talking to her in the lobby struck him as likely to be scandalized by using the wrong fork at dinner let alone the raucous life of Lord Byron.

"And we have readings of his work, several every day. Sometimes at the hotel but often at some of the local ruins—the Temple of Zeus or the agora. You have no idea how moving it is to hear someone recite *The Maid of Athens* or the *Song of the Greek Poet* in the shadows of ancient Greece. The first reading is tomorrow at the ruins of Hadrian's library. It will be most inspiring." She rose to her feet. "Many of the members write poetry as well—in the style of Lord Byron. A sort of homage if you will." She paused. "Admittedly, much of it is awful."

His lips twitched with the need to grin. "Do you?"

"No," she said quickly. "Well, not anymore. I gave up writing bad poetry quite some time ago." She picked up her hat and moved to a wall mirror. "The original poetry is always read here in one of the hotel parlors on the last night of our gathering. It's very, oh, bohemian I would say."

"I can imagine." Although, judging by those society members he'd seen clustered around Violet in the lobby, *bohemian* was the last word that came to mind. More likely the evening of recitation of original poetry was pretentious, endless and extraordinarily dull. Surely there was a way to avoid it.

Violet tied her hat into place.

"Didn't you just take a hat off?"

"I did, but this one is more sensible."

He frowned. "Are you going somewhere?"

"*We're* going somewhere." Her gaze met his in the mirror. "Unless you prefer not to join me."

"It depends." He narrowed his eyes. "Does it have anything to do with poetry?"

"No."

He grinned. "Then I'd be delighted to accompany you."

She glanced at his feet. "You might want to change

your shoes. Did you bring anything sturdier? More practical, perhaps."

"More practical for what?" he asked cautiously.

She inclined her head toward the balcony. "The Acropolis."

"It's a bit late in the day for sightseeing, don't you think?"

"Nonsense, we have a good two hours before sunset. The view from the Acropolis is the very best way to see all of Athens. Besides, there's nothing more glorious than observing the last rays of daylight vanish behind Mount Aigaleo with the Parthenon at your back. And then watching the stars rise. For more than two thousand years people have observed the sunset from the top of the Acropolis. Why, one can practically feel the presence of all those who have gone before, the ghosts of antiquity if you will. It's the perfect way to begin a stay in Athens. And goodness, James." She flashed him a grin. "It's an adventure."

"Oh, yes, that does sound enjoyable," he muttered. "It's rather a climb, isn't it?"

"Only for the faint of heart. Surely you're made of sterner stuff than to let a little thing like a bit of a climb dissuade you?"

"I'm not the least bit dissuaded," he said resolutely, although he could think of a dozen things he'd rather do. "And I'm sure my shoes will be just fine."

A few minutes later they met Marcus and Mrs. Ryland in the lobby.

"We're off to the Acropolis," Violet told them. "Why don't you join us?"

"Oh…" Marcus frowned.

"He was just confessing to me today that he doesn't like heights," Mrs. Ryland said quickly.

"That's it." Marcus shook his head. "Even the thought of being at the top of that block of stone…" He shuddered.

"Well, then, it's best you avoid heights at all costs." James took Violet's arm and steered her toward the door.

Somewhere between discovering their destination and meeting the others, James had come to the realization that seeing the Acropolis and the Parthenon, and whatever else was up there, alone with Violet would indeed be rather perfect. After all, she'd said moonlight on the Parthenon was most romantic.

He had always been fond of romance.

JAMES HATED THESE SHOES. Oh, they were fine for walking the streets of London, but climbing to the top of the Acropolis was another matter altogether. If he ever got off this blasted hill, he'd make buying appropriate footwear a priority.

They'd reached the summit of the flat-topped limestone hill that towered over Athens shortly before sunset. By the time they'd admired the Parthenon and the views and who knew how many other remains of temples or outbuildings, the sun was sinking below the mountains. The last rays of sunlight cast intriguing shadows over the grounds littered with broken pieces of the ancient world. Occasionally, a fragment of marble carved with a face stared up at him from the rubble. He jumped more than once and attributed it to his shoes, but looking at the ground and having it look back was unsettling. While at first he was annoyed that they were not the only visitors to the ancient site this evening, now it was nice to know they were not entirely alone. It was hard to dismiss Violet's comment about *ghosts of antiquity*.

Along with a blanket they spread on the stairs at the base of the Parthenon, the hotel had provided a lantern as well as a basket with a bottle of wine, bread and cheese. Their driver would wait at the bottom of the hill.

They shared the offerings in the basket, and Violet continued her tutorial on ancient Greece while James gazed at the stars. It was a long time since he had done nothing but gaze at the night sky. The stars weren't nearly as bright at home, obscured by fog and smoke and city lights. But here, starlight negated the need to light their lantern although he suspected they would indeed need it to negotiate the stairs and walkways on the way down.

"There was no French count or Italian sculptor or Greek poet, was there?" he asked when she paused to think of yet another obscure fact about ancient Athens.

"Of course there were." She shrugged. "Simply not any whose bed I shared."

"And yet, you let me think you had."

"Did I?" Doubt sounded in her voice. "I don't recall saying anything of the sort."

"You didn't deny it."

"I didn't know I needed to deny it," she said in a lofty manner, then paused. "I suspect you now know how I felt about the other women who occupied your life. Unpleasant, isn't it?"

"Yes." He blew a resigned breath. "I would do anything to have made different choices."

"I know." She took a sip of wine.

He stared at her. "Is that possibly forgiveness I hear?"

"Possibly." She smiled out at the night sky and the flickering lights in the buildings of Athens below them. "There is something about being here, looking down over the city, as the ancient gods might have, that puts things in an entirely different perspective." She paused. "'Maid of Athens, I am gone. Think of me, sweet! When alone.

Though I fly to Istambol, Athens holds my heart and soul. Can I cease to love thee? No!'"

He tried, but couldn't hold back something that sounded like a cross between a snort and a laugh.

"You don't like that?" Indignation rang in her voice.

"No, sorry, I don't." He sipped his wine. "It's Byron, isn't it?"

She nodded. "From 'Maid of Athens, ere we Part'."

"I never have liked him. I find his work…" He tried to find the right words. "Overly done, perhaps. Too flowery and somewhat pretentious."

"I think it's quite romantic," she said staunchly.

"I'll grant you that. Women in particular seem to love it." He grinned. "Even I have spouted him on occasion."

"To great success, no doubt."

"Well…" He shrugged modestly.

"You are incorrigible." A reluctant smile curved her lips. "And unrepentant."

"In that you're wrong, my dear Violetta." He chuckled. "Repentance is my sole purpose in life."

"Utter nonsense." She huffed. "Even so, you must admit some of his writing is quite compelling."

"Changing the subject, are we? We're back to Byron, then."

She ignored him. "As was his life."

"I'm not sure *compelling* is the right word to describe his life. Didn't someone call him mad, bad and dangerous to know?"

"Lady Caroline Lamb. One of his many lovers," she added casually. "You were once considered mad, bad and dangerous to know if I recall."

"Was I?"

"You needn't look so smug about it."

"I'm not the least bit smug. Proud perhaps. You just compared me to your favorite poet."

"In the worst possible way."

"Those days were quite some time ago." He chuckled. "I haven't been mad, bad or even remotely dangerous for years now."

"I don't know. I suspect you're still dangerous," she said softly.

He wasn't sure if that was bad or very good. He studied her profile, silhouetted against the star-filled sky. Byron might have been right. "'She walks in beauty, like the night,'" he said softly. "'Of cloudless climes and starry skies. And all that's best of dark and bright meet in her aspect and her eyes.'"

Violet's gaze jerked to his and she stared at him for a long moment. "We should go," she said abruptly, tossing back the rest of her wine.

And wasn't that interesting. "All right."

"It's been a long day of travel and I would prefer to retire early." Her words tumbled out as if there was so much to say there was no time to take a breath and she quickly packed the basket. "Travel is always tiring, you know, and there is a reading in the morning—at the Library of Hadrian—not far from the hotel. I don't know exactly what poem will be read—but I don't want to miss it. It is the first day, after all."

James tossed the blanket in the basket, then lit the lantern.

"It might be best if I took the lantern," Violet said. "As I am more familiar with the area."

"By all means." He stifled a chuckle. Apparently, his recitation of one of Byron's works affected her in a way he did not anticipate. Although he hadn't really anticipated anything at all. The words had simply come to him when he'd seen her lovely face against the starry night. Regardless of his overall opinion of Byron, those words were nothing short of perfect. The man could have had Violet in mind when he put pen to paper.

Violet continued to babble about nothing of significance all the way down the hill and on the short ride back to the hotel. If one didn't know better, one might think the confident, sophisticated Lady Ellsworth was distinctly flustered.

She disappeared into the bedroom the moment they reached their suite, again claiming exhaustion and noting what a long day it had been. All obvious excuses to escape his presence.

A few minutes later the door opened and she thrust an armful of blankets and pillows at him. "You'll need these."

"My dressing gown would be nice, as well," he said, accepting the bundle of linens.

"It's under the pillow." She adopted a cordial smile. "Good night, James." She turned and hurried back into the bedroom as if the hounds of hell were at her feet.

"Sleep well, Violetta," he said, just as the door closed.

He chuckled. He'd wager a considerable amount she would sleep no better than he. He stripped off his clothes and put on his dressing gown. He might be willing to sleep on a sofa, but he was not about to sleep in his clothes. He tossed the pillow on the sofa, turned off the lamp and lay down, pulling the light blanket over him. Aside from the fact that the sofa was a bit too short and he had to prop his feet on the armrest, it was fairly comfortable.

Violet was right. It had been a long day. Travel, together with the hike up and down the Acropolis, had taken their toll and he too was tired. Pity it seemed to make no difference.

Knowing she was in the next room was almost worse than her being on the other side of a row of pillows. Light showed under the door to her room for a long time then at last extinguished. But he could hear her bed creak with her attempt to sleep. Good, she was as restless as he. Was she as aware of his presence as he was of hers? Was she too wondering at his feelings for her as he was wondering about hers for him? Did she ache for his touch as he did for hers?

Good God, the woman was driving him insane. If he hadn't been such an idiot they would have been together long before now. If he had made an effort six years ago to claim her heart they would even now be living happily together. No, he wasn't ready for marriage then—wasn't ready for the feelings he'd refused to acknowledge then. Not beginning a life with her when they'd first married might well have been the only intelligent thing he'd ever done when it came to Violet. They would have both been miserable.

Bloody hell, it was stuffy in here. He shoved off the blanket, got to this feet and threw open the doors to the balcony. A slight breeze whispered over him. The night was clear, the air refreshing and the stars were bright. He could just make out the dark shadow of the Acropolis rising over the city. He braced his hands on the railing and gazed out at the night.

He heard the bedroom door swing open.

"Why did you do that? Was it just something to say? Something you've said before to women?"

"Why did I do what?" He glanced over his shoulder.

The light was on in the bedroom behind her. Violet wore that ridiculously charming kimono of hers. "That *she walks in beauty* nonsense."

"Nonsense, is it?" He raised a brow. "I thought you liked Byron."

"I do and 'She Walks in Beauty' is one of my favorites."

"It's the favorite of many women." His gaze shifted back to the Acropolis. "It's the only poem of Byron's I know. And I'm afraid I have said it before."

"I see." Faint disappointment edged her words.

"But never on the top of the ancient world with the stars as a backdrop. Never when it was significant. And never did the words ring true before. Before tonight it was simply something to say."

She was silent, but he heard or perhaps simply sensed her approach.

"I'm not sure I can ever forget your dalliances with other women. Nor the fact that you never came after me, never attempted a proper marriage with me, never fought for me."

His stomach twisted. "I understand."

She was silent for a long moment then she took a deep breath. "But I might possibly be able to forgive you."

He nodded. "Well, I do know now how you felt."

"I suspect it was worse for me than for you."

"I doubt it." He started to turn.

"No, wait, please don't turn around."

He paused.

"This is difficult enough without having to face you."

"Go on." He held his breath. Was she about to confess something he'd prefer not to hear?

"Yes, well, you see, it was harder for me because I was—" resignation sounded in her voice "—I *am* in love with you."

"Are you?" His heart leaped.

"I'm afraid so." She huffed. "And I'm rather tired of

pretending that I'm not. I've been telling myself that I wasn't in love with you for six years. Apparently to no avail."

"You needn't sound so distraught." In the back of his mind he noted how calm and collected he sounded, as if this was a conversation of no particular importance. Interesting, as he was not the least bit calm or collected. Indeed, he wasn't sure he'd ever felt so, well, overjoyed in his entire life.

"This is difficult, James." She drew a deep breath. "I too have my pride. I have just confessed my feelings to you. Honesty is not the least bit easy, you know."

"I am all too aware of that." He smiled slowly. "Perhaps I can make it easier."

"I doubt that." Her brow furrowed as if she were making a decision, then she nodded. "I'm going back to bed now." She swiveled and left the room before he could stop her. The door closed firmly behind her.

"Bloody hell." He moved to the door. "Let me in, Violet."

"I'm going to bed, James."

He tried the door handle and pushed the door open. "If you want to keep someone out, locking the door is a good idea."

She stood near the bed and crossed her arms over her chest. "I didn't think you'd be so impolite as to follow me. You've never been good at following."

"And yet here I am. It seems to me we have a great deal to talk about."

"And it seems to me there's nothing more to say." She shrugged.

He moved toward her. "Don't you want to know what I think? You certainly had a lot to say when I confessed to you about the incident."

"That was different." She waved off his comment. "That was something you did, not something you felt."

"Still, aren't I allowed the courtesy of a reply?"

"Yes, I suppose." She rolled her eyes toward the ceiling. "Go on then, say whatever it is you wish to say."

He stepped closer. "I simply think it's a remarkable coincidence, that's all."

"A coincidence? What on earth do you mean by that?"

"It's quite simple, my dear wife. My Violetta." He pulled her into his arms. "I am in love with you, too. I suspect I always have been."

Her breath caught. "You needn't say that if you don't mean it. If you're just saying that to keep me abiding by the terms of the will. It's not necessary."

"Oh, but I think it is. And I mean every word." He gazed into her endless green eyes. "The inheritance means nothing without you. You are the true prize. I've known it for quite some time."

Her eyes widened.

"I was a fool not to come after you, not to try to win you back long before now. Not to fight for you. It was stubborn and stupid of me. Uncle Richard knew we belonged together. As do I."

"James, I—"

Before she could say another word, he pressed his lips to hers. She froze for no more than an instant, then her arms slid around his neck. He gathered her closer, the heat of her body searing him through her clothes and his. Her mouth opened to his and she tasted of rich red wine and starry skies and forever after.

She pulled away. "Good Lord, James." For an endless moment she stared up at him. "We've wasted a lot of time."

CHAPTER TWENTY-FOUR

VIOLET PULLED HIM closer and again met his lips with hers. An awful ache of need and desire and longing swept through her. She clung to him, desperate for the taste of him, reveling in the heat of his body pressed to hers. He slanted his mouth over hers, deepening their kiss, her tongue tangling with his. A tiny voice in the back of her head whispered at last.

He wrenched his lips from hers to trail kisses along the line of her jaw, and she moaned softly. Her head fell back and he rained kisses down her neck to the base of her throat in a sensual exploration, as if he wanted to taste every inch of her. His hands roamed over the contours of her back and drifted lower to caress her derriere through the silk of her robe. A shiver of pure hunger raced through her and she pressed her hips tighter against him, the evidence of his arousal hard against her stomach. Oh God, she wanted this, wanted him. She clutched at his shoulders, reveling in the feel of hard muscle beneath the silk of his dressing gown.

She raised her head and shifted to place her lips at the hollow of his throat. He groaned with need, the sound vibrating through her and wrapping around her soul. She slid her hands over his chest, opening the dressing gown to the exploration of her lips and her touch. He tasted of heat and spice and promises as yet unmade.

Her fingers fumbled with the sash tied at his waist

until it fell free and her hands moved lower to lightly caress the hot hard length of his erection.

"Violet." He caught her hand, and she looked up at him. His eyes burned with a reflection of her own desire. "There is no turning back from this."

"I don't want to turn back." She pulled her hand free, untied her sash and let her kimono fall to the floor in a puddle of silk at her feet. She'd never stood naked in front of him before. Or in front of any man, for that matter. She pushed aside a momentary twinge of doubt. No, she raised her chin and gazed into his eyes. She wanted this. Wanted him.

His eyes darkened as if he realized she'd come to talk to him with only a whisper of silk between them. She rested her hand on his chest and gazed up at him. "Do you?"

"Never." The word was barely more than a murmur, as if saying even a word required effort he refused to squander. He shrugged off his dressing gown, sank down on the edge of the bed and pulled her between his legs. "I want to worship you."

He cupped her breasts in his hands, feasting on one then the other until her nails dug into his shoulders and her eyes rolled back in her head and her knees threatened to collapse. And she realized the odd, whimpering sound in the room came from her.

"James," she whispered. "Please…"

He wrapped his arms around her and pulled her onto the bed in a tangle of arms and legs, of hunger and demand. Need, urgent and unrelenting, consumed her and all restraint between them shattered. His hands, her lips were everywhere at once. An exploration—no, a conquest of taste and touch and merciless sensation. Tension coiled deep within her and she wanted—no, she needed—no, she demanded more. Her body, her very being was frantic for the feel of his heated flesh beneath her fingers, against her tongue. She stroked him, and he groaned against her neck. He slid his hand between her legs, and she could feel her own wet, slick need as his fingers caressed her. She moaned, and her back arched upward and she pressed against his hand.

He slid down her body, his mouth searing a trail over her, teasing her with lips and tongue and teeth. Until his head rested between her legs and his tongue flicked over that center of sensation only she had ever touched.

"Oh, God, James," she cried, her hips raising up to meet his mouth. Dear Lord, he hadn't done this on their wedding night. Why in the hell not? Her fingers tunneled through his hair and her very being narrowed to the unexpected pleasure and sheer torture of his tongue and his mouth claiming her.

When she thought she would surely die of the merciless onslaught of his mouth, when she hovered at the edge of something unknown, something the aching tightness with her yearned for, he stopped and shifted his body over her. The hard hot length of him pressed against her. And she quivered with the need, so long denied, to have him inside her. And the oddest moment of clarity seized her.

"Wait!"

"Wait?" Sheer disbelief shone in his dark eyes, glazed with passion and need. "Now you want me to wait?"

"I just thought you should know…" He was right. This was not the time. Still… "It's been a long time since I've done this."

He smiled into her eyes. "It's been a long time since I've done this, too."

"Oh, well, then." She brushed her lips against his. "Carry on."

His lips crushed hers and he guided himself into her. Her muscles tensed. It had been somewhat painful the first time they had done this. Since then, of course, she had been told it was only painful once. She wasn't entirely sure she believed it.

He slid into her with a slow, measured stroke as if he knew how very inexperienced she really was, and her tension eased. She was certainly tight but there wasn't so much as a twinge of pain. She'd nearly forgotten how odd the feeling was of him being inside her, filling her. Odd and…good. He pulled back and thrust into her again, his movements unhurried and deliberate, which only served to fuel her impatience. She wanted—needed—more. She wrapped her legs around his and rolled her hips against him, and their rhythm increased.

She urged him on faster and deeper, and let herself be carried away by the throbbing sensation deep inside her. Her blood pulsed in her veins, her heart thudded in her chest and her breath came faster. And oh, dear Lord. She didn't remember it as being this all-consuming. This intense. Everything that was Violet vanished, replaced by a creature who lived only for the exquisite joy of their joining. Who existed only in the heat of his body searing hers, the feel of him inside her and the ever-tightening tension within her.

He thrust into her again and again, faster and deeper and harder. Until that coil inside her exploded with release and waves of pure pleasure rushed through her. Her body quaked against him and her back arched and she cried out his name. And through it all she felt his body tense and then shudder and her name sounded like a prayer on his lips. "Violetta."

And she realized with a certainty she'd never known

before, together was where they belonged, where they'd always belonged.

Uncle Richard was right.

For a long moment they lay silently, too spent to so much as move. At last he lifted his head, smiled down at her, kissed her gently, then shifted to lie by her side.

"Good God, James." She blew a long breath. "That was remarkable."

He chuckled. "Indeed it was."

"I don't recall it being quite that earth-shattering the last time."

"You don't?" he said slowly.

"Not at all. Oh, it was pleasant enough." She drew her brows together. "A bit uncomfortable at first if I remember correctly, but nice."

"Nice?" he repeated.

"Well, I'd never done it before. I would think *nice* is really a rousing endorsement."

His brow shot upward. "*Nice* is an endorsement?"

It was all she could do not to laugh at the indignant look on his face. "A *rousing* endorsement."

"And tonight?"

"My dear, silly man." She hooked her leg over his and rolled on top of him, folding her arms on his chest and staring into his eyes. "This was so much better than nice."

"Good." He didn't sound at all convinced.

"You did all sorts of things I never imagined you might do." She thought for a moment. "Certainly they had sounded interesting but—"

He frowned. "Just who have you been talking to?"

"Friends, other women. You know how women like to share."

"Apparently, I had no idea," he said wryly.

"But I do think by anyone's assessment this was remarkable. Of course, my lack of experience might play a part in my appraisal." She leaned forward and nibbled on his bottom lip. "After all, my only previous experience was nice."

Beneath her, his body tensed. He drew back and stared at her. "So, am I to take that to mean you've only done this with me?"

"Surprised?"

"I don't know," he said slowly. "You do know I thought you'd had lovers."

"Of course I do." She widened her eyes innocently. "I know you've had lovers."

"Yes, well, mine didn't mean anything."

She leaned and kissed the hollow at the base of his throat. "I'm confident if I'd had lovers, they wouldn't have meant anything, either."

"No," he said gruffly. "They probably would have meant a great deal. You're not the sort of woman to sleep with men you didn't care about."

She raised her head and gazed into his eyes. "Goodness, James, you do say the sweetest things."

"I'm serious, Violet." His brow furrowed. "I was wrong about the count and the sculptor."

She grinned. "Don't forget the poet."

"I should have trusted you." His gaze searched hers. "Yet another mistake on my part."

"You didn't know me well enough to trust me. Not really." She paused. "And I didn't know you well enough to trust you."

"Do you now?" He held his breath, his blue eyes intense.

"Know you well enough? Or trust you?"

"Both."

She stared at him for a long moment. "Yes, I believe I do."

"I swear to you, Violet, I will be worthy of your trust. I will never again do anything to make you regret trusting me."

"Good." She smiled. "Although I should confess..." She smirked. "I will miss having the moral upper hand."

"My apologies." He grinned and pulled her into his arms. "Maybe I can do something to make up for that."

And he did, more than once before morning. And when they did sleep, they were entwined in each other's arms. Violet couldn't remember ever feeling quite so content and never before had she felt so loved.

She woke to find him lying on his side, his head propped in his hand, a too satisfied grin on his face. "Good morning, Violetta."

She rolled over to face him. "Good morning, Giacomo."

"I believe after last night, you need to rethink your *what's in a name* comment."

"You think you're living up to the expectations set by Casanova? That's rather arrogant of you, isn't it?"

"Well, you did use the word *remarkable*," he said modestly.

She laughed.

"I'm starving." He leaned closer and nuzzled her neck.

She shivered with delight. "Then we should do something about that. Unfortunately, we would have to dress." She trailed her fingers down his chest. "I'm not at all sure I'm amenable to that idea."

He laughed, grabbed her hand and raised it to his lips. "We could stay here all day if you want. I can't think of anything I'd rather do. But then we'd miss all the treasures of ancient Athens."

"Goodness, James." She pulled her hand free, curved it around the back of his neck and drew him closer. "I've seen the treasures of ancient Athens." She brushed her lips across his. "I can tell you all about them."

"As inviting as that sounds," he murmured against her lips, "don't you have a reading to attend?"

"Blast it all." She heaved a resigned sigh. "That completely slipped my mind." She smiled in as seductive a manner as she could muster. "Your fault entirely."

"You're welcome." He cast her his wonderfully wicked grin. The very grin that made her heart skip and something flutter in the pit of her stomach. As it had six years ago.

"What time is it?"

He grabbed his pocket watch from the side table. "Half past nine."

She wrinkled her nose. "I have time to eat, but I do need to dress. Rather a pity, don't you think?"

He laughed. "I do indeed. But we can't make up for six years in one night, you know." He grinned. "Although I think we gave it an excellent try."

She laughed. "We certainly did."

He slid out of bed and got to his feet. "Isn't there a restaurant downstairs?"

She nodded. Goodness, the man had the well-shaped body of a Greek statue—all planes and valleys and shadows. She could skip this morning's reading…

He pulled on his trousers. "I'll go down and order something sent up."

Damn. "Excellent. I'll dress while you're gone."

He cast her a wicked look. "Only if you insist."

She laughed. Again. The man made her laugh. Was there anything more wonderful than that? Excepting, of course, when he made her moan and cry out and sent delicious waves of sheer pleasure coursing through her.

He finished dressing and she was content to watch him. No, content was a far cry from her feelings at the moment. She was…happy. Yes, that was it. Deliriously, madly, immensely happy. It was more than merely the lingering glow of their night together. The man she loved loved her. What could be more wonderful than that?

He leaned over the bed and kissed the tip of her nose. "I'll be quick." He hesitated for a moment. "I am truly sorry, you know, for my behavior after our wedding. Well, for everything, really. I regret it deeply."

"I can't say it wasn't upsetting but I certainly could have done whatever I wished, as well. The fact that I didn't…" She shrugged. "Entirely my choice. It was part of our agreement, after all. Going our separate ways, living separate lives.

"And while I was angry with you for not coming after me, not asking me to come home, I certainly could have made some effort. I could have insisted on seeing you. I could have written."

"Not my smartest moment." He paused. "That agreement, that is. If I could undo what I have done, go back to the day after our wedding—"

"I wouldn't," she said without thinking. Abruptly, the oddest thought struck her. James hadn't mentioned the kiss that started everything. He began his regrets with after they married. Her heart thudded. Was it possible that he didn't think that kiss, their marriage, was a mistake? "These six years have been beneficial for both of us. You grew up and learned to be the man Uncle Richard wanted you to be. I grew up and became the woman I wanted to be."

"Yes, well—"

She held out a hand to quiet him. "However, I do think we've wasted a great deal of time."

"As do I." He stared at her for a long time. "And I have no intention of wasting any more starting today. I'll be back as soon as possible."

"See that you are," she said primly. "Would you like to come with me this morning? For the reading?"

"Won't Mrs. Ryland be accompanying you?"

Cleo was no doubt having the same problem getting out of bed as Violet was. "Probably."

"Then I shall leave you to it. I'm sure there are any number of interesting ways to fill my time."

"You can scarcely walk down the streets in Athens without stumbling over something ancient and fascinating. And then there are the more notable ruins. Would you like me to make you a list? I noticed there wasn't any stationery in the desk but I'm sure the front desk—"

He laughed. "No, I don't need a list. And later, you can show me some of those notable ruins." He shrugged into his coat, kissed her again, then took his leave.

She slid back under the covers and stared at the ceiling. So this was what joy felt like. She could easily become accustomed to this. And why not? Her husband loved her and after all these years they were finally starting a life together. She sent a silent prayer of gratitude heavenward.

Thank you, Uncle Richard.

VIOLET GLARED AT the sparse offerings in the wardrobe and for the first time in years, really had nothing she cared to wear. Oh, her clothes were all fashionable and quite becoming, but she was firm about keeping their luggage to a minimum and refused to pack more than was necessary. A shame really. She would have liked something special today. To match her mood. Her lavender walking dress would have to do.

It was mid-May in Athens and spring was in full bloom. And Violet was beginning the rest of her life with the man she loved.

She'd no sooner dressed than a knock sounded at the door. Perhaps that was whatever James had arranged to be sent to the room, although in her experience, hotel restaurants were never that prompt. James hadn't even returned yet. Maybe he had run into Marcus. And Cleo. The very idea made her giggle.

The knock sounded again. A bit louder and definitely impatient.

"Coming!" She hurried to the door, pulled it open and sucked in a sharp breath. "What on earth are you doing here?"

Duncan stood in the corridor, a somber expression on his face. "I have information you need to know."

CHAPTER TWENTY-FIVE

THE RESTAURANT AGREED to send breakfast to their rooms and assured James it would be as quickly as possible. He started back to their suite but detoured to stop by Marcus's room. Violet had mentioned there was no stationery, and James had a brilliant idea. All it required was paper.

His friend was on a different floor, and James found himself grinning all the way to Marcus's room. What better way to show the woman he loved just how much he loved her than with a love poem written especially for her? In the manner of Byron, perhaps. Admittedly "She Walks in Beauty" was classic and inspired. But then James too was inspired. He'd never attempted poetry before, but really, how difficult could it possibly be to string a few words together and make them rhyme?

He found Marcus's door and knocked sharply. There was no answer. James knocked again.

"Yes?" Marcus's muffled voice sounded from behind the door.

"Morning, old man," James said jovially. "Let me in."

Marcus said something James couldn't quite make out but a few moments later the door opened a crack.

"What do you want?" Marcus wore a dressing gown and stood so as to block any view from the door.

"Stationery," James said slowly, then snorted back a laugh. "You're not alone, are you?"

"Of course I'm alone." Marcus scoffed. "I simply slept

late, that's all. Why, I was in bed when you knocked. Alone. I think I would know if I wasn't alone. I'm completely alone. I daresay I've never been more alone."

James's brow row. "Protesting entirely too much, are we?"

"For goodness' sakes, Marcus," a female voice called from behind him. A very familiar female voice. "Let him in."

"Come in, then." Marcus aimed James a warning look, then leaned close and lowered his voice. "Try to be, I don't know, pleasant." He stepped aside.

"Good day, my lord." Mrs. Ryland stood next to a wildly disheveled bed, tying the belt of a kimono very much like Violet's.

"Obviously, I'm interrupting," James said slowly. He already knew Marcus was interested in the woman, although he never suspected it had gone quite this far. Still, Marcus should have known better. Admittedly, he had changed every bit as much as James in recent years but few of Marcus's dalliances had ever ended well. If this went the way of the others—James didn't even want to consider how Violet would react to Marcus breaking her friend's heart.

Marcus glanced at Mrs. Ryland and grinned. "You could say that."

She choked back a laugh.

"I just needed paper and thought you might have some." He nodded cordially at Mrs. Ryland, grabbed Marcus's arm, pulled him toward the door where they could have a modicum of privacy and lowered his voice. "Do you really think this is wise? How do you think Violet is going to feel when she learns you seduced her closest friend? And if this does not end well…" He shuddered. "She's going to be furious with you and no doubt me, as well."

"Why would she be angry with you?" Marcus's tone was entirely too casual for the matter at hand.

"Because I'm *your* friend!" James snapped. "Beyond that she probably doesn't need a reason. This is bad, Marcus, this is very bad."

"Is it?" Doubt sounded in Marcus's voice.

"Good God, yes!"

"I'm not sure I agree, but I do see your point." Marcus crossed his arms over his chest. "What do you suggest I do about it?"

"I don't know." James huffed. "But you'll have to think of something."

"I could marry her, I suppose," Marcus said mildly.

"I suggested that months ago and you were not at all amenable to the idea."

"I believe I said I had no desire to marry anyone simply to make your life easier. However, I may have had a change of heart. Making your life easier is probably the least I can do as your friend and solicitor." He stepped back and raised his voice. "Cleo, will you marry me?"

"What? Again?" She arched a brow. "Do you think that's necessary?"

Marcus shrugged. "Sorry. She doesn't think it's necessary."

James shook his head in confusion. "What?"

"James, allow me to introduce Mrs. Cleona Cecily Davies." Marcus chuckled. "My wife."

"Pleasure to meet you, my lord," Mrs. Ryland—*Mrs. Davies*—said. Marcus grinned and moved to her side.

James's gaze shifted between the two of them. "Your wife?"

"I believe that's what I just said."

James stared in disbelief. "You're married?"

"Damn difficult to have a wife without being married."

"We can prove it if you'd like." Mrs. Davies smiled up at her husband.

"That won't be necessary. It's just something of a shock. I never imagined..." He drew his brows together and addressed his friend. "Why didn't you tell me?"

"I was protecting you." Marcus shrugged. "And I fully intended to tell you, I simply haven't had the chance."

"What do you mean—you were protecting me?"

"I knew you'd see my marrying someone who didn't like you as a betrayal of sorts. And I—" he cast a completely smitten smile down at his wife "—we thought perhaps you would get to know her a little better during our travels, although I daresay it hasn't turned out that way."

"I've been too busy to trying to get my own wife to like me." James paused. "And I don't dislike her exactly. But she doesn't like me."

"It scarcely matters whether or not I like you, does it?" she asked. "All that really matters is how Violet feels about you." She sighed. "However, I did promise to try to like you."

Marcus nudged his wife. "He's very likable, really."

"Thank you, Mrs. Davies," James said. "I shall do all in my power to earn your friendship."

"We shall see, my lord." She cast him a reluctant smile. "And I am Cleo to my friends."

"And I am James." This might work out well for everyone. Indeed, it was much better to have *Cleo* as Marcus's wife rather than as Violet's constant companion. His gaze shifted to Marcus. "And I don't need protection."

"Of course you do, you always have," Marcus said. "I've protected you for years. It's my job."

"I don't think so."

"Do you remember when that woman claimed—"

"Yes," James said quickly. "But that was years ago."

"Very well." Marcus ticked the points off on his fingers. "More recently, I've protected you from any number of financial disasters by staving off frivolous lawsuits."

James frowned. "I don't remember anything like that."

"Because I don't tell you." Marcus sighed. "There are things that come to my attention as your solicitor that I don't mention to you. It's what you pay me quite handsomely to do. I rarely bother you with minor difficulties with contracts or licenses or possible legal actions. It's for the best, really."

"How is keeping me in the dark for the best?"

"For one thing, it leaves you free to concentrate on more important matters. For example, if you knew the way to escape the stipulations of the will was with an heir—"

"What?" James stared.

Cleo's brow furrowed. "What?"

Marcus's eyes widened as if he had just realized what he said. "What?"

James narrowed his eyes. "What are you talking about?"

"Nothing," Marcus said quickly. "A slip of the tongue, that's all. Complete nonsense really. My mind is obviously muddled by wedded bliss. I would disregard it entirely if I were you."

"That's the clause you didn't want to tell me about, isn't it?"

Marcus winced. "Possibly."

"You're right," James said slowly. "Violet cannot know about this. Especially not now."

"Absolutely not." Marcus nodded.

"If she hears about this, she'll never believe last night—"

"Last night?" Marcus asked.

"You're not the only one whose mind is muddled by wedded bliss." James ran his hand through his hair. "We're agreed, then."

"I beg your pardon, *James*." Cleo crossed her arms over her chest. "I haven't agreed to anything. I think Violet needs to know about this."

"She'll think everything that has passed between us—"

"Last night," Marcus murmured.

"—was only because of Uncle Richard's will. She'll think I used her for my own purposes." He shook his head. "It's taken me this long to win her trust. That trust will shatter if she learns about this."

"I'll simply tell her I was present when you discovered this," Cleo said.

"Do you really think she'll believe that I didn't know about something this important? That Marcus never told me?" James shook his head. "Even if she does believe you, there will always be doubt."

"Regardless, she is my dearest friend in the world. How on earth can I not tell her about this?"

"This revelation will ruin everything. It will ruin us." He met Cleo's gaze. "Bloody hell, Cleo, I love her. I can't lose her."

Marcus inclined his head toward his wife. "Have you ever seen any man more sincere? He really is a good sort. And this is all my fault. I would never forgive myself if I was the one to ruin my best friend's future happiness. Especially when I am so blissfully happy myself."

"That's not the least bit fair, Marcus." She glared at her husband.

"I know."

For a long moment Cleo didn't say a word. "Very well, then," she said at last, "I won't tell her." Her firm gaze met James's. "But you must."

His preference would be that Violet never know about this at all. Oh, certainly, someday in the far distant future, when their children were grown perhaps, then he could tell her. Why, she might even laugh about it, although he doubted it. It would be an entirely different matter if he had told her before last night. Now, however... Apparently, he had no choice.

"Agreed." He nodded. "Will you at least allow me to tell her when I think the moment is right?"

Cleo hesitated. Marcus nodded hopefully at his wife. She sighed. "Yes, I suppose." She met James's gaze. "But I would not wait too long, if I were you. The longer it takes you to tell her, the more awkward it's going to be."

"I realize that." Relief washed through him. "Thank you."

"I suppose this is the sort of things friends do for each other." She cast him a reluctant smile.

"Don't muck it up," Marcus added.

"I shall try not to." He turned to leave, then turned back. "Oh, I came for paper."

Cleo picked up a few sheets of stationery from the desk and brought it to him. After all, the poem was still a brilliant idea.

"Thank you." Again, he turned toward the door and again he turned back. "One more thing." James smiled at his old friend and perhaps his new one. "I forgot to offer my congratulations. I wish the two of you every happiness."

"Thank you, James." Cleo smiled.

"Good luck," Marcus added.

James thanked him and took his leave.

The smartest thing to do would be to tell Violet at once. Get it over with. Be completely honest. Tell her exactly when he found out about this clause. The fact that it was after they made love was definitely a point in his favor. If, of course, she believed him. It appeared her declaration that she trusted him was about to be tested.

And the stakes in the game they played had never been higher.

JAMES DREW A deep breath, opened the door and stepped into the suite. And pulled up short.

"Welles?"

Viscount Welles stood engaged in what appeared to be a discussion with Violet, who was visibly upset. What on earth was he doing here?

Welles nodded. "Ellsworth."

James glanced at Violet, then back to Welles. "Always a pleasure to see you," he said slowly, placing the stationery on the desk. "I had no idea you were planning to be in Greece."

"Oh, I've been to Greece before."

"I see." *With Violet?* He ignored the thought. Trust apparently went both ways.

"Duncan had something he thought was imperative for me to know." Violet clasped her hands in front of her.

"And a telegram was not sufficient?" There was something going on here. It hung in the air above them like a dark fog. And apparently James was the only one who didn't know what it was. "You came all the way to Greece?"

"I thought this information best delivered in person."

James raised a suspicious brow. "You don't write poetry, do you?"

"No." The man had the nerve to look indignant.

Violet cast him an annoyed glance, then turned her gaze to James. "Duncan tells me there is a clause in Uncle Richard's will that if there were to be a child on the way, we no longer have to abide by any of the stipulations. And you get your inheritance. All of it."

James dismissed the immediate urge to ask Welles how he'd uncovered that information. That would reveal his own knowledge and did not seem wise at the moment. He wasn't sure he had many cards in his hand at this point, but he'd rather hold back the ones he had. "Go on."

"I want to know if you knew about this?" Violet asked.

He started to respond. Without warning the truth hit him and he stopped. He chose his words with care. "You said you trusted me."

She nodded. "I did say that, yes."

"Then trust me now."

She frowned. "I simply want to know if you knew about this or not."

"Before last night, you mean."

"Last night?" Welles asked.

James ignored him. "Because if I did, last night was nothing more than a ploy on my part to get my inheritance. And last night meant nothing."

Violet hesitated.

"If you trust me, you shouldn't have to ask."

"It's a simple question, James. Why won't you answer it?"

"Because I'm tired, Violet. I've had enough. I've done everything I can to win your trust. And I have just realized, if you don't trust me now you never will." Weariness washed through him. "And I no longer wish to play this game."

"This was never a game for me."

"Either you trust me or you don't." He shook his head.

"I have tried to prove myself to you. To prove that I have changed. That I'm not the same man you married. That I can be trusted."

"I said I trusted you," she said sharply.

"Then it's your turn to prove something."

Their gazes locked for an endless moment.

"You're not going to answer me are you?" she said.

"I don't see the need to."

"And on that we disagree." She drew a deep breath. "Very well. We can continue this discussion later. I have a reading to attend."

"You're running away." He stared at her. Why hadn't he realized this before now? "Again."

"Utter nonsense. I'm not running away." She raised her chin. "I'm going to a reading."

"You ran away after we married. You ran away after we kissed."

"You kissed?" Welles frowned.

"And now you're doing it again."

"Don't be ridiculous," she said dismissively. "I am expected to attend this morning's reading and I intend to do exactly that."

"I can't guarantee I'll be here when you get back," he said without thinking, then realized he meant every word.

"Goodness, James, don't be so melodramatic." She grabbed her hat and gloves. "I shall see you in a few hours."

"I'm serious, Violet." He'd had quite enough of trying to prove himself to her. What more could he possibly do?

"Then go!" she snapped, turned on her heel and was out the door before anyone could protest.

Was this it, then?

Welles cleared his throat. James had almost forgotten

he was there. He'd always liked Welles—he considered him a friend. Until now.

"What are you really doing here, Welles?" Silly question. It was obvious he and Violet were involved in some manner.

"I thought it was important that Violet know about this," Welles said in a superior manner. Far too superior for a man trying to steal an old friend's wife.

"In the event I seduced her?"

Welles's expression tightened. "She may trust you, but I do not."

"She told you about the will?"

Welles hesitated then nodded. "In London, yes."

"So you asked a few questions and greased a few palms in the hopes of finding something to work to your benefit."

"It wasn't quite as easy as that, but yes, in a manner of speaking. And my intention was only to protect Violet." His tone was firm. "I intend to marry her."

"She's already married." James's jaw tightened.

"For the moment." Welles paused. "She'll never be able to truly trust you, you know. Not after this."

"I don't believe that." James clenched his fists by his side, but it was impossible to ignore the truth of Welles's charge.

"And I believe she just proved it." Welles's gaze locked with his. "Which means neither of you will ever be happy. Do you want that for her?"

"I can make her happy."

"Can you?" Welles shook his head. "You've already taken six years of her life. Does she deserve to waste the rest of it, too? She believes she owes you some sort of debt because you enabled her to see the world. I can't believe you want her to stay with you out of gratitude."

James's stomach clenched.

"The kindest thing you can do for her is to let her go. You said you wouldn't be here when she came back. I suggest you live up to your word."

"I love her."

"Then save her from a life of doubt and misgiving. Release her from years of wondering whether she can trust the one man she should trust. She doesn't deserve that." His tone softened slightly. "Neither do you." He hesitated then nodded. "Good day, Ellsworth." With that he took his leave.

For a long moment, James stared after him. How had everything gone so horribly wrong with Violet? Less than an hour ago, the future—*their* future—looked bright. Perhaps if James had simply answered her question...

No, either she trusted him or she didn't. And if she didn't trust him now, she never would. And without trust, was even love enough?

He'd told her he wished to be her hero. Maybe letting her go was the way to be that hero. Certainly he'd lose everything, but all that mattered was losing her. His heart twisted in his chest. Even if she was never really his.

Welles had followed her across a continent. He'd take care of her. Regardless, she had the funds Uncle Richard had given her. She would be fine financially.

He grabbed his clothes from the wardrobe and dresser and threw them into his portmanteau. He'd return to England and figure out what he was going to do with the rest of his life. That too scarcely mattered.

Even if it had taken him a long time to accept it and even longer to admit it, deep in his heart he had always known what Uncle Richard knew. He and Violet belonged together.

Pity they never would be.

CHAPTER TWENTY-SIX

RUNNING AWAY? What an absurd charge.

Violet walked briskly down the street leading from the hotel. She'd dismissed the thought of hailing a cab to take her to the ruins of Hadrian's Library. It was no more than a thirty-minute walk and walking was the best way to ease her annoyance and clear the jumbled thoughts in her head.

Why, she'd never run away from anything in her life.

Except James.

Nonsense. Her step slowed. The idea had never so much as entered her mind before but James might possibly have a point. Wasn't she even now trying to walk off the dreadful sense of fear that had gripped her the moment Duncan told her about the will? Hadn't the horrible ache inside her insisted she flee? Even so, she was not the one in the wrong here.

Was she?

She approached the remains of the ancient library where chairs had been arranged in front of the columns still standing for today's reading. Violet greeted some of the society members already here, although her mind was anywhere but on exchanging pleasantries. Mr. Tibbets of the Berkshire Tibbets and distantly connected to an extinct dukedom—which he bemoaned and yet insisted on mentioning every time they met—always gave the first reading. Violet had no idea why—he wasn't particularly good at it.

She took a seat in the back and tried to focus on the reading—one of the cantos of *Childe Harold's Pilgrimage*—although if asked she would have been hard-pressed to repeat even a single word of whatever was just recited.

Why wouldn't James just answer her question? Unless of course he had known about the clause *before* he'd slept with her. Maybe the question wasn't so much if she trusted him, but if she trusted herself. Last night had been everything she'd ever dreamed of. Everything she longed for. She'd confessed her feelings to James and he'd said he loved her, as well. There hadn't been a doubt in her mind last night. Or this morning.

Why on earth should she doubt him now?

Good God! She sat up straighter in her chair. James was right. Either she trusted him or she didn't. Didn't she know him well enough by now to know he wouldn't take advantage of her in order to claim his inheritance? If she didn't believe that, they had nothing. Everything inside her told her this was a man she could trust. And if indeed she did trust him, she didn't need to know if he knew about the clause in the will. It simply wasn't important. The man loved her and she loved him and in the end, that was all that really mattered.

"Are you all right?" Duncan sat down beside her.

"What are you doing here?" she said in a low voice.

"Why does everyone keep asking me that?"

"Because your presence here is unexpected." She sighed. "And unwanted."

"I came to help you." Indignation sounded in his voice. "At no little expense I might add."

"I understand that and I do appreciate it, but I don't

need your help." She hesitated, but it had to be said. "Nor do I welcome it."

A lady in the row in front of her turned and cast Violet a chastising look. Violet smiled weakly in apology.

"Come on," she said to Duncan, stood and picked her way through the sparse grass and pebbles to the street. It really was pointless to try to listen to poetry when what she really needed to do was find James. And apologize. And perhaps grovel a bit. Good Lord, what a mess she'd made of this.

"You'll never be able to trust him," Duncan said, moving into place beside her. "But you can always trust me."

"You have no idea how much that means to me," she said absently. Surely James didn't mean what he said about not being there when she returned. It was the sort of thing one said to make a point—no one ever took it literally. It was like *I should smack you for that*, or *I refuse to speak to you ever again* or—

I never want to see you again.

Bloody hell. She picked up her pace.

"Violet!" Duncan's hard tone jerked her attention. "I'm trying to talk to you."

"And I am listening, but I do need to get back to the hotel. There are matters I need to set right." She glanced at him, but didn't slow down. "It's rather difficult to go from being the victim to being the one in the wrong."

"I can't believe you've done anything wrong."

"Perhaps you don't know me as well as you think."

"I do know you, Violet. Far better than he does. And you know me, as well. You just said you trust me—"

"Not exactly," she muttered. Good Lord, did men only hear what they wished to hear?

"I love you, Violet. I can make you happy."

Apparently, they did. She stopped and turned to him.

"I thought I was very clear in London but perhaps not." Under other circumstances, this wouldn't be easy and she would try to be as gentle as possible. But right now, she needed to find her husband—the one man in the world who thought stupid comments like *I never want to see you again* were irrevocable edicts. And right now, Duncan was in her way. "You will always have a special place in my heart, but I'm afraid trust alone is not enough."

"But I love you."

"Yes, you said that. I am sorry if this is unpleasant to hear, but I don't love you." Violet drew a deep breath. "I do apologize, but I love my husband. And I trust him."

"In London, you said you didn't love him."

"London was a lifetime ago." She placed her hand on his arm. "You wouldn't have been happy with me and deep inside you know that. You deserve someone who wants to make you as happy as you want to make her."

"Violet—"

"Please, Duncan, I need to catch my husband before he does something stupid." She started off, then realized Duncan wasn't beside her. She swiveled back. "Are you coming?"

"It might be best if I don't accompany you. I said some things to Ellsworth…" He grimaced. "I might have encouraged him to leave. In your best interest, of course."

"Lord save me from stupid men who want to help," she snapped and started toward the hotel. "No wonder Shakespeare said the first thing we do is kill all the men."

"I believe the quote is *kill all the lawyers*," he called after her.

"Close enough!"

"WE WERE JUST coming to find you." Cleo and Marcus met her outside the door to her suite.

"Dare I ask why?" She forced a casual note to her voice. Judging by the looks on their faces, they were not looking for her to join them on a tour of the sights of Athens. A heavy weight settled in her stomach. She unlocked the door, pushed it open and stepped into the suite, Cleo and Marcus right behind her. The parlor looked no different than it had when she left, but she knew without question if she looked in the wardrobe his clothes would be missing. "He's gone, isn't he?"

"I'm afraid so." Marcus winced. "He left me a note. Slipped it under the door. We only found it a few minutes ago."

"Well?" She braced herself. "What did it say?"

"It said you didn't trust him." He paused. "And you probably never would. So he decided it would be best for you if he released you from any obligation to him. As it's fairly certain you will be apart for more than the thirteen days you have allocated for this year, he will lose everything. You will no longer have to follow the dictates of the will. You will be free to live your own life."

"The note said it was the best thing he could do for you." A distinct note of sympathy sounded in Cleo's voice. "It was quite noble of him."

"The man is trying to be my hero. He's giving up everything to ensure my happiness. It's not the least bit noble—it's stupid." She twisted her hands together. "And pointless. How can I be happy knowing he gave up everything for me? Knowing he'll forfeit not only the money, but the house in London where Richard made a home for them. And the manor in the country that's been part of his family for generations, the place that's filled with memories of his parents." Her throat ached and her voice rose. "How can I be happy without *him*?"

Cleo's eyes widened. "You do love him."

"Yes!" The word was barely more than a cry. "I do.
I always have."

"Dare I ask what happened?" Caution edged Marcus's voice.

Violet forced a note of calm to her voice. "I asked
James if he knew about the clause in the will that would
allow us to escape the stipulations."

"How did you know about that?" Marcus asked.

"It's not important at the moment." Violet waved off
the question. "James refused to answer. He said either
I trusted him or I didn't." She shook her head. "He was
right."

"I see." Marcus considered her thoughtfully. "Do you
still want to know the answer?"

"No." She raised her chin. "There's no need. I trust
him completely."

Marcus smiled. "Excellent answer, Lady Ellsworth.
Now, what do you intend to do about Lord Ellsworth?"

"You have to do something, you know," Cleo added.
"You can't simply mope."

"I have no intention of moping." Violet waved away
the comment. "Certainly I deserve a moment of despondency, but now action is called for. I've barely been away
an hour—he can't have gone far."

"I checked with the front desk. His lordship booked
passage on the ferry to Brindisi. It was scheduled to leave
a quarter of an hour ago." Cleo winced. "And there isn't
another ferry until tomorrow. If he takes a ship from
Brindisi we'll never catch up to him."

Violet scoffed. "He won't take a ship." She shot Marcus a pointed look. "Will he?"

"Probably not. He has a slight problem with ships."
Marcus grimaced. "And on occasion trains."

"I suspected as much." She thought for a moment.

"You're right. Even if he goes back the way we came we'll never catch him. How long—"

"Retracing our steps will take a minimum of a week to return to London," Cleo said. "And that only if there are no delays or missed connections. You and I both know that's impossible. As he's not an experienced traveler, even if all goes well, I would be surprised if he made it to London in less than—" she shook her head in regret "—fourteen days."

"Marcus." Violet pinned him with a direct look. "Mrs. Higginbotham is the sole authority on whether we have violated the terms of the will, is she not?"

He nodded.

"Then we need to get back to London before James does."

"I don't understand." Marcus frowned.

Cleo stared at her for a moment then grinned. "Violet has a plan."

"Well, the beginnings of one at least." She drew a deep breath. "But we can't do anything until we return to London and it's imperative we arrive before James."

Marcus's brow furrowed. "Why?"

"To speak to Mrs. Higginbotham, of course."

He shook his head. "I don't understand."

"You don't have to, dear." Cleo patted his arm, then turned to Violet. "If we take a ship directly from Athens…" She smiled. "I shall look into it at once."

"Good." Violet nodded. "For six years, I've been angry with James for not following me, for not fighting for me. For us." Determination rushed through her. "Now it appears it's my turn to fight for him. And I intend to do just that.

"Sometimes." She squared her shoulders. "Even the most stalwart of heroes needs a little help."

CHAPTER TWENTY-SEVEN

Fifteen days later

"GOOD HEAVENS, MY LORD." Andrews stared as if he'd seen a ghost. "Where have you been?"

"Good to see you too, Andrews," James said wryly and dropped his portmanteau in the entry. Bloody hell, it was good to be home. There were moments when he didn't think he'd make it. Of course, it wouldn't be home for much longer. His heart twisted. Still, it couldn't be helped and it did no good to dwell on his loss.

"My apologies, my lord." Andrews's brow furrowed. "It's simply that we have been concerned. Nor did we expect you tonight."

"And yet, here I am," James said with a weary sigh. "As to where I've been, I started my journey home in Greece where I boarded a ferry to Brindisi, Italy, and at once realized I had made yet another terrible decision. Unfortunately, it was too late and I was forced to complete the voyage. Upon my arrival in Italy, I immediately took the ferry back to Greece where, again, I was too late."

Andrews was apparently too stunned to speak.

"So I once more boarded that vile, creaking, deathtrap on water and returned to Italy. Do you have any idea how many people in Italy do not speak English?"

"A fair number I would imagine, my lord."

"An understatement, Andrews." James snorted. "And inevitably when you find someone who does speak your language and agrees to translate, he absconds with the money you've paid him and leaves you on the wrong train."

Andrews winced.

"In Italy, I changed trains in Naples, Rome and Milan. Did you know Italian trains are notorious for never being on time and it's impossible to count on connections?"

"No, my lord."

"Somehow, I ended up in Switzerland." James shook his head. He still wasn't entirely certain how that had happened. "There I encountered a group of elderly female travelers from Sheffield on a Thomas Cook tour. They took me in hand and accompanied me to Paris. From there, I managed the trip to London."

A muffled laugh sounded from the open doors of the parlor.

He narrowed his eyes. "Is that...?"

"Lady Ellsworth has been waiting for you," Andrews said. "She returned over a week ago."

Good. This would save him the effort of tracking her down. But the very fact that she was here... For the first time in two weeks, something that might well have been hope surged in his veins.

"Did she?" He braced himself. "And was she alone?"

"No, my lord."

James's heart sank.

"She was accompanied by Mr. and Mrs. Davies. They too were quite concerned as to your whereabouts."

"Has Lord Welles come by?" he asked casually as if it was of no importance.

"No, my lord."

And wasn't that good to know.

"The only callers since Lady Ellsworth's return have been Mr. and Mrs. Davies, and Mrs. Higginbotham and her friends." Andrews cast a quick look in the direction of the parlor, leaned closer and lowered his voice. "Lady Ellsworth has been beside herself awaiting your return. She insisted Mr. Davies hire detectives to locate you, but as no one had any idea what route you might have taken, the idea was dismissed. All Lady Ellsworth has done since her return is pace, mostly in the parlor and the library. The maids fear she'll wear out the carpets."

"I see." That too was good to know.

James adjusted his cuffs and straightened his tie—not that it made a significant difference. He no doubt looked every bit as weary and bedraggled as he felt. Still, Violet was here, which could only be a good sign. Regardless, they'd been apart longer than the time allotted in the will. Not that his legacy mattered anymore. Violet was the only thing he wanted. The only thing worth having. But he was through trying to prove it to her.

He strode into the library and right past her. Violet rested against the open door, her eyes twinkling with amusement. She had obviously heard every word.

"Welcome home." She grinned and closed the library doors.

"You find this amusing, do you?"

Her eyes widened. "It is amusing. But I'm not laughing because I'm amused. I'm laughing because I'm relieved that you're finally back."

"What are you doing here?" He strode across the room to the whiskey decanter, mercifully nearly full.

"I live here," she said in an offhand manner. "And I was waiting for you."

"Why?"

"Because I was worried. I wasn't entirely confident you could find your way home."

"Like any respectable retriever I managed."

"And because I was wrong." She stepped toward him. "Dreadfully, horribly wrong. And you were right."

"Oh?"

"You don't intend to make this easy for me, do you?"

"Making this easy for you has no great appeal at the moment."

"I see." She took his glass, tossed back the contents, then returned the glass. Obviously she was nervous about this. Good. "First, I owe you an apology."

He refilled his glass. "I know."

"I should not have doubted you. Even for a moment. And I don't," she added quickly. "Nor did it take me long to realize that. You, however, were already gone."

"It seemed a good idea at the time. Sacrificing everything to guarantee the happiness of the woman you loved. A grand gesture, that sort of thing." And then he'd spent the endless journey home trying to figure out where everything had gone wrong and what to do next. He hadn't been more than an hour out to sea on the first trip to Brindisi when he realized he was being an idiot. That he was doing exactly what he'd accused her of—running away. That regardless of his honorable intentions, this was akin to giving up.

"I thought it endearing of you." She paused. "And stupid."

"Stupid is perhaps the kindest thing you can say. I will admit I was blinded by the realization that no matter what I did, you might never trust me. Even so, my leaving Greece was not well thought out. I'm not sure what got into me." He raised his glass to her. "I blame you."

"It was possibly my fault," Violet admitted.

"Possibly?"

"Very well." She squared her shoulders. "It was entirely my fault."

"I have come to some conclusions on my endless journey home."

"As have I."

"Then this will be fun." He sipped his whiskey and studied her. "I am in love with you."

VIOLET NODDED COOLLY, but relief washed through her, dispelling the fear that had gripped her since she'd returned to the hotel. "You said that in Greece."

"What I didn't say is that I have always been in love with you." He swirled the whiskey in his glass and stared at it for a moment, obviously choosing his words. "All this started when I kissed you six years ago and I realized—"

"Yes?"

"Let me finish," he said sharply. "When I kissed you, I had intended it to be nothing more than a kiss. The kind of kiss I'd shared with any number of girls. But when I kissed you…"

"Bloody hell, it's you," she murmured.

"You remember that, do you?"

"I shall never forget it. I thought you were disappointed as you expected me to be Marie." She drew a deep breath. "I was crushed, heartbroken really. I thought you had finally realized I was the right woman for you."

"I did." He met her gaze directly. "When I kissed you, I was struck by the sure and certain knowledge that you were the right woman—the only woman—for me."

She stared.

"It terrified me." He blew a long breath. "I didn't know what to do. I had already come to the conclusion that I wasn't ready for marriage. I had no idea I wasn't ready for love, either. So I ignored it and did exactly what you do—I ran. Only my way of running was to put figurative distance between us—that idiocy about living separate lives. Then you left and for a long time I put you out of my head. Or tried, anyway. It's remarkable how alcohol and disreputable behavior can help you forget how badly you've messed everything up."

"Go on." She held her breath.

"It wasn't until I began taking on the responsibilities I always should have shouldered, and Uncle Richard began his campaign to reunite us in earnest that I started to suspect how I felt about you, how I had always felt. But I didn't know what to do. How to fix things between us. You never wanted to see me again."

"Well, yes, I said that, but—"

He held up his hand to quiet her. "I know now I should not have let that stop me and yet it did. In not knowing what to do, I did the worst thing possible." He shrugged. "I did nothing." He pinned her with a hard look. "Those days are over."

She swallowed hard. "Are they?"

"Because of the length of our separation, we have now lost Uncle Richard's legacy. I shall seek employment immediately and we will have to find a new residence." He looked around the room, regret in his eyes. "I shall miss this place, but in the end, it is only a house. The property, the fortune, none of it matters without you."

She started to speak then held her tongue. Best to let him finish.

"I understand you have a trust that has become a tidy fortune." He paused. "That is your money to do with as you wish, but you will not use it for our support. That is my responsibility."

She nodded. Perhaps someday she would tell him how

her money had been lost and then found. On the trip home, Cleo had spent hours going through the papers Gerard had given her and had discovered Violet hadn't lost anything, her funds had simply been the subject of clever manipulation by the comte, apparently at Uncle Richard's posthumous direction. Clever, diabolical old men.

"I will not spend the rest of my life trying to prove myself to you."

"Nor do you need to," she said quickly.

"I do, however, plan to spend the rest of my life making you happy or trying, anyway."

An ache settled in her throat and she nodded.

"I daresay I shall continue to make mistakes."

"Terrible decisions and dreadful mistakes?"

"I hope not but I can't guarantee that I won't." He shook his head. "I have a lot of experience with terrible decisions and dreadful mistakes."

"I imagine it's a difficult habit to break."

"I am sorry about losing everything."

"You were trying to be my hero."

"Not very well, I'm afraid."

"On the contrary, James." She swallowed against the lump in her throat. "I once told you I had stopped believing in heroes." She gazed into his eyes. "You made me believe."

After a long moment, a slow smile spread across his face. "I've worn you down, haven't I? Worked my way back into your affections."

"Don't be smug, James. After all, I do love you."

He reached her in one stride and pulled her into his arms. "We shall have a wonderful life, Violet. Filled with love and laughter and the family we shall have together. I am sorry that it will not be quite as affluent as we are accustomed to, but we will be rich in all that matters."

"Yes, well, about that." She hesitated to choose her words. "We have both made terrible decisions and dreadful mistakes. My greatest was not realizing I bear as much responsibility for the past six years as you. I wanted you to fight for me, but I failed to fight for you. So I did—in a manner of speaking, anyway."

"Oh?"

"When Mrs. Higginbotham, Lady Blodgett and Mrs. Fitzhew-Wellmore called, I told them how travel did not agree with you and how dreadfully ill you'd been—entirely true, I might add." She wrapped her arms around him. "I might also have implied that you had taken to your bed. Here."

"You lied to sweet old ladies?" he said slowly.

"Nonsense. I didn't lie. I *implied*." She tried and failed to look innocent. "And I had excellent legal advice."

He laughed. "So much for the moral upper hand."

"Nor do I feel the least bit guilty about it." She sniffed. "Uncle Richard's stipulations were for no other purpose than to bring the two of us together. They have done so. He would see no reason for you to lose everything now. Nor do I."

He laughed then hesitated, his gaze sober. "Welles said you were grateful to me and that's why you agreed to abide by the will. Is that true?"

"Of course it is." She leaned close and brushed her lips across his. "You gave me the world and for that I will be forever grateful. Now, I expect you to give me so much more, as I plan to give you."

"About the clause in the will—"

She pressed her fingers to his lips. "I don't need to know. I thought I didn't have the courage to trust you. What I didn't have was faith. At least not in the beginning. Now…" She gazed into his blue eyes, her heart thudding with pure joy. "You are my hero, Giacomo, and you always will be."

He smiled. "The game is over, my darling Violetta."

"Shall we call it a draw?"

"Oh, I'm fairly certain I won."

"Did you?"

"Without question." He pulled her closer and whispered in her ear, "Bloody hell, Violetta, it's you."

EPILOGUE

Nearly six years later

"EVEN AFTER ALL these years, I must confess it still bothers me." Poppy sighed and gazed out at the children playing in the gardens from her seat on the terrace of Ellsworth House.

Effie and Gwen traded long-suffering glances. They joined Lord and Lady Ellsworth and an assortment of their friends every year in late spring to mark not their official anniversary but the anniversary of their reunion. And every year Poppy allowed her conscience to pop up like a unrepentant dandelion.

"You know the letter Richard wrote was very specific about how I was to oversee the stipulations in the will," Effie said. Again. "His real purpose was true love. Richard had no desire to take away his nephew's birthright."

"Still, we ignored the fact that they had been apart more than the allocated time." Poppy's brow furrowed. "Not that they knew we knew of course, but it wasn't at all difficult to figure out."

"Poppy dear." Gwen leaned forward and met her friend's gaze firmly. "The end is all that matters, not how we came to be here. Would you change this if you could?"

"No, I suppose not." Poppy smiled weakly.

"I didn't think so." Gwen settled back in her chair and watched the children tumble about the lawn. It seemed

there was one or two more every year between Lord and
Lady Ellsworth and Mr. and Mrs. Davies. There was
nothing like seeing the future in the faces of children to
lead one to reflect upon the past.

And every year, life itself was more poignant, more
precious. All three friends were well into their eighties
and their time was nearly at an end. It was pointless to
deny the inevitable. They talked about it on occasion.
Rather more frequently than perhaps was wise, wondering about reunions with those who had gone before them.
Poppy with her beloved Malcomb, Effie with her dear
William and Gwen with Charles, the great love of her
life. Death would be well worth it to see his face again.

"It's been great fun, hasn't it?" Effie said abruptly, as
if she knew what Gwen had been thinking.

"What has?" Poppy asked.

"Oh, all of it. Founding the Lady Travelers Society."
Effie chuckled. "Selling the Lady Travelers Society. Traveling to Egypt. The people we've met. The schemes we've
hatched. The matches we've had a hand in."

"The hearts we've brought together." Poppy smiled
with the memories. "All those people we've nudged—"

Effie snorted. "Pushed."

"—toward happily ever after. All those lovely end-
ings."

"Goodness, dear, happily ever after is never the end."
Gwen smiled, her mind's eye skimming over the past—
these women who had been her sisters. Those friends
they had helped. Charles far in the distance.

"It's only, always, just the beginning."

* * * * *

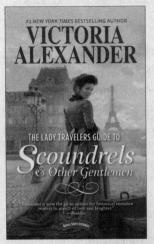

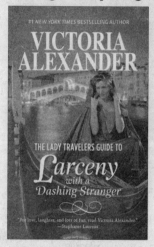

**Set sail for love in this sparkling
new adventure in
#1 *New York Times* bestselling author**

VICTORIA ALEXANDER'S

Lady Travelers Society series.

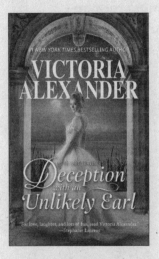